I0612237

REPLICATION
A Kid Sensation Novel

By

Kevin Hardman

REPLICATION

Copyright © 2019 by Kevin Hardman.

Cover Design by Isikol

Edited by Faith Williams, The Atwater Group

This book is published by I&H Recherche Publishing.

ISBN: 978-1-937666-42-2

Printed in the U.S.A.

REPLICATION

As I zoomed down the corridor, I didn't see anything unusual initially, but towards the end of the passageway (which terminated in a dead end), I noticed that the walls on both sides gave way to what appeared to be jail cells – two on each side – with bars at the front.

Thinking that one of them might contain Dream Machine's power generator, I peeked into each. All of them, however, were completely barren except the last one on the left, which contained someone that I took to be a homeless man from his appearance. All around him were empty liquor bottles, and from the way he smelled, it didn't take a genius to figure out that he probably took his breakfast, lunch, and dinner in liquid form.

Leaving him there, I quickly ran back to Mouse.

"There's nothing down there," I said. "No machines, equipment, or anything that struck me as capable of generating power."

"So it's completely empty?"

"Well, there *is* a guy down there," I admitted. "Some wino."

"Show me," Mouse practically demanded. Without hesitating, I teleported us down the hallway.

We popped up directly in front of the homeless man's cell. The Geiger counter on Mouse's tablet immediately became louder, producing infinitely more static.

"Where is he?" Mouse asked, not realizing that he was actually facing the wrong way.

"Over here," I said, tapping him on the shoulder to get him to turn around. The fellow in the cell, now awake, was in the process of putting one of the empty liquor bottles up to his mouth. "As I said, it's just some wino."

Mouse took one look at the guy and drew in a harsh breath. "That's not just some wino – it's Atomic Bum!"

REPLICATION

Kid Sensation Series
Sensation: A Superhero Novel
Mutation (A Kid Sensation Novel)
Infiltration (A Kid Sensation Novel)
Revelation (A Kid Sensation Novel)
Coronation (A Kid Sensation Novel)
Replication (A Kid Sensation Novel)

Kid Sensation Companion Series
Amped
Mouse's Tale (An Alpha League Supers Novel)

The Warden Series
Warden (Book 1: Wendigo Fever)
Warden (Book 2: Lure of the Lamia)
Warden (Book 3: Attack of the Aswang)

The Fringe Worlds
Terminus (Fringe Worlds #1)
Efferus (Fringe Worlds #2)

Boxed Sets
The Kid Sensation Series (Books 1–3)
The Warden Series (Books 1–3)
Worlds of Wonder

Short Stories
Extraction: A Kid Sensation Story

REPLICATION

ACKNOWLEDGMENTS

I would like to thank the following for their help with this book: GOD first and foremost, who continues to bless my endeavors; my family; and my readers, who have been very kind and generous with their support.

REPLICATION

Thank you for purchasing this book! If, after reading, you find that you enjoyed it, please feel free to leave a review on the site from which it was purchased.

Also, if you would like to be notified when I release new books, please subscribe to my mailing list via the following link: http://eepurl.com/C5a45

Finally, for those who may be interested, I have included my website, blog, Facebook, and Twitter info:

Website: http://www.kevinhardmanauthor.com/

Blog: http://kevinhardman.blogspot.com/

Facebook: www.facebook.com/kevin.hardman.967

Twitter: @kevindhardman

Chapter 1

"Stay close," Mouse muttered softly. "I'm gonna need you."

I gave a terse nod in response but didn't say anything.

We were currently downtown in the city, on the street. Mouse — my mentor — was wearing a buttoned-up but loose-fitting beige trench coat, under which he sported the well-known black-and-gold uniform of the Alpha League, the world's greatest superhero team.

Since we were attempting to be inconspicuous, I also wore my uniform under ordinary daywear, which in my case consisted of jeans, a long-sleeved T-shirt, and a light-weight jacket. Initially, however, I had pressed the notion of wearing a trench coat as well, but Mouse had nixed the idea.

"One guy in a trench coat is inconspicuous," he'd said. "Two is a couple of TV detectives, looking to bust a case wide open."

"So why do *you* get to wear the cool outfit?" I'd asked.

"Because I can actually pull off the look," he'd declared. "Besides, don't kids your age *like* looking scruffy and scraggly? Just wear some sweats or ripped jeans, and you'll be the epitome of cool."

And so we had come to be dressed in our current attire. From all indications, our attempt to keep a low profile was working, as no one seemed to be paying particular attention to us as we walked. More to the point, as I reached out empathically, I didn't sense any out-of-the-ordinary emotional vibes coming from any of the people around us.

After a few moments, we came to one of the city's many subway entrances. Mouse and I ducked inside, stepping onto an escalator that appeared to descend a good hundred feet, at the very least. Once at the bottom, we found ourselves in the midst of throngs of people trying to get through the turnstiles and onto the subway platform.

Welcome to rush hour, I thought, as bodies hemmed us in on all sides.

Tapping my shoulder to get my attention, Mouse suddenly tilted his head to the side, indicating I should follow him. We then began heading to one of the side walls, cutting a path through those around us that was perpendicular to the flow of foot traffic, causing shouts of frustration (and more than a few obscenities) to be voiced in our wake.

A few seconds later, we found ourselves at the wall. Nearby was a somewhat narrow gate which displayed an official "Metro Employees Only" sign. Needless to say, this was an entrance reserved for subway employees, a means of allowing them to quickly access the subway platform in order to go about their official duties rather than having to wait in line with the unwashed masses. And next to the gate — just to make sure no subway passengers temporarily forgot who they worked for — were a couple of transit cops.

Mouse approached the two officers and flashed what appeared to be a card made of plastic. One of the transit officers — a big fellow who made a show of twirling his nightstick — glanced at the card and simply nodded. Mouse then hustled through the gate, with me on his heels.

REPLICATION

At that juncture, a train was just pulling into the subway station. There was a high-pitched squeal of brakes as it slowly came to a halt; a moment later, a two-tone chime sounded, followed by the subway doors opening, and a mass of people began filing out.

He didn't say anything, but I sensed a slight twinge of frustration coming from Mouse, and I understood why. We were on a tight timetable, and although using the employee gate had allowed us to sidestep the wait and crush of bodies going through the turnstiles, we were still near the rear of a sizeable crowd. Even more, it was evident that we probably wouldn't make it onto this particular train, which would really throw our schedule out of whack.

As the last of the exiting passengers stepped off the train, those waiting to enter surged forward — a tidal wave of bodies that rushed ahead, almost heedless of anything and anyone around it. If it wasn't clear before, it was pretty certain now that getting on this particular train was out of the question. Unless we temporarily abandoned our efforts to be low-key.

"Hang on," I said to Mouse as I telescoped my vision in order to get a good look at the interior of the last train car. Then I teleported us, popping us into the subway car in question, but right in front of a middle-aged woman in a dark pants suit.

She jumped a little, obviously startled by our sudden appearance, then muttered, "I'm sorry. I didn't even see you there."

"No problem," Mouse assured her, then turned to me and gave a subtle nod of his head. I smiled slightly, taking this as acknowledgment that — although we were trying to avoid drawing attention to ourselves — using my powers had been the right decision.

REPLICATION

The car quickly filled up with passengers, and the press of bodies forced Mouse and me back to the very rear of the train car. At last, the chime sounded again, and the subway doors closed in the face of numerous disappointed patrons who hadn't been able to squeeze in. A moment later, we began moving, and within seconds we entered the tunnel, quickly picking up speed as the train moved toward its next destination. Glancing through a window set in the train's rear door, I watched as light from the platform we'd just left quickly receded into the distance.

I turned to Mouse, who — unlike me — was looking out the side windows instead.

"Scrubber room…" I heard him mutter softly. "Signal room… Communications…"

I followed his gaze, but already knew what he was doing: calling out the names of specific areas in the subway tunnel as we passed them.

Basically, the tunnel didn't just consist of steel tracks laid down in a passageway carved through the earth. There was a narrow, railed walkway on both sides which — at discrete intervals — intersected with the entrances to various areas that provided support functions. Most subway commuters had almost no idea how much was required in terms of manpower and equipment in order to keep the trains running in a timely and efficient manner.

"Heating and cooling should be next," Mouse stated, bringing my attention back to the task at hand. This was confirmed a few seconds later when I caught a glimpse of "HVAC" written on a door near the left-side walkway as we sped past.

"Okay, get ready…" Mouse droned. "Now!"

Telekinetically, I placed a firm grip on Mouse. At the same time, I phased us — making the two of us

4

physically insubstantial. Then I floated about an inch into the air (lifting Mouse as well), at the same time gently moving the two of us backward.

With our momentum now the opposite that of the subway car, the result was that we phased through the rear door. A second later, we were floating in the semi-darkness of the subway tunnel, watching the train swiftly moving away from us.

Empathically, I stayed in tune with the passengers for a moment, trying to make sure that our sudden disappearance hadn't caused any distress in those around us. Frankly speaking, I could have saved myself the trouble; I detected no more than mild surprise at our unorthodox departure. (Apparently, subway passengers adopt a mind-your-own-business mantra, although in all honesty I couldn't be sure how many of them had actually been paying attention to us in the first place.) This reaction actually served our current purpose, but at the same time it left me slightly disheartened with respect to human nature: two guys disappear from a moving subway train, and no one's concerned enough to raise an alarm?

"So far, so good," Mouse muttered, bringing me back to myself.

I moved us over to the railed walkway to our left, then made us substantial again and gently set us down. At the same time, I cycled my vision through the light spectrum until I could see almost normally. On his part, Mouse donned a pair of night vision goggles that he'd obviously brought with him.

"Let's go," he said, heading towards a nearby set of double doors. Unlike the previous areas we had passed (which had had the names of the respective rooms written on the entryways), this one was unlabeled.

Mouse tried the handle; unsurprisingly, it was locked. I phased the door without being told, and we stepped inside. We found ourselves on a landing at the top of a set of straight stairs that descended for about thirty feet.

We hustled down to the bottom of the staircase, which opened up into a square room roughly thirty-by-thirty feet in size. There was some type of equipment pushed against a couple of the walls, but none of it was familiar to me. Straight ahead of us was the entry to a narrow corridor. Mouse pulled out his computer tablet (which he always seemed to carry with him) and began walking towards the passageway. I immediately fell into step beside him.

Several hallways seemed to branch off from the one in which we found ourselves. Apparently using his tablet as a map, Mouse began guiding us through a honeycombed network of rooms, corridors, and even tunnels (with me occasionally using my phasing ability to get us past locked doors, blocked entrances, and the like).

"What is this place?" I asked softly a few minutes later as we walked through what appeared to be an abandoned subway line.

"Subterranean tunnel," Mouse answered with a snarky grin. "I'd have thought that was obvious."

"Funny," I replied sarcastically. "I meant why is it here, wise guy. Any of it, in fact. I mean, we've passed through a dozen places since we left the subway train that look like nobody's visited regularly in years."

"Yeah, well, it might shock you to know that there are scores of deserted underground sites throughout the city."

REPLICATION

"But again, why? It just seems weird to me to build out all these spaces and then simply abandon them."

"There are actually lots of reasons why people would simply walk away," Mouse declared as we left the subway line and entered a connecting passageway. "Maybe a tunnel collapsed or became too unstable to keep digging. Maybe they hit a pocket of gas or somehow lacked the ability to get fresh air far enough underground. In at least one instance, they upgraded the subway cars and then found out they wouldn't fit with the existing platforms. And in some cases, they just ran out of funding for the project."

I nodded in understanding. In the not-too-distant past, I had actually visited a town that had been evacuated years ago because of alleged exposure to some virulent biological agent. Thus, I could accept that there were occasionally valid reasons for abandoning places that had been built. Still, what I was currently seeing around me seemed like an incredible waste of effort, and I stated as much. This sparked a conversation between me and Mouse about the relative merits of cutting's one losses versus seeing a questionable project through to the end.

"Regardless of how you feel about them representing the squander of resources," Mouse finally said, "you have to admit that these underground spaces are a boon in terms of our task today."

"Yeah," I agreed. "Assuming we can get to the end of this rat maze."

"Sounds like someone's losing faith in the mission," Mouse chided as we rounded a corner. "How about a bit of cheese for encouragement?"

He pointed to the far end of the hallway we had just entered. There were still no lights (at least none that were on), but — with my vision set to the current band of the light spectrum — I didn't need them to see what Mouse was indicating: an elevator.

I smiled as we began heading toward it, as the presence of the elevator was an indicator that we were still moving in the right direction. Not that I had ever doubted Mouse or his ability to guide us through the underground labyrinth of tunnels and passageways. He was pretty much the smartest person on the planet and was rarely ever wrong about anything. Still, when the strategy for this particular mission was being planned, one of the drawbacks had been the lack of complete maps for the underground sites. That being the case, the path Mouse and I had taken to reach our current destination had — to some extent — consisted of guesswork and extrapolation. In short, it was nice to know we hadn't taken a wrong turn somewhere or gotten lost.

We stopped at the elevator doors, and Mouse began taking off his trench coat. This hinted at two things: first, that we were close enough to our final destination that the need to remain inconspicuous didn't matter. It also implied that Mouse didn't want excess clothing restricting his movements in any way.

Unlike my mentor, I didn't bother taking off my outer clothing. I merely phased myself and my Alpha League uniform, and everything else fell to the ground.

"We in a race?" Mouse asked accusingly, as if my method of changing clothes was a crime.

I laughed out loud, then sobered immediately as the sound echoed through the hallways around us.

My focus now back on the mission, I asked, "Do you think he knows we're here?"

REPLICATION

"Dream Machine?" Mouse said quizzically as he tossed his trench coat down. "If he doesn't, he will soon enough, so get your game face on."

I nodded and then, assuming that Mouse was ready, gripped him telekinetically again and phased us. I then moved us through the doors (which looked as though they hadn't opened in years) and into the elevator shaft.

Several floors below us was the elevator itself, but judging from the condition of the equipment in the shaft — rusted cables, exposed wiring, dilapidated pulleys, etcetera — I doubted that it was still functional (or would be safe to use even if it were). Like the elevator doors, everything around us probably hadn't seen use in a generation and was covered with dust and cobwebs.

Slowly, I began lowering us down the shaft. As we descended, I spent a few moments thinking about what lay ahead of us.

Despite having gone up against bad guys before, this was officially my first mission, the first one where my presence was actually sanctioned by the Alpha League. However, because of the individual we were about to face off with — Dream Machine — putting me (or someone like me) on the mission roster had almost been a foregone conclusion.

Technically, Dream Machine wasn't a person. He had started off as an artificial intelligence — a set of complex computer programs designed to help people with dementia, especially those having problems perceiving reality, through direct interface with the human brain.

Initially, the project was considered a roaring success. Somehow, however, the AI not only outgrew its original programming but also became self-aware. Moreover, through its incipient work with those suffering from dementia, it had somehow developed the ability to manipulate human perception. In short, it could cause people to see hallucinations, among other things. Taking on the name Dream Machine (and a masculine persona), the AI had decided that it could best fulfill its original purpose of helping people by conquering humanity. Thus, since escaping several years ago from the computer network where he was housed, Dream Machine had made world domination his top priority.

All of this flitted through my mind as we got closer to the elevator. Phasing through the roof, we found the interior of the elevator just as pulverulent and cobwebbed as the shaft we'd just left. Changing direction, I now moved us forward, taking us through the rusted-shut elevator doors.

The first thing I noticed when we emerged was light. Previously, we had been making our way through the subterranean tunnels and hallways in almost complete darkness. Now, however, there was a fair amount of illumination.

Glancing around, I saw that we were in a sizeable chamber that seemed to extend about a hundred feet ahead of us, as well as rise several stories in height. The light I had noticed apparently stemmed from two sources: electric bulbs that seemed to have been placed haphazardly throughout the area, and steel drums being used as burn barrels.

Much to my surprise, there were people scattered throughout the place — some old, some young, some alone, some with families. I had no idea where they had come from or how they'd managed to find their way this far underground, but one look at their threadbare clothing, well-worn footwear, and the multitude of sleeping bags made it clear to me that they were homeless.

Picking up a minor twinge of surprise from Mouse, I leaned towards him and whispered, "They're real."

Mouse merely gave a solemn nod in response as he removed his goggles. Like me, he had clearly not expected to find people here, and my statement was an indication to him that these people actually existed, as opposed to being illusions fabricated by Dream Machine.

This was the real benefit of having me on this mission. In essence, Dream Machine's illusions only appeared within the visible light spectrum. In other words, they only manifested within the range of the spectrum that was visible to the human eye. Ergo, people with normal vision were susceptible to the hallucinations he created, but someone like me — with my vision currently *outside* the visible light spectrum — couldn't see them at all. That meant I could tell what was real and what wasn't. Moreover, my empathic abilities also served as a differentiator, since illusions don't have feelings.

At the moment, I was picking up the usual emotions that one might expect from people dealing with homelessness: worry, fear, dread, and so on. At the same time, however, I picked up on feelings of comfort, hope, friendliness, and the like. Basically, on an overall basis, it wasn't much different than the sentiments I'd pick up from any random group of people. Thus, convinced that we were in no immediate danger, I placed Mouse and myself on the ground and made us substantial again. By that time, however, our presence had been noted.

Up to that point, there had been a multitude of conversations going on, but they quickly ground to a halt as those assembled became aware of strangers in their midst. Slowly, like the tide inexorably crashing on the shore, a wave of silence seemed to wash over those around us as all eyes turned in our direction.

I didn't pick up on any indications of malice, but the sea of staring eyes made me wary. Then, almost simultaneously (and so closely in unison that it might have been choreographed), everyone around us pointed to the far end of the chamber, where another set of double doors was located. Quite plainly, they knew who we were (or at least why we were there).

Taking our cue, Mouse and I began heading toward the doors. As we walked, I couldn't help but feel a slight bit of guilt as I noticed those around us huddling close to the burn barrels for warmth. Although we were on the verge of spring, it was still cold outside. Assuming there was some kind of ventilation system down here — and there had to be for these people to get air (not to mention preventing the burn barrels from filling the place with smoke) — it was probably cold air that was coming in. Thus, while not as wintry as being on the streets, it was quite likely that it could get cold enough down here to get uncomfortable.

For Mouse and me, the League uniforms that we wore were not just well-insulated, but also loaded with so much technology that getting a chill was the last thing we had to worry about. Needless to say, we hadn't done anything wrong, but I felt guilty all the same about being warm and cozy.

In addition, I noticed that the space we were in wasn't actually designed to be the huge chamber I initially took it to be. Upon closer inspection, I saw that Mouse and I were actually on the ground floor of what had been a multi-story facility of some sort. (In retrospect, I actually remembered floating past several floors as we had come down the elevator shaft.) From all indications, some portion of the structure had collapsed, leaving several rooms on multiple floors open and visible, thereby creating the semblance of a large space. Frankly speaking, it put me in mind of a wrecking ball that had smashed into the side of a building, leaving much of the interior exposed to the outside.

We were about a quarter of the way to the double doors when everyone — again, in synchronized fashion — dropped their hands. Presumably we knew which way to go at that juncture, so the chamber's occupants (at least those on the same floor as us) busied themselves with hurriedly stepping out of our path, as if we had a disease they might catch. They still didn't speak, however; they merely continued to watch us in stony silence.

We had almost reached the double doors when a young girl — about eight years old or so — dropped a doll she was holding as she stepped out of our path. I had just come abreast of her at the time, so I bent down to retrieve her plaything at the same time that the girl herself did. Our simultaneous action resulted in us almost bumping heads, but our comic timing was slightly off. Thus, although we didn't inadvertently head butt each other, her face did wind up close to my ear.

"Watch the shadows," she hastily whispered, at the same time taking her doll (which I had reached first) from my hand.

I stood up, frowning slightly over what I'd just heard and trying to discern the meaning. I glanced at the girl, who had just been gripped firmly by the arm, pulled back, and shushed by a woman who presumably was her mother. Still pondering her words, I stepped forward to join Mouse, who was already at the doors (which appeared to be locked). My mentor looked at me expectantly. Knowing what he wanted, I phased the doors and we stepped through.

We now found ourselves in a spacious tunnel. The place was modestly lit with a few incandescent lights, which provided enough illumination that Mouse didn't need his NVGs. A couple of darkened, recessed spaces in the tunnel walls indicated the presence of several corridors that presumably led to other areas.

"There," Mouse said, pointing at what appeared to be a metal post with some blinking lights that stood in the middle of the tunnel. He ran towards it, with me right on his heels.

As we approached, I realized that the blinking lights were actually diodes on a small black box about the size of my palm. It was attached to the pole at a height of about four feet. The pole itself was about nine feet tall and was not just in the middle of the tunnel, but also centered between two railway tracks.

"This is it," Mouse said, pulling a thin cable from a pouch at his belt. "One of the computer hubs connected to Dream Machine."

"That's a computer?" I asked in surprise as Mouse used the cable to connect his tablet to a port on the black box.

"Yeah," Mouse assured me. "Why?"

I shrugged. "I guess when I think 'computer,' I envision things like a keyboard and monitor."

"Dream Machine is an AI. He doesn't need that kind of interface to interact with a computer program or software."

REPLICATION

"So why have lights down here? He obviously doesn't need those either."

"That's for our benefit — so we can see whatever he sends at us. Now get ready. Even with the distraction provided by the others, we can't expect to go undetected."

I nodded in agreement. Mouse's last statement alluded to the fact that the two of us weren't the only Alpha League contingent currently engaging with Dream Machine. Somewhere well above us and miles away, another team was making a direct assault on an isolated warehouse that had been identified as the AI's main base of operations. With any luck, he'd be so preoccupied with the main team knocking down his front door that he wouldn't pay close attention to us slipping in the back. In short, what Mouse and I were doing could be generally construed as a sneak attack on Dream Machine's unprotected rear.

What we were hoping to do, of course, was put a stop to the AI's current machinations, which included uploading a malicious code to an orbiting communications satellite. Simply put, in order to manipulate what a person was seeing or hearing, Dream Machine usually had to be in close proximity to the affected individual. However, if he could take control of the satellite in question (which is what the code was designed to do), it would give the AI a much broader reach — global, in fact. In brief, he'd be able to influence the perception of almost anyone, anywhere on the planet. And if Mouse's calculations were correct (which was usually the case), the upload would be complete in about fifteen minutes.

Needless to say, the easiest way to stop Dream Machine would have been to simply shut down the satellite. Unfortunately, permission to do so hadn't been forthcoming. Apparently the satellite in question had certain military applications, and making it go dark — even temporarily — would have compromised several sensitive operations. (The requisite bureaucratic decision-makers had pretty much dismissed the suggestion out of hand.) Thus, we had been forced to employ our current stratagem.

I thought about all of this as Mouse went to work, typing on his tablet. In addition to giving us access to Dream Machine's systems, hubs like the one Mouse had connected his tablet to were used by the AI as an escape hatch — a means for him to make a quick getaway to the internet when necessary. Thus, we were not only hoping to use it to disrupt his current plans, but to also trap him by shutting down his exit route.

Without warning, I heard a noise like the growl of a large predator coming from somewhere nearby. Quickly, I spun around in a circle, trying to pinpoint the source of the sound, but couldn't see anything. Moreover, I wasn't picking up any emotional vibes from anything other than Mouse.

The growl sounded again — closer, and in a way that hinted at anger...or hunger.

"Polar bear," Mouse announced in answer to my unasked question.

"Where?" I asked, still looking around.

"Right in front of me," Mouse stated, continuing to type without missing a beat. "Just took a swipe at my head with a massive paw."

"I don't see anything."

"Good," Mouse declared. "That's the entire reason you're here."

I didn't respond, but his words reminded me of why I had been included on this mission: my ability to see outside the visible light spectrum, which meant that I would be unaffected by any hallucinations that Dream Machine might employ. Being able to separate fact from fantasy was absolutely critical at this juncture if we were going to stop him.

Unfortunately, although I wasn't visually vulnerable to Dream Machine's illusions, I was affected on an auditory level. In essence, I could still hear them, even though they weren't visible to me. Thus, when I looked to where Mouse indicated the polar bear was located, I didn't see anything other than my mentor's shadow cast against the wall. With his fingers flying across the tablet as he typed, the image on the wall gave the impression of a mad composer trying to complete his *magnus opus* within the span of a few minutes.

After a few seconds, the sound of the growling polar bear melted away. It was replaced almost immediately, however, by an ominous creaking, followed by the sound of numerous heavy items thunderously striking the ground.

"Cave in," Mouse said by way of explanation.

And so we continued for the next minute or two, with me hearing an odd new sound every few seconds, and Mouse identifying it for my benefit. It could almost have been a game of sorts, were the situation not so serious, because Dream Machine obviously knew we were here and was trying to run us off. But if this was the best the AI could do, we probably didn't have much to worry about.

Out of the blue, a deafening, animalistic roar sounded in front of me, catching me off guard.

"What was *that*?" I practically demanded.

"A dragon, by the looks of it," Mouse replied.

"A *dragon*?" I repeated, unable to hide my surprise.

17

"Yeah — a fire-breathing one, at that."

Okay, this I have to see, I thought. I cycled my vision back to the visible light spectrum, and sure enough — just as Mouse had said — there was an enormous, fire-breathing dragon right in front of us. It was winged and covered in gold-and-green scales, with a long, supple tail that whipped back and forth. As I watched, the creature's nostrils flared and its diaphragm expanded; a moment later, its mouth opened and a stream of fire shot out, bathing me and Mouse in flames.

I had to give Dream Machine credit: his creation was beautiful and incredibly life-like. Even knowing that it wasn't real, I still half-expected us to get burnt to a crisp. Thankfully, that didn't happen, and when the flames died down, the dragon was gone.

A moment later, however, I heard an odd clicking noise coming from overhead. Looking up, I'm sure my eyes bulged as I saw a bloated, man-sized spider descending towards us on a silky line of webbing from its spinneret. Almost completely black and with mandibles clacking together spasmodically, it reached for Mouse with long, spindly legs. Unexpectedly, it lunged in an apparent attempt to bite my mentor's head off. It was all I could do not to shout out a warning, but just before its fangs made contact, the spider disappeared.

Mouse gave me a quick sideways glance, but didn't say anything. It was a sure bet that I'd given him some non-verbal cues that I'd switched my vision to the visible spectrum. (Plus he was no longer giving me a play-by-play overview of Dream Machine's illusions, which suggested he knew that I could see them myself.)

A light suddenly began shining at the far end of the tunnel directly ahead of us. As I watched, it seemed to move closer towards us, like someone with a flashlight walking in our direction — except the light seemed to be held in a steady position. A moment later, a noise like an air horn reverberated through the tunnel.

No, not an air horn, I thought. *A* subway *horn!*

As if in confirmation of this, the rails on either side of us began to vibrate, and I heard the sound of a train car in motion — metal wheels grinding on metal tracks. Dream Machine's latest illusion was headed right for us.

With the light shining in our faces, I wasn't able to get a good look at the AI's latest fabrication, although I imagined it was a full-length subway train. However, as it drew closer, the lights in the tunnel caused the train's shadow to form on the wall, and I was a little disappointed to note that it was seemingly just a single subway car.

Shadow!

With klaxons going off in my head, the word leaped to the forefront of my brain — along with the dire warning of the little homeless girl. Thoughts racing, I reflected back on the illusions I had seen and suddenly realized that neither of them had cast shadows. That meant…

I immediately — almost simultaneously — did three things: I cycled my vision away from the visible spectrum; shouted a warning to Mouse that consisted solely of the word "Real!"; and phased the two of us.

The subway car — which was in no way an illusion — was almost on us at that point. The fact that he had sent something real (and capable of causing us grievous harm) was a sure indicator that Dream Machine was no longer fooling around. He was intent on stopping us by any means necessary.

Thankfully, I had phased us in time for the subway car to pass through us harmlessly. Unfortunately, in my haste, I forgot to phase the metal post with the computer hub attached (although I had phased Mouse's tablet). The train hit it at ramming speed, ripping the post up from the ground and dragging it along with it down the tracks. Mouse, who — to his credit — had never stopped working even when I'd shouted that the train was real, merely turned and watched as the post, now caught beneath the subway car's wheels, spewed forth a bright shower of sparks. A moment later, accompanied by the squeal of grinding metal, the train derailed and crashed into the wall of the tunnel with a sound like a bomb going off. The tunnel shook for a moment, causing the lights to flicker briefly as dust came cascading down from the ceiling.

A slight popping noise drew my attention to the floor, where I noticed some exposed wiring from several cables that had snapped when the post was dragged away. The popping noise sounded again, in concert with a few sparks from the wiring.

"Please tell me that you stopped the upload," I said as Mouse and I stepped back from what was obviously several live wires and I made the two of us solid again.

"Not enough time," Mouse said solemnly.

I let out a sigh of disgust, furious with myself. I had failed miserably. The entire reason for me being here was my ability to differentiate reality from illusion, and I had allowed myself to get so distracted that it affected the mission.

"So, that's it," I said, feeling wretched. "Dream Machine wins."

"Not necessarily," Mouse declared. "We just have to go to Plan B."

I frowned. "Huh?"

"We can't stop the upload directly, but maybe we can do it *in*directly."

"How?" I asked, nonplussed.

"By disrupting his power supply."

"What do you mean?"

"When I was in his systems, I noticed that all of Dream Machine's operations depend on a single power supply, and it's close by."

I thought about this for a second. "Wait a minute. You're saying he has an independent source of electricity that he uses to power everything?"

"Yep. I had always assumed that he was siphoning it from the city grid somehow, but apparently that's not the case. He's got some independent means of generating power, and if we find it, we can still stop him."

That was all I needed to hear. A few seconds later, we were dashing down one of the connecting corridors.

As before, Mouse dictated our course, using his tablet to guide us through the maze of passageways. After about a minute, however, he slowed his pace — then abruptly came to a halt.

"What's the problem?" I asked.

"The power source should be just up ahead," he said, pointing towards the end of the hallway we now found ourselves in. "But according to the readings I'm getting…it's nuclear."

I frowned. "Nuclear? As in 'nuclear bomb'?"

"Exactly," Mouse replied, then tapped a few keys on his tablet, which then began making a light, staticky sound.

"What's going on?" I asked, pointing at the tablet with my chin. "Some kind of interference?"

21

Mouse shook his head. "No. I've modified the tablet to act as a Geiger counter. It's reading the level of radiation down here."

I didn't need to hear any more. The fact that the Geiger counter was making any noise at all was an indication that we were currently being exposed to radiation of some sort.

"Are we in danger?" I asked.

"Not at the moment," Mouse answered. "Plus, our uniforms provide us with some level of protection. As long as the level of radioactivity doesn't get much higher and we don't experience prolonged exposure, we should be fine."

"Okay, but that means we need to find this power source fast."

"Agreed."

"Alright," I said, coming to a decision. "Hang back for a second."

Without waiting for Mouse to reply, I shifted into super speed and went zipping down the hallway. My assumption was that, as a speedster, I could swiftly check out the area and report back, while encountering only a miniscule amount of radiation (if any at all) in the process. That would hopefully keep my mentor out of danger, as well as make up, to some extent, for my blunder with the subway train.

As I zoomed down the corridor, I didn't see anything unusual initially, but towards the end of the passageway (which terminated in a dead end), I noticed that the walls on both sides gave way to what appeared to be jail cells — two on each side — with bars at the front.

Thinking that one of them might contain Dream Machine's power generator, I peeked into each. All of them, however, were completely barren except the last one on the left, which contained someone that I took to be a homeless man from his appearance.

His hair looked like it hadn't been combed in some time, and he had a shaggy, unkempt beard. Lying on the floor, he appeared to be asleep, and my read of his emotional state gave the same indication. All around him were empty liquor bottles, and from the way he smelled, it didn't take a genius to figure out that he probably took his breakfast, lunch, and dinner in liquid form.

Leaving him there, I quickly ran back to Mouse.

"There's nothing down there," I said. "No machines, equipment, or anything that struck me as capable of generating power."

"So it's completely empty?"

"Well, there *is* a guy down there," I admitted. "Some wino. I was going to teleport him to a shelter or something, but thought you might want to check him first to see if he's been exposed to radiation."

"Show me," Mouse practically demanded. Without hesitating, I teleported us down the hallway.

We popped up directly in front of the homeless man's cell. The Geiger counter on Mouse's tablet immediately became louder, producing infinitely more static.

"Where is he?" Mouse asked, not realizing that he was actually facing the wrong way.

"Over here," I said, tapping him on the shoulder to get him to turn around. The fellow in the cell, now awake, was in the process of putting one of the empty liquor bottles up to his mouth. "As I said, it's just some wino."

Mouse took one look at the guy and drew in a harsh breath. "That's not just some wino — it's Atomic Bum!"

"What?!" I exclaimed, eyes wide in surprise.

REPLICATION

Atomic Bum was a homeless man discovered in the middle of a huge, smoking, radioactive crater a few years back, following an explosion in a heavily forested area. In addition to Atomic Bum himself, investigators also discovered evidence that someone had been snatching homeless people off the street and experimenting on them — often with gruesome, horrifying results. After a few attempts at questioning him, it became obvious to investigators that the man they had found was mentally addled, but he provided enough information to make it clear that he had been one of those abducted.

It also became evident that he was a super, with a power set that seemed to mimic nuclear reactions. However, it was unknown whether this ability was something he possessed prior to being kidnapped or the result of an experiment after he was taken. One thing was sure, though: whoever had taken him ultimately found out that they had bitten off more than they could chew.

Because he didn't seem to have a name or permanent address — and grew agitated when he went too long without alcohol — the media nicknamed him Atomic Bum. He was generally considered to be harmless, but when upset or flustered, his powers would activate.

Looking at him in the cell now, as he set down the first bottle and tried to drink from another, a lot of things suddenly became clear. First and foremost was that this was Dream Machine's power supply — a living, nuclear power plant.

"What do we do now?" I asked as Atomic Bum tried to drink from yet a third empty bottle.

"Give me a sec," Mouse said, as he appeared to examine the exterior of the cell.

REPLICATION

The sound of glass shattering drew my attention back to Atomic Bum. Apparently frustrated at not having anything alcoholic available, he had thrown the last empty bottle forcefully against the back wall of the cell.

"Where's my bottle?!" he shouted angrily. All of a sudden, his eyes focused on me. "You! What have you done with it?"

"Huh?" I said.

"My bottle!" the homeless man screamed, spewing spittle as he came towards me. "I know you have it!"

Without warning, his eyes began to take on a mild red glow. At the same time, the Geiger counter began making even more noise and the temperature seemed to rise.

"Look," I said, trying to speak in a calm voice. "I don't have your bottle, but if you just stay calm, we can get you something to drink."

"Give me my bottle!" Atomic Bum screamed, making it clear that my words hadn't registered with him. Now at the front of the cell, he reached menacingly through the bars, causing me to take an involuntary step back.

His eyes were now a deep crimson, and the Geiger counter was going completely crazy. This guy was obviously starting to give off a ton of radiation, as well as oppressive heat. He was still rattling on about his bottle, and it was clear that no amount of talk was going to calm him down.

"Mouse!" I shouted. "Based on what the Geiger counter's saying, we need to get out of here!"

"Have you forgotten about Dream Machine?" Mouse asked. "If this is his power source, we can't just leave him."

"Then shut down whatever he's using to siphon power off this nut!"

"There's not enough time."

"Fine," I said. "Then I'll teleport this guy some place where he can go nuclear without killing anyone."

"No!" Mouse exclaimed. "If he unleashes some type of fission reaction, you don't know how big the explosion will be."

As usual, Mouse was right; I had no idea how much damage this guy could truly cause. Moreover, even without considering how big the blast radius would be, there would still be the other effects of a nuclear explosion to contend with — everything from radiation poisoning to flash blindness to nuclear fallout.

No, I couldn't teleport him without knowing more about the likely outcome.

"Phase the bars," Mouse suddenly ordered, catching me by surprise.

"What?" I said, not quite sure I'd heard him correctly.

"Phase the cell bars," he said. "Make them insubstantial."

I phased the bars as directed. Atomic Bum, who was leaning against them at the time, still reaching for me, fell forward off-balance and toppled to the ground.

Mouse stepped forward, and I simply watched, unsure of what he would do. *Maybe try to talk some sense into Atomic Bum? Or promise him a drink if he'd just calm down? Or —*

My thoughts were cut off as Mouse, planting a foot just as Atomic Bum came to his hands and knees, kicked the fellow solidly in the jaw. Atomic Bum flipped over onto his back, unconscious.

26

REPLICATION

Or that, I said to myself.

REPLICATION

Chapter 2

Mouse's kick sent Atomic Bum into dreamless unconsciousness, at which point he seemingly stopped generating radiation and heat. My mentor then spent a minute poking around the cell Atomic Bum had been in until he found what appeared to be a hidden panel. Behind it was a fair amount of sophisticated tech and equipment, which was apparently designed to siphon off radiation and — ultimately — use it to create electrical power.

"There," Mouse said with finality, after fiddling with the equipment behind the wall panel for a moment. "Dream Machine's power supply is no more."

"And the upload?" I asked, almost timidly.

"I'm not connected to Dream Machine's network anymore," Mouse admitted, looking at his tablet. "But I'm using a remote link to monitor the satellite's systems, and all indications are that the upload aborted."

I allowed myself a small grin, thankful that my earlier *faux pas* with the train had not had lasting repercussions.

"I think we're done here," Mouse added. "Why don't you head on back to HQ and get checked out? We can do the formal debrief tomorrow morning."

It was a kind gesture on his part. He knew that — aside from the mission — I had a lot on my mind.

Basically, I had just returned several weeks earlier from a sojourn to the distant planet Caeles — the homeworld of my maternal grandmother, an alien princess known as Indigo. My grandmother herself had been called home decades ago, leaving my grandfather to raise their infant daughter alone.

REPLICATION

My own visit to Caeles had been fraught with peril, and I'd almost been killed on more than one occasion. Needless to say, I was happy to have made it back to Earth in one piece. Even better, Queen Dornoccia — ruler of the Caelesian Empire — had allowed my grandmother to return home with me. (Indigo had essentially been under house arrest on her homeworld.) Unfortunately, the queen had also required me to come home with something else that was entirely unexpected: a fiancée.

To someone on the outside looking in, it probably appeared that I had won the lottery. My betrothed was a Caelesian princess named Isteria (although she preferred that I call her "Myshtal," which was one of her many middle names). She was a great-great-granddaughter — and favorite — of Queen Dornoccia. Because of the way Caelesian politics worked, Myshtal was not necessarily in line to inherit the throne, but she was heir to a considerable fortune. On top of all that, she was breathtakingly beautiful, with a sharp wit and lively personality that made everyone she met practically fall in love with her — everyone except my girlfriend, that is.

Frankly speaking, however, the arrangement with Myshtal was more of a business deal than anything else. On Caeles, it's not uncommon to use betrothals to cement commercial partnerships or political alliances. In my case, it had been the cost of getting Queen Dornoccia's support for my Caelesian family, which was under political attack, among other things. In exchange, I was to bring Myshtal home with me and look after her. (Myshtal had some budding super powers, and the queen had felt those abilities would be better developed on Earth, where such talents were more common.) Of course, I would have made Myshtal's well-being a priority even without the formality of an engagement, but apparently that's the Caelesian way of doing things, and when in Rome…

As might be expected, I wasn't wild about the situation — for quite a number of reasons. First of all, I was only sixteen, so marriage (even to someone who was quite fetching, and a princess) was one of the furthest things from my mind. Next, even though she was an adolescent by Caelesian standards, Myshtal was considerably older than me. (Caelesians live about five times longer than people on Earth.) Finally, as previously noted, I already had a girlfriend. The only good news was the fact that — once again — this was really nothing more than a business arrangement. That being the case, there was no guarantee that it would end in matrimony. (And even if it did, I had been assured that the date for any nuptials would be well in the future.)

All in all, I had a lot on my plate at the moment in terms of my personal life. Thus, the mission to deal with Dream Machine had been a welcome distraction. Now that it was seemingly over, however, my mind naturally began to turn once again to all the issues I was grappling with. Still, dealing with the AI and its machinations had made me acutely aware of how negligible my problems were: they were still bothersome, but compared to threats like world domination, they didn't carry a lot of weight.

My mind back on our present situation, I contemplated Mouse's suggestion that I take off only for a moment before discarding it. My mentor was a bright guy and I was confident that he could handle himself, but — from what I'd been able to glean — he had no discernable super powers. Thus, I wasn't about to leave him alone in what was obviously the lair of a supervillain (albeit one we had allegedly stopped), and I stated as much.

"Suit yourself," Mouse said with a shrug. "But support is en route, if that's what you're worried about."

He was proved right about a minute later when Buzz, the speedster of the Alpha League, zipped down the corridor and halted in front of us.

"You took your time," Mouse said, admonishing him.

"Hey, man, you're lucky I got here *this* fast," Buzz droned as he acknowledged my presence with a nod. "Do you know how many underground tunnels and hallways I had to search to find you? The homing beacon doesn't come with a map. It told me where you were, but not how to get here."

Buzz was, of course, speaking of the communicator that all Alpha League members carry with them as part of their standard equipment. It addition to allowing two-way communication, the device served a dual function by also operating as a tracker/homing beacon. Apparently Mouse had reached out to his colleague without me noticing. (Or, more likely, he had previously instructed Buzz to join us after the mission was over.)

Confident now that Mouse had adequate backup, I teleported back to Alpha League Headquarters.

REPLICATION

I popped up in the infirmary at League HQ. Because of the Dream Machine mission, an emergency response team was already on standby in case someone came back in dire need of medical attention. I didn't think possible radiation exposure was anything they were expecting, but you wouldn't have known it from the way they reacted.

In essence, the medical team operated like a well-oiled machine, switching immediately from idle into high gear from the moment I appeared — testing, probing, and evaluating my condition at a pace that was almost dizzying (even for a speedster like me). Within twenty minutes, I was pronounced fit and released. That might have seemed hasty by some standards, but the Alpha League — in keeping with their prominence as the gold standard for superhero teams — had the best doctors, the best equipment, and the best facilities available. If their medical team gave me a clean bill of health, then that meant I was good to go.

From the infirmary, I teleported to my room. Like all members of the League's teen affiliate, I had my own quarters at HQ — a comfy, one-bedroom unit with a cozy living room, a kitchenette, and a small breakfast area. (In truth, the League actually had several floors designated as on-site residences, so every League member had their own individual living quarters.) Historically, however, the teen apartments were seldom used; they were really only utilized the few times each year that teen supers were required to stay at HQ for extended training — usually during summer. That said, we could actually use them any time we liked.

REPLICATION

The first order of business when I arrived was to take a shower. Having just come back from a mission that took place almost wholly underground (and involving a lot of dusty places), I felt a little grimy. However, it was nothing that soap and water couldn't fix.

Fifteen minutes later, after a leisurely — but not overlong — shower, I felt ready to go out. Now dressed in a pair of khakis and a navy-blue sweater, I teleported to the teen lounge area of Alpha League Headquarters.

The lounge was a break room for members of the League's teen affiliate that housed, among other things, dart boards, video game consoles, and a billiards table. Needless to say, it was a favorite haunt of many teen supers, including me and my friends.

When I popped up, there were a fair number of people in the lounge, but not so many that you would call it crowded. But it was only early evening, and on a Friday at that — still lots of time for the place to fill up (which it probably would).

My sudden appearance caused a few heads to turn in my direction, but didn't really startle anyone. A couple of teens greeted me with a wave and I returned the gesture, all the while scanning the room for...

There!

Near the rear wall, striding towards a table at the back of the lounge, was my best friend, Smokescreen. I began walking in his direction, giving perfunctory greetings to several people that I knew as I moved through the room. By the time I reached him, Smokey (as he liked to be called) was already sitting at the table, which was square-shaped, with a chair on all four sides. I took a seat across from him.

"Hey," he said as I sat down. "That was fast."

"Huh?" I muttered, not sure what he was talking about. The mission, maybe?

"Never mind — I forgot who I was talking to," he stated with a self-deprecating shake of his head. "Anyway, here you go."

He pushed something across the table towards me — a bottle of soda. Now that my attention was drawn in that direction, I noticed that he had one as well.

"Good timing," I acknowledged, before taking a quick drink of soda.

Smokey gave me an odd look and for a moment, I sensed confusion coming from him. However, it vanished a moment later as he leaned in.

"So," he said in a hushed, conspiratorial tone, "can you tell me about the mission now?"

"Uh, sure," I answered. His phrasing struck me as a little odd, but I quickly forgot about it as I telepathically reached out and gave him a quick overview of events.

Although technically a telepath, I consider my abilities in that arena to be limited. While I can broadcast my own thoughts, I can only pick up the surface thoughts of others and anything they willingly want to share. True mindreading — being able to burrow into someone's brain and ferret out information — is not really one of my gifts.

That said, telepathic communication occurs much faster than actual speech, so it only took a few seconds to bring Smokey up to speed. Under normal circumstances, I probably wouldn't have been discussing the mission at all. It was classified, and I hadn't been debriefed yet. However, due to our playing a significant role in saving the planet a few times in the past, several of us teen supers — including myself, Smokey, and my girlfriend, Electra — had been given special clearances. Thus I wasn't violating any rules by talking to him about the Dream Machine mission. (To be honest, he was probably the only teen in the lounge who even knew about it.)

"Well," Smokey said when I concluded, "sounds like you learned a lesson."

I nodded. "Yeah — stay out of subway tunnels."

Smokey grinned. "I was thinking more along the lines of keeping your eye on the ball."

"That, too," I said noncommittally. "But trust me, I'll stay totally focused from now on."

Smokey gave me a skeptical look. "Totally focused, eh?"

"Completely, from this point forward. Nothing will get by me."

"Then in that case, you already know you've got inbound at eleven o'clock."

"What?" I mumbled, frowning.

With a sly grin, Smokey subtly tilted his head towards the main area of the lounge. Looking in the direction indicated, I didn't notice anything initially, but then drew in a sharp breath as I realized what Smokey was trying to draw my attention to — or rather, *who*.

Vestibule.

REPLICATION

Chapter 4

Vestibule was one of those people for whom life had seemingly pulled out all the stops. Born into a family of blue bloods, she'd known almost nothing but wealth and privilege her entire life. Moreover, she'd been blessed with classical beauty and an eye-popping figure, which she had parlayed into a successful modeling career. Last but not least, she had the rare ability of teleportation — a talent that had earned her a spot with the teen affiliate of the A-List Supers, who operated on the West Coast and were typically considered to rank second only to the Alpha League in terms of power and prestige.

Upon seeing her, I let out a slight groan of irritation that caused Smokey's grin to widen. Vestibule's presence was not something I wanted to deal with at the moment, but it should have been expected.

In the not-too-distant past, we had needed Vestibule's help to save the planet. Her assistance, however, had come with a price attached: a date with me. But as luck would have it, I had been summoned to my grandmother's homeworld before fulfilling that commitment. During my absence, however, Vestibule had apparently come by the lounge regularly looking for me. (Only a handful of people were aware of the fact that I was off-planet at the time, and she was not in the know.) Thus, the fact that she was here now shouldn't have been a surprise.

For a brief moment, I contemplated teleporting away (*any*where else would have been preferable), but then she caught sight of us and the opportunity was lost. A moment later, she was headed in our direction.

REPLICATION

She was dressed in a form-fitting, white-and-gray mini dress that was just long enough to reach an area that could — if one were feeling generous — be classified as her thigh. She also wore matching boots that came up just above the knee, and an unusual shade of metallic lipstick that would have looked odd on anyone else but suited her perfectly.

She strutted towards our table like she was on the runway, effortlessly drawing the attention of almost everyone present. (All the males, anyway.) She certainly knew how to work a room. Seeing her approach, Smokey began to rise from his seat, preparing to excuse himself on some pretext. I told him to stay put; he stared at me for a second, then sat back down.

When she reached our table, she took a seat without waiting for an invitation, then graced me with a smile that probably made most guys euphoric.

"Face-to-face at last," she said, eyes twinkling as she leaned back and crossed her legs. "You're a hard guy to catch up with, Kid Sensation — even for a teleporter like me."

"I typically go by 'Jim,'" I stated flatly. "And for the record, we've been face-to-face before, but you blew me off."

"That was on a previous occasion when I didn't know who you were," she clarified, referencing the fact that the face most of the world identified with Kid Sensation — a label the media had pinned on me — was not my true countenance. Thus, when she'd seen my "real" face, she hadn't recognized me.

I shrugged. "One of the hazards of cavorting with shapeshifters, I suppose. You never know when we're around or when you're dealing with us."

"Fair enough," she admitted. "But I think you'll agree that the last time we met — and I knew what you actually looked like — I didn't do anything close to blowing you off."

I frowned, thinking back. What Vestibule was referring to was the fact that she had kissed me — purportedly for luck — during the prior crisis when she had helped save the world. It was an incident I would have been happy to forget about, had it not happened in front of my girlfriend, Smokey, and a score of other people.

"Cat got your tongue?" Vestibule asked, bringing me out of my reverie. "Of course, if you don't recall what happened last time, I'd be happy to refresh your memory."

She raised an eyebrow suggestively. At the same time, Smokey began to cough like something was stuck in his throat — an act that reminded both Vestibule and me of his presence. (He had been completely silent up to that point, such that I'd almost forgotten he was there.) Fortunately, he stopped after a moment, making it clear that he wasn't likely to choke to death.

"Sorry," he rasped. "I think that last sip of soda went down the wrong way."

"Anyway," Vestibule said, crossing her arms as she turned back to me. "You owe me a date."

"An *outing*," I corrected, using my girlfriend Electra's terminology.

Vestibule waved her hand dismissively. "Whatever. You still have an obligation here."

"Which I plan to make good on tomorrow night," I declared firmly. "Didn't you get the invite?"

"I did," she answered. "But that's not a date. It's an event with tons of people."

"Well, if I were taking you to dinner, a movie, or a show, barring me renting out the entire venue, there would be lots of other people around. Tomorrow night will be no different, so it counts."

"The hell it does!" Vestibule practically hissed, leaning forward angrily. "First of all, you're not picking me up, which is what I'd expect — even for an *outing*, as you call it. I'm providing my own transportation. Second, I'd anticipate at least being by your side, if not on your arm, when we do this, but I doubt I'll see you for more than five minutes tomorrow. Third, I don't envision your little lightning rod being anywhere around when you finally decide to man up and keep your promise."

There was silence for a moment as Vestibule and I sat there scowling at each other. She had just voiced the reason for her displeasure, plainly stating her case. In addition, I felt frustration rolling off her in waves. On my part, I didn't care for the way that she was implying that I was trying to duck my obligations.

"Ah, just to be clear," Smokey said, breaking the silence, "a lightning rod doesn't actually *create* electricity, as was implied. What it actually does is…"

Smokey's voiced trailed off as Vestibule gave him a withering look that would have felled an oak. Her expression made it clear that she wasn't in the mood to entertain comments from the peanut gallery.

"Fine," I finally said, drawing Vestibule's attention back to me. "You don't like the arrangements I made for resolving this, so tell me how you see it playing out."

Her eyebrows shot up momentarily in surprise, and I could tell from her emotions that my comment had caught her a little unprepared. However, she recovered quickly.

"Well," she said, smiling impishly, "word on the street is that you took your little girlfriend to Paris a few months back."

Now it was my turn to raise my eyebrows. "You're kidding, right? You can't possibly want me to repeat the same date with you."

Vestibule shook her head. "No, but it shows you've got imagination. What I want is for you to apply that same creative spark to *our...*" — she spent a moment searching for the right term — "...jaunt."

I chuckled at her choice of words, which elicited a giggle from her in return. In addition to its traditional meaning, "jaunt" was a term that was generally accepted as a synonym for "teleport" in the realm of science fiction. Vestibule's use of it implied that there might be more to her than there appeared at first blush. (Plainly speaking, I had always considered her to be a bit vapid, but perhaps I needed to reassess that opinion.)

"Alright, we'll do it your way," I acquiesced. "Tomorrow is out of the question, so how about Sunday afternoon?"

"Sunday *night* would be better," she replied. "But I'll take what I can get. And who knows where the day may take us?"

I didn't respond to that directly, preferring instead to suggest we exchange contact info. (To be fair, Vestibule had actually written down her relevant information for me on a previous occasion, but Electra had taken possession of it almost immediately, and, well...enough said.) We were still in the process of entering our respective phone numbers on each other's cell phones when I heard a familiar voice.

"Please forgive me if I am interrupting, but I was hoping I could join you."

The speaker was Li, another friend and fellow member of the League's teen affiliate. Unlike the rest of us, however, Li wasn't human; he was an AI housed in an android body. That said, he looked like a typical teen and was ordinarily accepted as such (at least by me and my peers).

"It's fine, Li," I said as Vestibule and I returned each other's phones. "Have a seat."

"Yes, please do," Vestibule added as she rose from her chair. "I was about to leave anyway." She turned to me. "So, I'll see you tomorrow, and we're on for Sunday."

I gave a terse nod but didn't say anything. In reply, Vestibule gave me a wink, then vanished.

Chapter 5

"Well, that was interesting," Smokey said after Vestibule was gone.

"That's one way to put it," I offered. "At least now I can finally put this 'date' thing to bed."

"You know, I would have been happy to let you guys speak alone," Smokey assured me. "Why'd you tell me to stay?"

"Because when I tell Electra what happened, she's not going to be happy," I stated. "I'm going to need a witness to back up my version of events."

"*Your* version?" Li said, sounding nonplussed.

"Yes, *my* version," I replied. "Which is basically that I don't want this outing with Vestibule, and I'm doing it under protest."

"Electra knows that," Smokey chimed in. "She also knows that you need to honor the deal that was made."

"Speaking of Electra," Li said, "I assume that the lack of heated words while Vestibule was visiting means she is not here?"

"She mentioned something earlier about shopping for a dress," I answered somewhat sulkily. "Although I assumed she'd be back by now."

Smokey laughed. "What you really mean is that you thought she'd be so worried about you that she'd be waiting to make sure you made it back okay."

"Not exactly," I protested, although Smokey had accurately picked up on my mood. "I just—"

Still smirking, Smokey cut me off with a wave of his hand. "You've got a lot to learn about women. For instance, nothing interferes with shopping — not even boyfriends on deadly missions."

I chuckled slightly at that. He may not have been an empath or a telepath, but Smokey often displayed an uncanny ability to read the room.

"If I might offer my own analysis, Jim," Li added. "I think that Electra — being aware of your power set — feels little need to worry regarding your well-being. You have displayed on multiple occasions an innate ability to take care of yourself."

"Thanks, Li," I said. His words, however, reminded me of an oversight on my part.

"I'm sorry," I continued. "I didn't even ask — how did things go on your end today?"

"Very well, thank you," Li replied. "We encountered some issues, but nothing that jeopardized our ability to complete our assigned task."

I nodded. "Good to hear."

That was about as much as we could say in our current location. Li had been part of the team that had made a direct assault on Dream Machine's main base. Being an android, he wasn't susceptible to the AI's power, which had made him — like me — indispensable to a certain extent. Moreover, it was also his first official mission.

His group had obviously been successful in providing a distraction, and Mouse had relayed to me before I left that they were all okay. (The very fact that Li was here now was another indicator that things had gone well.) Still, he was my friend, and I suddenly felt bad that I had been so wrapped up in my own issues that I had failed to ask about the life-or-death mission he'd undertaken. Thankfully, Li did not seem offended.

"Anyway," I said, getting to my feet, "I've got a million things to do before tomorrow night, so I need to get out of here."

"You're not going anywhere," Smokey stated plainly. "Not until you finish that soda."

I blinked. "What?"

"Do you know what it cost to get that for you?" Smokey asked, pointing at the soda bottle. "And you've barely taken a sip."

"It was free," I countered, "from a fridge about fifty feet away, that's kept fully stocked. Exactly what did it cost you?"

"Time and effort," Smokey said. "But it's not about what it cost *me*, young man. It's about the waste. Do you know that there are little kids dying of thirst—"

"Alright, alright," I cut in, laughing.

Shifting into super speed, I grabbed the soda bottle, turned it up, and gulped down the contents in about a second.

"Satisfied?" I asked as I placed the bottle back on the table.

"Eh," Smokey muttered noncommittally, but with a smile. "It's a start."

I laughed again, enjoying the good-natured ribbing I was receiving. It made me mindful of the fact that Smokey and I really hadn't had a chance to talk since I'd been back. Other than my immediate family and Electra, I hadn't really made time for anyone lately, but I mentally made a note to remedy that situation at the earliest opportunity.

I turned to Li. "What about you? Anything *you* need me to do before I take off?"

Li shook his head. "No, but with respect to tomorrow night. Are you sure—"

"You're coming," I declared, not letting him finish. "Both of you. No excuses."

"Hey, man, I'm looking forward to it," Smokey clarified. "And it's still okay for me to bring my plus-one, right?"

"Of course," I said with a nod. "Sarah will enjoy it."

At the mention of his girlfriend, Smokey's brow creased slightly and I felt an odd mix of emotions from him: longing, sadness, affection, and more. Clearly something was off.

Maybe they're fighting, I thought.

Whatever the issue was, Smokey hadn't mentioned it and it wasn't my place to delve. Besides, he and Sarah had always seemed like a rock-solid couple, so I was sure they'd work it out.

So, assuming everything was fine for the most part (but promising myself I'd see if Smokey wanted to talk about it later), I said goodbye to my friends and teleported home.

REPLICATION

Chapter 6

Home for me these days was a three-story mansion in a tony residential district that was reserved for ambassadors and foreign dignitaries. In fact, the place where I now hung my hat was officially the ambassadorial residence of the Caelesian envoy to Earth (which, at present, was none other than yours truly).

The person who had originally filled that role was my grandmother, Indigo. However, due to her prolonged absence, I found myself unexpectedly saddled with the title a few months back. I hadn't wanted the job, but it had come with some nice perks (diplomatic immunity, for example) and virtually no duties, so I really didn't have much to complain about.

I popped up in my bedroom — an oversized space that would probably be better described as a suite since it had two connecting rooms (not counting the bathroom). One of those was a sitting room; the other was a small library with built-in bookshelves, an easy chair, and a small end table. The bedroom itself was about three hundred square feet in size, which was far larger than anything I'd ever had before. Populated only by my bed, dresser, and nightstand, the room looked almost barren.

Needless to say, I hadn't quite gotten used to having this much space, even though we'd been living here for several weeks now — almost from the moment my grandmother, Myshtal, and I had arrived. The modest house I'd previously occupied with my mother and grandfather had suddenly felt cramped with five people living there. (It had gone without saying, of course, that Myshtal would be staying with us.)

REPLICATION

More to the point, my grandmother and Myshtal were royalty (although, technically, my mother and I were as well). They were used to living in opulence: mansions, chateaus, palaces, and the like. Even when she had been under house arrest on Caeles, my grandmother had basically lived in the lap of luxury.

That said, I'd initially had no doubt that my grandmother would be able to downsize. She had done so before (when she first came to Earth and married my grandfather), and presumably wouldn't have an issue doing so again. Myshtal, on the other hand, had originally given me pause. I didn't know how she'd react to having to live among the masses, without a bunch of servants at her beck and call.

I needn't have worried, however. From the moment we set foot on Earth, my involuntary fiancée had made it clear that she was prepared to "rough it" to whatever extent necessary. (And from what I could read of her emotions, she was sincere in that regard.) So if that meant smaller beds (and bedrooms) than she was accustomed to, no servants, etcetera, then so be it.

Fortunately, it didn't come to that. A few days after our arrival from Caeles (and after we'd suffered through trying to live together in close quarters), all five of us jointly decided to move to the Caelesian embassy. It marked a compromise in size between what Gramps, Mom, and I were comfortable with and what Indigo and Myshtal were accustomed to. Even more, it had accoutrements and affectations of Caelesian high society, which would probably go a long way towards making Myshtal feel at home.

The process of actually moving had taken perhaps a day and primarily consisted of me teleporting our household goods and belongings to the embassy. This also necessitated that I teleport much of the original furnishings (the bulk of which I considered outdated) into storage — including the Louis XIV-style furniture that had originally been in my bedroom. After that, it had taken perhaps another day to get settled in, but since then we'd all adjusted pretty well to our new home.

Looking around now, however, I spent a moment wondering if it had been a mistake to get rid of all the furniture that had been in my bedroom before. Without it, the place really did look and feel empty. Un-lived in, to be honest, and I found myself contemplating what I might use to fill the dead space. (Apparently it's true what they say: nature abhors a vacuum.)

I was still picturing what I could do with my bedroom in terms of interior design when I felt someone mentally pinging me a minute later. Based on years of experience and familiarity, I automatically knew who it was: my grandfather.

Gramps was a telepath — at one time, the most powerful one on the planet. Although he had hung up his cape years ago, he still had formidable mental abilities. (He was also the primary person who had trained me in the use of my own telepathy.) Dropping my mental shields, I heard his voice ring out almost immediately in my brain.

<About time you showed up,> he admonished. <We're starving.>

Mentally, I let out a chuckle. My grandfather's statement referred to the fact that — since my return from Caeles — we tried to eat dinner together as a family every night. (It stood to reason; after all, our family unit had been broken up for decades.) Although humorous, and obviously an exaggeration, his comment about "starving" clearly conveyed that they had delayed eating supper for my benefit.

<Well?> he continued. <You coming, or do we need to head up to eat in your room?>

<Sorry,> I said sheepishly. <I'll be there in a sec. What are we having?>

<Pizza,> he replied. <The women were out shopping all day and I had some things to take care of, so nobody cooked. Unless *you* whipped something up...>

The only thing I had whipped up was a nigh-fatal screw-up of an important mission, but I kept that little nugget to myself.

<Not this time,> I said. <I'll put my culinary skills on display at a later date.>

<Great. I'll hold you to that. Now get down here.>

REPLICATION

Chapter 7

After quickly washing up, I headed downstairs to a small breakfast nook where we generally took our meals. There was actually a posh formal dining room on the premises, complete with a fireplace and chandelier, but we all found it to be too ceremonial. It was the kind of place that made me feel like all the men should be sporting monocles, and all the women should be wearing cage crinolines.

Everyone was already there when I arrived, sitting at a square-shaped, counter-height table that seated eight, and which currently had a couple of pizza boxes in the center. As had become typical for them, my grandparents were seated next to each other at what we had informally dubbed the "head" of the table. To their right were my mother and Myshtal; I took a seat to the left of my grandparents, giving me an entire side of the table to myself. My grandfather took a moment to lead the family in saying grace, and then we dove in. Glancing around the table as we began to eat, I couldn't help but notice a certain surreal quality to our mealtime.

First there were my grandparents, who — in addition to the contrast in complexion (with him being dark and her being fair) — also appeared to have a distinct age gap between them. Because Caelesians live much longer than Terrans, Indigo still looked as youthful as she had when they had first married. Gramps, on the other hand, had aged well but had still grown noticeably older during their decades apart. (Oddly enough, however, my grandmother was the older of the two.)

Next, seeing my mother and grandmother next to each other could cause the average person to do a double-take. My mother had inherited Caelesian genes in spades, which manifested themselves in an exotically beautiful appearance that included pointed, elfin ears and eyes that changed color with her emotions. In fact, she and Indigo were so similar in appearance that they were far more likely to be mistaken for sisters than mother and daughter.

Finally, there was Myshtal — the fiancée that had been forced upon me. With exquisite features framed by flame-red curls and a figure that swimsuit models dream of, calling her physically attractive would have been a severe understatement. She had an allure that went well beyond mere appearance and which exceeded the ability to be accurately described. Looking at her now, I couldn't help but think that under other circumstances...

"How was your day, *Sxibbo*?" my grandmother asked, interrupting my thoughts before biting into a slice of pepperoni pizza. She addressed me by a Caelesian appellation that loosely translated as "beloved and adored male progeny."

"It went well, *Sxahnin*," I replied, using a Caelesian term of affection for an older female relative. "But I don't want to bore you guys by talking shop."

Indigo gave me a subtle nod, indicating that she understood: I'd been involved in something that I wasn't exactly free to talk about. Mentally, however, she pinged me with a query asking if I was all right (as did Mom and Gramps). I telepathically assured them all that I was fine, and — thankfully — no one pressed me for details.

There was silence for a moment (at least audibly) as we continued to eat, but on a psychic level I was picking up lots of mental chatter. This wasn't unusual, as there would typically be at least five conversations going on when we ate, with at least four of them being telepathic.

REPLICATION

For starters, Gramps and Indigo were always connected; they were in constant mental communion (which was understandable since they had spent so many years apart). In addition, my mother and grandmother tended to keep an open line of communication as well. I knew that Indigo felt as though she'd never had a chance to truly nurture my mother, but it had taken them almost no time to develop a fierce and loving bond. Also, the three of them — my mother and her parents — spent a lot of time mentally yammering, clearly making up for lost time. Occasionally, I would get sucked into a conversation with the three of them, making it a full family affair.

In addition to the conversations noted, there was usually some oral discussion going on as well, to make sure Myshtal didn't feel left out or isolated. In fact, when I was growing up, Mom and Gramps generally made it a point to keep the bulk of our communications verbal (unless there was an emergency or a need to share information quickly). That might sound odd for a family of telepaths, but the truth of the matter was that, historically, Mom had rarely used her powers. (There was also the fact that I had seemingly been born without any special abilities, which had made verbal communication mandatory at one point in time.)

"This is delicious!" Myshtal exclaimed, obviously relishing her first taste of pizza. "This is one of Earth's delicacies, I presume?"

"Hardly," I chuckled, along with the rest of my family. "It's just pizza."

In response, Myshtal wrinkled her brow, and I felt confusion coming from her.

"I'm sorry," she said, eyes slightly downcast. "Did I misspeak?"

"Not at all," my grandmother assured her. "It's just that this isn't really a delicacy. It's something on par with *yraszin*."

"Oh," Myshtal muttered softly. Then she began snickering as well, realizing the term Indigo had used was the Caelesian version of "junk food."

I felt relief flooding through her, and I realized that she was more concerned about her language skills than anything else. Apparently, she didn't mind being confused on the concept (that is, confusing junk food with a delicacy); she was more bothered by the notion that she had picked the wrong word altogether — for instance, if she had said "shoe" instead of "delicacy." In short, she was fretting over the thought that she might not have mastered the English language.

She needn't have worried. She spoke with an adorable accent, but her English was perfect. She had practiced with me and my grandmother on the trip back from Caeles, but it had become immediately obvious that she had been tutored quite extensively on the subject. My guess was that plans had been made for her to visit Earth long before I came into the picture.

"Anyway," my mom said, taking charge of the conversation, "if you want to sample delicacies, there should be plenty of them tomorrow night."

Myshtal beamed upon hearing this. "Excellent. It will be my first formal Earth event, so I'm very excited."

"We all are," my grandmother added.

Not all of us, I thought. All of a sudden everyone turned to look at me, and for a moment I wondered if I'd telepathically broadcast my thoughts or expressed them vocally. I realized a moment later that I hadn't done either, but had still done something that made my feelings on the matter known: I had audibly groaned.

My grandmother raised an eyebrow. "You have something you wish to say, *Sxibbo?*"

I was on the verge of answering in the negative, then simply decided to be forthright.

Letting out a deep breath, I said, "I don't know. I just feel like this thing's gotten out of control."

"Hear, hear," said Gramps, surprising me with a show of support.

"John," my grandmother admonished. "Don't encourage him."

"I'm not encouraging him," my grandfather countered. "I side with the boy on this."

"What?" Indigo muttered, obviously caught a little off guard.

"Look, Indigo," Gramps said, "hiding my joy when you finally got back a couple of weeks ago was damn near impossible. I reached out to let a handful of old friends know you'd returned, then you and I agreed we'd have a small get-together with a few of them — just for old times' sake. A couple of other people got wind of it and wanted to join in, then some more, and before we knew it, our little get-together had transformed into a big party."

My grandfather glanced in my direction and I gave a slight nod to indicate that he had accurately summed things up. The only issue I might take with his narrative was that the term "big party" was inadequate to describe the upcoming affair. To me, that was like calling a hurricane a stiff breeze.

In short, as word circulated that my grandparents would be hosting an impromptu reception for some old acquaintances, the number of people wanting to drop in had broadened considerably. I had initially thought the attendees would include only their old ex-cape buddies, but I had seriously underestimated the level of society at which Indigo and Gramps had circulated in their prime. They had counted as personal friends everyone from celebrities to industrial billionaires to heads of state — many of whom would equate the lack of an invitation to being publicly snubbed. Thus, the guest list had grown.

However, it wasn't just past newsmakers who wanted to attend. Current media darlings — actors, singers, tech moguls, and so on (most of whom had probably never heard of my grandparents) — also wanted in. In essence, anybody who was anybody (or who thought of themselves that way) had been angling for an invite.

Moreover, it turned out that people were fascinated by Indigo's story: a long-lost superhero returning to Earth after a lengthy sojourn in outer space. (It didn't hurt that she was a beautiful, alien princess to boot.)

Long story short, what had started out as an intimate function with a few friends from my grandparents' heyday had morphed into a gala event, despite its impromptu nature. (Basically, this thing was being held just a few weeks after we got back to Earth, so it was being put together in record time.) Everyone's initial thought had been to have it at the embassy, but the ever-growing guest list had promptly squashed those plans. Now it was being held at a palatial estate owned by my father, Alpha Prime, who was generally considered Earth's greatest superhero.

"So in my opinion, Jim's right," my grandfather continued, bringing me back to the conversation at hand. "This thing's become so bloated and unwieldy that I'd almost prefer to skip it."

REPLICATION

"Well, all of our old friends will be there, so you're going," Indigo stated with finality. She then turned to me. "You, too, *Sxibbo*. There are some people coming I want you to meet."

"I appreciate that, *Sxahnin*," I replied, "and I was fine when it was supposed to be a small function. I was even okay when it became too big to hold here at the embassy. But now, it's not just a huge bash — it's exploded into an over-the-top, red carpet event."

"The boy hates the spotlight," Gramps explained in a conspiratorial tone, mostly for Myshtal's benefit.

"It's not so much that," I clarified, "although I do like my privacy. In all honesty, I was simply looking forward to me and my friends listening to you guys and some of your old colleagues talk about the adventures you had. Now it just feels like another pompous, overblown banquet full of pretentious stuffed shirts."

"Except — since we're throwing the party — *we're* the stuffed shirts," Mom noted.

"Something like that," I said.

Myshtal shook her head in confusion. "I'm sorry — 'stuffed shirt'?"

"A *turzzkon*," my grandmother explained. At the same time, she shared with everyone a mental image of a puffed up, self-conceited Caelesian royal. The figure was so blatantly haughty and vainglorious that we all had to laugh.

"Ahhh!" Myshtal exclaimed in understanding, still smiling. "It's clear now. But don't worry; I won't let Jim become a *turzzkon*. I'll make sure he has too much fun to stuff his shirt."

"Oh?" I said, chuckling at her phrasing. "And how will you do that?"

"Like this," she replied, then stuck out her tongue and crossed her eyes.

I was so surprised by the gesture (which I didn't even know she was aware of), that I just stared at her for a second — and then I burst out laughing, along with everyone else.

REPLICATION

Chapter 8

We spent the remainder of dinner idly chatting about the upcoming gala. Afterwards, we all retreated to the parlor to play board games, which had been one of my grandmother's favorite pastimes during her first visit to Earth. It was a form of entertainment that didn't really have an equivalent on Caeles, so she had missed it terribly. Given her predilection for it, we generally played a couple of times per week.

On this particular occasion, we settled on a game that required each player to build their own medieval kingdom. The game was won by achieving a certain amount of wealth, along with a stable (but sizeable) population and trade routes for specific goods. In most instances, it was easiest to achieve victory by forming alliances with other players, and — on the whole — it was a fun and challenging game. Playing with Indigo, however, took things to an entirely different level.

It turned out that my grandmother was incredibly competitive when it came to games like this and tended to adopt a win-at-all-cost mentality. Thus, with respect to the particular game in question, she would breach peace treaties, betray allies, and more if she thought it would give her an advantage. And heaven forbid that she should ever be losing! At that point, all bets were off, as she would adopt a scorched Earth policy: burning crops and fields, raiding villages, poisoning wells...

"If I can't win, no one will," was her philosophy.

It was an entirely different side of my grandmother — one that I hadn't even known existed — but to be honest, having a villain in the game (for lack of a better term) tended to make things more exciting. Tonight was no exception as Indigo quickly launched a victory-or-death style of play that kept us all on our toes. On this particular occasion, however, an alliance with me led to my mother winning the game not just once, but twice. Flush with victory after her two consecutive wins, Mom let out an excited whoop and began high-fiving everyone. She then turned to Indigo (who always sat next to her at the gaming table where we played) and blew a raspberry at her.

"That's it," Indigo declared, feigning disgust as she smacked her hand on the table. "We're playing again."

"No, we're not," Gramps said with conviction as he came to his feet. "You'll play all night if we let you, Indigo, but I'm an old man and I need my beauty sleep."

"You're not *that* old," my grandmother replied with a mischievous look in her eye.

"Oh, jeez," I muttered as I detected a noticeable uptick in the mental chatter between my grandparents. "Please leave — both of you. We'll put the game away. Just…go."

Laughing, my grandparents bid us goodnight and left.

Myshtal turned to my mother. "If you wish to leave as well, please do. I'll help Jim put everything away."

My mother didn't respond immediately. Instead, she gave me an inquisitive look.

"It's fine," I assured her. "Plus, you have a deadline to meet."

"Thanks for the reminder," Mom said.

My statement was a reference to the fact that my mother was a midlist author of superhero romance novels. She had a deadline that was approaching, and with everything going on lately — from my grandmother's return to the upcoming gala — it would be a minor miracle if she wasn't behind.

"Frankly speaking, I can use all the time I can get," Mom continued. "So, if you're sure…"

She trailed off, giving me one last chance to change my mind.

"It's no big deal, Mom," I stressed. "It's just game pieces and a game board, not rocket science. But if it makes you feel better…"

Rather than finish my statement, I let my actions speak for me. Shifting into super speed, I put away all the pieces of the game and then placed it back in the cabinet where it was normally kept before dashing back to my place at the table — all in less than a second. Thankfully, the room wasn't exceptionally large, so there was barely any wind following in the wake of my burst of speed.

"Well, that works for me," Mom said. She turned and headed for the door, shouting over her shoulder, "I'll be in my office if you need me."

That left me and Myshtal alone in the parlor, something that managed to fill me with both delight and dread. On the one hand, I found her fascinating; she was bright, had a ready wit, and we never seemed to lack for things to talk about. Plainly speaking, we had developed a strong bond almost from the moment we met.

That said, I was admittedly wild about my girlfriend Electra, and I worried immensely over how a growing friendship with Myshtal might affect our relationship. (It certainly didn't help that, technically, Myshtal and I were affianced.)

"Are you going to bed as well?" Myshtal asked, interrupting my thoughts.

"No," I replied, glancing at my watch. "Contrary to what my grandfather said, it's not that late, and I don't feel particularly tired."

All of that was true, but what I failed to mention was that I was actually feeling restless. Dinner and time with my family had been a welcome distraction, but now my thoughts were turning back to my earlier performance during the mission. Even if I had been ready to turn in, it would be a night of fitful sleep with those images in my head. (I also hadn't talked to Electra yet, which was one of the last things I did every night, but I tried to avoid bringing up my girlfriend in Myshtal's presence — and vice versa).

"I think I may just watch a movie or something," I added.

"Would you mind if I joined you?"

"Not at all," I said, practically beaming — and then immediately feeling guilty about it.

REPLICATION

Chapter 9

We ended up in the theater room — a windowless, soundproof chamber on the second floor. Rectangular in shape, the room had originally consisted of three identical, outdated couches lined up one behind the other and all facing a projector screen that covered an entire wall. The second and third couch had sat on risers, thereby allowing anyone sitting on either row to see over the heads of those in front of them. The walls had been covered with posters from classic films and autographed pictures of iconic movie stars from years past. Finally, a reel-to-reel projector had been used to show films on the screen.

Fast-forward to the present, and the couches had all been replaced with powered recliners — two to a row, with a hand-carved snack table between each pair. The reel-to-reel and original screen were gone as well, replaced by a state-of-the-art home theater system that included an upscale, high-definition projector, surround sound, and a one-hundred-twenty-inch projector screen. Last but not least, there was a red-and-white retro-style popcorn maker in a back corner, along with a mini fridge. About the only thing remaining of the original décor was the artwork on the walls.

The change in the room's look had come about at my grandfather's direction while I had been off-planet. The embassy had been badly in need of an upgraded security system (among other things), but to make it work with current technology had required a massive overhaul in a number of areas: rewiring the electrical system, installation of Cat 6 cable, and more. (There was also some physical damage to the embassy that had been inadvertently caused by my father Alpha Prime, who had voluntarily paid for the repairs.)

The end result of my grandfather's efforts was a smashing success, in my opinion — especially in terms of upgrading the home theater. It had been one of the few rooms in the house where I hadn't had to teleport a bunch of archaic furniture into storage. Looking around the room now as Myshtal and I entered, I couldn't help but think — and not for the first time — that Gramps had probably updated everything in here as part of a plan to use the embassy as his secret man-cave.

I let Myshtal pick the movie, and she chose a crime drama about a Robin Hood-esque gang trying to pull off a major heist. I felt it was a good choice, but Myshtal had probably picked it for reasons other than its entertainment value. While she understood that there was a lack of realism in films, she saw them as a way to learn more about Earth culture. There was a similar art form on Caeles, but it lacked the variation on themes that our movies embraced.

For instance, in a Caelesian "film," a thief would always be a bad guy. There would never be a situation whereby the audience's sympathies would be aligned with the person trying to commit a crime. It simply wasn't done. Likewise with other motifs; for example, a Caelesian movie about an arranged marriage would never lead viewers to wishing that, say, the prospective bride break off the engagement in order to marry her true love. (Not to say that those things never happened; they were just never represented in Caelesian films.) Bearing all that in mind, it's not surprising that Myshtal found this particular form of entertainment fascinating.

REPLICATION

I started the movie, then spent a moment firing up the popcorn maker. A few minutes later, we were seated in the front row recliners with a bowl of popcorn between us, as well as a couple of sodas from the mini fridge.

I had to admit that watching a movie with Myshtal was a treat. Almost as soon as the film started, she began making droll little comments about the on-screen action. For instance, one early scene showed a woman in a massive walk-in closet that was full of men's attire.

"That entire wardrobe is hideous," Myshtal declared. "She should just burn it."

Almost immediately, the woman on the screen pulled out a lighter and then walked through the closet, setting various articles of clothing on fire. (It turned out the woman was burning her husband's things after discovering he had a mistress.)

In another scene, a street musician was playing a guitar and singing, trying to entice passersby to place money in a tin cup.

"That instrument is completely out of tune," Myshtal stated. "Someone should smash it."

Within thirty seconds, a hard-nosed character snatched the guitar from the musician and smashed it into the ground several times until it broke into pieces.

After Myshtal made several more observations of this nature (and essentially predicted what the characters were going to do), I paused the movie.

"Stop. Just stop," I said, laughing. "You've obviously seen this film before."

"*Moi?*" she intoned mockingly, placing a hand innocently on her chest — a gesture that showed she was much more familiar with Earth culture than she occasionally let on.

"Yes, *you*," I stressed with a smile. "You're predicting every scene like you wrote the script."

"It's not my fault that Earth behavior is completely predictable."

"It isn't, due to the fact that we're a complex species."

"Of course you are," she said condescendingly. "I'm sure amoebas consider themselves a complex species as well."

I stared at her for a moment, and then we both burst out laughing. I'd been so wrapped up in other things lately, that I'd actually forgotten that Myshtal had a great sense of humor.

"Okay, you're right," she admitted after her laughter subsided. "I did see that film before. I've been watching a lot of them lately in my spare time in order to get more acclimated to Earth culture."

I thought for a moment. "Is that where you picked up a couple of the gestures you've used lately — like sticking out your tongue?"

"Yes," she said, grinning sheepishly.

"Well, keep up the good work."

She smiled at my words of encouragement, and I sensed something like pride coming from her in relation to a job well done.

With Myshtal promising not to foretell any more of the action, we went back to the movie. However, we'd only been watching a few minutes when the phone rang. There was a cordless extension in the theater room, and — knowing that Mom was working and that my grandparents were probably in bed — I teleported the phone into my hand.

65

I switched the phone on and gave a perfunctory "Hello."

"Hey, handsome," said a honeyed feminine voice on the other end of the line.

"Hey," I replied as I came to my feet, smiling at hearing my girlfriend's voice. I gestured to Myshtal that I needed to take this call, then began walking towards the door after she nodded in acknowledgment.

"What are you doing?" Electra asked.

"Thinking about you, of course." I stepped out of the theater room and closed the door behind me.

"Good answer," Electra said, giggling. As always, her laughter was intoxicating and infectious, making me chuckle along with her. "Seriously though, are you busy?"

"No — just watching a movie."

"Feel like hanging out?"

"Is that a trick question?" I asked, causing her to laugh again. I had rarely, if ever, turned down a chance to spend time with her. "Should I pop by your house?"

"No, not tonight," she said, causing me to frown in confusion. *Why ask me to hang out if she really didn't want to?* Then she added, "Just buzz me in."

"Huh?" I muttered, more confused than before.

"Buzz me in," she repeated. "I'm at the gate."

Smiling now, I pressed the digits on the phone that would cause the large, wrought-iron gate at the embassy entrance to open.

"Be there in a sec," I said, barely waiting for Electra to acknowledge my statement before hanging up the phone and setting it on a nearby table. I then teleported outside, to the bottom of a wide stoop that consisted of about a dozen stone steps that led up the embassy's front door.

REPLICATION

It was a rather dark night; what little illumination there was came mostly from a couple of ornate post lights — one at each end at the foot of the stoop. Looking down the driveway, I saw a pair of headlights headed in my direction. A few moments later, a car pulled to a stop in front of me, the engine turned off, and Electra got out.

She was dressed in jeans, black boots, gloves, and a hooded parka that neatly framed her face. Seeing her bundled up made me mindful of the fact that it was chilly outside and a stiff breeze was blowing. As was typical, Electra wasn't wearing makeup, but she had an inherent, natural beauty that didn't need to be enhanced by cosmetics.

We moved towards each other, both of us smiling, and then shared a short kiss as we met. Eyes twinkling, Electra moved closer and wrapped her arms around me as I embraced her as well.

"Well, this is disappointing," she droned a second later. Rubbing her hands quickly up and down the sides of my torso, she added, "Come on — do your thing."

I laughed, understanding what she meant. On cold days, when I haven't dressed appropriately for the weather, I tend to compensate by raising my body temperature. On this particular occasion, I had come outside without grabbing so much as a light jacket. However, I hadn't been outside long enough for the cold to start to affect me. Nevertheless, I did as requested and raised my core body temperature.

"*That's* my guy," Electra intoned, snuggling in close and placing her head against my chest. She had explained before that being next to me when I was like this was akin to cuddling next to a warm, cozy fire with a blizzard raging outside. "You're so nice and toasty that I could stay like this forever."

She then looked up and gave me a kiss — this time longer and more lingering than before. When we separated, breathless, a few moments later, she smiled and then pulled in close to me again.

"You know," I said, "you didn't have to drive all the way over here. I would have been happy to come to you."

"I know," she admitted, "but I wanted to. You shouldn't have to come to me *all* the time."

I smiled but didn't say anything, understanding what the meaning was behind her actions. In terms of spending time together, Electra had once equated dating me to having a rich boyfriend: sure, the guy could afford to pay every time they went out, but occasionally the girl wants to — if only to show the guy what he means to her. That's why she had chosen to drive and see me on a cold, dark night rather than have me come to her (which, frankly speaking, would have been much easier). Basically, it was a way of telling me I was worth it, and I loved her for it.

"So, how'd the mission go?" she asked, breaking my chain of thought. She also stepped back slightly as she posed the question, allowing us to see eye-to-eye.

"Uh…" I muttered. "It's a bit of a mixed report, to be honest."

I then telepathically shared with her the pertinent mission details. As expected, she groaned in disapproval at certain actions on my part. Upon finishing, I decided not to give her an opportunity to verbalize any criticisms.

"So," I blurted out, "how was your shopping jaunt?"

"Nice try at changing the subject," she said, making it understood that she knew what I was trying to do. "But it was fine. I think I found the perfect dress."

"Oh? What does it look like?"

She laughed. "No, no, no, no. You're going to have to wait until tomorrow. I want to see the look on your face when you first catch a glimpse of me in it."

I frowned. "Well, how does telling what it looks like change that? I still won't see you in it until tomorrow."

"Because I want your complete reaction. I won't get that if you have an idea of what to expect."

I shook my head, nonplussed. "Smokey's right. I really *don't* understand women."

Electra laughed at that. "Good. That's the way I like it."

I raised an eyebrow inquisitively. "You *want* me confused about women?"

She grinned. "No. I just don't want you thinking you fully understand *me*, because the second that happens, you'll—"

Electra stopped abruptly as the sound of hinges creaking drew the attention of us both. Almost in unison, we separated and looked toward the top of the steps — to the front door of the embassy. With light from the interior behind her, we watched in silence as Myshtal stepped out.

Almost immediately, there was tension in the air. More to the point, where there had been lighthearted mirth and amusement a moment before, I now felt a flurry of heated emotions coming from Electra that included resentment, spite, and annoyance (to name a few).

Myshtal wrapped her arms around herself against the cold. At that moment I noticed she appeared to be wearing something short, sheer, and form-fitting. She obviously hadn't dressed for the weather, which suggested she wouldn't be out here long — something I considered a blessing.

"Hello, Electra," Myshtal said, giving my girlfriend a congenial wave. "It's nice to see you again."

"Yeah — you, too," Electra said flatly, although her tone suggested that it was anything *but* nice.

It was undoubtedly a cool reception on my girlfriend's part, but about the best that could be hoped for under the circumstances. Ever since their initial meeting after I returned from Caeles — and had to tell Electra about my contracted nuptials — the relationship between the two had been nothing short of frosty.

"I'm sorry for intruding," Myshtal said, turning to me, "but I just wanted to ask if you wanted me to pause the movie, Jim?"

I felt, rather than saw, Electra jerk her head in my direction. At the same time, a volcano of emotions erupted within her — mostly bitterness and displeasure, blanketed by layers of anger and frustration.

"Uh, no," I said, purposely avoiding looking at Electra. "You can just let it play, or watch something else if you want."

"Okay," she said with a nod. "Goodnight, Electra."

My girlfriend grunted something inaudible in response as Myshtal turned and headed back inside. A moment later, the door closed.

"Is that what you were doing when I called?" she demanded. "Watching a movie, with *her*?"

"Yeah, we were watching a movie," I said defensively.

She gave me a smoldering look. "So the two of you were having a date night?"

"What?!" I asked, flabbergasted. "No! It was just a movie!"

"Really? So who else was there?"

I cut my eyes away in impotent anger. I didn't say anything, but I didn't have to.

"That's what I thought," Electra said as she indignantly crossed her arms.

"That still doesn't make it a date," I stressed.

"And what about what she was wearing?"

"What about it?" I asked.

"It was practically lingerie!"

I frowned in concentration for a moment. I hadn't really gotten a good look at what Myshtal was wearing when she came to the door. I suppose it *could* have been a negligee…

"That's not what she was wearing earlier," I insisted, and it was true. If memory served me correctly, she had previously been dressed in some kind of skirt-and-blouse combo.

"Oh?" Electra intoned, raising her eyebrows in faux surprise. "So you're saying that for the movie, she decided to slip into something more comfortable?"

"That's not what happened at all. You're twisting the facts into something sordid."

"Or maybe you're just being blind to the truth," she countered. "Can't you see what's going on here?"

"Yes, I can. And what I can confirm is that there's absolutely *nothing* going on."

She shook her head in disbelief. "You can't be that naïve, Jim. She's prancing around in front of you in a negligee — you think she's doing that for her health?"

I let out an exasperated breath. "Even if what you're suggesting is true — and I don't believe it is, but

71

even if it were — you can't possibly think I'd be more interested in her than you."

"In all honesty, I don't know what to think any more," she said softly. "You two could be doing anything, and I wouldn't have a clue."

I stared at her in dumbfounded amazement for a moment. "You're kidding, right? Between my mom, Gramps, and my grandmother, we've got like a million chaperones — all of them psychic! There's nothing going on in that house that they don't know about or condone."

Electra seemed to mull over my statement, then let out a long sigh and said, "Okay, but why does she even have to stay here, under the same roof as you?"

"Where else is she going to stay? She literally knows no one else on the planet."

"Just check her into a hotel or something. Plus, I hear they're fixing up a place for her at League HQ."

"Come on, Electra. Only a handful of super teens have ever stayed at the League full-time. And with her limited experience with Earth culture, I can't just stick her in a hotel — even a resort. I promised to look after her."

"Yeah," Electra scoffed disdainfully. "Dressed like she was a moment ago, I imagine you're doing a *lot* of looking — and not just after."

I bit my tongue to avoid blurting out my instinctive response, which was to deny what was being implied. Electra's last statement was bait, and any denial on my part would lead to her asking a question along the lines of, "So you're saying you're not attracted to her?" Having already been painfully hooked by that lure several times in the past few weeks, I wasn't falling for it again.

"Look," I said calmly, "in addition to everything else, Myshtal is a guest in my family's home. Even if I was willing, they wouldn't let me stick her away out of sight, any more than they'd let me do it to you if your positions were reversed. And in case you forgot, her great-great-grandmother rules an interstellar empire, and Myshtal is her favorite. You don't think the queen's having her watched? Having *me* watched?"

"There wouldn't *be* any watching if you hadn't gotten yourself into this mess," she stated stonily. "Did you even try to say 'No' to this shotgun wedding?"

"We've been over this before. This was the deal I had to make to get home. Or would you prefer that I be stuck on Caeles for decades like my grandmother?"

"What I would prefer—"

"Shhh!" I hissed, putting a finger to her lips. She immediately went quiet.

I looked around warily. Just as Electra had begun speaking, I had picked up an emotional spike from nearby — a mix of excitement and elation mingled with trepidation. Somebody was watching us. Acting on instinct, I stepped protectively in front of my girlfriend.

"What is it?" she whispered.

"We've got eyes on us," I answered over my shoulder.

"How many?"

"Just one, I think."

At the same time that I answered, I felt the hairs on my arm rising as the air became ionized. Electra was gearing up to use her power.

"Where?" she asked, trying to step from behind me.

"Not sure," I said, thrusting an arm back to make sure she stayed to my rear. "But give me a sec. I'll find them."

REPLICATION

I began reaching out empathically. For me, the uptick in emotional activity had been almost like a verbal shout, giving me a pretty good idea of where the person was.

The embassy sat on several acres, with nicely-manicured lawns and a number of good-sized trees. It was behind one of these — a thick, towering oak near the gated entrance — that I pinpointed our voyeur.

I telescoped my vision and then cycled through the light spectrum until I could see almost as well as in daylight.

"Got him," I said. "One guy, lurking behind a tree at ten o'clock, peeking around it every few seconds."

"I got him, too," Electra declared. It was a subtle reminder of the fact that her power allowed her to detect people by their bioelectric fields. "Does he seem dangerous?"

"I'm not picking up that kind of vibe from him, but he's holding something in his hand," I said, noting that our watcher had a tight grip on an object of some sort.

"Gun?"

I watched for a second, then let out a sigh of relief. "No — a digital camera with a telephoto lens."

Electra let out a disgusted sigh as she stepped from behind me. "Paparazzi."

I took a few steps forward and shouted, "Hey, you! By the tree! What are you doing?!"

The reaction was immediate: the fellow behind the tree took off, running towards a brick wall that framed the embassy grounds near the front gate. I gave Electra a telepathic heads-up, then teleported us.

We popped up a few feet behind our late-night visitor, who slipped a camera strap over his neck as he ran and then leaped for the brick wall, which was about nine feet tall. As he pulled himself up, Electra raised her hand, and I noticed that it was filled with a small, pulsing electrical charge.

<Wait,> I told her telepathically.

Emotionally, I could sense that she was still fired up about our argument, and — although she'd shown excellent control over her powers of late — I was a little worried that she might accidentally fry this guy. Nevertheless, despite obviously wanting to take her frustration out on someone, Electra mentally agreed to stand down.

I turned my attention back to our friend with the camera, who had just pulled himself up high enough to kick a leg up to the top of the wall. He was so focused on the task at hand that he didn't even notice us behind him (not that he would have expected us to close the distance that fast).

I phased the brick wall, making it insubstantial. With nothing solid supporting him, our visitor fell to the ground, landing on his back with a solid thud that knocked the wind out of him. As he began to cough, I telekinetically grabbed his ankle and pulled him farther inside the embassy grounds before making the wall solid again.

I teleported his camera, which had been attached to the strap around his neck, into my hand. Photography wasn't my forte, but from what I could tell it was a high-end model and had probably cost a pretty penny.

Taking his camera seemed to galvanize our visitor in some way, as he seemed to tap an inner reserve of sorts and struggle to his feet.

"Who are you?" I asked as soon as he stood up.

"Just a photographer," he said, sidestepping my question. As I looked him over, I noticed that he was young — early twenties at most. Dressed in corduroy pants and a fleece jacket, he was maybe an inch shy of six feet in height, with a slender build and sandy hair that was just a tad bit long.

"A photographer," I repeated, sounding skeptical. "What are you doing here?"

I sensed nervousness and anxiety coming from him, but he managed to answer in an even tone, saying, "Just hoping to get a picture of the princess."

I raised an eyebrow at this. "Indigo?"

"Yeah," he answered with a nod.

"Word on the street says she's staying at Alpha League Headquarters," I said. That was indeed the rumor, but one which we ourselves had started in order to have some privacy. "That being the case, why are you *here*?"

"There's an army of photographers over at League HQ," he replied. "They're entrenched around the place like they're conducting a siege. If Indigo takes one step outside, there's going to be a million pics of her posted across the internet in minutes."

"So shouldn't you be over there trying to make it a million-and-one?" I asked.

He shook his head. "It's the rare pics that are valuable — the ones that are unique in some way. I realized that if everyone had a photo of Indigo, then they wouldn't be worth as much. But if I could bring something to the table that others didn't have, my work would have added value. So I did a little research into her past and found out that this was Indigo's embassy back in the day."

I kept my face impassive as he spoke, but had to admit to being impressed. The records weren't exactly sealed but they weren't that straightforward either; thus, tracing everything back was a notable bit of detective work.

"So you came here on a hunch that Indigo might show up," I surmised as he finished speaking.

He shook his head. "No, I was honestly just hoping to get a few shots of the place that I could sell to anybody who might be interested in her backstory. It was just dumb luck that I was here when your girlfriend" — he nodded towards Electra — "pulled up."

"My girlfriend?" I repeated, frowning. He seemed harmless, but I really didn't like the notion of this guy knowing anything about me or Electra.

The fellow held up his hands defensively. "Hey, dude, it's just an expression. She could be your sister for all I know."

I didn't immediately answer. Instead, I took a moment to flip through the pictures he'd taken. The most recent ones were of me and Electra, but mostly her — about a half-dozen shots that actually looked very nice, despite the lack of adequate illumination. However, they also brought to mind that this guy might be some kind of crazed stalker (although I hadn't picked up that kind of vibe from him).

"It's not what you think," he said, almost reading my mind. He turned to my girlfriend. "I didn't recognize you initially, but I did after you got out of the car. You're Electra, right?"

On her part, Electra didn't say anything; she merely looked at me.

"Fry his camera, babe," I said, holding the camera out to her. A white ball of electricity immediately began to form in Electra's hand.

"No!" the guy screeched, almost in a panic. "Please, don't!"

REPLICATION

Neither Electra nor I said anything, but I felt raw, unrestrained anxiety rolling off the guy in waves.

"Please," he continued, pleading. "Don't destroy it. I'm freelance, alright? I'm not on salary anywhere. I take pictures and try to sell them to interested parties — newspapers, social media, what have you. But I'm not like paparazzi. I wasn't trying to peek into your windows, sneak into your house, or anything like that in order to get shots."

"But you *are* willing to trespass," I declared.

"I admit it," he said. "I slipped inside when the gate opened to let Electra in, but it's the first time I've ever done anything like that."

"Right," Electra muttered sarcastically. "That's what they all say."

"Look," the guy implored, "I'm just trying to earn enough to make my next tuition payment at the university. Taking pics is how I pay the bills. So you can take the chip out and destroy it if you want, or even wipe the hard drive clean. If you want to call the cops, I'll make a full confession to trespassing, illegal entry — whatever you want. But I'm begging you, don't destroy the camera. It's all I've got, and I can't afford another."

While he'd been speaking, I'd had my empathic abilities turned up to the max; from what I could discern, he was being completely sincere. More specifically, his plea brought to mind something I'd learned once in history class.

Back in the Old West, they used to hang horse thieves. It wasn't because horses were that valuable in and of themselves, but because the animals were used for everything from wrangling to farming. Thus, when you stole a man's horse, you often took away his livelihood.

You robbed him of the ability to earn a living, thereby making him destitute.

Our visitor's plea for his camera left me with much the same impression. Moreover, I developed a mental picture of what had likely happened earlier: after recognizing Electra, the guy had probably gotten excited about the money he could make from her picture (which had resulted in the emotional spike I'd detected). In short, I didn't really think this fellow was a stalker.

<What's going on out there?> Gramps asked telepathically, his unexpected intrusion bringing me back to myself. He had apparently picked up on our visitor's panicky thoughts.

Mentally, I gave him a quick rundown of what had happened, resulting in a short telepathic conversation that also included Indigo.

When we finished, I turned to our visitor, who had a deer-in-the-headlights look about him as he waited to hear the verdict regarding his camera.

"What's your name?" I asked, wondering if he'd try to dodge the question like before.

He gulped, and then seemed to struggle to find his voice for a second before finally stating, "It's Matt. Matthew Kroner."

I smiled. "Well, Matthew Kroner, today's your lucky day."

Chapter 10

I woke up the next morning not of my own volition, but due to someone psychically tapping on my mental shields. It was the telepathic equivalent of someone nudging me awake.

<Hurry up and get down here,> Gramps said. <There's a surprise for you.>

I mentally acknowledged that I was awake and promised to be down momentarily. I then grabbed my cell phone off the nightstand and checked the time. I groaned softly; it was still early.

In addition to noticing the time on my phone, I also saw that I had received a text roughly fifteen minutes earlier. It was from Smokey's girlfriend Sarah and said, "Have you talked to him yet?"

I stood up and stretched, contemplating Sarah's message as I did so. I hadn't talk to her in a while, so presumably her message was meant for someone else. (It wouldn't have been the first time that I received a text meant for another person, and probably wouldn't be the last.) After dwelling on it for a moment — and remembering Smokey's question about bringing a guest — I assumed it was meant for him. My guess is that Sarah was trying to reach her boyfriend and had inadvertently texted me instead.

Shifting into super speed, I then raced through my normal morning routine and got dressed. After looking in the bathroom mirror to make sure I was presentable, I went back to normal speed before heading down to the breakfast area.

REPLICATION

Only my grandparents were present when I arrived, sitting in their usual spot at the table with a newspaper between them.

"Come take a look at this, boy," Gramps said, excitedly waving me over.

"What is it?" I asked as I walked towards them.

Instead of responding, Indigo tapped the newspaper laying on the table. Taking a good look, I saw that the front page had a large color photograph of my grandparents. The background was obscured so that you couldn't tell where the picture had been taken, but it showed Gramps and Indigo staring lovingly into each other's eyes. It was a beautiful photo, effortlessly capturing the depth of emotion between the subjects in it, and I smiled as I noticed who was credited with the snapshot in the caption below the image: Matthew Kroner.

In brief, after hearing Kroner's plea, we had decided not to destroy his camera. Even more, my grandparents had come outside and essentially posed for him, giving him a photographic exclusive. (It was literally a money shot, since I assume he sold it for a nice chunk of change.)

"It's a nice pic," I stated truthfully, "although I'm not that surprised since Kroner seemed like a decent photographer."

Indigo laughed. "Oh *Sxibbo*, that's not the surprise."

My eyebrows went up, but before I could say anything, Myshtal entered the room wearing a cooking apron and carrying a plate of toast in one hand and a plate of cooked bacon in the other. She was followed by my mother, who carried a bowl of scrambled eggs.

"What's this?" I asked as Myshtal set both plates on the table.

"Myshtal made breakfast for us," Mom said.

"Oh, wow," I uttered, as this really *was* unexpected. "You didn't have to do that."

"So says the guy who rarely cooks his own meals," my grandfather chimed in.

"That's not true," I countered. "I make my own meals all the time."

"Cereal and sandwiches don't count as cooking," Indigo interjected.

"Fine," I said testily. "I'll fry my cereal in the skillet next time before I eat it."

That got a chuckle out of everyone as we sat down to eat, with me thinking that this was a nice gesture on Myshtal's part. It was a fairly basic breakfast and clearly wasn't a test of her culinary skills, but considering the fact that she had probably never prepared a meal before, I was suitably impressed.

"This is great," I said to Myshtal as I took a bite of toast.

"Thanks," Myshtal replied. "I wish I could take all the credit, but I did have help." She tilted her head towards my mother.

"You're being too generous," Mom said between bites of bacon. "All I really did was season the eggs."

"Well, my compliments to *both* chefs," Gramps said, to which Mom and Myshtal both muttered their thanks.

From that point, the breakfast conversation shifted mostly to generic topics, but with a focus on the gala to occur that night. There was a general question about my friends being invited, but no one asked specifically about

Electra attending. Our relationship was obviously in an odd place, but — despite the tense conversation we'd had outside the embassy — we had ended the night on something of a high note. Dealing with Kroner's unexpected appearance had given us something else to focus on, and watching my grandparents pose for him had reminded us of just how much we cared for each other. In short, after Kroner had gotten his photo and departed — and my grandparents had retired for the night (for the second time) — Electra and I had parted with a kiss as opposed to heated words.

Thinking of her now (and the fact that I'd be seeing her at the upcoming shindig) made me mindful of everything I had to do today. With my chore list now in the forefront of my brain, I quickly finished up breakfast and excused myself. Then — after promising that I wouldn't be late for the night's festivities — I ran upstairs, grabbed a jacket from my closet, and teleported.

Chapter 11

I popped up on a paved but mostly deserted two-lane road that could be accurately described as being in the middle of nowhere. The immediate surroundings were primarily featureless, frost-covered plains, although mountains were visible off in the distance. A cruel, wintry wind blew in from behind me, mussing my hair. Raising my body temperature to combat the obvious cold, I focused on the one notable feature of the landscape — a guard shack in the middle of the road about a thousand feet away — and began walking towards it.

I approached at a pace that was probably on par with power walking: too slow to be jogging or running, but too fast to be construed as my normal stride. This was basically to give the guards in the shack adequate notice of my presence. Telescoping my vision, I saw them through the window of the building — a couple of guys in matching uniforms that at first resembled military fatigues, but which didn't have name tags or identify a branch of service. Noting my approach, one of them spoke hastily into a handheld radio, and then they both checked their weapons — each carried a service pistol — before putting on overcoats. Afterwards, they simply watched me, plainly waiting until I got close enough to merit them coming outside.

Having been here before, I could easily have popped up right next to the shack, or zipped over to it at super speed. However, I didn't see any benefit in making guys with guns (and perhaps itchy trigger fingers) any more excitable than necessary. Therefore, I had made sure that my presence was conspicuous and kept my hands visible as I drew close.

REPLICATION

When I was about a dozen paces away, the two guards came out. One of them carried a small computer tablet; the other held an assault rifle (which I hadn't noticed before), although it was currently pointed at the ground.

The shack had barrier arms down, blocking traffic in both directions — an indication that most visitors probably arrived here via motor vehicle. However, if the guards found anything strange with respect to me being on foot, they didn't show it. It was either a sign of professionalism on their part, or they'd been briefed about me. (Or they could have been the same guards who had been on duty when I'd been here previously. Unfortunately, I hadn't taken note of their faces, and without name tags it was difficult to say.)

The two guards eyed me warily as they approached, and I felt suspicion emanating from both of them. That was to be expected in their line of work, but the feeling was interlaced with confusion and bafflement. Maybe my being on foot was surprising to them after all.

The guard with the tablet walked straight up to me, while the other took a position to my left and slightly to the rear. Practically speaking, the one with the assault rifle was in position to blow my head off if I did anything even slightly out of the ordinary.

"I'm on the approved visitor's list," I said to the one with the tablet. "Name's Jim Carrow."

"I haven't forgotten," the guy with the tablet grumbled, making me raise an eyebrow. Apparently these guys — at least the one in front of me — actually had been on duty when I'd come through here before. (And he seemed to have an excellent memory.)

"He's clear," the fellow with the tablet said to his partner, not even bothering to check the VIP list that I knew was on his computer. He then turned to me. "I assume I don't need to call a ride for you."

"Ah, no," I mumbled, thinking that this entire interaction seemed somewhat surreal. "I'm good."

The two guards returned to the shack without another word. I watched them for a moment, then teleported.

****

I had to pass two more similar checkpoints in the same fashion. In each instance, I appeared far enough away to give the guards on duty enough time to react to my presence. Oddly enough, on each occasion, I picked up on almost the exact same emotional sentiment as I had at the first shack: heightened suspicion accompanied by frank bewilderment. It was almost as if they weren't expecting me, even though the exact opposite should have been true. Being on the VIP list in question meant that there had been confirmation that I would be present.

Despite being curious about the situation, I put all thoughts about the guards aside after passing the last checkpoint and focused on my ultimate destination: a fenced-in compound consisting of numerous interconnected, windowless buildings, all of which appeared to have armed security personnel stationed on the rooftops. In addition, there were a few guard towers placed strategically around the premises, and the top of the fence was covered with razor wire.

Frankly speaking, the place gave off a distinct "prison" vibe, which is exactly what it was. However, it wasn't the kind of penal institution that you'd find on any map or falling under the jurisdiction of the Federal Bureau of Prisons. This was a black site — a place that didn't officially exist — and the people kept here weren't your run-of-the-mill criminals. They were supers, which meant that the normal rules of confinement went out the window.

Knowing where I was supposed to go, I headed to the side of a nearby building. When I was within a few feet of it, a seam appeared in the featureless expanse of wall. The seam grew in length, outlining the shape of a rectangle before swinging outward, revealing a doorway. I went inside and found myself in a long, narrow corridor.

On previous occasions, there had been an escort waiting for me just inside the entrance. This time there was no one, but I knew the drill well enough. As the door swung shut behind me, I began walking down the hallway, noting that it was warm enough inside for me to lower my body temperature.

Other than lights in the ceiling, the passageway appeared to be empty. However, I knew with certainty that there were hidden cameras watching my every move, as well as weapons packing significant firepower surreptitiously tucked away behind the walls.

As I drew close, a door at the end of the corridor opened, revealing what appeared to be a small lounge. It contained a sofa, a couple of easy chairs, a coffee table, and a flat-screen television attached to a wall. Sitting in one of the chairs, watching television, was the person I'd come here to see.

My brother, Paramount.

REPLICATION

Chapter 12

Technically, he was my half-brother, by virtue of us having the same father. Roughly two years older than me, Paramount had practically grown up in the limelight as the son of the world's greatest superhero. Moreover, he had spent most of his life being universally hailed as the brightest star in the next generation of superheroes, and with good reason. Not only had he inherited our father's movie-star looks and Greek-god physique, but also an impressive power set that included super strength, nigh-invulnerability, and an incredibly destructive ability known as the Bolt Blast.

Until very recently, Paramount had been completely unaware of our relationship. I had never sought him out, and no one — not even his father — had ever told him I even existed. To be honest, however, only a handful of people on the planet actually knew of my parentage. (Kid Sensation might be world-famous, but his pedigree was mostly a mystery, and that's the way I liked it.)

Even if he had known who I was, I don't think Paramount and I would have been fast friends growing up. My half-brother had been a brat and a bully, and on those few occasions when our paths had crossed, neither of us had gotten the warm fuzzy. Needless to say, our relationship hadn't improved by him going completely off the rails the previous year, including putting together a Gestapo of sinister teen supers, blowing up Alpha League HQ, and killing a bunch of people. (He had even tried to kill our father.)

Since then, he'd spent most of his time locked up in some place off the grid. I hadn't initially known or cared where he was, as long as they kept a nullifier around him (to strip away his powers) and threw away the key. However, an odd event had resulted in us reconnecting: Paramount lost his mind. Literally.

Basically, an explosion had occurred while he was in a nullifier, and as a result, the bulk of my half-brother's skull (and brain matter) had been blasted away. However, once out of the nullifier, his body began to heal — even going so far as to regrow his missing brain tissue. But the new Paramount seemed to be a different person; all vestiges of his old persona were gone, including his memories. He was now kind, thoughtful, and considerate — unquestionably an upgrade over the jerk he'd been before. More to the point, when recruited to help foil an alien plot that would have killed billions, Paramount 2.0 had not only saved the lives of Smokey and Electra, he had helped save the entire planet from destruction.

Although skeptical at first that it was a trick, I was now convinced that the current Paramount was indeed a separate and distinct individual from the person I'd known before. Thus, I had mostly let go of the past and now treated him as my brother, even going so far as to visit him in the pokey (as I was doing now).

"Hey!" Paramount blurted out as he finally noted my presence, thereby bringing me out of my reverie. He practically jumped to his feet and began walking towards me, saying, "You're back."

"Back?" I muttered in surprise as we shared a brotherly hug.

Paramount nodded. "Yeah. You were just here this morning."

I frowned. Paramount had been subject to random seizures since his injury. It was an indication that he still wasn't fully healed, and his doctors had warned that the spasms could affect his memories. Based on the statement he'd just made (and the fact that my last visit had been weeks ago), it was possible he'd had an episode very recently.

"You don't remember?" Paramount asked with a worried look on his face, plainly bothered by my silence.

"I guess it slipped my mind," I stated with a dismissive wave, deciding not to worry about it. "Anyway, how have you been?"

"Same as I said when I saw you earlier: good. No issues. If this keeps up, they'll probably put me back in a nullifier soon."

I nodded in understanding. Paramount's power set was what had saved his life after the explosion. (Medical science certainly wasn't advanced enough to have helped him.) In order to fully heal, however, he couldn't go back into a nullifier just yet. He had to stay "free" in that context until his health was back to one hundred percent (or close enough that it wouldn't matter). Once that happened, however, the powers that be were likely to toss him into a nullifier cell and weld the door shut. (After all, he was still guilty of horrific crimes.)

But in the meantime, his need to recover from his injuries had made guarding him problematic. Keeping him out of a nullifier meant that he'd have his full slate of powers and could break out any time he liked. Thankfully, our father had called in a few favors, and the end result was that — while he was being held at a black ops site — Paramount wasn't required to spend any time in a nullifier. (It probably helped that he was — as I understood it — a model prisoner as well. It was a sure bet that the second he gave his handlers any trouble, the deal was off.)

REPLICATION

"So what happens after that?" Paramount asked as we walked back towards the easy chairs.

"Hmmm?" I muttered as we sat down, not understanding his question.

"When they put me back in the nullifier," he explained, "what happens then?"

I felt deep-rooted anxiety emanating from him, a tight ball of apprehension and concern. He was really worried about this.

"You won't have your powers," I explained. "You'll be like a normal person, but it's not so bad. Billions of people manage without super powers every day."

Paramount let out a depressed sigh. "I'm not worried about that. I can deal with not having my powers. It's not like I'm using them anyway."

"Then what is it?" I asked, plainly curious.

He stared at me for a moment, and I sensed him struggling for words as a deep-welled sadness grew within him. After a few seconds, he lowered his eyes and softly said, "If they put me in a nullifier, I probably won't get any more visitors."

I blinked, caught by surprise but now understanding what was bothering him. He had no issue with being put in a nullifier himself, but that meant that anyone visiting him would have to enter a nullifier, too. In other words, if it was a super, visiting Paramount would mean willingly giving up their powers (if only temporarily).

The thought was disturbing, to say the least. For most supers, their powers are an intimate part of who they are; losing your abilities is like losing a limb. Moreover, from my personal point of view, having my powers stripped from me would leave me vulnerable in a way that I had a tough time contemplating — especially since it had happened to me before. (And I had vowed to myself that it would never happen again.)

I glanced at Paramount, who was watching me with sorrowful eyes. His expression made me wonder if my misgivings about being in a nullifier were an overreaction, so I spent a moment reflecting on what Alpha Prime and Electra would do in that situation. (To the best of my knowledge, they were the only other people who ever came to see Paramount, but because of some obscure rule about super-powered visitors, only one of us was allowed on the premises at any given time.)

I already knew that Alpha Prime, who had raised Paramount as a single parent, would enter a nullifier without hesitation to spend time with his son. Likewise, I felt the same was true of Electra; as an orphan adopted by the Alpha League, she and Paramount had grown up like brother and sister. She, too, would have no qualms about visiting Paramount in a nullifier. That left me as the odd man out.

Paramount was still looking at me with a melancholy expression, and empathically I could sense a pool of dread in him as he waited for me to say something. He was clearly more astute than I'd given him credit for, because he was vividly aware of how difficult it would be for me to socialize with him in a nullifier. In essence, he plainly expected me to say that I wouldn't be visiting him after he got better.

Surprising myself, I laid a hand on his shoulder and said, "Look, I can't say that I like the idea of visiting you in a nullifier. The very idea makes my stomach flip. But that said, I don't plan to stop visiting you. You're my brother, so I'll find some way to make it work. I promise."

Paramount's eyes practically lit up and I picked up something like exhilaration coming from him. Somehow, however, he kept his voice even and simply said, "Thanks, Jim. I'd like that."

REPLICATION

Chapter 13

I stayed with Paramount for about half an hour, splitting the time between general chitchat and watching television. For a guy who was likely to spend a good many years in the clink, he seemed to be in relatively good spirits for the most part — even cracking a couple of jokes. It was something I had trouble envisioning the old Paramount doing, and reinforced the notion that the current version of my half-brother was an entirely different person.

When it was time for me to leave, we parted as we had met — with a fraternal hug. Then, after promising to visit again soon, I left via the door and hallway by which I'd entered.

Upon exiting the building, I was immediately hit by a frosty wind and once again raised my body temperature in response. I was still wearing the jacket I'd brought from home, but it had essentially been just for show — so that I wouldn't look even more out of place at the checkpoints than I did by simply being on foot. I realized then that — during my visit with Paramount — I hadn't even taken the jacket off. It had probably given the impression that I hadn't planned to stay long (or didn't want to). However, I seriously doubted that Paramount had noticed or cared; he was just happy to have a visitor. Still, I made a mental note to take my jacket off next time and then teleported.

I reappeared at Alpha League HQ, just outside Mouse's lab. Ordinarily I would have just teleported inside, but I was trying to be more conscientious about things like that. (Basically, teleporting directly inside was like going to visit a friend and just walking into their home instead of ringing the doorbell.) Mouse had never complained — he probably didn't even care — but I didn't want to get into the habit of taking liberties in that fashion.

I pulled out my cell phone and dialed Mouse's number; he picked up on the first ring.

"Hey, Jim," he said. "Sorry — you're probably wondering where I am."

I wrinkled my brow in confusion. "Huh?"

"You're in the lab, right?"

"Uh, no. I'm actually outside. I thought it would be more appropriate if I announced myself instead of just popping up out of the blue."

"Oh," he said, sounding surprised, then jokingly added, "That's a first."

"I was trying to be considerate," I admonished. "But if you don't appreciate the effort…"

I trailed off as Mouse started laughing.

"Actually," he stated a moment later, still chuckling, "your popping up doesn't bother me. That said, it's probably good to get in the habit of announcing yourself first, so bravo."

"Thanks," I said, pleased at the fact that my mentor had complimented my behavior. "Anyway, I was coming by for the debrief, but we can reschedule if you aren't here."

He shook his head. "No, we can go ahead. I'm in the Alpha conference room."

I nodded. "Okay. Be there in a sec." I then hung up the phone and teleported.

I reappeared in a stately, rectangular room that was home to a large executive conference table. Mouse was seated at one end of it, with his computer tablet in front of him. I walked down and took a seat diagonally to his right.

"Been awhile since I've been in here," I intoned, glancing around. "Something wrong with the lab?"

Mouse shook his head. "No, but Vixen says I need to get out more."

I laughed. "I'm sure she meant 'out' as in fresh air, sunshine, and such."

"Probably, but she's my girlfriend, not my mother. She'll have to take what she can get."

I chuckled some more at that. Vixen — in addition to being Mouse's significant other — was also a member of the Alpha League. As a Siren, she had the ability to manipulate the opposite sex, but Mouse was somehow immune to her charms. I briefly wondered if she had tried to use her power to get him to take her advice about getting out and this was his way of defying her, but then dismissed the idea. Mouse wasn't like that, and it was my understanding that Vixen had moved beyond trying to control him the way she'd done other men in the past.

"Anyway," Mouse droned, changing the subject, "how do you think the mission went yesterday?"

I let out a disgusted sigh. "Everyone else seemingly did fine. I was a disaster."

Mouse shook his head. "Not true. You took your eye off the ball for a minute, but managed to recover."

"And almost got us killed in the process — not quite how I wanted my first official mission to go."

"Actually, it's a good thing that we were beset by a little mishap. It's better if something untoward happens the first time you're out in the field."

I raised an eyebrow. "How so?"

"Because after that you're more likely to be on your toes when you go on a mission. If it's a piece of cake the first time, you're more apt to let your guard down in the future."

"Well, you can bet that I'll be completely mission-oriented from now on. I'm just glad no one got hurt."

"Even if someone had gotten injured, it wouldn't necessarily have been your fault. What we do — stopping bad guys — is inherently dangerous, like being a cop, a fireman, or working high steel. Occasionally, people are going to get hurt. It's a professional hazard."

"I know," I said with a nod. "I suppose I should be grateful that Dream Machine only sent a train at us. I'd have thought he'd utilize something more lethal, but maybe he relied too heavily on his hallucinatory abilities — not that I'm complaining."

"Oh, he had more pernicious items at his disposal, like turrets and such in the walls, but I shut them down. It's the first thing I did when I connected to his system."

Well, that explains some things, I thought.

"Unfortunately," Mouse went on, "I wasn't able to shut down *everything*, as you saw. In addition, I didn't have time to cut off Dream Machine's escape route before my connection got terminated."

"You mean before I screwed up," I corrected, feeling awful.

Mouse laid a comforting hand on my shoulder. "Look, don't go beating yourself up about what happened. Even if everything else had gone perfectly, there's no guarantee that I would have been able to use my tablet to stop the upload or keep Dream Machine from hightailing it to the internet."

"Except there won't be a note that says 'Lacks focus' in your League dossier."

Mouse laughed. "We don't keep a tally of stuff like that around here. We're not some military school, tracking demerits to see if we need to kick you out."

"But there's got to be some kind of scoreboard — some way to rate mission performance."

Mouse contemplated for a second before answering. "It's really on a case-by-case basis, and individualized towards the person."

"So you're saying that if two people — say, me and Smokey — go on a mission, we might be rated on different things in terms of efficacy."

"Exactly."

I drummed my fingers on the table for a moment. "So what was I graded on this time?"

"You weren't really being evaluated. Based on everything you've been dealing with since you came back from Caeles, I was really just hoping the mission would give you a sense of perspective."

"You mean, did it take my mind off the raging trash fire that's my personal life?"

Mouse chuckled. "The key word you were supposed to focus on was 'perspective,' wiseacre."

"Oh. You're asking if the mission made me realize that the raging trash fire I mentioned was really more of a sputtering matchhead. In that case, the answer is yes. My personal problems pale in comparison to the threats the League faces on a daily basis."

Mouse nodded. "Bingo. All of our personal problems — breakups, bad investments, car in the shop, what have you — they're mostly inconsequential when you look at the big picture of what we do."

"Agreed," I said, knowing he was right.

"Great. That's one important aspect of the mission covered."

"Uh," I mumbled hesitantly, "before we move on to anything else, can we talk about the people we saw underground?"

Mouse's brow creased. "What about them?"

I leaned forward, unsure of how to phrase what I wanted to say. "It bothered me when I saw them. I mean, they looked like they were having a hard time — especially some of the children. Isn't there anything we can do to help them?"

"You don't need to do anything to help them," Mouse said flatly.

I stared at him for a moment, unsure that I'd heard him correctly. "Excuse me?"

"I said that you don't need to do anything for those people," he repeated in a sincere tone.

I blinked, so confused that I had trouble articulating my thoughts. "I'm sorry…I don't…I'm not…"

I was beyond bewildered. Mouse was one of the most compassionate people I knew, so I was having a real issue coming to terms with his statements. I'd never seen him voice this kind of callous disregard for others. Hoping for answers, I reached out empathically and sensed something unexpected: mirth, and a self-satisfied air of contentment.

"Wait a minute," I muttered, still trying to make sense of everything as a sly smile crept onto my mentor's face. And then the truth hit me.

"You already did it," I asserted, more a statement of fact than anything else.

Mouse responded by bursting into laughter.

"Yes," he said a few moments later, after regaining his composure. "After you left, I made some calls to a few shelters and humanitarian organizations. We got most of the people placed, but a few stubbornly refused to leave, so we arranged to have some meals and blankets sent down to them. So, as I said, there's nothing you need to do because it's already been done."

"Thanks," I said. "For a moment there, I thought you were serious."

"You should have seen the look on your face," Mouse chuckled. "It was hilarious."

"Well, I'm glad you were entertained," I stated with mock indignation. "Hopefully you'll consider me for the position of League jester. But in the meantime, if we're done with the debriefing, I'll take my leave."

Mouse nodded, still grinning. "Yes, we're done. However, I could use your assistance with something else."

REPLICATION

Chapter 14

I teleported Mouse and myself to my father's mansion — the palatial estate where the gala for my grandparents was going to be held. We popped up in the foyer, which opened into a lavish great room that was characterized by marble floors, exquisite furnishings, and rare artwork.

Even though we were hours away from the night's festivities, the place was already bustling. The great room was filled with an army of staff and personnel, hurriedly trying to do a million things: bring in food, set up tables, install temporary bars, and so on.

"You see BT anywhere?" Mouse asked.

"No," I replied, "but give me a sec."

I reached out empathically, searching for the familiar emotional vibe of Braintrust (whom Mouse had casually referred to as "BT").

"She's out by the pool," I announced a moment later. "Hang on."

I teleported us again, this time taking us to an exotic, poolside terrace at the rear of the mansion that was home to, among other things, an outdoor fireplace, lavish furnishings, and a built-in bar. The pool itself was oversized, with various amenities, including a waterfall and hot tub.

"Hey, you two," said a feminine voice from behind us.

We both turned almost in unison and found ourselves facing a stunning blonde wearing jeans and a sweatshirt: BT.

It was a little breezy on the terrace, but Braintrust didn't appear uncomfortable (and probably wasn't).

REPLICATION

Although she looked like a normal person, BT was actually an extensive array of clones all sharing a single hive mind. I had known BT most of my life, but during the bulk of that time the clone I'd dealt with had been male. Thus, even though I had been interacting primarily with this new blonde for months now, I was only just reaching the point where I could think of Braintrust as a "she" (although I'd always known that BT had clones of both genders).

"Jim," she said in greeting. "Let me guess: Mouse has recruited you for our little project."

I nodded. "Yeah, but he's been skimpy on the details."

She smiled. "Well, allow me to enlighten you."

She gestured towards a couple of open wooden crates that I hadn't noticed before. Standing just a few feet from BT, the first was rectangular in shape and roughly five feet in height. The second was smaller — approximately two-by-two feet in size — and sat on a table next to the first.

Curious, I walked over and took a look inside the larger crate. It was full of cylindrical metal rods that reminded me of tent poles. The crate on the table contained some kind of advanced machinery that seemed to have more than an ample number of buttons and dials, as well as a screen and small keyboard. I couldn't immediately identify it, but the equipment in the crates all seemed familiar — and then it hit me.

"A force field generator?" I asked hesitantly.

Mouse and BT both grinned at that, with the latter saying, "No, but close."

"It's a localized temperate clime converter," Mouse added. "It *does* generate a field, but — unlike a force field

102

— one that's permeable, and within which we can make subtle alterations to atmospheric conditions."

I wrinkled my brow for a second, trying to make sense of what Mouse's words. A moment later, the clouds parted in my mind.

"Oh," I said solemnly. "It's a weather dominator."

BT laughed. "That's what *I* said!"

"No," Mouse insisted. "It's a temperate clime—"

"Weather. Dominator," BT plainly declared in a surprisingly loud voice as she cut my mentor off. Still laughing, she held up a hand, palm outward, in my direction. Chuckling as well, I promptly high-fived her.

Shaking his head in disgust, Mouse mumbled something incoherent about "amateurs" and "belittling my work."

My mentor then cleared his throat, getting our attention. "Well, if you two are done congratulating yourselves on your equally inept skill at nomenclature, we can get started."

****

<There,> I telepathically announced with finality as I pushed the last of the metal rods into the ground. <That's the last one.>

<Activating,> BT stated in response.

Almost immediately, the rod began extending, stretching up until it reached a height of about nine feet. At the same time, a small diode — previously unnoticeable — began flashing near the upper end as a small metallic canopy opened up, covering the top of the rod like a conical hat.

REPLICATION

This was the same scenario that had played out with all of the other rods, which I had — at BT and Mouse's direction — placed equidistant from each other around the edge of my father's estate. As I understood it, the metal poles generally framed the area that would fall under the control of the weather dominator, which was the device that had been in the smaller crate.

The work had naturally gone a lot faster with me involved, since I could essentially teleport to each spot where the rods needed to be placed. Moreover, rather than having to dig or force the poles into the frost-hardened earth, I simply phased the necessary portion of the ground and then slid the rod into it before making it solid again.

<It should be working now,> BT continued, bringing my mind back to the present. <Are you noticing anything different in the weather?>

I thought about his question for a moment. <The wind. It was gusting the entire time I was putting up the poles, but now it's gone.>

<Good,> BT declared. <I think you're done. You can come back now.>

<Roger that,> I affirmed. A second later, I was back on the terrace with BT and Mouse, who was busy typing on the keyboard of the weather dominator.

"Good job," Mouse said, barely looking up.

"Thanks," I replied. "How soon before I can whip out the T-shirt and shorts?"

"The immediate cessation of wind was expected," Mouse explained. "The actual temperature change will be more gradual, but should be comfortable by the time of the party."

That sounded good to me, and I was about to say as much when a deep baritone sounded from the direction of the mansion's interior.

"How's it going out here?"

I looked around to find Alpha Prime, dressed in a black thermal shirt and dark khakis, stepping out to join us.

At six-foot-seven, my father typically stood at least a head taller than anyone else around. On most occasions, however, he appeared even taller because — rather than walk — he usually just floated from one place to another. Thus, it still occasionally caught me by surprise whenever I saw him trudging along the ground like the rest of the mere mortals.

"I think we're good," BT asserted in answer to my father's question. "This entire place should be nice and cozy — at least in terms of temperature — by the time guests start arriving."

"I've also locked the controls," Mouse added, "so no one will accidentally turn this place into a burning desert or a landlocked iceberg. Still, we probably need to put this" — he pointed to the weather dominator — "somewhere safe."

Alpha Prime nodded. "I've got a couple of places that should work. You can let me know which you think is best."

"Any place will do, as long as there's no general access."

My father turned to me. "Jim, can you put that in Storage Room B?"

"No problem," I said, then teleported with the weather dominator.

I popped up in a darkened, windowless antechamber, holding the weather dominator aloft

105

telekinetically. After a moment, automatic lights came on, revealing my current environs to be a room about a hundred square feet in size. The place was practically bare except for a built-in desk in one corner, on which sat a computer, monitor, and keyboard. There were also four interconnected viewscreens — two on each side of the monitor. The only other feature to the room was what appeared to be the entrance to a narrow hallway.

I heard something click and immediately went still. My father's mansion was equipped with automatic defenses, some of which could cause serious injury. Although he had obviously shut them down in other parts of the estate, it was possible he had left the security system active in my current location with the intention of making this area off-limits.

Of course, I wasn't too worried; my biometrics had been fed into the system database so that my presence on the premises was always deemed authorized. (And even if that weren't the case, with my particular powers I was unlikely to be in any real danger.) Nevertheless, I stood still, trying to avoid making any sudden moves while allowing whatever system might be scanning me to establish my bona fides.

Fortunately, the click I'd heard turned out to be nothing more than the computer turning on. As I watched, the viewscreens all came to life, with each showing various parts of my father's mansion and estate. After a few seconds, each screen cycled to another image; a few moments later, the pattern would repeat.

Basically, I was in a panic room — one which my father had shown me when I first visited him here. His mansion actually had three such rooms, each of which had a secret entrance; the one I currently found myself in was located in a sub-basement and could only be entered through a hidden door in the main garage. ("Storage Room B" was, of course, a code phrase. A panic room loses its effectiveness if people know you have one.) Since my father and I were probably the only two people who knew about this place, the weather dominator — which I quickly and securely tucked under my arm — should be safe here.

I watched the screens for several moments, noting all kinds of activity and understanding that what I was seeing was live. However, it was essentially what Mouse and I had noted when I first teleported us to the foyer: people hurriedly preparing for the night's festivities. That said, the hustle and bustle reminded me that I still had things to do myself, including the task at hand.

I turned from the screens to the hallway entrance, which I knew connected to a modest living space comprised of a small suite of rooms: kitchen, bedroom, bathroom, etc. I quickly hurried through the passageway, with automatic lights once again coming on as I entered the main suite. Glancing around, I noticed an end table located at the junction of a sofa and loveseat. I placed the weather dominator on it, and then, after looking around a final time, teleported back to the terrace.

Upon reappearing, I noticed that my father, Mouse, and BT had been joined by yet another person — a hypnotically beautiful woman whose angelic face was set off by a cascade of gorgeous blonde curls. I recognized her right away: Hippolyta — Paramount's mother.

"Jim!" she screeched in delight after noticing me. She raced over to give me a hug, which I returned. "I'm so happy to see you! How are you?"

"I'm fine," I said. "And it's great to see you as well. How have you been?"

She seemed to ponder this for a second before answering. "Good. Better, at least."

I nodded in understanding, but didn't say anything. A generation earlier, Hippolyta had been one of the foremost supers on the planet. Incredibly powerful and almost invincible, she had been a pillar of the Alpha League. However, the birth of my brother had done something to her, opened up a fault line that no one would have guessed even existed. In short, constant worry over her child, among other things, ultimately caused her to have an emotional breakdown from which she never fully recovered. She had essentially disappeared, leaving Alpha Prime to raise their son, but had come back after the explosion that almost killed her child.

"Anyway," Hippolyta continued, "I can't wait for the party tonight. I honestly haven't been to anything like this in ages. Which reminds me…"

With that, she turned to Mouse and BT and began asking what sounded like questions about proper decorum for formal events these days. In my opinion, she was asking the right individuals, because Mouse and BT were the two smartest people I knew — probably the most brilliant duo on the planet (and presumably someone had advised Hippolyta of that fact).

As the other three spoke, I reached out to my father telepathically.

<So she's coming tonight?> I asked.

<Yeah,> he answered. He seemed to ponder for a moment, then asked, <You think it's inappropriate?>

I frowned. <What do you mean?>

<Well, your mother will be there…>

I had to fight to keep from laughing out loud as my father trailed off.

<Ha!> I mentally barked. <Mom stopped caring who you dated ages ago.>

<We're not dating,> he countered. <She just needs to get out more, start being around people again on a regular basis. I'm simply trying to help.>

<Well, for starters, it's your plus-one, so you can bring who you want. In addition, it's being held at your house, so I'd feel awkward telling you who couldn't accompany you. Finally, I like Hippolyta, so if this helps her, I'm in favor of it — and I'm sure Mom would be, too.>

<Thanks, son. It means a lot to me to hear you say that.>

Empathically, I felt him beaming with pride and knew he had spoken with sincerity. It made me reflect on a time in the not-too-distant past when being a source of pride for Alpha Prime would have meant less than nothing to me. Now, however, our relationship had dramatically changed, and — although knowing he was proud of me made me glad — I didn't quite know how to express it. Thus, I merely mumbled a brief mental "Thanks," and then broke the telepathic connection.

REPLICATION

Chapter 15

After the telepathic conversation with my father, I only stayed long enough to confirm with Mouse and BT that they would both be in attendance at the party. After receiving their assurances, I teleported.

I reappeared outside a small apparel shop that specialized in men's formal wear. I dashed inside and emerged a few minutes later holding two tuxedos — one for me and one for Gramps. (Once it had become apparent that my grandparents' little shindig had escalated into a formal event, Gramps had insisted that the two of us get new attire for the occasion.) With black tie vestments now in hand, I teleported back to the embassy.

I popped up in the main living room. I laid my grandfather's tux across the back of a sofa, then mentally reached out to let him know where to find it. After receiving a telepathic acknowledgment from him, I teleported to my room, where I proceeded to hang my own tux in the closet. Once that was done, I felt that I was finally caught up on all my current tasks.

Taking advantage of the momentary break, I kicked off my shoes and stretched out on the bed. Bearing in mind everything that had happened in the past twenty-four hours — from the Dream Machine mission to visiting Paramount to my debriefing (not to mention getting ready for the upcoming gala) — I felt like I'd barely had a moment's peace. Physically I wasn't particularly tired, but mentally I was exhausted.

I closed my eyes and rubbed my temples, simply trying to relax. It seemed as though everything in my life had been going at a hundred miles per hour lately, and my strained relationship with Electra wasn't helping. However, there really wasn't a lot of blame I could lay at her feet; she was dealing with an incredibly awkward situation, and handling it with more poise than could reasonably be expected. She really was special, and it suddenly occurred to me that I should probably do something to convey that to her.

Maybe flowers, I thought, yawning. *Or candy…or…*

****

I awoke with something of a start. I had clearly dozed off, and — judging from the dimness of the light coming through my window — had slept for several hours. Checking the time on my cell phone, I noted that it was nearly time for us to leave for the gala. There was maybe half an hour left before we were supposed to depart.

For a moment, I wondered why no one had bothered to wake me — and then almost laughed at my own oversight. There was probably little concern that I would be late, even if I woke up only five minutes before our anticipated departure time. As if needing to prove this, I shifted into super speed and zipped into the bathroom. Two minutes later, I had not only emerged — freshly showered and well-groomed — but was also dressed in my tuxedo and ready to go.

As I prepared to leave my room, I spent a moment glancing in the dresser mirror to make sure I was as presentable as I thought.

Hair combed, I said to myself. *Tie straight.*

Out of the blue, my stomach rumbled loudly, reminding me that I hadn't eaten since breakfast. (And in truth, I *was* feeling a mite peckish.) However, recalling that there was to be a lavish spread at the gala, I decided to forego eating anything for the nonce and instead tweaked my internal physiological systems so that I wouldn't be bothered by hunger pangs. Satisfied now that neither my appearance nor growling belly would cause me any embarrassment, I left and went downstairs.

I made my way to the main living room, but didn't see anyone. My grandfather's tux was gone, indicating that he had retrieved it at some point while I was napping. Reaching out empathically, I sensed my mother and grandparents in their respective rooms, presumably still getting dressed. Myshtal, on the other hand, was on the ground floor with me. Rather than wait alone, I decided to see what she was up to.

I found her near the parlor, standing in front of an alcove that was home to an oddity: a weird contraption that looked something like a medieval suit of armor with supple, spider-like limbs.

I frowned, as I always seemed to these days around the bizarre device. Its formal name was the Beobona Onufrot (or simply "Beobona" for short), and within its frame was an incredibly ancient and unbelievably powerful relic — the Beobona Jewel.

The Beobona had actually saved my life on several occasions — most recently during my trip to Indigo's homeworld of Caeles — so one would think that I would be happy to have it around. But, in truth, there was a very real possibility that the Beobona had manipulated events (and perhaps even *me*) for its own ends. Thus, I tended to be wary around it to some extent.

As I watched, I saw Myshtal reach towards the Beobona's torso, an area that appeared to be a smooth metal surface but which would occasionally spiral open to reveal the Beobona Jewel inside. On this occasion, however, it stayed shut.

I must have made some noise, because Myshtal suddenly spun in my direction. As she did so, I took note for the first time of what she was wearing.

She was sporting a floor-length, halter neck dress that was navy blue in color and exceptionally form-fitting. The halter itself seemed to be made of some type of bejeweled material that was an amalgam of silvery metal and cloth, while the bodice was adorned with tiny gemstones that — amazingly — appeared to move in some unknown fashion. Finally, her hair was done up in something akin to French waterfall braids and adorned with a goddess headpiece that culminated in an exotic azure jewel that rested on the center of her forehead. All in all — even without a crown — she looked like nothing less than a fairy-tale princess.

"Reminiscing?" I asked, gesturing towards the Beobona as I walked to her, trying to sound casual.

Myshtal smiled at me. "Not exactly. I was just thinking that — even though I saw it before — I never actually got to hold the Beobona Jewel. I couldn't help wondering what it would feel like." She looked at me expectantly, causing me to understand that she was hoping for a response.

I reflected for a moment. "The first time I held it, it didn't really feel like anything out of the ordinary, but there was a piece of it missing at the time. Later, after it became whole, I picked up a kind of…energy."

To be frank, I was downplaying the truth. What I had actually sensed in the Beobona Jewel (after it became replete) was almost indescribable — an infinite and unfathomable power so intense that it boggled the mind.

Myshtal gave me a skeptical look, plainly aware that I was holding something back. "There has to be more to it than that. I know what the Beobona is capable of."

Her comment caught me off guard. I had forgotten that Myshtal was more than just a pretty face; she was fairly astute.

"Alright, I may have understated the facts," I admitted. "In simple terms, what I felt when I held it was power — pure, potent, and without peer."

"And you didn't feel comfortable telling me that?"

I shrugged. "Very few people are truly aware of what the Beobona is capable of. If it ever became common knowledge…"

"Wars have been fought for far less," Myshtal noted as I trailed off, clearly picking up on my meaning. "I can see why you would try to deemphasize its might. I shudder to think what might have happened had Vicra gained control of it, in addition to his time travel abilities."

I nodded, but didn't immediately comment. Vicra had been a Caelesian prince who had used time-travel technology to further his own ambitions. After purportedly traveling to the future and seeing me sitting on the Caelesian throne, he had tried to kill me (and probably came closer to doing so than anyone ever had — even managing to temporarily strip me of my powers). But although Vicra had managed to get his hands on the Beobona, I seriously doubted that he could have wielded its power in the manner Myshtal imagined. It was the Beobona that controlled and manipulated — not the other way around. In some ways, it was almost as if the thing were alive.

"Anyway," I said, changing the subject. "I don't think I apologized for kind of deserting you last night in the middle of the movie."

"No apologies necessary," she assured me. "Once Electra came by, it was only natural that you'd want to spend time with her. Plus, I heard about our unexpected visitor from your grandparents."

"Yeah, it turned out to be a late night, so thanks for understanding," I said. Then, ruminating on another issue, I added, "By the way, did you change clothes last night?"

She frowned, obviously confused. "Excuse me?"

"When you came to the door to ask about pausing the movie, you seemed to be wearing different attire than when we'd been in the theater room."

"Oh," she muttered. "I didn't exactly change, but my attire may have looked different."

"Huh?" I spouted in confusion.

"I should probably explain, and hopefully not sound too vain in the process," she said, then paused for a moment before continuing. "As you know, due to my position as Caelesian royalty and my relationship to the queen, I've grown up with a fair amount of excess. I've always had an overabundance of anything I wanted, from toys to jewelry to clothes."

"I can understand that," I assured her. "We have people with similar upbringings here on Earth." (Of course, Vestibule immediately came to mind.)

"But not you." She uttered it as more of a statement than a question.

I burst into laughter. "Hardly. It's only within the past six months or so that my royal lineage has had any effect on my life at all. The kind of regal lifestyle you're talking about is almost completely foreign to my personal experience."

"I see," she said as a pensive look crossed her face, and I could sense uncertainty brewing in her.

"But please," I insisted, "go on with what you were saying."

She stared at me for a moment, then let out a deep breath before continuing. "In brief, it has to do with my clothes. Because Earth is essentially an alien culture for me, I wanted to make sure I fit in as much as possible — including having the proper attire for any occasion. However, I couldn't bring everything from the homeworld that I would have liked; there simply wasn't enough room on the ship. So I made a compromise of sorts."

She paused for a second, prompting me to ask, "In what way?"

"I don't think you have it on your planet, but there's technology on Caeles that can be infused into garments to make it sensitive to the wearer's temperament and frame of mind. It's exorbitantly expensive, but the end result is raiment that can change or alter itself to suit one's disposition."

"Wait a minute," I said, catching on. "Are you saying that you have 'mood' clothing?"

She frowned. "I'm not sure I understand."

I took a moment to explain the concept of mood rings to her — novelty items that allegedly change color based on the emotional state of the person wearing it.

"Yes," she finally agreed. "I'm speaking of a similar reaction, but for attire."

"So," I summed up, "you're saying that rather than transport enough clothes to fill a department store, you brought along some garments that can become almost anything you need them to be."

"Correct."

"So when you came to the door last night, your clothes had changed based on your mood."

"Right again."

"So were you sleepy or something?"

Myshtal's brow creased in confusion. "Excuse me?"

"When you came outside, I think you were wearing something like a nightgown. Your clothes had changed to that because you were getting ready to go to bed, right?"

"Ah...no," Myshtal replied, casting her eyes sheepishly towards the ground.

"No?" I repeated, somewhat surprised. "Then I don't understand. Why would your clothing take on that appearance if you weren't about to turn in?"

Myshtal suddenly looked at me with an odd expression on her face. Emotionally, I could sense something like anxiety within her — butterflies in her stomach and an abundance of nervousness. Her lip trembled, slightly, but then she steeled herself and prepared to speak.

However, before she could utter a word, a familiar voice cut in.

"There you are, boy," muttered Gramps.

I turned to find that my grandfather had entered the room. Dressed as I was in a tuxedo, he actually cut a rather dashing figure, and it was easy to imagine what he must have looked like in his prime.

Gramps turned to Myshtal. "I hope you don't mind, Princess, but I was hoping to have a quick word with my grandson."

"Not at all," Myshtal replied, sounding almost relieved before hurriedly stepping from the room.

After she was gone, Gramps gave me a once-over, eyeing me from head to toe.

"Very nice," he said, brushing a piece of lint from my shoulder. "You look good."

"Runs in the family," I replied with a wink, causing us both to chortle. "I'm sure Indigo's return dashed a lot of women's hopes."

"Ha!" Gramps guffawed. "I took myself off the market long before your grandmother came back, so any hopes got dashed decades ago." He then took a moment to clear his throat, and I noted that his demeanor became more somber as he added, "However, that does segue into what I wanted to talk to you about."

I nodded. "Okay. What is it?"

"We really haven't talked in depth about this situation you have with Myshtal. It basically seemed like a business arrangement — a deal you had to make in order to get you and Indigo back here. That being the case, it appeared to be a reasonable choice, and I didn't fault you for it. In fact, it showed a level of maturity and decision-making that would have been beyond most people your age."

"Thanks," I mumbled. This was all stuff he had told me before, so it really wasn't news. Obviously there was more on his mind, and it didn't take him long to get to it.

"Anyway," my grandfather droned, "I didn't think much of it. I mean, it struck me as peculiar, but apparently it's standard operating procedure for Caelesians. Plus, it wasn't bothering your grandmother, so I saw no need to worry."

"So what's changed?"

He gave me a curious look, but — rather than answer my question — asked one of his own. "So what did you think about breakfast?"

"Uh…" I mumbled, not sure where this was going. "It was okay, I guess. I enjoyed it."

"I meant, what did you think about Myshtal preparing it?"

"Oh. She did fine. I mean, it was essentially eggs and toast — kind of hard to mess that up."

My grandfather let out a weary sigh, and I sensed a slight bit of exasperation in him. "Let me ask another way: how many times do you think Myshtal has prepared breakfast for anyone, including herself?"

I frowned. "What — in her life?" I let the question roll around in my head for a second. "As a Caelesian princess, probably a handful at most, since that kind of stuff is usually done by servants. In fact, I wouldn't be surprised if today was the first time she ever touched a skillet."

"That's precisely my point," Gramps stated with a nod.

I stared at him in confusion for a moment, still not understanding. "What exactly are you getting at?"

He didn't answer immediately. Instead, a wistful expression settled across his features, and after a moment he said, "Years ago, shortly after we met, your grandmother decided to do some ironing for me one day. It wasn't an activity she was familiar with to any degree or something she'd shown a knack for. Still, it came as a bit of surprise when she burned a hole in my favorite shirt."

Needless to say, a laughing fit took hold of me at that juncture. Telepathically, I sent my grandfather an image of himself wearing an expensive designer shirt riddled with scorched holes.

"Hilarious," Gramps said with a deadpan expression, although I could tell that he really was amused. "And while you're yucking it up, you'll be happy to know that's exactly what happened — I wore the shirt."

"What?" I nearly exclaimed, his admission cutting short my mirth. "You did?"

"Of course. Because I knew what it represented."

"Which was what — that alien princesses are terrible at domestic labor?"

"Well, that's a given," he admitted with a smile. "But what it really showed was how your grandmother felt about me."

"How's that?"

"Because in ironing my shirt, she did something for me that she didn't ordinarily do for anyone, even herself. In essence, she was saying, 'This I don't do, but I'll do it for you.'"

I blinked as it suddenly started to dawn on me what my grandfather was talking about.

"It's a symbolic gesture among Caelesian royalty," he continued. "Something you do for someone you consider special — usually an action or activity you wouldn't normally undertake. Doing their laundry, for instance, or washing their clothes."

"Or cooking them breakfast," I mumbled, the scales falling from my eyes. "But we don't have a bunch of servants running around doing any of that stuff, so eventually she'd have to do it anyway — if only for herself. Why can't this morning's breakfast simply be an example of Myshtal being a good houseguest?"

"Because your grandmother says that the person performing the act traditionally makes certain kinesic expressions, and she noticed Myshtal engaging in some of them as we ate."

I contemplated this for a moment. "So something in Myshtal's body language conveyed to Indigo that this symbolic gesture was being made towards me?"

"Yes."

"What was it?"

Gramps shrugged. "I don't know, boy. We're talking about Caelesian versions of winks and nods. It may be things too subtle for the rest of us to notice, or if we did see something unusual, we'd probably just chalk it up to alien eccentricities."

"But the upshot of what you're saying is that Myshtal may be expecting this pact I made with Queen Dornoccia to result in actual matrimony."

"No, not at all," Gramps declared, shaking his head emphatically. "That would be like expecting you to marry Electra simply because you like her. So even if Myshtal does have feelings for you, it doesn't mean that she's already picked out her wedding dress."

"Thank heaven for small favors."

"Look, the main thing I want you to understand is that this is clearly more than just a simple business deal now. There are real feelings involved, real emotions. That means you're going to have to figure out what's the right thing to do here very soon, or someone's bound to get hurt."

"So basically, you're telling me I need to man up."

"That's one way to put it," he said laughingly as he clapped me on the shoulder. "But you've got excellent judgment, Jim, so I've got all the confidence in the world that you'll make the right decision."

"That makes one of us," I stated glumly, causing my grandfather to chuckle again.

REPLICATION

Chapter 16

Shortly after the conversation with my grandfather, we all left for the gala. Our ride was a chauffeured limousine, courtesy of Alpha Prime. It was a bit more pretentious than we had planned, but my father had insisted. Thus, we had all piled in after the car and driver showed up at the embassy gate.

The limo's interior configuration was along the lines of what I expected, with two rows of seats set across from each other. My grandparents and mother took the forward-facing seats, while Myshtal and I sat on the rear-facing row, with our backs to the partition separating our group from the driver.

As we drove, Myshtal began peppering my grandparents with questions about proper Earth etiquette in social settings. This was, for all practical purposes, going to be her public debut, and she obviously wanted to make a good impression. However, she invariably charmed almost everyone she met, so in my opinion she was worrying over nothing.

On my part, I couldn't stop thinking about what my grandfather had said to me. Myshtal and I had gone through a crisis together on Caeles, so it was undeniable that the two of us had a bond that had nothing to do with our marital pact. However, what Gramps had told me changed the entire landscape between me and the princess. I mean, it was one thing to imagine how things would be between us if I didn't have a girlfriend. It was something else altogether for her to actually have romantic feelings for me (although it would certainly explain a few things).

<Hey,> my mother's voice telepathically cut into my thoughts. <You okay over there?>

<Yeah,> I replied. <I'm fine.>

<You sure? You look like something's got you worried.>

<No, I'm good.>

<Then what's with the frown?>

I was about to ask what she was talking about, then realized with a start that she was right: my brow was distinctly furrowed. Smiling at my own gaffe, I relaxed my features.

<That's much better,> Mom noted with approval. <With that scowl off your face, you actually look nice.>

Mentally, I chuckled. <Thanks — so do you. All of us, in fact.>

<Yeah,> she agreed, glancing around at our group. <Never let it be said that the Carrows don't clean up nice.>

I nodded in agreement. Like me, Gramps, and Myshtal, my mother and grandmother had also dressed up for the occasion. Now bedecked in formal attire and with their hair styled in a similar fashion, they looked more like siblings than ever.

<Anyway,> my mother continued, <I was hoping you would do me a favor.>

<Sure,> I replied. <What do you need?>

She seemed to contemplate for a moment before responding. <I know you're busy, but just make sure you leave enough flexibility in your schedule to spend time with your grandparents.>

<I will. I mean, I do. I think we have either breakfast or dinner together just about every day.>

<I'm not talking about meals. I'm talking about *real* time, where you do something together.>

<Well, we do play board games.>

<That we do,> she admitted. <But I want you to do more than that. I'm talking about things that will create memories — maybe going to see a show, or taking in a ballgame.>

As she spoke, I sensed an odd vibe in her, something like dolefulness mingled with disquiet.

<Alright,> I stated flatly. <What is it?>

She gave me a bewildered look. <What do you mean?>

<What is it that you're not telling me?>

My mother simply stared at me, and for a moment it seemed as though she wasn't going to answer. Then she let out a telepathic sigh and simply announced, <They're leaving.>

<What?> I mentally muttered. <Who?>

<Your grandparents, of course! Haven't you been paying attention? They're leaving.>

<You mean like on vacation or something?> I asked, then had to choke back laughter. <You make it sound like it's the end of the world. Where are they going — Europe or someplace like that?>

Mom gave a mental shake of her head. <No, they're going a bit farther abroad than simply overseas.>

Now the frown was back on my face as I concentrated, trying to figure out what my mother was getting at. She helped me out by telepathically sending me a clue: an image of a black field stretching out in all directions, covered with twinkling lights.

<Outer space?!> I mentally blurted out, unable to hide my surprise. <They're leaving the planet?>

<Not right away, but yes.>

<How? The ship that brought us back from Caeles is long gone.>

My mother mentally shrugged. <Mom's made arrangements of some sort.>

<But *why*? Are they unhappy here?>

<No, it's not that.>

<Then what is it? Why are they leaving?>

<Because they've already seen everything Earth has to offer. They got to travel all over the place years ago when they were with the Alpha League. In short, Dad got to show Mom his world; now she wants to show him hers.>

I sat there for a moment without responding, still somewhat stunned by what I'd heard. Losing Indigo — the grandmother I was still getting to know — would be bad enough. But Gramps?

Along with my mother, my grandfather had raised me. Trained me. Taught me how to use my powers. I had a tough time imagining him suddenly gone.

And if it was hard for me, it had to be incredibly difficult for Mom. She'd have to say goodbye not only to her father — the only parent she'd ever known until a few weeks ago — but also the mother who had just come back into her life.

Overwhelmed with sympathy for my mother, I reached out to her empathically and detected an unusual potpourri of emotions: doleful sentiment mingled with bittersweet reflection and somber resignation, all encased in a shroud of wistful yearning so powerful that it was almost palpable.

The thought of not having her parents around was clearly distressing to my mother, and I wished that I could do something to ease her pain. I just found it hard to believe that my grandparents would simply take off like that — just when we were finally a family.

And just like that, understanding dawned on me. I knew exactly how I could help my mother.

<Go with them,> I stated flatly.

My mother's eyebrows went up in surprise. <What?>

<You should go with them,> I repeated.

Telepathically, she shook her head. <No. I couldn't.>

<Sure you could,> I insisted. <And it's not like it would be forever, right?>

<No, but we're probably talking a long time, regardless. A year, possibly — maybe even two. I can't just walk away from everything for that long just to tag along with my parents like a bratty kid.>

<Look, I've had you and Gramps my entire life, and I've bonded with Indigo a lot better and faster than I would have thought possible. But the three of you... You never had a real chance to be together, to become a family unit the way you would have under normal circumstances. You deserve to have that, even if the opportunity for it is coming a couple of decades late.>

My mother seemed to contemplate this for a moment, but then gave another sad shake of her head mentally. <But what about you? I can't just leave you behind. What kind of mother would I be if—>

<Mom, I'll be fine,> I said, cutting her off. <Have some faith in the job that you and Gramps did as far as raising me. I can take care of myself, and if I do need help there's plenty of people I can call on: Mouse...Braintrust...> I gulped and then added, <Alpha Prime.>

She didn't respond immediately; instead, she just stared at me for a few seconds, mentally wrestling with a decision as she pondered what I'd said. Then she gave me a bright smile and a telepathic hug.

<You know, you've got to be the best son on the entire planet,> she declared, beaming.

<Of course,> I replied, grinning. <The best son for the best mom.>

REPLICATION

Chapter 17

For the remainder of the ride, Mom and I joined in the conversation with Gramps, Indigo, and Myshtal. Before I knew it, we had reached my father's subdivision, passing through a gated and guarded entrance into an exclusive neighborhood of million-dollar homes and sprawling estates.

From that point, it should only have taken us about fifteen minutes to reach my father's mansion. Unfortunately, we were still in view of the neighborhood entrance when our limo slowed to a halt behind a long line of equally ostentatious vehicles.

"Apparently we should have come early," Indigo commented, prompting a grunt of annoyance from my grandfather. "Hopefully the line will move quickly."

My grandmother's hopes in that regard were soon dashed, as ten minutes later we had moved forward only a few hundred feet.

"This is ridiculous," Gramps finally barked. "What's the hold-up?"

I shrugged. "Don't know. There's supposed to be a valet service, but I'm guessing they're overwhelmed."

"Half these vehicles are chauffeur-driven stretch limos," my grandfather shot back. "They don't need a valet."

"So," Mom mused, "you've got a bunch of oversized vehicles dropping people off and then trying to maneuver around in spaces that were probably designed for much smaller cars."

Gramps seemed to ruminate on that for a moment, then let out a sigh of resignation, saying, "Okay, maybe I'm just being impatient, but it seems like we could have walked there by now. Or…"

He trailed off as he turned towards me, a suggestive glint in his eye.

Knowing what was being implied, I merely nodded. "Yeah, I could teleport us, but I wouldn't in our current position."

"Why not?" asked Myshtal.

"Because you're all sitting," I replied. "If I took us there now, you'd all flop down on your butts when we appeared, like some synchronized clown routine. Of course, I could hold everyone in their current posture telekinetically, but you might find it awkward."

"Well, there's a simple solution to that," Indigo said, reaching for the door handle. A moment later, we were all standing outside the limo.

"Everyone ready?" I asked.

"Wait just a minute," Gramps said, reaching for his wallet as he began walking towards our driver's window. I then noticed him give the man a tip and then mutter something — probably letting the chauffeur know that we'd call him when we were ready to go.

After getting a curt nod in response from the driver, my grandfather turned and walked back to us, saying, "Okay, let's go."

Taking that as my cue, I teleported the five of us.

****

We popped up in a French formal garden — a broad concourse consisting of exotic flowers and carefully manicured shrubs. In addition, there were fabulous water terraces interspersed throughout the area, and it was all arranged in an eye-catching symmetrical design.

I sensed a deep wonder welling up in Myshtal as she looked around, and I couldn't blame her. Frankly speaking, the garden was spectacular and worthy of a spread in some national home-and-garden magazine, as the architect had clearly outdone himself.

As to Mom and my grandparents, I felt that they were suitably impressed but not overly awed by our present surroundings. (Now that I thought about it, it was possible that they had seen this garden — or others on the same scale — before.) In terms of location, it was notched off the rear of Alpha Prime's mansion, a bit farther out than the pool area where I had spoken with Mouse and Braintrust earlier. I had chosen to teleport us here instead of directly into the mansion in hopes of being less conspicuous. That said, there were a few people in the garden when we appeared, but none took particular notice of us.

"Come on," I said, and began marching towards the rear of the mansion. A few minutes later, we were inside.

REPLICATION

Chapter 18

We were able to get inside my father's mansion without a lot attention or fanfare. In fact, we were probably there a good ten minutes — with my grandparents inconspicuously greeting old friends and the rest of us following in their wake — before people in general began to realize that the guests of honor had arrived. (Apparently they had been expecting us to come through the front door.)

After our presence became known, we quickly found ourselves hemmed in on all sides by what looked to be scores (if not hundreds) of people. The atmosphere was a little madcap for the next few minutes, as various folks in front, behind, and on both sides of us tried to get a word in with my grandparents. Thankfully, Mouse — who had seemingly arrived early — was on hand, and quickly took charge. Bringing order to chaos, he placed the five of us into something akin to a receiving line in the mansion's ballroom and then whipped the crowd into an orderly queue.

For the next fifteen minutes, it seemed as though I was incessantly glad-handing a long string of people, like a political incumbent who was worried about re-election. In truth, however, it wasn't that bad.

I was fourth in the receiving line — after my grandparents and mother, but just before Myshtal (who was generally identified merely as my "friend"). Unsurprisingly, a good number of those I met were my grandparents' contemporaries. Thus, they'd spend a quick minute chatting with Gramps and Indigo about the old days, devote a brief moment to Mom (whom many of them remembered as a child), and then briefly shake my hand —

the grandson that few of them even knew existed. (And it was pretty much a certainty that none of them knew I was Kid Sensation.) But in all honesty, I think everyone gave me short shrift in order to get to Myshtal, who was as engaging as she was beautiful. In fact, it was difficult to say who the guests preferred speaking with — her or my grandparents.

I managed to obtain a brief respite from handshaking when one guest — a rotund, middle-aged fellow with a handlebar moustache — spent more than the average amount of time with Mom. Worried that she might be getting bored, I took advantage of the opportunity to check on Myshtal.

"Having fun yet?" I joked as I turned to her. "Hopefully it's not too tedious." I actually addressed her in Caelesian, which would give her a chance to give a frank response without worrying about anyone understanding what she was saying.

She giggled slightly before answering in her native language. "Oh, this is nothing. You should see the lines I have to endure when I attend an event with the queen."

I nodded in understanding, having actually seen Queen Dornoccia and Myshtal at a formal event and noting how many people they had to greet on such occasions.

"So," Myshtal went on, "how many of the people here are supers?"

I took a quick glance around before answering. "Most of those on the guest list don't have any special abilities to speak of, but there are a good number of people with powers present. For instance, that lady over there" — I pointed to a silver-haired woman who appeared to be in her sixties — "can shoot lasers from her eyes. That fellow by the far wall in the cowboy outfit and ten-gallon hat has a magic gun — or magic bullets, I forget which…"

I went on in that manner, pointing out a few other supers in the vicinity that I recognized.

"What about the gentleman speaking to your mother?" Myshtal asked, nodding at the guy with the moustache.

"Apparently he *thinks* his super power is charming women half his age," I replied stiffly.

Myshtal erupted into laughter at my comment, the outburst making several nearby guests turn in our direction — including the man who had been talking to Mom. Thankfully, we had still been speaking in Caelesian so he surely hadn't understood us, but his attention only made Myshtal succumb further to her giggling fit. A moment later, I joined her, chuckling heartily at my own quip. I was about to make a further attempt at humor when a familiar voice sounded behind me.

"You two," said my grandmother, who had apparently stepped out of the receiving line without me noticing. "Come with me."

Her tone was somewhat stern, and immediately brought our jocularity to an end. Without waiting for a reply, she turned and walked away; Myshtal and I quickly fell into step behind her.

Indigo marched determinedly across the ballroom, heading towards an empty patch of wall on the far side of the room. Once we reached it, she halted and turned to me and Myshtal.

"This should be fine," she announced. "You're discharged — both of you."

Myshtal and I exchanged a confused glance; neither of us had a clue what my grandmother was talking about.

REPLICATION

"Discharged?" I repeated quizzically. "I'm sorry, *Sxahnin*, I don't know what you mean."

"It means you're both released from your duties in the receiving line. From what I could overhear of your conversation, it's pretty obvious the two of you are bored."

I felt my cheeks turn slightly red as I realized I had overlooked the fact that at least one other person here was fluent in Caelesian: my grandmother.

"Our apologies, N'd'go," said Myshtal solemnly, emphasizing the Caelesian pronunciation of my grandmother's name. "We meant no harm."

My grandmother reached out and gently patted Myshtal's hand. "It's fine, my dear." Then a crafty smile crept onto her face and she added, "To be honest, I wish there were someone to discharge *me* from the receiving line."

We all got a laugh out of that.

"Anyway," Indigo continued a moment later, "if anyone should ask" — she looked pointedly at me — "especially your grandfather, I gave you both a stern lecture about—"

My grandmother abruptly stopped speaking, as if she'd suddenly lost her voice. At the same time, I noticed a faraway look come into her eyes as she tilted her head slightly to the side, as if listening for music only she could hear.

Concerned, I focused my empathic senses on her and picked up the sensation of curiosity mixed with bewilderment. A second later, it was all overridden by a cavalcade of surprise, joy, and exuberance.

Practically beaming now, Indigo belted out, "Come on!" Reaching for us, she gripped my wrist in one hand and

Myshtal's in the other, and then took off — practically dragging us behind her.

"Wait…" I muttered, trying to get her attention. "*Sxahnin*…"

I was hoping to get an explanation of some sort for her behavior. Unfortunately, my words fell on deaf ears as my grandmother hastily pulled us towards the ballroom entrance, heedless of the people we inadvertently bumped into. She was clearly on a mission. Hoping to get an indication of what was so important, I looked in the direction we were headed.

At first, I didn't see anything of note. The column of guests waiting to get through the receiving line stretched out the door, but there were lots of other people milling about as well: servers walking through with trays of refreshments, friends laughing merrily at each other's jokes, visitors gawking in awe at the scale of the mansion, and so on. And then I saw him.

He appeared to be young — late twenties or early thirties — and was remarkably handsome. He was a few inches taller than my six-foot height (making me peg him at about six-three), and had dark hair that was combed back. Like just about all the other men present, he had on a tuxedo, but his seemed to fit and wear in a way that went beyond simply being tailor-made or handcrafted. It was like it was a part of him.

More than his physical appearance, however, was his presence. He had a panache you could sense even without empathic abilities, but at the same time exuded a *sangfroid* that was almost tangible. It was as though he brought his own atmosphere into the room with him, something that allowed him to radiate confidence without being overbearing, to appear poised while simultaneously relaxed. In short, he exuded an effortless cool that many attempt, but few actually achieve.

Around this time, my grandmother noticed him as well. Almost squealing in delight, she suddenly released Myshtal and me from her grip and then raced towards the stranger. Eager to see what the fuss was about, I followed quickly on her heels, with Myshtal doing much the same.

Seeing Indigo approach, the corners of the man's mouth drew up into a dazzling smile. My grandmother virtually leaped into his arms, giving him a fierce hug that was probably only rivaled by the one she gave my grandfather after we returned to Earth.

After a few moments, Indigo and the young stranger separated, but still gripped each other by the forearms. They both then leaned forward, each grinning broadly, and placed their heads next to each other so that my grandmother's right ear touched the newcomer's left. It was then that I noticed something that had escaped my attention until now: the guy's ears were pointed.

He's Caelesian! I thought. A moment later, my brain started becoming frothy with questions. *Who was this guy? Why was he here? Did Queen Dornoccia send him? Had the queen changed her mind about allowing my grandmother to return to Earth?*

Those and a thousand other questions were racing through my mind when Indigo and the stranger drew their heads back, although still gripping each other's forearms.

"You got my message!" my grandmother exclaimed excitedly.

"Of course," the fellow replied in a sanguine tone that matched his demeanor. "Why do you think I'm here?"

"I'm sorry," Indigo muttered, shaking her head. "I simply didn't expect you to come yourself."

The newcomer raised an eyebrow. "You expected me to entrust this to an underling?"

Before Indigo could respond, I coughed softly in an attention-getting manner. My grandmother turned to me, looking as if she'd forgotten where she was for a moment.

"Forgive me — I've been rude," she declared, releasing her grip on the stranger's arms. Waving a hand in my direction, she then said, "Please allow me to introduce my thrice-child, Prince J'h'dgo." She then swung her hand towards the newcomer, saying, "J'h'dgo, this is my cousin, Prince Nobaxlin."

"Cousin?" I mumbled, trying to hide my surprise.

"On the maternal side," Indigo explained. "He's the son of my mother's brother. We practically grew up together."

I frowned, trying to process this. Indigo's mother had been Fleodin — a people who were of the same race as Caelesians but who maintained a separate (but equally powerful) interstellar empire. My grandmother had occasionally mentioned her maternal relatives, but personally I'd never given them much thought.

"So," Nobaxlin droned, breaking in on my thoughts and flashing another smile as he looked me over. "This is the Prince *Dranilac*."

"Excuse me?" I said, plainly a bit confused by the conversation. "Prince Landrax?"

"The Prince *Dranilac*," my grandmother corrected before speaking to me telepathically. <It's not a name, but rather a title that you have among my mother's people — one of them, anyway. It loosely translates as "Sovereign Supreme," but don't let it go to your head — all Fleodin

titles are along the lines of the-greatest-*this* or most-wonderful-*that*.>

Mentally, I shook my head, not quite able to make sense of what I was hearing.

<I'm sorry, but I really don't understand,> I admitted after a moment.

<As I told you before, my mother's family rules the Fleodin Demesne. As a member of that family, you are considered a Fleodin Royal and have a number of formal titles.>

That came as something of a surprise. I mean, I'd known about my great-grandmother's family being the Fleodin governing authority, but I had never thought about it in the context of positions or titles. Before I could respond to my grandmother's comment, however, Nobaxlin spoke — interrupting the telepathic conversation between me and Indigo.

"I've been given to understand that you visited Caeles recently," he said. "What did you think?"

His question caught me flatfooted, and I didn't have an immediate answer ready. The truth of the matter was that my sojourn to Caeles had resulted in me being stripped of my powers, accused of treason, and almost dying. However, I thought it prudent to give a more tactful — but equally candid — response, so I concentrated for a moment and then stated, "I enjoyed my time there for the most part. The food was delicious, the people were congenial, and the architecture was inspiring."

Nobaxlin harrumphed. "Well, if you were impressed with those mudhuts they call castles and that swill they brazenly label as food, then you're going to be awed by what you encounter in the Demesne. Wait until you see it. You'll love—"

He stopped abruptly, and I noticed Indigo giving him a piercing stare along with a subtle shake of her head. No words passed between them, but I suddenly had a strong indication of the arrangements my grandmother had made for leaving Earth.

Nobaxlin cleared his throat. "Please forgive me. I tend to go overboard when discussing the highlights of Fleodin society and can be a bit boorish in that regard."

Indigo laughed. "You're always boorish, but I'm glad you stopped short of completing denigrating my homeworld's culture, since we have another Caelesian royal present." She inclined her head towards Myshtal, saying, "This is Princess Isteria, the quint-child of Queen Dornoccia."

My brow creased slightly, as hearing Myshtal addressed by her first name sounded odd to me. That said, it struck me as appropriate under the circumstances, as this was a formal introduction.

"Pleased to meet you," Nobaxlin stated, gesticulating with his hands in a manner that I recognized as a Caelesian greeting.

Returning the gesture, Myshtal said, "Actually, we've already met."

A look of surprise crossed the Fleodin's face. "We have?"

"Yes," Myshtal insisted. "Years ago, when I was much younger, you came to Caeles as part of a trade delegation when I was visiting the queen."

A fervent but faraway look came into Nobaxlin's eyes — as if he were staring at something on the horizon that was close enough to be seen, but too distant to be made out clearly. You could almost see the wheels turning in his mind as his brow wrinkled in concentration. After a moment, however, the look of intensity vanished and he gave Myshtal a bright smile.

"Blue dress with a white sash," he said. "Along with a black-and-silver tiara."

"Good memory," Myshtal admitted, obviously impressed. "That's exactly what I wore when we previously met."

Nobaxlin laughed. "My recollection was likely helped by the fact that you're one of the few children I ever met on Caeles — certainly the only one I ever encountered in the presence of the queen. The next time you see her, please give her my regards."

"I certainly will," Myshtal assured him. "Especially in relation to our swill and mudhuts."

Nobaxlin blinked, clearly taken aback — and then exploded into riotous laughter. A moment later, the rest of us joined him. I had been worried for a moment, but it was pretty clear that the Fleodin prince could take a joke.

"I like this one," Nobaxlin announced once he could catch his breath, smiling at me while pointing at Myshtal. "She's a — what's the Terran phrase? — a keeper."

I sobered almost immediately, Nobaxlin's innocuous comment making me keenly aware of the fact that Myshtal was my titular fiancée. Given what my grandfather had said earlier, I didn't need anyone entertaining the notion that we actually made a cute couple. (Moreover, I knew that Electra would go completely bananas if she ever found out I let a remark like that slide by without comment.) Thus, I spent a few anxious seconds trying to think of an appropriate response that would set the record straight in an unobtrusive manner. I came up empty, but fortunately, my grandmother came to my rescue.

Shaking her head, Indigo teased, "Nobaxlin, you've always had a gift for languages, but in this instance your use of local idioms leaves something to be desired."

"Oh?" Nobaxlin muttered, raising an eyebrow in surprise. "I was certain I had it right."

Indigo laughed. "You can regale my grandson with your mastery of Earth colloquialisms later. For now, I want you to come say hello to my husband and daughter."

With that, she looped her arm into Nobaxlin's and began leading him away. He spared a short wave for Myshtal and me before being dragged into the sea of bodies present.

"So," Myshtal said after my grandmother and her cousin vanished into the crowd, "you're a Fleodin royal?"

"So it appears," I answered dispassionately.

"You don't seem particularly pleased about it."

"To be honest, I'm still digesting the news. I mean, I've had enough on my plate just learning the ropes in terms of being a Caelesian prince. I don't even want to think about having a separate and distinct regal role right now."

"Well, why don't we do something to take your mind off it?"

"Such as?"

She made a Caelesian gesture that was the equivalent of shrugging one's shoulders. "I don't know. How about a tour?"

"With pleasure," I said with a smile.

REPLICATION

Chapter 19

Over the next twenty minutes, I took Myshtal on a quick jaunt through my father's mansion. I didn't want to be away from the main party for too long, so I focused on showing her what I considered to be the most notable features, such as the bowling alley and indoor basketball court. (The place was monstrously huge, to be sure, and it would have taken hours to see every part of it.)

That said, I had no doubt that the grandeur of my father's home made little impression on Myshtal. After all, her great-great-grandmother, Queen Dornoccia, lived in a palace that was the size of a city. My father's place probably looked like a lean-to by comparison. In truth, she seemed more fascinated by the novelty of what she was shown than the scale of the mansion, as Earth forms of leisure and recreation varied greatly from what she was used to.

Mentally, I had put a thirty-minute limit on this particular excursion. The last thing I needed at this juncture was for a rumor to start circulating that Myshtal and I had disappeared together for an extended period of time. Fortunately, my father had made much of the mansion accessible, so we bumped into other guests almost everywhere we went. (In other words, there were witnesses if — for some reason — I needed proof of my whereabouts later.) In fact, it was one of the other attendees who pretty much brought our tour to an end.

We were headed towards the indoor pool (which also contained a two-story waterfall) when Myshtal stopped dead in her tracks, drawing in a sharp breath that was practically a gasp.

Turning to her, I noticed that she had a look of complete surprise on her face. Emotionally, I could sense that she had received quite a jolt. Following her eyes, I looked in the direction of her gaze, trying to get a glimpse of what had startled her.

There was a man approaching us. Like most of the other male guests, he was wearing a tux — in this instance, a single-breasted jacket with a peaked lapel. However, that's where adherence to Black Tie standards ended. Instead of the traditional black-and-white color scheme, this fellow's attire incorporated brilliant hues of shocking pink and psychedelic purple. The chromatism didn't just encompass his jacket, pants, and shirt, but also his gloves, socks, and shoes. Needless to say, his ensemble garnered considerable attention.

But even more intriguing than his wardrobe was the man himself, as his entire face seemed to be covered with strange designs: ancient symbols, weird hieroglyphs, and obscure characters — all of which seemed to move eerily across the surface of his skin.

I smiled as he sauntered towards us. This was Rune, one of the members of the Alpha League. He was generally considered to be a magician of some sort, but I knew that he was something much more. He was an Incarnate — the physical embodiment of certain powers that were beyond the ability of most people to comprehend.

"*Gzint msint!*" Myshtal hissed, cursing mildly in her native language. "It's the *Visiwigon!*"

I frowned. Her voice had brought me back to myself, but she still seemed somewhat spellbound and had used a Caelesian term I was unfamiliar with. However, before I could delve into what was bothering her, Rune stopped directly in front of us.

REPLICATION

"Language, Princess," he chuckled. "That kind of verbiage isn't appropriate for a member of the royal family."

I raised an eyebrow in surprise. "You speak Caelesian, Rune?"

"Somewhat," he replied, waffling a hand from side to side in a so-so gesture. "I've had the privilege of meeting a few visitors from there, and apparently I resemble an infamous character from Caelesian mythology."

"The *Visiwigon*," Myshtal repeated, although she seemed to have recovered to an extent from her earlier surprise. "A legendary thaumaturge and notorious trickster, easily recognizable by the cryptic symbols etched all over his body."

Now I understood Myshtal's reaction a little better. Seeing Rune was probably the equivalent of me going to Scotland and catching a glimpse of the Loch Ness Monster. From her perspective, he was a fabled character seemingly come to life.

"Well," Rune droned, "I hope you'll reserve judgment until you actually get to know me — assuming we're ever introduced."

He gave me an expectant look, but it still took me a moment to catch on.

"Oh, I'm sorry," I muttered a second later, then hastily made formal introductions. However, it was obvious that Rune already knew who Myshtal was, as he had called her "Princess" just a few moments earlier. (Frankly speaking, it probably hadn't been difficult to put two-and-two together: to anyone familiar with her race, she was obviously Caelesian, and word of our "arrangement" had spread like wildfire through the League.)

REPLICATION

After exchanging pleasantries with Myshtal, Rune leaned forward unexpectedly and whispered something in her ear. I couldn't make out what he said (although I could tell that it was in Caelesian), but whatever it was caused Myshtal to start giggling almost hysterically. And just like that, the ice melted and — on an empathic level — I sensed her going back to normal, emotionally.

"Anyway," Rune said, "I won't keep you any longer, but I didn't actually bump into the two of you by accident. I was actually looking for Jim."

"Oh?" I mumbled, openly curious.

"I have an issue that I might need your help with," he explained.

He said it nonchalantly, like he needed a hand taking out the trash or something, but Rune's statement caught me a little flatfooted. His own abilities were extraordinary: among other things, he could travel to a dimension outside of space and time, project himself astrally, warp reality... Simply put, there weren't a lot of scenarios where I could envision him needing help — even from someone with a power set as singular as mine. If he was asking, it was clearly important.

"Um, sure," I said, uncertain of what I was getting myself into. "Just let me tell my mom and—"

"No, no, no," Rune insisted with a shake of his head. "It's not anything that needs to happen right now, and I might not need you at all. Even if I do, it probably won't be for a couple of days. I simply wanted to put it on your radar — just in case."

I nodded. "That's fine. Just let me know."

"Will do," Rune stated with a grin. He then turned to Myshtal. "And if I didn't say so before, Princess, please accept my apologies for startling you with my appearance.

I sincerely hope it won't prevent you from enjoying the rest of the party."

"It won't," Myshtal assured him, smiling. "And please accept my apologies as well. My reaction was more juvenile than I would ever have expected."

Rune laughed. "No worries. It's not the first time someone has responded in that fashion, and probably won't be last."

"That may happen sooner than you expect," Myshtal stated. "I'm not the only Caelesian here."

Rune seemed to ponder that for a moment before responding. "Well, I wouldn't want my appearance to shock anyone else tonight, so I suppose I could make myself less conspicuous."

"That would be great," Myshtal said.

"Done," Rune declared a moment later. As he spoke, his entire body seemed to go fuzzy for a second, as if I was seeing him through the lens of a camera that was out of focus. The effect only lasted for the blink of an eye, but when he came back into focus (for lack of a better term), he was no longer wearing the outlandish pink-and-purple outfit. Instead, he was dressed in the time-honored, traditional tuxedo colors of black and white.

"Better?" Rune asked, holding his arms out and turning in a slow circle.

"Uh…" I droned. "I think the princess was referring more to your symbols." I made a twirling motion in front of my face.

"Oh, that," Rune said in a casual tone. "How about now?"

I blinked. I hadn't noticed anything happen, but all of the mobile characters previously on Rune's face (and presumably the rest of him) had vanished. They had disappeared, literally, before my eyes.

"That's excellent," Myshtal replied, while I merely mumbled something.

In truth, it could probably be said that the cat had my tongue. I had never seen Rune without his namesake symbols on his body. Seeing him without them came as a bit of a shock, because I suddenly realized that I hadn't really known what he looked like. The characters covering his skin had always been so visually distracting that I'd never taken note of his actual features until now.

He had what would probably be described as roguish good looks, which went well with the devil-may-care attitude he often seemed to exhibit. Coupled with the cocksure grin he was now giving us, the overall effect was the addition of a rakish quality to his appearance.

"You two should probably get back to the ballroom," Rune said, interrupting my thoughts. "I'd hate for you to miss anything."

There was a percipient tone to his voice, as if he knew something we didn't — which, with respect to Rune, could very well be the case.

"Come on," I said to Myshtal. "Let's head back."

With that, we said goodbye to Rune and began making our way to the ballroom.

REPLICATION

Chapter 20

When we returned to the ballroom, I was almost disappointed to find that nothing of particular note seemed to be happening. The place was full of people and the air was alive with chatter, but I didn't notice anything that had been worth hustling back for. Glancing around, I saw my mother and grandparents still greeting guests, with Mom currently in the process of hugging a couple of dark-haired young women who had come through the receiving line — and then I almost did a double-take when I realized who the two women were. Smiling, I shot a quick telepathic message to one of them.

<Hey, Avis,> I said casually. <Glad you could make it.>

The woman in question quickly jerked her head around, scanning the crowd as she excitedly responded, <Cuz! Where are you?>

I sent her a mental ping to indicate where I was in the ballroom, then gave a quick wave as her gaze turned in my direction. A broad grin broke out on her face, indicating that she'd spotted me. Then she grabbed her companion by the hand and began dragging her towards me. A moment later, they were both in front of us.

"Jim!" Avis exclaimed as she gave me a fierce hug (albeit with only one arm, since I now noticed she had a drink in her other hand). "It's so good to see you again!"

"Yeah," said the other woman, giving me a quick but forceful embrace as well. "We heard you took a little sabbatical, so it's wonderful that you're back."

"I'm happy to *be* back, Vela," I announced, grateful that she'd been circumspect in her description of my off-

149

planet escapades. I didn't think anyone was listening to us, but it didn't hurt to be discreet.

"Well, the time away obviously didn't hurt you," chimed in Avis. "You look great."

"As do the two of you," I replied, "although I have to admit that I almost didn't recognize you at first."

The two of them laughed, with Vela noting, "Yeah, it's a different look for us."

Her comment (as well as my own) alluded to the fact she and Avis were wearing formal dresses rather than superhero costumes. In truth, the two women were actually my cousins — the daughters of my father's brother, Megaton — and supers in their own right. Avis (who was formally known as Rara Avis) was typically considered to be one of the most powerful supers on the planet, but was known just as much for a social life in which she partied like a rock star. Vela was formidable as well, but as a member of a mid-level superhero team based in the Midwest, she didn't receive as much press as her sibling.

"Where's Monique?" I asked, referring to my other cousin — Avis and Vela's sister. "Will she be here? And what about your father?"

"Monique can't make it," Vela replied. "But she sends her love."

"Little Miss Homemaker has a conflict," Avis almost sneered. "Some event she needs to attend with her husband."

I nodded, but didn't say anything. The disdain in Avis' voice was centered around the fact that Monique — who could probably go toe-to-toe with any super on the planet — had eschewed the family business in favor of being a housewife, which she enjoyed immensely.

REPLICATION

"As to Dad…" Avis continued, then merely shrugged her shoulders as she trailed off. The gesture hinted at the fact that our fathers were generally estranged (as brothers sometimes are), so it was unlikely that Megaton would put in an appearance tonight.

"Anyway," Vela interjected, gracefully changing the subject, "who's your friend?" She inclined her head towards Myshtal.

"Sorry," I mumbled apologetically. "This is Princess Isteria of Caeles. Princess, please allow me to present Vela and Rara Avis."

Mentally, I frowned as I made the introductions, which involved a couple of judicious decisions. First, I had chosen to introduce Myshtal by her formal name. It was what my grandmother had done with Nobaxlin, so I thought it important to follow suit.

Next, I had sidestepped mentioning that Vela and Avis were my cousins. In truth, almost no one knew that the two women were sisters, and even fewer were aware of the fact that they were related to me. Basically, there was a deliberate practice in my family to avoid disclosing familial relationships, for both privacy concerns and to avoid the inevitable comparisons that would result if the information became known. Of course, that hadn't stopped Avis from announcing on social media that Kid Sensation was her cousin; the only silver lining at that juncture was the fact that few people knew that Jim Carrow and Kid Sensation were the same person. (On my part, I'd only recently found out that I even had an uncle or cousins, so keeping that info under wraps had never really been an issue for me.)

Naturally, no one seemed to notice or appreciate the shrewdness I'd displayed in acquainting Myshtal with my cousins. My affianced bride greeted Avis and Vela warmly, and it became immediately apparent that she was going to charm them as quickly and completely as she did almost everyone else. However, the three of them had barely exchanged a dozen words before someone else cut in.

"Aren't you going to introduce *me*?"

Recognizing the voice, I groaned inwardly and then glanced around until I laid eyes on the speaker: Vestibule.

Chapter 21

She was standing just a few feet behind Avis and Vela, dressed in a simple but elegant teal gown. She also sported a subtle shade of pink lipstick and lightly-applied eye shadow, and had her hair braided into a fishtail. All in all, it was a much more subdued look than most other occasions when I'd seen Vestibule. (Usually, she looked as though she were headed to or coming from a modeling gig, and strutted around like she was the peacock with the largest plume.)

Hurriedly replaying the last few minutes through my mind, I had a vague recollection of seeing her in the receiving line, as well as following in my cousins' wake as they came over to greet me. Obviously, I had been so focused on Vela and Avis that I hadn't truly noticed her. And even though I'd known she'd be here, her sudden appearance, having come somewhat out of the blue, caught me a little unprepared.

"Introduce me?" Vestibule repeated, bringing me back to myself.

"Oh, um, sure," I muttered half-heartedly. "I think you already know Avis —"

"We've met," Vestibule cut in sharply, giving me an odd look. Her expression probably stemmed from the fact that she and Avis were both part of the A-List Supers and traveled in the same social circles, which was something I knew.

"There's also Vela," I continued.

"We're acquainted as well," Vestibule declared.

"Okay, great," I said flatly. "Well, this is Princess Isteria." I gestured towards Myshtal. "Princess, meet Vestibule."

It was short and to the point, but apparently represented the intro that Vestibule had been angling for, as, smiling, she immediately moved forward to greet Myshtal. However, they had done little more than say "Hello" to each other before Avis spoke up.

"Please excuse us for a minute," she said. "I need to speak to Jim about something."

She then placed a firm hand on my elbow and practically marched me a dozen paces away, not releasing me until we were safely out of earshot.

"Look," she stated firmly, "I know that you and Vestibule have some kind of thing going, but —"

"No," I interrupted, "we have *no* kind of thing going."

"Well, aren't you supposed to be dating?"

"No!" I declared emphatically. "Did she tell you that?"

Avis shrugged. "She mentioned something along those lines."

"Well, it's not true. We're supposed to go on an outing — a single, solitary outing — but it's not a date."

"Fine — date, outing, whatever. I just need you not to tick her off. She's my ride home tonight. Vela's too."

"So she teleported you here. Big deal. Vela can run at like a thousand miles per hour, and you can fly at Mach speed. Why does either of you need a ride home?"

"Well, I can't speak for my sister, but I'm not sure I'll be in any condition to fly at the end of the night." With that, she knocked back her drink, finishing it off. "Plus, I'm not keen on zipping back through the air in this dress, and I'm sure Vela feels the same about running on the road in hers."

"Well, in case you've forgotten, *I'm* a teleporter, so I can get you home."

"You mean you can get me close, since you don't know exactly where I live. Same thing for Vela."

"Unless you're passed out or slurring your words so badly that I can't understand you, I can get you there. But even if I can't, you're forgetting something else: this is your uncle's house. If you don't think you can make it home, you can always crash here."

"Yeah, that's a *great* option," she quipped sarcastically. Noticing the puzzled look on my face, she explained, "Your old man has rules about overnight guests that a young lady with a social life would probably describe as…antiquated."

"Oh," I mumbled softly, now understanding. Then I frowned. "Wait a minute. Why would that rule bother you? Aren't you dating some tech billionaire?"

"We broke up," Avis said casually. "He found board meetings and business trips more interesting than hanging out with me."

"In other words, he had a business to run," I concluded. "Come on, Avis. You can't expect a guy's heart to go all aflutter and have him drop everything on his plate every time you call."

"I can, and I do," she retorted. "But speaking of setting hearts aflutter, who is *that*?"

There was an extremely attentive look on my cousin's face, and emotionally I detected a sudden and very focused interest — like a kid who had just seen a toy he simply had to have for Christmas. Following the direction of her gaze, it only took me a second to figure out who she was referring to, and the realization of who it was caught me more than a little by surprise.

REPLICATION

I let out an exasperated sigh and muttered, "You've got to be kidding."

"What?" Avis asked. "You know him?"

I nodded, frowning. "That's Prince Nobaxlin."

"A prince?" Avis repeated with a smile, sounding immensely pleased. "It's been awhile since I've dated royalty. Can you introduce me?"

I was silent for a moment, debating on how best to explain the situation. Needless to say, there was nothing really problematic about making an introduction. Moreover, technically, there would be nothing wrong if — after becoming acquainted — Avis and Nobaxlin decided to pursue a romantic relationship. After all, they weren't related to each other. They were, however, both related to *me*, which made the situation awkward from my point of view.

Thankfully, I was saved from having to deal with what would have been a ticklish scenario by the abrupt appearance of a scabrous, crimson line a few feet from us. It parted the air vertically from the floor up to a height of about six feet. A few people nearby quickly stepped back, unsure of what was going on. Personally, I smiled, understanding what was happening. A moment later, three people stepped through the scarlet slit, which quickly closed behind them.

Grinning broadly, I stepped forward, exclaiming, "You made it!"

"Of course," said the first of the new arrivals — a boyish-looking youth with an odd assortment of rings on his fingers. Returning my smile, he reached out and gave me a firm handshake.

"Yeah, we couldn't miss *this*," said one of his companions, a willowy young blonde with a wicked scar that cut across her right eye. Dressed in a floor-length gown, she gave me a hug and a quick peck on the cheek. "Thanks for inviting us."

"And my thanks again for inviting *me*," said Li, who was the third member of the newly-arrived trio. "Kane and Gossamer" — he indicated the youth and the blonde, respectively — "were kind enough to allow me to travel here with them."

"Actually, we insisted," said Kane.

"And it was no problem to swing by Alpha League HQ and scoop him up," Gossamer added.

I merely made a grunt of acknowledgment, as I now found myself looking at Gossamer almost in disbelief.

"What is it?" she asked, noting my attention and giving herself a once-over. "Is there something wrong with my clothes?"

I shook my head. "No, I—"

"Is it my weapons?" Gossamer continued, as if she hadn't heard me. At the same time, she reached towards a couple of ceremonial daggers that she always wore at her waist. "Because I can—"

"No, no, no," I insisted, cutting her off.

"Then what?" she asked imploringly.

"It's nothing," I declared. "It's just that…I don't think I've ever seen you in a dress before."

Kane burst into laughter. "I know, right? But you have to admit that my girl cleans up rather nice."

Blushing slightly, Gossamer's response was to punch her boyfriend lightly on the arm, causing Kane to mutter an exaggerated, "Ow." This was typical behavior for them, along with regular squabbling (which had initially begun as a way to mask their growing mutual attraction).

Gossamer turned back to me. "So it's not my daggers?"

I shook my head. "No. To be honest, I barely noticed them."

It was a sincere statement on my part. Although Gossamer was indeed wearing them, the daggers subtly and effectively blended in with her ensemble. Also, the fact that she seldom wore dresses was not a reflection on her femininity, but more indicative of the fact that she was always ready to spring into action.

Plainly speaking, Gossamer was an elf and incredibly beautiful — even with the scar across her eye. (In fact, the scar, which was a souvenir from a run-in with a supervillain, gave her a certain appeal, in my opinion.) As to the daggers, they were not just weapons, but one of the ways in which she wielded magic. This had resulted in a friendly rivalry with Kane — who employed sorcery — as to whose magical abilities were superior.

"Everything good here?" asked a familiar voice, bringing my attention back to the present. I turned and saw that my father had joined us without me even noticing. (In fact, I hadn't even realized he was in the room.)

Of course. The magic that my friends had used to come here had drawn some attention. At this point, it was clear that it had been an innocuous event, as most of the nearby guests were going back to their prior conversations, but my father had come over to investigate anyway.

"Everything's fine," I assured him. "You remember Gossamer and Kane."

"Yes, of course I do," my father said, then greeted the two of them, as well as Li. "I hope you're all enjoying the party."

REPLICATION

"We only just arrived," Gossamer stated, "but this place seems beautiful. Do you know who it belongs to?"

"Some nouveau riche lout who thinks that money equals taste," I quipped facetiously.

"I'll pass your comments on to the owner." My father deadpanned, but I could tell that he was amused. "Anyway, you kids have fun, and stay out of trouble."

With that, Alpha Prime left us, winding his way through the throngs of those present.

"So when do we meet your grandmother?" Gossamer asked, her voiced laced with excitement.

I laughed. I had almost forgotten that Gossamer was a big fan of Indigo.

"Soon," I promised. "After she finishes with the receiving line. But in the meantime, there are some other people you guys should probably meet."

With that, I led Kane, Gossamer, and Li back to where I'd left Vela and Myshtal. A few minutes later, they had all become acquainted and were chatting amiably. (I didn't need to introduce the newly-arrived trio to Vestibule — who was still present — as they had previously met. The same was true of Avis, who had disappeared without me noticing around the time my friends showed up.)

Unexpectedly, Vela excused herself. Stepping in my direction, she motioned me aside, overtly indicating that she wanted to have a word with me.

"Where'd Avis go?" she asked without preamble.

I shrugged. "I don't know. She was there one second, gone the next."

Vela let out a sigh of frustration. "That's just great."

My brow wrinkled in confusion. "What's the problem?"

"I'm supposed to be keeping an eye on her," Vela stated, looking around. "She's kind of vulnerable right now."

"Vulnerable?" I repeated, somewhat shocked. Did Avis have some weakness I didn't know about?

"*Emotionally* vulnerable, dingbat," Vela said playfully. "Her boyfriend recently dumped her."

"He dumped her? She made it sound mutual."

"Yeah, well, when you're ranked as one of the world's top supers, you don't have the privilege of moping over failed relationships or lack of closure."

"So what do you do?"

"In my sister's case, she tends to rebound — usually quite quickly, but not always with the right kind of guy."

Nodding, I followed Vela's lead and began scanning the ranks of nearby guests, saying, "In that case, I think I might know where she…there!"

I inconspicuously pointed to an area on the opposite side of the room, where — unsurprisingly — Avis was engaged in deep conversation with Nobaxlin. Suddenly, she threw her head back, laughing gaily at something the Fleodin had just said.

"Okay, that's my cue," Vela declared. "Later, cuz."

Giving me a short wave goodbye, Vela began making a beeline towards her sister. However, she had barely stepped away before I sensed a sharp flare of excitement and elation coming from my rear. Having been privy to this scenario before, I knew what was about to happen. Therefore, fighting the temptation to turn around, I decided to play along and stayed in the same position. A moment later, someone stepped directly behind me and placed a hand over my eyes.

REPLICATION

I felt the person behind me lean in close, then grinned as a soft, feminine voice murmured, "Guess who?" next to my ear.

Chapter 22

It was, of course, my girlfriend, Electra. Smiling, I spun around — and then blinked as I took a good look at her.

She had her hair pinned up in an intricate, luxurious chignon that incorporated braids, layered curls, and waves. (I could tell just by looking at it that adopting this particular hairstyle had taken a significant amount of time and effort.) With respect to attire, she wore a strapless, full-length black dress. It was an exceptionally form-fitting little number, with a beaded, sweetheart neckline and a wide slit on one side that showed an ample — but not excessive — amount of leg. As to makeup, she'd stuck to her habit of using very little, with the most prominent application thereof being an alluring shade of deep red lipstick.

All in all, it was a more suggestive ensemble than she'd ever worn before, and I found it completely bewitching.

"Well?" she said, plainly inviting me to comment on her appearance.

Rather than respond verbally, I leaned in and kissed her.

A few seconds later, she pulled back, beaming, and said, "I'll take that to mean you approve."

"What, his drooling wasn't enough of an indicator?" Kane joked, causing me to note that he, Li, and the others had come closer during the few moments when Electra and I had been…distracted.

Laughing along with everyone else at Kane's comment, Electra patted me on the cheek and remarked, "Well, my baby only drools for the best."

REPLICATION

This elicited another round of chuckles, but I noticed that as she spoke, my girlfriend had cast a sharp but almost imperceptible glance in Vestibule's direction. At the same time, I picked up on a pleased and self-satisfied emotional vibe coming from Electra, making it clear to me that her statement was only being made partially in jest. However, the overall message being conveyed was plain enough to anyone paying attention: fashion model or not, Vestibule was out of her league when it came to my affections.

Internally, I let out a sigh of relief. Based on what I'd heard about the last time those two had met (which had involved my girlfriend releasing a ball of electricity over Vestibule's head), I wasn't exactly sure they'd avoid locking horns at the party. Thankfully, both seemed to be in relatively affable moods. More importantly, if innuendo and intimation were all I'd have to deal with (especially on Electra's part), it suggested that everyone would at least be civil to one another.

Sadly, all hopes for comity hit an abrupt speedbump a moment later when Myshtal said, "Hi, Electra. Your dress is lovely."

****

Later, when I replayed the scene in my mind, I should have realized there was a reason why Myshtal had been spared getting the same severe look from my girlfriend that Vestibule had received. It was because she wasn't in the immediate vicinity at the time. (Apparently my betrothed was actually a few feet away from our little group, talking to someone with her back to us.) She had presumably stepped away for a few moments while I was

163

talking to Vela, or around the time Electra had crept up behind me. Regardless, it seemed obvious that Electra had not initially noticed that the Caelesian princess was nearby.

Upon rejoining us, Myshtal had attempted something that she'd seen women on Earth do to break the ice when they met other females: compliment each other's appearance. Needless to say, it's probably more effective when the ice in question is more like a cube in size. What was between Myshtal and Electra was absolutely glacial in scope, as evidenced by the emotions the latter was broadcasting (which were far more intense than her feelings about Vestibule).

As if to confirm this, Electra muttered a chilly, nigh-inaudible "Thanks" in response to Myshtal's comment.

Her remark was followed by an uncomfortable silence — a blatant indication that the mood of our group had definitely been altered. Of course, I hadn't contemplated a scenario whereby Electra, Myshtal, and Vestibule would be in close proximity to one another, and it was a lot like transporting nitroglycerine and dynamite in a keg full of gunpowder. Basically, it felt like simply breathing the wrong way would set something off.

Seeking to reestablish the jovial atmosphere that had existed just moments earlier, I racked my brains for something to say but came up empty. As luck would have it, however, we were saved from having the situation become too awkward by one of my friends.

"So, Jim," Gossamer intoned, "any chance you can make good on that promise to meet your grandmother?"

"Uh, sure," I answered, trying to keep the relief out of my voice. "It might take us a minute to make our way through the crowd to get to her."

"No need for that," Electra chimed in. "Here she comes."

I looked in the same direction as Electra and noticed that she was correct. My grandmother was indeed headed our way, walking with purposeful determination.

"There you are," Indigo said when she reached us. From the way she said it, I got the impression that she had been looking for me.

"Did you need me for something, *Sxahnin*?" I asked.

"It can wait a moment," she replied. "Who are your friends?"

Taking that as my cue, I introduced my grandmother to those among us that she didn't already know (which was essentially everyone except Myshtal and Electra). Indigo then spent a few minutes chatting amiably with everyone, which actually did a lot to ease the tension in the air.

"Anyway," she said after a minute or two, "I've got to get back to meeting-and-greeting folks, but it was very nice meeting you all."

"Wait," I said, almost too eagerly. "I think you mentioned needing me for something?"

"Actually," she replied, seeming to contemplate, "I believe I'd prefer to take the girls with me."

I frowned, nonplussed. "The girls?"

"I think she means *us*, genius," Electra replied. "Me, Myshtal, Gossamer, and Vestibule." She then turned to Indigo. "How many of us do you need?"

"All of you, to be honest," my grandmother replied.

You didn't need any special powers to know that Electra was a little crestfallen at Indigo's response. My girlfriend had obviously been hoping to get rid of her rivals (for lack of a better term) — at least for a little while tonight. Unfortunately, it appeared that she and Gossamer would be going with them, and a moment later they were off, following close behind my grandmother as she worked her way through the crowd.

<I hope you don't mind me stepping in like that,> Indigo said telepathically, not bothering to turn around as she led the others away. <But you looked like you were in trouble.>

<No problem,> I assured her. <I appreciate the assist.>

<Happy to help. Plus, I think if these girls spend some time around each other without any…distractions, they may find that they actually have a lot in common.>

I smiled as Indigo, Electra, and the others headed back to the receiving line, now understanding that my grandmother's arrival hadn't been completely fortuitous. Apparently she'd been keeping an eye out to some extent.

"So," Kane droned, bringing an end to my musing, "what should we men-folk do while the women are preoccupied?"

"There is much we could do to entertain ourselves," Li noted, "but should we not include Smokescreen?"

"Smokey can join us when he gets here," Kane stated firmly.

"I think what Li meant to convey is that Smokey is *already* here," I said, pointing.

Kane looked in the direction indicated, where I assume he saw what I did: Smokey working his way towards us. After realizing we'd seen him, he gave us a quick wave. At that point, I noticed that Smokey had his

166

other arm extended behind him, as if leading someone by the hand — presumably his girlfriend, Sarah. Thus, it came as somewhat of a shock to me when they cleared the crowd and I realized that his date was someone else entirely. Even more telling, they continued holding hands as they headed in our direction, not letting go until they reached us. Last but not least, Smokey's date was actually someone I knew — a powerful teen super called Atalanta.

I kept silent as Smokey introduced Atalanta to Kane and Li. Truth be told, seeing her again was a little awkward for me, because the first time we met I was operating under a love spell that caused me to become wildly infatuated with her. Thankfully, very few people (including Atalanta herself) knew about the spell that had been cast on me, but I still found it embarrassing. Thus, I simply stood by quietly while the others chatted and probably would have been content to remain that way indefinitely had not Atalanta unexpectedly engaged me in conversation.

While Smokey was busy explaining something to Li and Kane, she suddenly turned to me and — speaking with a slight accent — said, "So, it appears that you've had some type of adventure lately."

I frowned. "What do you mean?"

"Your aura. It's changed significantly."

I nodded. Atalanta had the ability to sense auras around other people — an atmosphere which she claimed reflected their inner qualities in the form of a few basic colors. My aura, however, had been different in that — per Atalanta — it pulsed through a wild kaleidoscope of chroma, among other things.

"So what's different?" I asked after a few seconds.

REPLICATION

She seemed to spend a moment looking me over before responding. "There's still a wide range of colors, but they're richer, more vibrant, than before."

"What does that mean?"

She shrugged. "Your aura is still unlike anything I've ever seen, but at a guess I'd say that some new power or purpose has taken root in you."

I fought to keep a look of surprise off my face. In truth, I actually had developed a new power on Caeles — a healing ability that I'd used to save Queen Dornoccia after she had been poisoned and shot. My new talent had not only made her hale and hearty, but also seemed to rejuvenate the queen — making her years younger. It was, without question, a unique ability; it was also a power that I hadn't been unable to manifest since. Still, the idea of discussing it with someone who wasn't part of my inner circle wasn't that appealing to me, so I desperately wanted to change the subject.

Letting out a slight chuckle, I said, "As far as I know, I'm still the same guy. But enough about me. What have you been up to? I didn't think the Argonauts spent much time away from home."

Now it was Atalanta's turn to be circumspect. She hailed from a small but wealthy island nation called Argo, and was a member of the Argonauts — her country's team of supers. In the past, she had been incredibly judicious regarding the information she shared about her home and her teammates, so I assumed she would stay true to form and clam up. Much to my surprise, she gave what felt like a sincere and unrestrained response.

"I believe there's an adage in your country about all work and no play," she said, smiling. "We Argonauts work

168

hard, so we play hard as well, taking downtime when we need it."

"So this is downtime for you? Attending stiff formal events?"

She let out a slight giggle. "Actually, I like to travel, and my visit just happened to coincide with this party. But don't members of the Alpha League do something similar in terms of taking time off to unwind?"

I reflected on her question for a moment before responding. "Different people do different things. Like you, some travel. Others might take up a sport, like golf. A few simply just look for a quiet place to retreat from the world for a little while."

That last comment brought my father to mind. Alpha Prime had a secret base that he used as a refuge of sorts when he wanted to get away from everything.

"What about you?" she asked. "What do you do to de-stress?"

I shrugged. "Just hang out with friends, I guess."

"What, no hidden sanctuary where you can get away from it all?"

"Not really," I replied, although it wasn't exactly true. I did have a place — a small condo unit that had served as a sort of base of operations for my superhero antics before I joined the Alpha League. I still had a decent number of clothes there, along with a few personables, but I had pretty much avoided the place after someone was murdered there the previous year.

Thankfully, I was saved from having to dwell on such dour thoughts by Kane, who turned to Atalanta and announced, "By the way, this isn't a stag party, in case you were wondering."

Atalanta's brow wrinkled. "Excuse me?"

"It's not just you and a bunch of guys," Kane clarified. "Jim and I actually have dates."

"Oh?" murmured Atalanta. "Where are they?"

"They got drafted," I joked. "Our hostess needed help with something, so she recruited them."

Atalanta appeared to contemplate this for a second, then asked, "In that case, should I join them?"

"Um, sure," I mumbled. "I don't know exactly what they're doing, but I'm sure they'll appreciate the help."

"I just don't want to come across as being too good to lend a hand," she explained.

I gave a candid shake of my head. "Trust me, no one would think that. But if you'd still like to join them, they're right over there."

I tilted my chin in the direction of the receiving line, where Electra and the others were standing.

"You know what, why don't I walk you over?" Kane interjected. "I see Gossamer motioning for me to come anyway."

"Thanks," Atalanta said with a smile. "That's very kind of you." She then reached out and gave Smokey's hand a gentle squeeze, saying, "I'll be back as soon as I can."

With that, she and Kane began meandering towards the receiving line, joined — much to my surprise — by Li. Smokey watched them, his eyes glued to his date and with an infatuated grin on his face. I didn't need to employ my empathic abilities to know what he was feeling.

"So," I said. "You and Atalanta."

Smokey glanced down at the floor for a second before responding. "Yeah. It's complicated."

"Well, I obviously can't relate, because I know nothing about complicated relationships."

As I finished, I gestured towards the receiving line, where Vestibule, Electra (with arms sullenly crossed), and Myshtal stood next to one another, in that order.

Smokey, looking where indicated, merely nodded, conceding my point. Taking a deep breath, he stated, "It's something that happened around the time you came back. It's not anything that either of us aimed for. We just sort of…connected."

"And what about Sarah? You guys have been dating forever."

Smokey's brow creased as he gave me a fiercely intense look, and I felt muted anger flowing from him. Maybe he felt I was needling him too much, but — when I was fawning over Atalanta as a result of the love spell I'd been under — he had raked me over the coals regarding what he perceived as my mistreatment of Electra. Frankly speaking, he was my friend, but if he could dish it out, he could take it.

"That's over," he announced with finality after a few seconds.

"So you're just going to dump her? After all this time?"

Smokey tilted his head up, and his face took on a faraway expression, as if there were something in the distance that only he could see. Then he let out a pent-up breath and turned to me with a pained expression on his face.

"She went out with another guy, Jim."

I blinked, almost sure that I'd misheard him. Sarah and Smokey had always been wild about each other. He'd even gone so far as to tell her that he was a super in order to maintain their relationship. And she had always seemed devoted to him. I'd spent a great deal of time around her, and never once picked up on the slightest indication that she was interested in anyone else. Ergo, Smokey's statement came as something of a shock.

Nevertheless, from everything I could sense, what he was saying was true. Moreover, I suddenly understood that the anger he'd exuded earlier hadn't been directed at me, but at Sarah.

Struggling for words of comfort, I blurted out, "I'm sorry, man. Why didn't you say anything?"

Smokey shrugged his shoulders. "I guess we just really haven't had a chance to talk since you've been back. Plus," — he glanced back to where Electra and the others were standing — "as you pointed out a few minutes ago, you've got your own issues to deal with on that front."

"It's worse than it looks," I stated, almost despondently. "There's a chance Myshtal may have actual feelings for me."

"Wait a minute," Smokey said. "Wouldn't you have picked up on that — sensed something?"

"Well, let's keep in mind that despite how she looks, the princess is actually an alien. So, while I've become somewhat adept at reading their emotions, I'm not perfect."

"In other words," Smokey summed up, "you had no clue."

I let out a weary sigh. "I picked up on affection, but I didn't think anything of it. I categorized it to what you probably feel towards Electra. You like her and you care about her, but you don't have romantic intentions where she's concerned. In that same vein, I recognized that

Myshtal was fond of me, but I would never have pegged it as full-blown amore."

"You know," Smokey chuckled as Kane and Li began heading back our way, "between Electra, Myshtal, and Vestibule, I honestly didn't think your situation could get any more complicated, romantically. Somehow, though, you managed it."

I shrugged. "It's a gift, I guess."

REPLICATION

Chapter 23

After Li and Kane rejoined us, the four of us spent about half an hour engaging in guy talk — sports, action movies, etc. — before the girls returned. Apparently my grandmother had used them to ferry exclusive gifts, consisting of handcrafted Caelesian jewelry, to a select group of old friends. (On a related note, it seems Gossamer had called Kane over to ask if it was appropriate to use magic to deliver the gifts, but he had wisely told her that Indigo probably wanted a personal touch.)

All of the recipients appeared to be exceptionally delighted and honored by my grandmother's largess — including Electra and the other girls, who also received Caelesian jewelry as a sign of Indigo's gratitude for their help. Much to my surprise, the experience did seem to ease some of the tension that had been present earlier. For instance, as they came back to rejoin our group, I noticed Myshtal and Electra comparing the Caelesian brooch and ring they had each been given, respectively. I didn't fool myself into thinking they were going to be BFFs from that point forward, but I did garner the impression that everyone would be civil enough to keep things from getting awkward. Oddly enough, it turned out to be a fairly accurate assessment for the most part; even Vestibule felt comfortable enough to continue hanging out with us.

With everyone ostensibly willing to put forth an effort to be cordial, the party quickly became a lot more enjoyable. Conversation and commentary were a little guarded at first, but before long we were actually having fun. We laughed, joked, danced — we even started a conga line that almost everyone in the ballroom joined.

REPLICATION

After our efforts on the dance floor, someone made a comment about the room being stuffy. With the ability to control my body temperature, among other things, I was still comfortable, but the statement made me conscious of the fact that a couple of the girls were fanning themselves with their hands. At that juncture, our group made a joint decision to step out and get some air.

It took us a few minutes to press our way through the crowd, but we eventually made our way outside. It was a beautiful, starry night, and we spent a little time wandering aimlessly, with my friends admiring the architecture of my father's manor and the meticulous landscaping of the surrounding grounds, much of which was illuminated by lamps. Although we had no particular destination in mind, we ultimately found ourselves near the pool at the rear of the mansion.

That's when *he* entered the picture.

REPLICATION

Chapter 24

He was the Pelagic Prince — a teen super who claimed to be the heir to an undersea kingdom. I didn't know him personally, only by reputation, but he'd always struck me as being a bit pompous. That said, he wasn't really a bad guy and didn't intentionally do anything wrong, but his presence had an indirect effect on the rest of the evening.

We had only been at the pool for a few minutes when he sauntered over in our direction. He was dressed in tuxedo pants, but that's pretty much where his attempt at formal attire came to an abrupt halt. Rather than a shirt and coat, he wore what appeared to be an open vest, displaying bare arms, washboard abs, and pecs so overdeveloped it looked like he had inflated balloons under his skin. Now that I thought about it, he always seemed to be bare chested to some extent. (Apparently the same thought occurred to Smokey, who leaned towards me and whispered, "Seems someone is allergic to shirts.")

In truth, the Pelagic Prince had spent the bulk of his life in the water (or more appropriately, *under* it), where shirts weren't exactly en vogue. Thus, he couldn't truly be blamed for never really growing accustomed to them. Presumably, like many others in attendance, he had come to the party as the guest of an invitee — in this case, his grandfather, who had been a contemporary of Gramps and Indigo.

For a moment, it appeared that he was going to approach and speak to us, but instead the Pelagic Prince walked by, merely giving us a short, friendly wave for the most part (although I noticed him wink at Myshtal). He stopped at the edge of the pool, and then shrugged in a way that caused the vest to drop from his shoulders. Looking back in our direction, he gave us a cocky grin and then suddenly leaped up and out over the water.

From the way his body was positioned, I got the impression that he was attempting a belly flop of some sort. That being the case, I expected to hear an audible "plop" as he hit the surface of the pool and see water splash explosively. What actually happened, however, was quite a surprise.

While still in the air, the Pelagic Prince acrobatically performed a double backflip, then somehow managed to straighten out before hitting the water. Remarkably, he went in with a sound that was barely above a whisper, and which scarcely caused a ripple on the surface. Once under the water, he zipped away like he had a motor attached to him, swimming the length of the pool and back, then completing the circuit again — all in under ten seconds (and while still wearing his tuxedo pants).

"Wow," murmured Gossamer. "I don't think I've ever seen anything like that before."

Kane nodded in agreement. "Me either. I didn't even know they made aquatic tuxedos."

That caused a general round of laughter, and a moment later, normal conversation resumed. In truth, however, I only halfway paid attention to what was being said, as I was still keeping an eye on the Pelagic Prince. I lost track of how many times he swam the length of the pool over the next few minutes, but there was one thing I did take note of: he never once broke the surface for air. It was an effective display of his talents, and I'd be lying if I said I wasn't impressed.

After a few minutes, the Pelagic Prince exited the pool. He came out almost the same way he'd gone in —

jumping straight out of the water with a muted sound like a knife leaving a sheath, and barely disturbing the surface of the pool. Landing next to his vest, he suddenly shuddered in a weird way — and then again — and for a second I wondered if he had caught a chill or something. It took me a moment to realize what he was actually doing was shaking water off his body, but in a very controlled manner that didn't send droplets flying everywhere. A minute later, he was generally dry except for his pants and hair.

Apparently swimming did something to improve his social skills, because the Pelagic Prince — still shirtless — swiftly strode over to us purposefully and introduced himself. We responded in kind, with each member of our group individually greeting him. Although he responded politely to each of us in turn, it became obvious almost immediately that he was really only interested in one person: Myshtal.

Even before she introduced herself (using her formal name, Isteria), the Pelagic Prince seemed to have eyes for no one but my betrothed. On her part, she seemed to note his attention, but emotionally I could sense that she wasn't interested — a fact that gave me peace of mind, for some reason.

Lacking empathic abilities, the Pelagic Prince clearly didn't realize that his feelings weren't reciprocated. (Or if he did, maybe he didn't care, thinking he could win her over.) Intentionally engaging Myshtal in one-on-one conversation, it only took him a minute or two to casually maneuver her a few feet away from the rest of us and out of earshot. From that aspect, he had his technique for getting a girl alone, so to speak, down to a science.

REPLICATION

Telling myself that I was responsible for her, I kept an eye on Myshtal and her new suitor, only half-heartedly participating in the discussion the rest of my friends were engaged in (which currently focused on the merits of an up-and-coming social media site). I couldn't hear what was being said between them, but I could sense Myshtal slowly growing annoyed and frustrated with the Pelagic Prince, as he clearly wasn't getting the message.

I spent a brief moment debating about whether I should come to her rescue, but immediately dismissed the idea. Anything along those lines was sure to reignite the fuse on a stick of dynamite that had already been doused once tonight. Everyone in my current circle of friends — particularly Myshtal and Electra — had managed to peacefully coexist since the girls had returned from delivering gifts on behalf of my grandmother. (In fact, the only notable event of an untoward nature had been when Myshtal introduced herself to the Pelagic Prince by her formal name, which caused Electra to frown — presumably because she hadn't heard it before.) In short, I made a conscious choice to do nothing where Myshtal was concerned.

In the end, standing down turned out to be the right decision, as Myshtal apparently handled the problem on her own. I don't know what she said, but she uttered something that caused the Pelagic Prince to smile broadly as he responded, and then he quickly retrieved his vest and shuffled away towards the interior of the mansion. Myshtal rejoined us a moment later, glancing over her shoulder as if to make sure her admirer was gone.

"Well, someone has a fan," Gossamer noted.

"Not by choice," Myshtal assured her. "He's somewhat overbearing."

179

"It goes with the territory," Vestibule chimed in. "He's a prince, after all, and it's not every day that a girl has royalty courting her."

Myshtal frowned. "Are princes that uncommon here?"

This elicited more than a few chuckles, with Li responding a few seconds later, saying, "They are somewhat rare."

"Then a double-prince must be singularly unique," Myshtal announced conclusively.

Her statement caused almost everyone except me to display a look of confusion.

"A *double*-prince?" Smokey echoed a few seconds later.

Rather than respond Myshtal merely gestured towards me.

My thoughts raced furiously as I wrestled with what to say. Most of those in our current circle were my close friends and knew many of the intimate details of my life. Vestibule and Atalanta, however, were acquaintances at best. How much did I really want them knowing about me? Then again, I had spent the early part of the evening in a receiving line being introduced as Indigo's grandson. Thus, the cat was out of the bag to a large extent where my background was concerned.

Mind made up, I let out a sigh and then quickly summed up how I was both Caelesian and Fleodin royalty. There was stunned silence for the most part when I finished.

"Wait a minute — you're a prince in not just one but two interstellar empires?" Kane finally said after a few seconds. "How's that fair? Someone please explain to me how that's fair."

He asked the last two questions in a tone of mock frustration, causing all of us to laugh.

"Truthfully," I said with a grin, "it's not all it's cracked up to be."

"Yeah, right," Smokey stated sarcastically. "We're not buying your uneasy-lies-the-head-that-wears-a-crown routine." He turned to Myshtal. "Anyway, what did you say to the Pelagic Prince to get him to leave?"

"Nothing much," Myshtal replied. "I just asked him if he would get me something from the dessert bar inside."

"There's a dessert bar here?" Kane asked, obviously intrigued.

"No, there isn't," Myshtal replied.

Her comment was met with perplexed looks — and then a raucous outburst of laughter as everyone figured out the joke at about the same time. Myshtal had sent her would-be Romeo on a snipe hunt.

"That's awesome!" Gossamer chirped between giggles.

"You think so?" Myshtal inquired.

"Oh, yeah," I insisted, grinning broadly. "That was classic."

"Do you think he'll be back?" Myshtal asked.

I shrugged. "Who knows? But if he does, just tell him he needs to put on a shirt if he wants to continue the conversation. I doubt that's an option for the Pelagic Prince."

"More like the *Pectoral* Prince," Myshtal harrumphed.

This caused even more chuckles. Or rather, I thought it did, but after a few seconds I realized that Myshtal and I were the only ones laughing. Everyone else was just staring at us as if we were speaking gibberish — especially Electra, who was suddenly giving off an unsettling vibe.

"Oh, come on," I said, trying to reestablish a congenial atmosphere. "You have to admit that was funny."

"I don't know, Jim," Electra blurted out testily. "Maybe if we'd heard it in *English*."

I blinked, trying to make sense of her statement — and then it hit me. The last bit of dialog between Myshtal and me had actually been spoken in Caelesian. Somehow we had switched to my grandmother's native tongue without me even noticing.

I opened my mouth to explain — to say anything — but had seemingly taken too long to gather my thoughts, because at that point I was looking at Electra's back as she stormed off.

REPLICATION

Chapter 25

I took off after my girlfriend, urged on by Kane making a surreptitious shooing motion with his hand and Smokey doing something similar with his eyes. It didn't take me long to catch her, as she only had a few seconds of a head start and never got out of my line of sight.

She hadn't marched towards the mansion. Instead, she had gone past the pool, heading for the expansive, lamplit grounds of my father's estate. Needless to say, she was fitfully irate, and it was visibly evident on her face.

I initially tried to talk to her — asked her to speak to me, why she was so angry, and so on. She essentially ignored me, continuing to walk without breaking stride. After a few minutes, I gave up on trying to engage with her verbally and attempted to hold her hand. The first time, she shook my hand off like it was more disgusting than a dung beetle. The next time I tried it, she gave me a mild electrical zap that had my fingers stinging for about thirty seconds. Following that, I just fell into step beside her, following where she led and keeping my hands to myself.

She didn't seem to have a particular destination in mind — just away from the pool area where I had seemingly committed the unforgiveable sin of speaking in another language. At this juncture, however, we were well away from the site of my transgression and had just begun walking down a path that I recognized.

"Um…" I began, thinking I should tell Electra what lay ahead. However, a withering look from her made me reassess, and I stayed quiet.

After a few moments, the path we were on began to bisect a pair of well-trimmed hedgerows. The shrubbery comprising them was initially about four feet tall, but within a few steps had stretched up to about seven feet in height. Moreover, the path we were on (which was well-lit by lamps) began to fork every five or ten paces.

I smiled to myself, thinking how distracted Electra must be not to realize what was happening, to not recognize where we were. Nevertheless, I kept my mouth shut, understanding that sooner or later she would notice what was already obvious to me.

She got her first hint when the path we were on suddenly came to a dead end at a wall of hedges. She frowned for a second, plainly confused, then tried retracing our steps. Moments later, we hit another dead end, causing me to smile momentarily. When we hit our third dead end a minute later, I couldn't keep the grin off my face.

Having reached her limits, Electra finally declared, "If you're going to be following me around all night like a stray hoping to be adopted, the least you can do is help me instead of standing there smirking."

I chuckled. "We're in a hedge maze."

"I know that, professor. I'm looking for the way out."

"Well, there are two options. Number one, I could phase you, and then you could simply walk straight through the hedges until you're out."

I was silent for a moment, prompting her to ask, "What's option two?"

"We work together to actually find our way out of the maze."

****

It took about ten minutes of concerted effort to find our way out of the maze. In truth, it was actually a lot of fun working together to solve what was effectively a giant puzzle, and a few times we bumped into other people who were also trying to locate the exit. By the time we made our way out, Electra was speaking to me again in something akin to her usual tone. Making a bold gamble, I reached out to take her hand, and this time she let me (and also rewarded me with a smile).

"We should probably head back," I said, and immediately regretted it as I sensed tension and ire rising in Electra.

"Or not," I quickly added.

Electra looked as though she wanted to make a comment, but before she could someone softly cleared their throat nearby. We both turned in the direction of the sound. Facing us, camera in hand and dressed in a tux, was the photographer we'd met the night before.

"Matt Kroner," I said flatly, trying to hide my surprise. "If you're trying to avoid being confused with paparazzi, crashing private parties is not how it's done."

He chuckled a little nervously. "Believe it or not, I actually have an invite."

"Oh?" said Electra, sounding somewhat skeptical.

Kroner nodded. "Yes, Indigo asked me to come. They never lined up an official photographer, and she decided at the last minute that she'd really like some keepsakes."

I kept my face passive, but internally I felt that what Kroner had said was reasonable. It actually sounded like something my grandmother would do. More to the point, from what I could sense of his emotions, Kroner was being truthful.

"So why are you out here wandering around instead of being inside where the party is?" Electra asked.

"There are folks partying outside, too," Kroner countered, glancing around at others who were also taking the air. "Plus, I've been snapping pictures of people inside all night. But the real reason I'm out here is *you*."

Electra's eyebrows rose in surprise. "Me?"

"The two of you, actually," Kroner answered. "Indigo told me to make sure that I got a picture of you and the quick-change artist" — he nodded at me — "so I tracked you down."

Quick-change artist? I frowned for a moment, trying to make sense of his comment, but decided not to dwell on it as Kroner gave a quick rundown of how he'd found us. Essentially, my grandmother had told him to look for the famous teen model Vestibule, who in turn had pointed him in the direction where Electra and I had last been seen. (The rest was elementary, although he'd had to wait a few minutes for us to come out of the hedge maze.)

After he finished speaking, Kroner had us quickly strike a few poses — standing side-by-side, face-to-face, back-to-back, etc. — and then hurriedly bid us adieu.

"Well, that was fast," Electra whispered as we watched Kroner walking away. "I guess there's some bigwig inside whose picture will sell for more money than ours."

"It's more likely that he's just trying to give us some privacy," I said. "Remember how he announced himself by clearing his throat? He obviously realized he caught us at an awkward time."

She nodded. "Good point."

"Anyway," I said, changing the subject, "where were we before Kroner captured us on camera?"

"You were about to apologize."

186

"I was?" I droned, raising an eyebrow. "For what, exactly?"

"For what?" she repeated. "For being an a—"

She stopped in mid-sentence as a young couple appeared nearby. Holding hands and looking starry-eyed, they hurried past us towards the entrance to the hedge maze.

Electra was silent for a moment as the couple went around a hedgerow and vanished from our line of sight.

"Look, is there some place where we can talk in private?" she asked.

"Of course," I assured her, and then teleported us.

Chapter 26

We popped up on a high veranda facing the rear of the mansion and enclosed by a decorative stone railing. It not only let us look down on the poolside terrace where our friends were, but also provided an epic view of the grounds and surrounding area. All in all, it was a stunning panorama that was difficult to absorb with a single glance.

"Wow," Electra muttered, taking in the view. "Where are we?"

"One of the upper balconies," I replied. "But this wing is one of the few parts of the mansion closed off tonight, so we won't be disturbed."

"Balconies, wings, mansions," she said teasingly. "Someone's growing accustomed to haute living."

"On the contrary, my lifestyle's finally catching up to my taste," I quipped.

She giggled merrily at that, the sound of her laughter making my heart race. Then, still smiling, she stepped close and kissed me, catching me a little unprepared but I quickly recovered.

She pulled back a few moments later, a coy grin on her face as she tucked a stray lock of hair behind her ear. Then she took me by the hand and led me to a couch that was part of an outdoor furniture set, along with a couple of armchairs and an ottoman. She took a seat in the middle of the couch and drew me down next to her.

She didn't say anything at first, just sat there with a thoughtful expression on her face. Knowing that she was working up to something, I simply stayed quiet, perfectly content to merely hold her hand.

After a minute or so, she let out a deep breath and said, "I don't really dislike her — Myshtal, that is." She added the name hastily, as if I wouldn't have known who she was referring to. "And I don't think she's a terrible person because of this…situation that you're both in."

"Then what is it?" I asked.

"It's the fact that you live in the same house with her, you sleep under the same roof, you're both royalty, you've had adventures together, and the two of you speak a language that no one else understands."

"Well, that's not exactly true. I mean, not that many people on Earth speak Caelesian, but —"

"You know what I mean," she interjected, cutting me off. "Basically, the two of you connect in ways that you and I can't."

"Look, I can't deny that Myshtal and I have a rapport," I admitted. "You can't go through what we did on Caeles and *not* develop a bond of some sort, but it's not like what you and I have."

"Yeah, what you and I have is very different," she stated in a huff, letting go of my hand and crossing her arms. "I'm the one you're *not* engaged to."

I laughed. "You say that like it's a competition."

She gave me a steely look. "You said that, not me."

"Fine, *I* said it. So will it make you feel better if I even up the score?"

She frowned. "What do you mean?"

"I'll just get engaged to you, too," I announced with a smile, wrapping my arms around her and pulling her close.

Electra burst out laughing. "Ha! That's your idea of evening up the score?"

"Sure," I insisted with a nod as Electra leaned towards me and lay her head against my chest. "If I'm engaged to *you*, that'll be an additional connection that you and I have."

"Well, I hate to disappoint you," she said, feigning a stern tone, "but on Earth, we don't just arrange marriages at the drop of a dime. Maybe on Caeles they sell women off as brides for a candy bar when they want a snack, but here we do it differently."

"Well, in that case, I'll do it the old-fashioned way," I stated. "I'll just ask your father for your hand."

Suddenly, Electra went stiff. Although I had meant for my statement to be generic, I had inadvertently touched upon a sensitive subject.

Electra had been raised by the Alpha League since she was an infant. However, she had recently found her birth parents, and the details about them had been sobering, to say the least. For starters, her biological father was in prison, while her mother had suffered a psychotic break shortly after Electra's birth. Even worse, the entire maternal side of her family — but for one notable exception — were essentially bad apples whose calling card was synonymous to "Supervillains R Us."

The only silver lining was the fact that her father, Vir, was actually a good guy who — from what I had been told — didn't deserve to be behind bars. That said, it didn't appear that parole was likely to happen any time in the near future. (It certainly didn't help that Vir had recently broken out. There had been extenuating circumstances and he had willingly turned himself back in, but he clearly hadn't earned any brownie points with that maneuver.) Nevertheless, Electra and her father had started developing a relationship and had grown close, but it was obviously an area in which my girlfriend was pretty touchy.

Fortunately, Electra plainly realized that my *faux pas* was completely unintentional, and after a few seconds I felt the tension drain out of her.

"I think you might be putting the cart before the horse," she finally said, a little snarkily.

"How's that?" I asked.

"Well, anything like that is obviously years away, but before you start asking anybody for my hand, you might want to figure out whether I'll say 'Yes' when you pop the question."

REPLICATION

Chapter 27

Electra and I didn't return to the party. We simply stayed on the balcony, talking and spending some much-needed quality time together. (And it's just as well that we didn't go back, since I'm sure something else would have happened to sour the mood. It just seemed to be a recurring theme whenever Myshtal and my girlfriend drifted into each other's orbit.)

Thankfully, our friends weren't offended when I gave them a telepathic heads-up that they were on their own, so to speak. Likewise with my mother and grandparents, who made sure Myshtal got home safely. In fact, the only person not too keen on the idea of me and Electra being off by ourselves was Esper, another member of the Alpha League who generally served as Electra's de facto guardian. (It had recently come to light that Esper was also my girlfriend's aunt, which explained why she had a tendency to be overprotective on occasion.)

I hadn't seen her at the party, but I'd known she was present and had no trouble making mental contact with Esper, who was typically ranked as the most powerful telepath on the planet. She, in turn, had given me very specific instructions on when I was to have her niece home — and how swiftly I was to depart thereafter. To someone on the outside looking in, it might have appeared that Esper didn't like me. In truth, however, she actually approved of me as Electra's boyfriend. That said, I clearly hadn't done myself any favors in her sight by returning from Caeles with a fiancée in tow.

Thus it was with Esper's directives still fresh in my head that I teleported Electra home at the appropriate time. A big smooch before she went inside let me know I was pretty much forgiven for any transgression, and I teleported home and went to bed in a generally good mood.

✳✳✳✳✳✳✳✳✳✳✳✳✳✳✳✳✳✳✳✳✳✳✳✳✳✳✳✳✳✳✳✳✳✳✳✳✳✳

I woke up the next morning to the sound of my cell phone ringing. Still groggy, I checked the time and noted that it wasn't exceptionally early, but — after a late night — I had actually planned to sleep in a little longer. I then looked to see who was calling me, and saw a message saying, "Caller ID Blocked."

I immediately became wide awake, all signs of drowsiness gone.

Among the various applications and programs on my phone was a feature known as Anonymous Caller Rejection. In essence, if someone attempts to phone me while blocking their own number, their call won't go through. That said, there was one person who seemingly had the ability to circumvent the anonymous caller feature, phoning me at will while keeping their own caller info private.

I debated for a moment on whether to answer as the phone continued ringing. The person calling wasn't a friend — far from it. And it was a sure bet that he wasn't calling with good news. More than likely, he wanted something. However, in the past, taking a similar call had ultimately worked to my advantage. In short, if I was careful, there was a possibility that I could derive a benefit from speaking with my caller.

Mind made up, I answered, uttering in an uninterested monotone, "Gray."

"You know," replied my caller, "I'm not so young that I would be offended if you chose to use an honorific when addressing me. Something like 'Mister' or 'Monsieur' or—"

"What do you want, Gray?" I demanded, cutting him off.

"Straight to the point, as usual," he said, sounding a little disheartened. "Fine. I'm actually calling to see if I can assist with this situation you've gotten yourself into."

Situation? I thought, frowning. Was he talking about Myshtal? It was pretty much a given that my caller, Gray, knew about her. Although he had no super powers to speak of, Gray had been granted nigh-limitless, global authority — ostensibly to maintain peace and order (among other things) — and it made him one of the most powerful men on the planet, as well as one of the most dangerous. More importantly, it was within his mandate to eradicate anything he determined to be a threat. It was a label that had seemingly been applied to me in the past, but Gray's statement made me wonder if the definition might now include Myshtal, since his jurisdiction also extended to extraterrestrials.

"Are you talking about the princess?" I asked, deciding to address the matter head-on.

"What?" Gray replied, momentarily confused. "Heavens, no. That's a mess of your own making. You'll have to clean that one up yourself."

Tension I wasn't aware of suddenly left my body, and I let out a deep breath. It was one thing to personally be the target of Gray's machinations. It would have been something else entirely if Myshtal had somehow been central to one of his schemes. Knowing that wasn't the case came as a great relief.

"Okay, so we're back to my original question," I said. "What do you want?"

"The same as I said in my original answer: to help you with this issue that's come up."

"What issue? I have no idea what you're talking about."

He seemed to contemplate that for a second. "I suppose it really hasn't popped up on your radar yet, which is why it would be best if we deal with it now."

"We?" I repeated. "So we'd be working together?"

"Surely you don't object? I mean, I'm only trying to help."

"Yeah, right," I muttered sarcastically. "Assuming that you really are calling to lend me a hand with some undefined problem that I'm completely unaware of, you wouldn't do it for nothing. You want *some*thing."

Gray chuckled. "Astute as always. All right, I do want something, but it's the same thing I've sought in the past. I want you to work for me."

"Forget it. Conversation over," I declared. The last thing I wanted or needed was to be indebted to a man like Gray. Working for him was completely out of the question.

"But don't you even want to hear what the problem is?" he asked.

"Doesn't matter," I replied definitively. "Whatever it is, I'll handle it on my own. I don't need your help."

"And you know that for a fact?"

"I do."

"Then you don't know *Jack*!" he blurted out, laughing, and then hung up on me.

I sat there for a moment, frowning. The way he'd uttered that last statement had struck me as odd — as if there had been some inside joke I was unaware of.

However, before I could devote any more time to it, I felt my grandfather reaching out for me mentally.

<Jim,> he said, with something of an urgent tone, <I need you to get down here asap.>

REPLICATION

Chapter 28

At super speed, it took me less than a minute to shower, get dressed, and make myself presentable. Dashing downstairs, I found my grandfather in the main living room, but not alone.

With him was a man who I pegged to be in his early forties, but in great physical condition. He stood next to my grandfather with his hands behind his back in a position I recognized as parade rest. His dark hair was just starting to show a hint of gray, and was cut in a high-and-tight style. Finally, he wore a dark uniform that appeared to be military, although it didn't conform with the standard attire for any of the armed services that I was familiar with. All in all, despite the unusual uniform, everything about him screamed "career soldier."

"Jim," my grandfather said, motioning me over. "This is Colonel Drake Dreiser. Drake, this is my grandson, Jim."

"Colonel?" I repeated. "What branch of service?"

"Drake's part of a special unit," Gramps cut in, not giving our guest a chance to reply. "He's here to talk about an issue that's come up."

"I'll get straight to the point," the colonel said. "As you're both aware, the government maintains several discreet high-end superstructures for the purpose of containing sentient threats that can't — for a variety of reasons — be housed in ordinary facilities."

Supermaxes for supervillains, I thought, but didn't say anything, choosing instead to simply nod as Gramps did.

"Last night," Dreiser went on, "one of these structures was breached."

"Someone broke out?" Gramps asked.

The colonel shook his head. "No, someone broke *in*. But it's probably easier to show you than tell you."

Dreiser shifted his stance, bringing his arms from behind his back and revealing a small object in one hand. He stepped over to a nearby table where a laptop computer sat open. I didn't recognize it as one of ours, so presumably the colonel had brought it with him. Gramps and I approached and stood next to him as he plugged the object in his hand (which I now recognized as a flash drive) into one of the ports on the side of the computer, then pressed the Enter key. A moment later, the screen began to play some type of video.

It only took me a moment to recognize what I was seeing: security footage of some sort, showing two soldiers in the same type of uniform that Dreiser was wearing — except for the fact that the duo in the video also wore sidearms. They were sitting at a couple of side-by-side desks, with their backs to the camera that had filmed them. On each of the two desks was a standard computer monitor and keyboard. Mounted on a wall directly in front of the soldiers were several large security monitors, each of which had a screen that relayed images from multiple cameras.

Based on what Dreiser had told us — and scenes from a million movies and TV shows — we were looking at a prison control room. It was also safe to assume that this was where the break-in previously mentioned had occurred, and we didn't have to wait long for that to be confirmed.

The two soldiers — guards, really — were doubtlessly going about their normal routine when a third person abruptly appeared in the room. He pretty much came out of nowhere; one second he wasn't there, and the next he was standing directly in front of the two guards' desks. (Actually, if the date/time stamp in the corner of the screen was correct, it didn't even take a second for him to appear.)

The newcomer was facing the camera, and I suddenly found myself leaning in close, not quite believing what I was seeing.

The fellow who had just shown up had *my* face.

REPLICATION

Chapter 29

I hit a button on the laptop, pausing the video.

"What is this?" I practically demanded.

"Let's just let it play out first," Dreiser replied, tapping a key that caused the video to resume.

I was going to protest, but a subtle shake of my grandfather's head made me hold my tongue.

<Don't say anything,> he instructed me telepathically, <no matter what you see.>

I gave a mental nod to acknowledge that I understood. Turning back to the footage, I saw the two guards suddenly take note of the newcomer's presence. They reacted as anticipated, coming to their feet while simultaneously reaching for their sidearms. However, they had barely drawn their weapons before some unseen force unexpectedly snatched the guns from their hands and flung them out of view of the camera. The two guards exchanged worried looks — and then they themselves were gone. They vanished into thin air, like some sort of parlor trick, leaving the new arrival alone in the control room.

Next, the new guy himself disappeared, only to materialize almost immediately in front of one of the desks. Based on what I'd seen, it didn't take a lot of effort to understand that the fellow on the screen was a teleporter.

Without hesitation, the newcomer leaned across the desk, but at an angle that gave the camera a profile view of his visage. He then began tapping on the keyboard, occasionally glancing at an image on one of the security monitors. After about ten seconds of this, he simply stood up straight and seemingly stared at the security monitor image he'd been watching earlier. He then crossed his arms, and I observed the corner of his mouth slowly turning up into a smile. I couldn't pick up any emotions, of course, but I got the distinct impression that he was feeling a sense of smug satisfaction.

"What's he doing?" Gramps finally asked.

"Admiring his handiwork," Dreiser replied. My grandfather and I both gave him blank looks, prompting him to add, "Hang on. This will clear things up."

Without waiting for questions or commentary, the colonel hit a few keys, and the image on the screen changed.

We were now looking at a small room — maybe seventy square feet in size — that was austerely furnished with a plastic chair, a sink, and a bed that was more accurately described as a cot bolted to the wall. The sole occupant was a young blonde about my age who was dressed in an orange coverall. Surprisingly, I knew who she was.

"That's Incendia," Dreiser announced, confirming my own assessment. "She's a super whose power set revolves around fire."

<You recognize her?> Gramps asked telepathically.

<Yeah,> I confirmed. <She's the one who torched our house.>

My grandfather gave a barely-perceptible nod, and I picked up on a nostalgic vibe that suggested he was reminiscing. Around the time I joined the Alpha League, a group of supervillains had decided I was a threat to one of their schemes, so they had sent Incendia to deal with me. She had then used her power over fire to burn our house to the ground, destroying many of my grandfather's keepsakes in the process.

<She's supposed to be locked up in a nullifier somewhere off the grid,> I continued.

<Looking at this, I'd say she is,> Gramps replied.

I had to agree with my grandfather. Everything about the scene, from Incendia's wardrobe to the Spartan furnishings, shouted "prison cell."

All of a sudden, Incendia's head jerked up towards the ceiling, then left-to-right once, but in rapid fashion, as if she had noticed something perplexing. I was curious as to what was happening, but the camera in her cell was not angled in a way to give a view of what she was seeing.

Without warning, something like a jet of water seemed to splash the front of her coverall from above. Incendia appeared to gasp, like someone being unexpectedly doused with a garden hose. At the same time, the liquid seemed to crystalize on her clothing.

Incendia then arched her back wildly, her face wincing in pain. She then spun around, with one hand reaching over her shoulder, as if trying to grab something in the middle of her back. As she turned, I noticed that another stream of water (or whatever it was) had struck her back and crystalized there as well.

"What's that liquid striking her?" Gramps asked.

"A modified form of liquid nitrogen," the colonel replied. "Chemically altered to be more concentrated and pernicious than the industrial grade. It freezes on contact, and there are spouts placed in hidden cubbies all around her cell that will smother Incendia with that stuff if the nullifier fails for some reason and she gets her powers back."

As if to prove up what Dreiser was saying, it suddenly appeared as if someone had turned a firehose on Incendia, with jets of liquid hitting her and becoming frozen solid almost immediately. She dashed madly around the cell, trying to get away, but there was nowhere to run. (There was no audio, but from the way her mouth moved, I could tell she was screaming.) After about thirty seconds, she hunkered down in a corner with her back to the camera as she continued getting sprayed. Within a minute, she looked to be little more than a block of ice.

Dreiser tapped a key on the laptop, ending the video.

"In case you were wondering, Incendia survived," he stated. "But just barely. She'll spend the next few weeks being treated for severe hypothermia. Hopefully she'll regain consciousness soon, and she'll be lucky not to lose any fingers or toes."

"She has our sympathies," my grandfather said sincerely, "but what does this have to do with us?"

The colonel gave him a frank stare. "You're kidding, right? Were we looking at the same video? Our facility got breached by a perp who's a dead ringer for your grandson."

"I saw a young man with a passing resemblance to Jim," Gramps acknowledged. "But nothing definitive."

"Really?" Dreiser droned sarcastically. "What about the part where he telekinetically disarmed a couple of my men, and then teleported them two miles away?"

Well, that explains what happened to the guards, I thought.

Gramps shrugged. "They were doing tricks like that with cameras forty years ago. These days, they've got apps that can make you look like a dog or turn you into the opposite sex. Making a couple of guys disappear on video is child's play."

"Come on, John," Dreiser said, almost sounding exasperated. "This visit is off the record, so I'm not here in an official capacity. I'm here as a friend."

Gramps stared at him for a moment, and then nodded. "Alright, off the record. So tell me, what do you have?"

"Just what I said," the colonel answered. "Your grandson teleporting into a high-end facility last night, accosting two guards, and almost killing a prisoner."

"That's not Jim on that video," Gramps firmly insisted.

Dreiser held up his hands defensively. "Look, John, I believe you, but let's face facts. Your grandson is Kid Sensation. That info isn't publicly known, but enough people at certain echelons are aware of it. And on the surface, we've got a guy displaying both telekinesis and teleportation — two of Kid Sensation's well-documented abilities — not to mention the fact that he could be your grandson's twin."

My grandfather crossed his arms. "I get it. People above you on the totem pole think Jim's a criminal now. Even if that were true, what can they do? Technically, he's the Caelesian ambassador to Earth, which means he's got diplomatic immunity. They can't touch him."

The colonel nodded. "True, but even if you can't arrest a diplomat, you can always give them the boot — kick them out of the country. Or in this case, off the planet."

"Make him leave Earth?" Gramps asked, raising an eyebrow.

"That would be one option," Dreiser confirmed.

Gramps frowned. "Is there another?"

Dreiser made a vague gesture. "Being born on Earth, your grandson is considered to have dual citizenship, from a planetary perspective. He could voluntarily relinquish his Caelesian status."

"Which would open him up to arrest and prosecution," Gramps added. "So he can go to jail or leave the planet. It's a bit of a catch-22."

"Pretty much," the colonel acknowledged. "Unless he can prove it wasn't him."

"Of course he can prove it wasn't him!" Gramps declared. "He's got an alibi."

Colonel Dreiser's eyebrows went up slightly in surprise. "Oh?"

"He was at a party last night," Gramps said. "He was seen by hundreds of people."

"John, your grandson's a teleporter," Dreiser stated flatly. "He could be here one second and on the dark side of the moon the next. Bearing that in mind, it doesn't matter if a million people saw him at that party. He's got no alibi for anything. Not now. Not ever."

Chapter 30

Dreiser left shortly thereafter, with my grandfather walking him to the door. I stayed put, still trying to make sense of everything I'd seen and heard. In fact, I was replaying the video in my head when my grandfather came back into the room, albeit a few minutes later than expected.

"Permission to speak, sir?" I asked.

"Funny," Gramps said sarcastically. "I didn't want you talking because I didn't want you to say anything that might inadvertently incriminate you."

I acknowledged his comment with a nod. "So you took longer than necessary to show the colonel out. What were you two talking about?"

"I was getting a better lay of the land."

"And?"

"Drake's a friend, as you could probably tell. Since the facility that got breached is under his authority, I asked him to do what he could to help us."

"Which is what?"

"Well, some people above his pay grade think the case against you is pretty clear-cut. The situation is still being looked into, but they want to fast-track the investigation. However, your standing as a Caelesian dignitary complicates things. Drake's going to use that to insist on a deliberate, by-the-books approach to the investigation, which he's heading up. He'll buy us some time to figure this thing out, including what we want to do."

My brow crinkled in thought. "How much time are we talking about?"

"A week — two, max."

"Not a whole lot of time," I noted. "And what happens after that? They show up with manacles and a rocket ship, giving me a Hobson's Choice?"

"Ha!" Gramps chortled. "With your mother and grandmother around, I'd love to see them try."

"That reminds me," I said, noting that I couldn't detect any nearby emotions besides my grandfather's, "where is everybody?"

Gramps shrugged. "They went off to do some post-party, Caelesian princess thing. Your mother doesn't know anything about it, so Indigo and Myshtal are teaching her."

That news came as a bit of a relief. Basically, I was glad that they hadn't been around to see that footage of what appeared to be me doing something heinous.

"Anyway," I said, "did Dreiser say anything else?"

"No," my grandfather replied, shaking his head. "But he did give me this."

He held out a hand, palm open, in which sat the flash drive with the incriminating footage.

Chapter 31

It went without saying, of course, that the data on the flash drive was a duplicate. Dreiser wasn't foolish enough to carry the original of something that important around with him, and he certainly wouldn't have given it to Gramps, no matter how close their friendship was.

"So what's our next step?" I asked.

"We try to get a better handle on what's going on here," my grandfather replied. "See what more there is to the story."

"How?"

"I'll reach out to some old friends. Make a few phone calls. If I can get in contact with the right people, maybe I can even stop this crazy talk about kicking you off the planet."

His statement brought Gray to mind, who had once threatened to deport me off the planet as well. I hadn't even told Gramps that he'd called me, but I did so now, swiftly bringing him up to speed on the conversation we'd had.

"You don't think he's behind this, do you?" I asked when finished.

My grandfather shook his head. "It's really not his style. Gray tends to tackle things like this head-on."

"In other words, he would have shown up and tried to toss me in the paddy wagon."

Gramps chuckled softly. "Probably. But even if he isn't directly involved, he obviously knows something. The timing of his call couldn't have been a coincidence."

"Agreed," I said with a nod. "But back to your friends — do you really think they'll help?"

"Of course. I'm still owed more than a few favors by some high-ranking individuals. I just need to call in some markers."

"Great," I effused. "What do you need me to do?"

"Nothing. Just sit tight while I go get my phone and start making calls."

With that, he began walking out of the room while I smiled to myself, thinking how lucky I was to have such a great grandfather. He typically had good contacts, so it was almost a certainty that they'd be able to help us. I hated to think what would have happened if this mess had occurred a little later, after my mom and grandparents had left the planet. I'd be on my own then, and have to deal with the problem myself.

Suddenly I frowned as an entirely new line of thought pushed itself to the forefront of my brain.

"Wait," I practically ordered, causing Gramps to turn around just as he was leaving the room. "Don't do it."

My grandfather frowned. "Do what?"

"Don't call."

Gramps seemed to ponder this for a moment, then asked, "You don't want me to call my friends?"

I shook my head. "No."

"Why wouldn't you want…?" he began, and then his eyes grew big as I felt something like dread arising in him. "Jim, you didn't do this, did you?"

"What?!" I exclaimed. "No! We both know that's not me on that video."

"Then I don't understand. Why don't you want me to have my contacts look into this?"

I closed my eyes for a moment and let out a deep breath, trying to figure the best way to explain. "You, Mom, and Indigo are leaving soon. If this had happened

209

when you were gone, it would be *my* problem. *I'd* have to handle it."

"Well, we aren't gone yet," Gramps said, "and we're not leaving before this thing gets resolved."

He made his statement in a matter-of-fact tone, not even fazed by the fact that I knew about their plans. (Presumably Mom had told him, since he didn't register any surprise when I mentioned her going with them.)

"Regardless," I stated, "this is something *I* need to take care of. More to the point, you need to be comfortable with the idea of me tackling issues like this — and worse — while you're gone, because that's what's going to happen. And if you can't adjust to the notion of me dealing with these types of problems on my own, then maybe you shouldn't leave."

I had spoken more fiercely than I intended, and felt a little ashamed for talking to my grandfather in that tone. He hadn't really done anything but offer to help, but it had suddenly occurred to me — as I'd stated — that I wasn't going to be able to lean on him for much longer. I needed to start handling my own problems.

On his part, Gramps merely stared at me for a moment. Then he extended a hand in my direction, and I realized that he was holding out the flash drive. As I reached out and took it, he still didn't say anything, but I felt a powerful emotion surging through him: pride.

REPLICATION

Chapter 32

As with most dilemmas, I turned to the place where I was most likely to get answers: Mouse. Dismissing with formalities, I teleported straight to his lab (after promising Gramps that I would keep him and the rest of the family apprised of any developments).

I popped up in an exceptionally large room with numerous oversized worktables covered with highly sophisticated and specialized devices. An extensive array of complex computers and machinery were lined along one wall. Finally, an uninterrupted stream of data flowed nonstop across more than a dozen large, flat-screen monitors placed strategically around the room.

This was Mouse's lab. Much to my dismay, however, Mouse himself was nowhere to be found and didn't answer when I called him on his cell phone. Feeling frustrated and thwarted, I left him an urgent voicemail asking that he call me back asap.

I hung around for a few minutes afterwards, hoping that my mentor would quickly return my call (or better yet, show up in person), but it didn't happen. Impatience quickly got the better of me, and simply for want of something to do, I teleported to my Alpha League quarters.

My suite, like all the other teen units, was furnished, but in a strictly utilitarian manner — with chairs, a bed and so on. There were no pictures on the walls, no photos, no memorabilia or knickknacks. In short, it lacked a lot of the homey features that make a place feel cozy and inviting.

Obviously, being my quarters, it was left to me to select the items that would fill that particular void and give the place character. Not trusting my judgment in that arena, Electra had volunteered to help me decorate, but thus far we hadn't been able to find the time.

Looking around the place now, it occurred to me that I probably had some things at home that could be used to enhance the aesthetics. In fact, I probably had suitable items in a couple of the places I called home. Now that I thought about it, there were at least three locations — other than my quarters at HQ — where I could lay my head at night: the Caelesian Embassy (where my family currently lived), my father's mansion, and my condo unit. (That last, however, was probably out, as I hadn't truly felt comfortable in the condo since the murder that took place on the premises.)

Still, having even two choices seemed like an embarrassment of riches, and I was still contemplating what I should bring to liven the place up when Mouse called me back.

"Where are you?" I asked without preamble after tapping the "Talk" button on my phone.

"Well, hello to you, too," Mouse said nonchalantly.

"Sorry," I muttered apologetically, "but I've got a situation and could really use your help. Are you back at HQ yet?"

"Just got here. I had to gather up the weather rods from Alpha Prime's mansion."

The weather rods! I'd forgotten all about them. Of course, there had been no explicit agreement that I'd assist in taking them down, but since I'd help put them up…

I began apologizing to Mouse for the oversight, but he cut me off.

"Don't worry about it," he assured me. "You did enough just helping us get them in place. Plus I'm sure you had a late night and were planning to sleep in."

"Well, the sleep-in didn't happen," I stated, then gave a quick overview of the morning's events.

"Alright," Mouse said when I finished. "Meet me in my lab in five minutes."

I hung up and teleported to the lab immediately, too impatient to wait any longer.

REPLICATION

Chapter 33

"That's not you," Mouse said, the first words he'd spoken after watching the footage from the flash drive three times in total silence.

"Really?" I droned mockingly, then wiped imaginary sweat from my brow with the back of my hand. "Whew! That's a relief. I was worried there for a minute."

My mentor gave me a sideways look as he tapped a button, pausing the clip. "I was trying to be supportive."

"Sorry," I muttered. "Thanks."

We were in Mouse's lab, standing at a worktable and watching the video of my doppelganger on a laptop. I had expected all along that Mouse would discount what the footage seemed to imply, but it still felt great to hear him say it.

"So what makes you say it isn't me?" I asked, blatantly curious.

Mouse shrugged. "Aside from almost killing Incendia — which would be out of character for you — the guy in the video just seems to exhibit a sort of callousness that isn't part of your personality. He's got cold eyes."

"Thanks, but I don't think the fact that I've got a more bubbly nature is going to mean anything to the people investigating this."

"Well, let's give them something they can sink their teeth into."

Noticing an odd gleam in Mouse's eye, I asked, "What are you thinking?"

"For starters," he said, "I'm going to tear into this footage and make sure it's a hundred percent legit."

"Sounds great. Let's do it."

Mouse seemed to contemplate for a moment. "It's going to take a little while."

"How long?"

"A couple of hours to do everything I'm thinking," he stated. "If you want to take off, it's fine. I can call you when I'm done."

"I've got nowhere to be," I said firmly, then immediately realized that it wasn't exactly a true statement. I had an outing scheduled with Vestibule.

"Suit yourself," Mouse said, then went to work.

****

As Mouse predicted, it took several hours for him to fully examine the footage. From what I could tell, his analysis included — among other things — applying some advanced algorithms to the video and feeding the clip into a specialized program that broke the images down frame by frame.

Initially, I attempted to help, but quickly realized I was out of my depth. I then settled for asking questions about what he was doing, which Mouse willingly answered. (Far be it from my mentor to pass up a teaching moment when it came to me.) A good portion of that was also over my head, so ultimately I decided to just sit quietly to the side and let him work.

About the only thing I personally accomplished during that time was sending a text message to Vestibule telling her she'd have to take a rain check on our outing, but without going into detail. Her response was an emoji involving an animated waffle that couldn't decide if it preferred syrup or jam. I rolled my eyes at the image. I'm sure from her perspective it did look like I was waffling, but my current situation obviously took precedence over her petty wants.

After that, I turned my attention back to Mouse, attempting to wait patiently while he finished up. From my perspective it seemed to take forever, but eventually he looked up from his computer tablet (on which he appeared to have done most of the work) and I — sensing a certain decisiveness in him — realized that he was finished.

"Okay," he said. "All done."

"So what's the verdict?" I asked eagerly, hoping Mouse would immediately declare the video a flat-out fake.

"Well first, let me explain a little about what I did," he replied. "That way you'll hopefully have confidence in my conclusion."

"Okay," I responded, slightly surprised. Mouse knew I trusted him implicitly; he didn't have to explain his rationale to me. However, the fact that he'd decided to do so did not bode well.

"I had to engage in some image and video forensics," he began. "Without going into excessive detail, I examined the footage in various ways to try to determine the authenticity of the images."

"And?"

"I didn't see any of the usual telltale signs that the video had been edited or photoshopped. No blurring, no warping, no distortions. No unusual displacement of light. No misalignment of objects and their shadows. Optically, the footage was consistent from start to finish."

"In other words, it wasn't doctored or altered," I concluded, feeling downcast.

"No, it wasn't," Mouse agreed. "But I didn't stop there. I also looked at the video's metadata."

"The metadata?" I echoed in surprise.

"Yeah, the metadata," Mouse stated. "You do know what metadata is, right?"

I nodded. "It's data about data — at least, that's how my computer science teacher described it. So I can look at the metadata of, say, a book report I've written, and it'll show me data about the doc, like who created it, when they created it, when it was last modified, and so on."

"That's good," Mouse said, sounding impressed. "From the look on your face a moment ago, I would have sworn you'd never heard of metadata."

"Oh no," I countered. "I've definitely heard of it. I just didn't realize that videos also had it."

"Well, they do. In this instance, it shows — among other things — the time and date the video was made."

"Let me guess," I said. "The date and time of the footage coincides with last night's party."

Mouse nodded. "Correct. Even more, it doesn't look like the metadata has been tampered with."

I groaned slightly in frustration. "For anyone else, that would be an alibi, but not for a teleporter."

"Well, would it help you if the time and date had been altered or was actually different from the time of the party?"

My brow crinkled as I focused on his question.

"Not really," I said after a moment. "I'm still a teleporter, so regardless of when the attack occurred there's no alibi to be had, according to Dreiser."

"Exactly," Mouse said.

I was nonplussed. "So why even bother looking at that?"

"Because if it was altered in any way — for example, if the metadata time was changed by a single second — the whole video is tainted and shouldn't be used as evidence against you."

"Well, that doesn't appear to be the case. Based on everything you've said, the footage appears to be authentic, so we're back at square one."

"Not square one, per se," Mouse corrected. "You're forgetting about the guy."

"Huh?" I mumbled in confusion. "What guy?"

"Your long-lost twin in the video."

I shook my head, not comprehending. "I'm sorry. I don't follow you."

"I also checked *him* out to see if *he* was fake."

I frowned. "I thought we just agreed that the entire video was authentic."

"We agreed that the *images* are authentic in that they haven't been edited. With respect to our friend, however, I also looked to see if his physiognomy is credible."

Mentally, I chewed on this for a moment, trying to pick up on what was obviously an extremely subtle nuance. After a few moments, I thought I had it.

"So," I began, "you're saying that his presence in the footage is legitimate, but how he *looks* in the video may not be."

"Good job," Mouse declared, smiling. "In essence, he looks like you, but is that really his face?"

"Okay, I follow you. So what's the process for showing he's faking my face?"

"Well," Mouse began, slipping into teaching mode, "I first enlarged and examined every image of his visage from all angles. From what I could see, there was no unnatural smoothness or excessive bunching that you'd expect if he was wearing one of those face-masks that you see in the movies."

I nodded. "I know what you mean — like a spy movie where the main character is also a master of disguise."

"Right," Mouse stated in agreement. "And from what I could see of things like his pores, hydration, and pigmentation, there's nothing anomalous or aberrant about his skin."

"I get it — that's his actual appearance and not some kind of disguise," I concluded. "So could this be the result of something like a face transplant?"

"A face transplant," Mouse droned, somewhat mockingly. "So did you wake up yesterday with your face missing? Did you walk around all day with bones, nerves, and blood vessels exposed — maybe without eyelids or lips?"

"Okay — enough with the imagery," I said firmly, my face wrinkled in disapproval.

Mouse chuckled. "Since when did you get squeamish?"

"I'm not," I insisted. "I just don't like visualizing myself with my face ripped off."

Mouse laughed again. "But you see my point?"

"Yes. Aside from the fact that I've seen too many movies, you're saying that the only place to get a copy of my face is *me*, so the odds of a facial transplant are nil."

"Actually, a transplant of that nature would go beyond simply getting a copy of your face and slapping it on someone else. The facial contours would also have to match."

"What do you mean?" I asked, intrigued.

Mouse seemed to reflect for a moment. "Imagine you've got a couch that's covered with a sheet. You can't see the couch underneath, but the sheet gives the outline of it."

"Okay," I said, understanding but still not sure where he was going with this.

"Now imagine you take that same sheet, remove it from the couch, and then cover up another piece of furniture with it — say, a table. Is the sheet still going to have the shape of a couch?"

I shook my head. "No. It's going to take on the shape of the table."

"Exactly, and the same is true of your face."

"So just putting my face on another person isn't going to necessarily make them look like me."

"Correct. The underlying features of their face will have to match as well."

"What would that entail?" I asked.

"A good bit of surgery," Mouse replied. "We're talking about altering tissue, cartilage, bone structure and more. But I don't see evidence of surgery of any sort, let alone what we're discussing. For instance, there are no scars, nothing to indicate a surgical incision of any type."

"But what if he had a really good plastic surgeon?"

Mouse let out a sigh. "Apparently I'm not explaining this very well, so I'll try again. *All* surgery leaves a scar. So if a woman gets a facelift, she's going to have scars. A good plastic surgeon is just adept at hiding them — like around the ear, in the hairline, or in natural folds of the skin. Scars can also fade and become less noticeable, but they don't disappear entirely."

"What about you?" I asked.

A baffled expression came across Mouse's face. "What *about* me?"

REPLICATION

"You once told me you had an arm chopped off," I explained. "But I've seen your bare arms, and you don't have any scars."

Mouse seemed to reflect for a moment. My statement referred to a time when a group of aliens had taken him prisoner. It was before the two of us ever met and I'd never gotten the full details, but I'd never known Mouse to have anything less than a full complement of limbs, so something must have happened for him to get his arm back after the aliens hacked it off.

"Okay," he said a few seconds later. "I'll revise my earlier statement and say that surgery *almost* always leaves a scar. However, there are some pieces of sophisticated, avant-garde medical tech out there that can leave skin completely unmarred after surgery. But that type of gear is uncommon, and rarer still is the person with the knowledge and skill to operate it."

"Give me a head count."

"There's maybe five people on the planet with the resources and know-how to do what you're suggesting," Mouse said. "But I know their handiwork, and I'm not seeing any sign of it here."

"Well, if that's the case," I concluded, "you're saying that this guy really is a dead ringer for me."

"What I'm saying is that his face isn't a graft or the result of surgical modification. Assuming he's not naturally your doppelganger, the most likely conclusion is that he's a shapeshifter."

"There is another option," I chimed in. "Magic."

As I mentioned it, I thought back to when I'd first met Gossamer and Kane. To help fool some bad guys, Kane had cast a glamour over me back then which made me look like someone else.

"It's a good thought, but I've already looked into it and don't think that's the case here."

I raised an eyebrow in surprise. "You were able to assess and discard the possibility of magic just by looking at the video?"

"What I did was examine your twin's fingerprints using an advanced form of photogrammetry," Mouse clarified.

"I'm sorry," I said, shaking my head in confusion. "Photo-what?"

"Photogrammetry," he repeated. "It's an area of science focused on taking measurements from images. It's used a lot in the field of mapmaking, as it allows you to survey and measure land using things like aerial photographs."

"Okay, so how does that apply to the current situation?"

"The guy in the video doesn't do anything to hide from the camera, so there's adequate footage of his hands," Mouse stated, at the same time tapping on his computer tablet. "Using some cutting-edge photogrammetric algorithms, I created a 3-D model of his fingers — more specifically, his prints."

As he finished speaking, Mouse gestured towards the laptop where the video of my lookalike had been playing. The footage was gone now, replaced by a three-dimensional image of a hand. (Obviously my mentor was controlling the laptop remotely.)

Mouse, continuing to fiddle with his tablet, went on, saying, "I then enlarged the image, which allowed me to see all kinds of ridge detail on his fingerprints — loops, whorls, arches."

REPLICATION

As he spoke, the image of the hand on the laptop vanished except for the fingertips, which lined up in a row before growing large enough in size to go from one side of the screen to the other. Leaning in for a better look, I noticed the patterns Mouse had mentioned.

"Alright, I can see different shapes on these prints," I acknowledged.

"Good," Mouse said. "I then compared those prints to yours."

In conjunction with Mouse speaking, the prints on the laptop shrank in size and shifted to the left side of the screen. On the right side appeared another set of prints, which I intuitively understood to be mine. I frowned for a moment, wondering where and when Mouse had lifted my prints — then almost laughed at my own mental lapse. I was in Mouse's lab all the time; he could get a copy of my prints practically without effort. (Not to mention the fact that he had cameras in his lab, and could have used photogrammetry to create a model of my prints within the last few minutes.)

I turned my attention back to the two images on the screen. "They're about half the size they were a moment ago, but I can still identify features on the first set of prints, as well as the second."

"And?" Mouse asked expectantly.

"I'm not an expert, but I can make out enough differences between them to say that they're not a match."

"Expert or not, you're right on that point," Mouse declared. "Now, back to the issue of magic being involved. Typically with a spell that's intended to mimic another person's appearance, you need to infuse the enchantment with something that embodies their physical characteristics."

REPLICATION

"DNA," I said in summary.

"Right," Mouse agreed. "Something as simple as a strand of hair will serve, and if done right, you can create a spell that will seemingly replicate a person right down to the cellular level."

I nodded, already aware of this information. When Kane had cast the glamour on me before, it so effectively duplicated the other person's appearance that I was able to pass a retinal scan (which was why we had resorted to magic instead of my shapeshifting ability).

"So the gist of all this is that if magic were involved you would expect the fingerprints to match," I concluded.

"And the face as well," Mouse added. I gave him an odd look, causing him to expound. "As with his hands, I did the same photogrammetry on our mystery man's face, and it doesn't square up with yours. However, we're talking minutiae — things that are essentially negligible, like eyes that are a billionth of a millimeter farther apart than yours. It's nothing you can tell with the naked eye, but it's another indication that this isn't you."

"Maybe," I mumbled, unconvinced. "But I'm not certain that any of this is enough to sway anyone who sees that footage. The simple truth of the matter is that I'm a shapeshifter, so the fact that my eyes aren't as far apart, or my cheekbones aren't as high, or I have loops instead of arches in my fingerprints isn't going to carry the day. Plus, I'm just having trouble making sense of all this."

Mouse frowned. "What do you mean?"

"I mean that on the surface, it looks like a frame job — like someone's setting me up. But why go through the trouble of mimicking my face if you're not going to change the fingerprints to match? Any shapeshifter worth his salt can do that. The fact that this person didn't just confuses me — it's like a shapeshifting amateur hour. All it does is create doubt about who's in that video, and doubt about who you are is something shapeshifters try to avoid."

Mouse seemed to chew on that for a moment. "Maybe it's someone who only recently developed that ability."

"Then I wouldn't expect him to be that good at replicating faces. I'd expect…"

I trailed off as my mentor's statement took my thoughts in a new direction.

"Do you think the SuperStore could be open again?" I asked after a few seconds.

A look of grave concern crossed Mouse's face, and empathically I could sense that my question had jarred him a little.

"I suppose," he replied a moment later, "but who would be crazy or desperate enough to transact with them?"

I nodded, conceding his point. The SuperStore wasn't an actual store or a physical location, but a black market where super powers were bought and sold. Sounds cool — until you realize that it's not a regulated area of commerce, none of the merchandise is warrantied, and it comes with a fair degree of risk. Case in point: some wealthy hedge fund manager thought it would be awesome to have the power of atmokinesis — that is, the ability to affect the weather. (Apparently he dealt with weather derivatives in the financial markets, and thought atmokinesis would give him a leg up on the competition.) It's unclear what process he underwent to obtain his purported powers, but the end result was not to his liking: every time it rained, he would get struck by lightning.

There were lots of similar stories — some comical, some horrifying — about the experiences of shoppers at the SuperStore. Ultimately, an international task force shut them down, but there were rumors that the marketplace was simply driven further underground — not out of business.

Bearing all the facts in mind, I would wager that Mouse was right, and I admitted as much.

"So, assuming it's not the SuperStore," I said, "where does that leave us?"

"Back to where we were before," Mouse replied. "Trying to get a lead on this guy who not only looks like you, but mimics your powers."

"Sounds good," I said. "I was so focused on his appearance that I practically forgot that he has powers similar to mine, like telekinesis and teleportation."

Without warning, Mouse suddenly got an odd glint in his eye. Recognizing the look, I knew that something new had occurred to him. He then spent a few seconds hastily tapping on his tablet.

A moment later, Mouse glanced at the laptop, which was now frozen on the image of the fake me, then gave me an intense look. "Jim, could you have done this?"

"What?!" I exclaimed, aghast that he could even ask that question.

"I don't mean whether it's possible that this is you," he clarified, pointing to the screen. "I mean, *physically*, could you have done this? Could you have teleported back and forth between the party and this…facility?"

"I suppose it's possible I could have done that, but there were people with me all night. I was always in the presence of someone."

226

"Well, can you go back and forth between two locations such that it seems like you're in two places at once?"

"You mean go back and forth fast enough that no one can tell?"

"Yeah," Mouse answered.

I thought about it for a second, then shook my head. "I don't think so. I still need a moment to visualize where I'm teleporting to. Trying to go back and forth like you're suggesting would probably just result in me flickering in and out like an old light bulb about to go dark."

"What if you did it at super speed?" Mouse asked.

I rubbed my chin in thought for a moment, letting Mouse's question roll around in my brain. I didn't often teleport while at super speed — didn't have to. Teleporting took me wherever I needed to go instantaneously. Thus, there was rarely (if ever) a need to be at super speed when I used that particular ability.

That said, when I'm in speedster mode, everything about my body operates at an accelerated pace, including my thought processes. Therefore, at super speed, I could conceivably visualize the place I'd like to teleport to a lot faster than I could normally. That being the case, I felt that I had the answer to my mentor's question.

"Theoretically," I began, "I think I could do it if I was at super speed — that is, teleport so quickly that I appeared to be in two places at once. But practically speaking, I don't think I could pull it off."

"Why not?" Mouse asked.

"Think about it. Suppose I were to try it by having a conversation here with you, while at the same time meeting Electra in the lounge."

"Okay, what would happen?"

"Well, let's say I'm about to use the word 'little' during our conversation, but I'm greeting Electra with a 'Hello.' With you, I start pronouncing the 'L' in 'little,' then teleport to Electra where I begin enunciating the 'H' in 'hello.' Then I teleport back to you to pronounce some more of the 'L' before going back to her to continue verbalizing the letter 'H.' And that back-and-forth continues nonstop until I've spoken both words."

"It does sound rather complicated — even more so when you add movement to the mix."

"Huh?" I said, not really following his train of thought.

"While you're speaking, you'd also have to maintain consistency with your physical actions," Mouse explained. "For example, if you're in the process of raising your hand while speaking to me but you're reaching out to hold her hand while talking to Electra, you've got to keep those motions respectively congruent."

"So, using your example, every time I teleport back to you, I've got to raise my hand fractionally higher, while each time I go to Electra, I've got to extend my hand a little farther toward hers. And it all has to be seamless, without either of you able to tell that I'm actually teleporting from one place to the other."

Mouse nodded. "Yep — virtually a real-life version of stop-motion animation. But it's even more problematic than that."

I stared at him in disbelief. "I can't imagine how."

"Well, you'd actually be doing all this stuff — speaking and moving — at super speed, but from your perspective you'd have to carry out those actions at a decelerated pace so that it appears normal to me and Electra."

"No way," I muttered, shaking my head. "Taken altogether, it's too much. I take back my claim about it being theoretically possible."

Mouse laughed. "No, it's just not *probable*, but it's still *possible*."

I shrugged. "Maybe, but you're talking about multi-tasking to the nth degree."

"True, but if anyone could accomplish it, I'd bank on you."

"Thanks for the vote of confidence. Now, what's our next move?"

"Well, I'm going to think about this footage some more and see if there's anything else we can glean from it."

As he spoke, he bent down and appeared to reach for something under the worktable. When he stood back up, he was holding a mid-sized box in his hands.

"You, on the other hand," Mouse continued, "are going to study."

"Study?" I repeated as Mouse placed the box next to the laptop on the worktable. "Study what?"

"Physics," Mouse answered as he opened up the box and took out what appeared to be a textbook. He then removed a second book from the box. "Calculus." He took out a third text. "World History."

"What is all this?" I asked.

"In case it escaped your notice, when you took off for Caeles, you basically dropped out of school. Now that you're back, we can't have you truant, so I talked to your Mom and grandparents, and we decided that homeschooling for the rest of the year was probably the best option."

I nodded, as this was a conversation I'd already had with my family, but a new issue immediately rose up in my brain.

"So who's going to teach me?" I asked, then explained about how — if all went as scheduled — the rest of my family would probably be leaving the planet soon.

Mouse smiled. "Lucky for you, there's a local guy who's experienced with most of the subject matter. He's agreed to step up in this instance and be your instructor."

"Who —" I began, then noticed the smirk on my mentor's face. "*You*, Mouse? Really?"

"For classroom purposes, you can refer to me as *Professor* Mouse."

I rolled my eyes. "Okay, so why wait so long to get this started? I've been back for weeks."

Mouse suddenly looked pensive. "Honestly, I didn't like any of the textbooks on the market or their treatment of the relative subject matter, so I had my own books made up."

"What?" I muttered, somewhat stunned. I grabbed one of the texts and looked at the author's name. Sure enough, it read *Professor Mouse, PhD*.

I would have laughed if the situation wasn't so disheartening. It's one thing to be taught by a guy who's probably the smartest man who ever lived. It's something else to be taught by him out of textbooks that he authored. I groaned in frustration at the thought of it.

"Stop being a baby," Mouse said. "It's not that bad. Smokey's not complaining."

I raised in eyebrow in surprise. "Smokey?"

"Yeah — he missed some time in school, too. Not as much as you, but enough so that you two get to go through my class together."

"Probably less of a class and more like a crucible," I said, at the same time wondering what exactly Smokey had been up to lately. A new girl, missing school… I guess he and I really *did* need to catch up.

"Class or crucible," Mouse droned. "Sounds like a good topic for your first English essay. I'll expect a draft in a week."

I groaned again, making Mouse laugh heartily.

REPLICATION

Chapter 34

After confirming with Mouse that his comment about the English essay was a joke (and that any homeschooling could wait until the current situation was resolved), I spent a little time chatting with him about next steps. Specifically, I asked what *I* could do with respect to solving the mystery of my evil twin, because the idea of just waiting around until my mentor came up with a solution didn't appeal to me.

Mouse's suggestion was that I make a detailed list of everyone I'd spoken to at the party, along with the relevant times. It wouldn't be an ironclad alibi (especially since I was a teleporter), but it would lend support to my argument that the guy in the video wasn't me. With those marching orders, I teleported home, taking the textbooks with me at Mouse's insistence.

I popped up in my room. Almost immediately, I felt a mental bombardment as my mother and grandparents telepathically barraged me with questions. (Obviously Gramps had brought Mom and Indigo up to speed during my absence.) Tossing the textbooks on my dresser, I quickly gave them an overview of my conversation with Mouse and what I'd found out.

With their appetite for information sated, my family finally left me alone. I took advantage of the opportunity to grab a notepad and start jotting down everything I could remember about the people I'd interacted with the night before, starting with those in the receiving line. I went at it for about an hour, at which point Gramps sent me a telepathic message to come down for dinner. Thinking that I could do with a break, I washed up and went downstairs to eat.

REPLICATION

On this occasion, the meal was light on conversation. It went without saying that I had a lot on my mind, and everyone seemed to eat mostly in silence in deference to me. Even Myshtal, who was typically effervescent, had little to say. I didn't know whether my family had told her what happened or if she simply knew how to read the room, but I was grateful to her for leaving me to my thoughts.

After dinner, I raced back to my room to finish working on my witness list (for lack of a better term). Forty-five minutes later, I thought it was pretty much complete and was looking it over for the third time when my cell phone rang. It was Electra.

I felt a sudden degree of shame as I realized that I hadn't really thought about my girlfriend all day. Given the circumstances, it could probably be forgiven, but I still felt that I'd been neglectful.

Embarrassed by my oversight, I quickly answered with a perfunctory, "Hello?"

"Did I misread the situation?" she asked without any kind of preface.

"Huh?" I mumbled in confusion.

"Well, I thought we ended the night in a positive place," she said. "But then a whole day goes by without me hearing from you."

"Sorry, babe," I said, now recognizing that she was speaking tongue-in-cheek. "Something came up, and I've been dealing with it all day."

Her tone immediately became more somber. "Is it serious?"

"Serious enough."

"You want to talk about it?"

"Yeah, but not over the phone. How about tomorrow?"

"Oh, um, okay," she said, my response catching her a little off guard. It was clear that she had expected me to teleport to her asap so that we could talk, which is what I normally would have done. The fact that I had suggested waiting until tomorrow was a bit out of character for me and had thrown her off.

In truth, however, I was mentally exhausted. I had been dealing with the issue of my apparent double all day, and it had taken its toll.

"Tomorrow's fine," Electra continued, bringing my thoughts back to the present.

"Thanks," I said, then hurriedly wished her goodnight and hung up.

REPLICATION

Chapter 35

The next morning, for the second day in a row, I was awakened by the ringing of my cell phone. Still a little groggy, I started to sit up and noticed that there was a notepad on the bed next to me, and suddenly everything came back.

After getting off the phone with Electra the night before, I had taken a quick shower with the intent of going over my witness list again afterwards. However, the info wasn't particularly stimulating and I had already scrutinized it a number of times at that point. Long story short, I fell asleep in the middle of reviewing everything for the umpteenth time.

Remembering what the info on the notepad represented jolted me wide awake. Grabbing my phone, I noted that the caller was Sarah — Smokey's girlfriend. (Or rather, *previous* girlfriend.)

I answered the phone, but didn't get a chance to say a greeting before Sarah blurted out, "Did you talk to him?"

"Excuse me?" I said, not sure what she was talking about.

"Smokey," she stressed. "You said you'd talk to him for me."

I was completely confused now. "I'm sorry but when did I say that?"

"Friday, when we spoke."

"Friday?" I repeated, completely befuddled by this conversation. "You and I didn't—"

The words froze in my throat as I happened to glance at my witness list and got a terrible feeling in the pit of my stomach.

REPLICATION

"Where are you?" I asked, trying to keep my voice on an even keel.

"At home," she replied. "About to leave to catch the bus to school."

"Meet me outside in one minute," I practically ordered, then hung up.

****

It took me even less time to get through my morning routine than the day before, with the only difference being that on this occasion I ripped a page from the back of the notepad and hastily scrawled a message saying that I was going out, then left it on the kitchen table. I then teleported to the embassy's garage, which housed — among other things — a ten-year-old clunker that served as my car. I jumped behind the wheel, phased myself and the vehicle, then teleported.

The car and I popped up on a street in a well-kept, middle-class neighborhood. Making myself and the jalopy solid again, I turned the key in the ignition and began driving down the road.

I didn't know Sarah's address, but she and Smokey had been on numerous double-dates with me and Electra, and — having dropped her off after a few of those — I knew where her house was located and what it looked like. Thus, almost exactly when I said I would, I pulled up in front of a two-story house with a mixed stucco-and-stone exterior and waited. A few seconds later, the front door opened and Sarah came out.

She was wearing jeans, a sweatshirt, and a jacket. In addition, she was sporting a backpack, and also had a small purse in her hand. Her dark hair hung loose, framing a remarkably beautiful face with Asian features. The only thing that seemingly marred her appearance were her eyes, which were red and puffy — a sure indication that she had been crying.

If she thought it odd that I had shown up in a car, it didn't show in her demeanor. (The truth of the matter is that I felt a vehicle would afford some degree of privacy for the conversation I wanted to have. Popping up a little ways from her house had been an attempt to be low-key.) Upon reaching the car, she opened the front passenger door, slid her backpack off, and dropped it on the floor. She then slipped inside and shut the door.

"So, did you talk to him?" she asked eagerly, repeating the question she'd asked on the phone as I began driving, heading towards her school.

"Uh, not exactly," I said, not sure how to begin.

"This is all a mistake," she suddenly stated. "I'll admit it's my fault, but it's not what it seems."

I cleared my throat. "Look, I know you said we talked on Friday, but—"

"It's my fault," she repeated, cutting me off. "Plus, I really didn't tell you everything."

"I need to stop you," I chimed in. "You and I didn't—"

"I really love Smokey, you know?" she interjected, as if she hadn't heard me. I realized then that she wasn't really listening to anything I was trying to say. Moreover, I could sense empathically that she was racked with guilt and almost consumed by melancholy and depression. Whatever was going on, she obviously needed to talk to someone about it. I probably wasn't the ideal candidate since I had my own agenda here, but the best course of action at the moment seemed to involve lending a sympathetic ear.

"So what happened?" I asked.

She looked at me askance. "Didn't I tell you all this on Friday?" I opened my mouth to speak, but she went on without waiting for an answer, saying with a sigh, "It all started with my family."

I waited a few seconds, but she didn't say anything more, just stared out the window.

"What do you mean?" I prompted after a few moments.

"My parents are immigrants," she said. "Came here from the old country. They also brought some of the old traditions with them — notions about courtship and relationships."

"Such as?"

"Arranged marriages."

Taking my eyes off the road for a second, I looked at her in shock, finding it difficult to believe that another teen could have the same matrimonial problem I did. "They want you to get married?"

"No," she replied, shaking her head. "I mean, someday, but not soon. The real issue is that they want me to be with someone from a similar background."

"What?"

"It's like that movie about the Greek wedding," she explained. "They want me dating someone from the same culture."

"So your family doesn't like Smokey?"

"They like him well enough. I mean, they know he's a nice guy and that he treats me well. They just don't see me with him long-term."

"Isn't that *your* choice?"

"Not exactly. They're my parents and I have to obey them, so in order to date Smokey, I had to make a deal."

"What kind of deal?" I asked, not sure where this was going.

"I'm free to date Smokey, but if they find someone who they feel is appropriate for me, I have to go out with him."

"You mean they make you date someone else while you're going out with Smokey?"

"It's complicated. I only have to go out with the guy they pick once, and if I don't like him that's the end of it. They're basically banking on me having so much in common with one of these guys that I'll dump Smokey."

"What do you mean, 'one of these guys'?" I asked. "How many times have you done this?"

"Too many," she admitted, sounding despondent.

"Does Smokey know about this?"

"Of course. In terms of dating me, it was the cost of doing business. But he always knew when it was happening, where we were going, what we were doing, and so on. And I'd always tell my parents I didn't want to see the guy again."

I shook my head in confusion. "Then I don't understand. Smokey said you went out with another guy, but if he's aware of this deal you have with your parents and has made his peace with it, I'm confused about what the problem is."

Sarah lowered her eyes. "The problem isn't that I went out with one of these guys. It's that I went out with him a second time."

"Okay," I droned, letting that roll around in my brain. "Well, what did Smokey say when you told him about the second date?"

She looked up at me but didn't say anything, and I could see tears streaming down her face. In that moment, I knew what had happened, and didn't even need my empathic abilities to figure it out.

"You didn't tell him," I concluded as she pulled a tissue from her purse. "You didn't tell him about the second date."

"No," she admitted, wiping her tears with the tissue, "but somehow he found out about it and now he won't talk to me."

My first inclination was to say, "Can you blame him?" but I held my tongue. Sarah appeared to be suffering greatly, but there seemed little doubt that this girl had mistreated my best friend.

"It's not what you think," Sarah said, as if reading my mind. "I didn't like the guy — not like that, anyway. I mean we hit it off, but it was completely platonic."

"Well, if that's all true, why go out with him a second time? Why keep it from Smokey?"

She put her hands to her face, then pushed them up and back, running her fingers through her hair. "I just needed a break from the pressure," she said.

I gave her a stunned look, then quickly turned my attention back to the road, as I was still driving. "Wait a minute. Smokey's been pressuring you?" I'm sure the surprise showed in my voice, because what she seemed to be suggesting was something I never would have suspected. "Has he been pushing you to—"

"No, no, no," she stressed forcefully. "It's not pressure from *him* I'm talking about. It's pressure from you guys — his friends."

I had trouble hiding my astonishment. After a few moments, I said, "I'm sorry, but you're going to have to explain that."

She sighed. "You, Electra, Li — you guys are all Smokey's friends and you're all supers, with cool powers. On top of that, you go on amazing adventures together. By comparison, I can't help but be boring."

"That's not true," I insisted. "You're lots of fun, and we love hanging out with you."

"Yes, but I have to be 'on' *all* the time. I don't have any amazing abilities, so I have to compete on personality. I have to constantly be smiling, bubbly, charming and so on — especially when we're around you guys."

"Sarah, I'm sorry," I said sincerely. "I apologize if we ever made you feel like you had to be or act in any way contrary to what you feel."

"And that just makes it worse," she intoned. "It would be a lot easier if you guys were aloof snobs, arrogant jerks, boorish imbeciles, or something along those lines. Then it wouldn't matter to me because I wouldn't want to be your friend anyway. But you're all friendly and funny and nice, which just makes me feel like I have to do even more to appear interesting."

I nodded. "I think I understand, and again I apologize if we did something to make you feel you couldn't be yourself around us."

"You don't need to apologize for being a nice guy, or for having nice friends."

"Well, if it'll take some of the pressure off, I could always be a jerk and backhand you — rough you up a bit," I said, and raised my hand mockingly.

She laughed, the first sound I'd heard from her today that didn't come out heavy with gloom.

"I appreciate the offer," she commented, "but I'll manage."

"Anyway," I said, "this guy you went out with?"

She sighed. "As I said, we hit it off, but it was platonic. I just had a good time hanging out with someone without feeling like I had to compete or perform. I went out with the guy again because of that reason, not because I had feelings for him, so it wasn't a *real* date, in my opinion. I didn't tell Smokey because I wasn't sure I could properly explain it without making him feel like he had to choose between me and his friends. That's not a choice I wanted him making, because…"

She trailed off without finishing, but from her emotional vibe, I knew what she was feeling.

"You think that if Smokey has to make that kind of choice, you'll lose," I concluded.

She nodded. "It's like you're a poor kid whose best friend has a rich neighbor who's always inviting him to big parties, offering him limo rides, and so on. How do you compete?"

Her face took on a pained expression, and emotionally I noted an ache in her so potent that it almost equated to physical pain. She felt completely dejected, like she was drowning in a sea of hopelessness and despair.

I desperately wished that there was something I could do for her, that I had some ability to cure what ailed her. I did have a healing ability, but it didn't come at my beck and call, and even if it did, it only worked on a physical level. It wouldn't do any good here.

And then, I suddenly realized that there *was* something I could do for Sarah. I pulled over to the side of the road, and then turned to her, opening my arms. Without a word, she leaned over and buried her face in my shoulder, sobbing fitfully as I gave her a hug.

Chapter 36

It only took Sarah a few minutes to get it all out and then regain her composure. I had pulled over maybe a block from her school and then waited patiently in case there was more she wanted to say, but she had seemingly said her piece. Subtly checking my watch, it appeared that Sarah was in no danger of being late, which meant we had time to address the real reason I'd wanted to see her.

"Look," I began, "I'll say something to Smokey, but I can't promise he'll listen to me."

"I know," she said with a nod, dabbing her eyes with tissue again. "But if you can just get him to talk to me, it'll be enough."

"Okay, in the meantime, though, there was something I needed to ask you about. Remember when you said something about having talked to me on Friday?"

****

It didn't take long to explain the situation to Sarah, and get the story out of her. Although plainly unnerved by the thought of me having an evil twin, she detailed what had happened in fairly succinct terms.

"You dropped by for a friendly visit on Friday after I got in from school," she said. "The conversation naturally turned to Smokey, and you promised you'd talk to him for me."

"Did I say anything else?" I asked, noting how odd it was to be speaking of my lookalike as if he were *me*.

Sarah shook her head. "No, you mostly asked questions."

"Questions? What kind of questions?"

She shrugged. "I don't know — all kinds of stuff. How everyone had been while you'd been away, had anything unusual happened, what everyone was up to, etcetera. Just a hodgepodge — you kind of jumped around in terms of subject matter."

I frowned but didn't say anything. Being a shapeshifter myself (and therefore knowing how they operate), I understood that my double's visit to Sarah had had one primary purpose: to get information. She had given it willingly, but couldn't be blamed since she'd been under the impression she was talking to a friend.

Rather than continue grilling Sarah, I put an end to the questions and finished driving her to school. Once there, she made me promise one last time that I'd talk to Smokey, then got out of the car and headed inside just before the bell rang. I pulled away, driving another few blocks before turning in to the lot of a strip mall and parking. Then I teleported, car and all, back to the garage of the embassy.

Chapter 37

I teleported back to my room and flopped down on the bed, thinking about what I'd learned. The fake me had gotten a decent amount of information from Sarah. None of it was earth-shattering, but it was enough to allow him to do what shapeshifters do best: get close to people without arousing suspicion. But who else, exactly, had he gotten close to?

That was a difficult question to answer. Anyone who saw my double would probably assume it was me, as Sarah did. I'd only discovered that my evil twin had approached her because she called me and referenced a conversation that we'd never actually had.

Hmmm. Had anyone else spoken to me in a way that suggested we had interacted when we actually hadn't?

I grabbed the notepad containing my witness list and started scanning the names. However, I stopped about halfway through as a new thought occurred to me: my list only contained the names of people from the party on Saturday, but my doppelganger had been in business since at least the day before that, when he had met with Sarah.

Letting out a despondent sigh, I flung my mind back yet another twenty-four hours in time and tacked onto the list the names of people I had interacted with as of Friday afternoon. There weren't many, so within a minute or so, I felt I finally had a complete list of all the people I had crossed paths with over the past few days.

Looking at the names, it quickly became apparent to me that, from the standpoint of the fake Jim, a good number of them wouldn't have been worth talking to. The bulk of them were folks that I didn't associate with on a regular basis — case in point, the people who had come through the receiving line. They wouldn't have enough information about me to merit a conversation. (Of course, all of this rested on a hypothesis that *I* was somehow the focus of my double's actions, but since he was walking around with my face and basically setting me up to take a fall, it didn't seem too much of a stretch.)

Next, I started eliminating those whom my double was unlikely to have made contact with, such as my family. As they could all read minds and generally kept a mental tab on me when I was at home, my mother and grandparents had a pretty good idea of what I "looked like" telepathically. Fooling them would be next to impossible, so I would have heard about it if they'd been approached. Likewise, there were others who would be hard to hoodwink.

In the end, I was left with a short list of people who might have been contacted by my lookalike. In fact, upon reflection, there was at least one person whom I was all but certain had interacted with my double, and I made a phone call to BT asking her to look into it for me. After eliciting a promise from her to get back to me asap, I called Mouse.

My mentor answered after the first ring, stating, "If you're calling for a status update, I don't have anything."

"No problem," I said. "I was actually calling to update *you*." I then gave him a quick overview of what Sarah had told me (sans the part about her issues with Smokey), and my efforts to narrow down the list of people whom my evil twin may have reached out to.

"That's not bad detective work," Mouse admitted grudgingly. "It'll be interesting to see what BT comes back with, but what about the others? Have you contacted them?"

"Uh...not yet," I said a bit timidly.

"Get on it," Mouse ordered. "I'm still at home, but I can be at HQ in an hour. Meet me in my lab when you're done."

He then hung up without waiting for any acknowledgment.

REPLICATION

Chapter 38

There were three names for me to check out: Li, Smokey, and Electra. I decided to take them in reverse order and started with my girlfriend.

In an ideal world, I would simply have called her on her cell phone. However, like Sarah, I expected Electra to be in class by this point, and since cell phone use was prohibited during the school day, I had to go to Plan B.

I teleported to her school, popping up in the student parking lot at the rear of the campus. Electra actually attended a different high school than I did, so — while I had a vague notion of her schedule — I didn't know exactly where she was.

It was chilly out and I hadn't worn a jacket, so I adjusted my body temperature to compensate. Unbothered now by the weather, I reached out empathically, extending my ability in the direction of the school. Almost immediately, I started picking up a number of typical adolescent sensations: teen angst, high school crushes, simmering rebelliousness... In a similar vein, there were vibes with a more mature undertone that presumably originated from faculty and administration, including pent-up frustration, joy of accomplishment, and hopefulness mingled with worry.

Much like I could recognize her voice, being around Electra on an almost daily basis had allowed me to become attuned to her empathically. Thus, it only took me a minute to lock in on her emotional vibe, so to speak, and thereby pinpoint her location. I phased and simultaneously turned invisible (which automatically switched my vision over to the infrared), then flew towards the school building

— bypassing the doors in favor of simply going through the walls.

I found her in what appeared to be a math class. Still invisible, I floated up into a corner of the room and hovered there for a second while I cycled my vision through the light spectrum to something approaching normal. Then I spent a moment looking at my girlfriend.

She was dressed in jeans and an oversized, maroon turtleneck sweater. Her hair was pulled back into a ponytail, revealing a pair of tear-shaped earrings that I had brought back for her from Caeles. As to cosmetics, the only thing I noted appeared to be a light application of shiny lip gloss. All in all, while not as stunning as she had been at the party, she was still storybook beautiful — and as it turned out, I wasn't the only one who felt that way.

Electra was actually watching the teacher, who had his back to the class and was writing something on the board about polynomials, when a girl at the desk next to her passed her a note. Obviously surprised, Electra took the note, which had been folded over several times and had a little heart drawn on the outside. She turned to the girl who had given her the note with a perplexed expression, and emotionally I sensed genuine confusion coming from her.

Rather than reply, the girl who had passed the note hooked a thumb over her shoulder. Glancing in the direction indicated, I saw a guy sitting there and took a moment to look him over.

Even though he was seated, I got the impression that he was tall, and he had dark hair that he'd allowed to grow to his shoulders. Good genes had blessed him with a handsome face, and he had a physique that suggested he worked out regularly. He wasn't wearing a letterman jacket, but I got the sense that he belonged to one of the school's cool cliques — probably the football team, or something along those lines. Emotionally, I detected a degree of confidence that maybe just crossed the line into the region of arrogance, along with smugness and a roguish sense of entitlement. All in all, he exuded something of a bad-boy element that girls probably found attractive.

Like me, Electra had followed her classmate's thumb-pointing with respect to who had sent the note. Seeing that he had my girlfriend's attention, the guy winked at her and flashed a thousand-watt smile. Based on what I was picking up empathically, he was probably used to that routine melting hearts, and thus expected Electra to give him an encouraging smile or something along those lines. What he got, however, was a response he likely hadn't seen in a while (if ever).

Rather than smile back, Electra frowned in irritation and rolled her eyes. She then crumpled up the note without reading it and flung the wadded ball of paper back at the guy. It hit him in the chest and then flopped to the floor, despite his valiant attempts to catch it.

I smiled. *That's my girl.*

A general round of snickering followed Electra's actions, causing the teacher to turn around. By that time, however, Electra was sitting face-forward again and stone-faced. The teacher eyed the class warily, knowing that something had happened but unable to discern what, then turned back to the board and continued with the polynomials instruction.

I waited a few seconds and then reached out to Electra telepathically.

<Hey, cutie,> I said mentally.

Slightly startled, Electra promptly looked around, head jerking about as she replied. <Jim? What...What...Where are you?>

<Front of the class, near the ceiling.>

She looked up, then almost immediately turned her head towards the upper right corner of the room, where I was hovering. She had obviously used her powers to pinpoint my location, and confirmed the fact by giving me a surreptitious wave. <Just pinged you. What are you doing here?>

<Just had to see you, babe. Missed you.>

<Yeah, right,> she replied sarcastically, but smiling in a way that let me know she liked my answer. <Now why are you really here?>

<You remember yesterday when I said something came up?>

<Are you kidding?> Electra asked incredulously. <You want to talk about it now? I'm about to have a quiz!>

<It's important,> I insisted.

She sighed mentally. <Okay, but make it quick.>

<You got it.>

I quickly explained to Electra what had happened. Using telepathy, it only took a few seconds to make her fully aware of the entire situation involving my evil twin. Needless to say, she was quite surprised.

<So there's a guy running around out there with your face?> she asked.

<At least in the one instance,> I corrected. <If he's a shapeshifter like we think, we don't know what he really looks like.>

<Still, that can't be good.>

<Agreed, which is why I'm reaching out to people my double may have contacted.>

<He hasn't approached me yet, but he will get quite the surprise if he does.>

I frowned, not sure what she meant, then the truth hit me: Electra was one of the people my double wouldn't be able to fool. Her power let her recognize people by their bioelectric fields — for her, it was as good as a photo. Thus, unless he could change his bioelectric field to match mine (which was a tall order), he'd be wasting his time trying to siphon info from Electra.

And bearing that thought in mind, I suddenly realized I was wasting *my* time. It was good to have warned Electra about my double, but she was in no danger of being conned by him. That being the case, I wished her well on her quiz and teleported.

Chapter 39

The next person on my list was Smokey. Initially, I tried to locate him the same way I'd pinned down Electra: by going to his school and searching for him empathically. It didn't work; Smokey wasn't at school — at least not as far as I could tell.

Strike one, I thought.

Reflecting on it, I supposed he could have been on a field trip, out sick, or anything in between. In essence, there are lots of reasons why a student might not be in school on a particular day. That said, the situation was serious enough that it warranted me putting a little thought into trying to ascertain my best friend's whereabouts. And then I laughed as the truth hit me.

Of course Smokey wasn't in class. I had completely forgotten what Mouse had told me: Smokey was in the same boat I was in terms of being AWOL regarding his academics. He and I would be going through the crucible of being instructed by Mouse together, so he wouldn't be wandering the hallowed halls of his high school any more. More than likely, he was at home.

Pulling out my cell phone, I gave him a call. It rang several times, then went to voicemail. The same thing happened when I tried a second time.

Strike two. I put my phone away without leaving a message and then spent a moment thinking about what to do next.

The fact that Smokey hadn't answered didn't necessarily mean anything. In today's society, with technology so prevalent (especially communication devices, like cell phones), it's easy to simply assume that people are always in a position to take a call. That, however, is far from true. The person you're calling could be in the shower, taking out the trash, or just have their phone off. Thus, Smokey failing to pick up wasn't anything I could assign meaning to, but I still needed to talk to him.

With that thought in mind, I teleported to Smokey's neighborhood, popping up about a block from where he lived — evidence, once again, of my attempt to avoid excess attention. I then sauntered towards my destination in a leisurely fashion, thinking about the conversation I'd had with Sarah.

In truth, it wasn't my business, but I had promised I'd speak to Smokey on her behalf. He might tell me to butt out (and that was his prerogative), but I didn't think he would. Previously, when he'd thought I was mistreating Electra, he hadn't hesitated to let me know what he was thinking. I felt certain he'd appreciate the same candor from me.

By this time, I was on the sidewalk in front of Smokey's house. I put the issue of Sarah on the backburner momentarily as I reached out empathically in the direction of my friend's home.

Strike three, I muttered internally a few seconds later. No one was home.

That shouldn't have been completely surprising. Smokey's parents worked and his siblings were, presumably, at school. That just left one question: where was Smokey?

I stood there on the sidewalk for a moment, debating. Smokey could take care of himself, so I wasn't too worried — plus I had the issue of my evil twin, which was the whole reason I was here. I didn't need to get distracted, but at the same time this was all so uncharacteristic of Smokey that I couldn't help being slightly worried.

The sound of footsteps striking the ground in a rhythmic pattern drew my attention. I turned in the direction of the sound and saw what I assumed to be a fairly new mother, jogging towards me while pushing a stroller. She eyed me with deep suspicion as she went by, and I suddenly realized what I must look like: a kid who obviously should be in school but instead was standing out there on the sidewalk, unmoving, not dressed for the weather, seemingly staring at a house whose occupants were all gone for the day. She probably thought I was planning to burgle the place, and would call the cops as soon as she put some distance between us. (In fact, she appeared to be pulling out a cell phone at that very moment...)

I sighed. I didn't need any more misunderstandings regarding who I was or my intentions. That being the case, I decided to put the Smokey question on the backburner for now and began swiftly walking — almost high-stepping — in the opposite direction of the jogger. I turned as soon as I reached the corner, and teleported the moment I was out of her line of sight.

Chapter 40

I popped up at League HQ — in the residential section. More specifically, I was outside Li's apartment. I rang the bell and then waited. Approximately fifteen seconds later, it was answered.

Li opened the door wearing a black Mandarin shirt with matching pants — pretty much the same ensemble that he was wearing when we had first met. I smiled, thinking back to that time, when Li had proven himself to be a strong and resourceful ally, as well as a great friend.

"Please come in, Jim," he said, motioning for me to enter.

"Thanks," I said as I went inside. His quarters were generally a replica of mine in terms of layout, so I went to the living room and plopped down on the couch.

"Is this a social call?" Li asked as he closed the door.

"Not exactly," I replied as Li came over and took a seat in an easy chair. "I'm dealing with an unusual issue…"

As he was an android, I couldn't share anything with Li telepathically. Still, it only took a few minutes to lay everything out for him, including the reason for my visit.

Li seemed to ponder for a moment after I finished, then said, "So you think this individual may have attempted contact with your friends and associates in an effort to glean information about you?"

"I'm not sure if information about me, per se, is his endgame, but I'd wager he wants to know enough to be able to present himself as me without anyone knowing the difference."

"I see," Li murmured thoughtfully. "In any event, I can assure you that he has not attempted to make contact with me."

I frowned. "How can you be sure?"

"Because I have means of establishing identity that go beyond the mere visual."

"What do you mean?"

Li appeared thoughtful for a moment. "I know that I appear human and everyone treats me as such, but I am not. For instance, what you designate as eyes are ocular implants which allow me to see well outside the visible light spectrum. What you denote as ears are auditory devices that let me perceive sound well beyond the scope of human hearing."

"I don't think that would surprise anyone. We're all aware that you have enhanced senses."

"That would probably be an understatement," Li noted. "In essence, I have internal systems, constructs, and configurations that permit me to detect, observe, and examine the world around me in ways that most of your contemporaries cannot. By way of example, when I look at you, it is not merely your physical traits I see — your height, weight, the shape of your face, and so on. I hear your heart beat, the rush of blood in your veins. I note your respiratory rate as you breathe, the air capacity of your lungs. As I speak right now, I sense the bones in your middle ear vibrating."

I stared at him, almost in shock. "Li, are you saying that you perform an X-ray of some sort when you see me?"

Li shook his head. "No, that would be dangerous. X-rays pose a risk of harm due to radiation. I would never expose my friends to perils of that nature. What I have described is, practically speaking, just taking an assessment of certain bodily functions at a particular point in time. If necessary, I can compare those to an established baseline to determine if there are notable variations."

I frowned, concentrating on what I'd just heard. "So basically, you take biometric readings every time you see me?"

"Biometrics typically refers to verification of identity through unique signifiers such as fingerprints, facial recognition, and earlobe geometry. What I can do goes well beyond that, but the short answer to your question is yes. And it is not just you for whom I take these readings — it is everyone. But it is not with a specific purpose in mind; it is simply the way I am designed."

"But if we apply that to the issue we were originally discussing, you're saying that my doppelganger couldn't mislead you because, biometrically, you know what I look like."

"Precisely."

"But I'm able to alter my biological systems at will — tweak things internally so that I can go without sleep, don't feel hunger, and so on. What if my double can do the same thing and tries to match the internal functions you monitor when you see me?"

"Any attempt to replicate the biometrics of your internal physiology is doomed to fail."

Li's statement caught me a little by surprise. Intrigued, I asked, "Why is that?"

"Because your heredity is unprecedented, which lends itself to a biology that is not only extraordinary, but particularly anomalous and exceedingly rare."

I nodded, but stayed silent. Li's statement alluded to the fact that my father was actually from another dimension. That, combined with the fact that I also had alien DNA, meant that I pretty much made up my own species. In short, if I ever needed a blood transfusion, the odds of finding a match were going to be pretty low.

Interrupting my thoughts, Li went on, saying, "You have internal organs and systems that no one fully understands and which don't exist anywhere else in nature. In essence, you are sui generis — one of a kind."

"And that being the case," I concluded, "the fake Jim isn't going to be able to mimic my biometrics. For instance, if I've got a supernova for a heart, he can't replicate my biometric readings unless he has a supernova heart, too."

"I sense hyperbole in your analogy, but your statement is generally correct."

"Great," I said sincerely. "That means two of the three people I've been hunting for can't be fooled by my evil twin. Now I just need to find Smokey."

"Smokey?" Li echoed, sounding perplexed.

"Yeah. I need to talk to him about my evil twin, but he's not at school and isn't at home. Apparently he's missing in action."

"But he is not missing," Li stressed. "He is here."

REPLICATION

Chapter 41

"So this is where you've been hiding out," I said to Smokey.

We were in his apartment at League HQ, sitting at a small table in the breakfast area, where my friend — still dressed in pajamas — was eating a bowl of oatmeal. After Li had advised me of his whereabouts, I had quickly reached out to Smokey — via the internal landline as opposed to his cell phone — and moments later, I had teleported to his quarters. Now, watching him enjoy his morning meal, I was reminded of the fact that I had missed breakfast myself, so I tweaked my internal systems to stave off any hunger pangs.

"First of all," Smokey began, after swallowing a bite of oatmeal, "I've only been staying here a couple of days — not long enough to be considered 'hiding out' by any standard. Next, I'm here solely because Sarah keeps coming by the house to visit, and I don't want to deal with her."

"So you're here to avoid her."

"Pretty much."

"By staying some place she's unlikely to find you."

"Yeah, so?"

"That's the very definition of hiding out."

He gave me a sideways look, as if there were something he wanted to say, and then we both started laughing.

"Okay, you got me there," Smokey admitted a few seconds later. "Maybe it *is* hiding out. But she was calling me ten times a day and leaving twice as many texts — still is. I'm at the point where I don't even bother looking at my phone anymore because nine times out of ten, it's her."

261

Well, that explained why he hadn't answered when I called.

"Then, since I wasn't responding to her calls, she started dropping by the house unexpectedly," he continued. "My family would do as I asked and tell her I wasn't home, but they like Sarah and didn't care for lying to her, and I hated putting them in that position."

"So you basically moved out."

Smokey shrugged. "I told my family that I had to check into HQ for some training, which isn't exactly a lie since I'm going to be homeschooled by Mouse. And if Sarah asks, the League isn't going to tell her anything about who's in residence at the moment."

"Speaking of Sarah," I said, "full disclosure: I spoke with her today."

Smokey dropped his spoon into the oatmeal, then pushed the entire bowl away before leaning back, looking annoyed. "I suppose she asked you to talk to me."

"Something like that."

"And I take it that's why you're here."

"Not the complete reason, but yeah," I confirmed. "Obviously it's none of my business, but for what it's worth, I think you should at least hear her out."

Smokey looked away for a moment, shaking his head in a woebegone manner before turning back to me. "Did she tell you about our arrangement — the concessions we had to make to her family in order to date?"

"She told me."

"I guess you think it's weird."

I held up my hands in a hands-off fashion. "Hey man, you're talking to a guy who had to get engaged to someone in order to get home to see his girlfriend. I'm not in a position to judge anyone."

"True," Smokey acknowledged with a chuckle.

"So is that why you started missing school, too?" I asked. "Trying to duck Sarah?"

"No," he stated, shaking his head. "I skipped school because of Atalanta."

I frowned. Needless to say, his statement bothered me. Playing hooky — even for a pretty girl — was well out of character for my friend.

"Wait a minute," I said. "You skipped school to hang out with her?"

"Not exactly," Smokey stated. "She had a problem that she needed some assistance with. Helping her caused me to miss some class time."

I took a moment to let his statement soak in, not saying anything. Based on what I was picking up from him emotionally, there was more to the story, but I probably needed to get it another time.

"Anyway," I said, "my talking to Sarah about you was really sidebar to another conversation and segues into the real reason why I'm here."

I then reached out telepathically to explain about my evil twin — and much to my surprise, hit pay dirt.

Chapter 42

"So Smokey actually interacted with this guy?" Mouse asked.

I nodded. "Yeah, but in a very limited fashion. As far as he was concerned, though, it was *me*."

We were in Mouse's lab. After getting the story from Smokey, I had immediately called my mentor. At that juncture, Mouse was onsite at HQ, so I'd simply teleported and here we were.

"So let me see if I have this right," Mouse said. "The fake Jim shows up in the teen lounge, sees Smokey, and approaches him. Smokey thinks it's you, and immediately asks about the mission. Your evil twin says he has to leave, but states he'll be back in a few minutes and asks Smokey to grab him a soda in the meantime. He then teleports."

"And about thirty seconds later, *I* walk in," I added. "The *real* me, that is."

Thinking back on it, it certainly explained why the initial part of the conversation with Smokey seemed odd — as if he were following up on something that had been said before. (And from his point of view, that had been the case.)

"So," Mouse concluded, "while he seemed to have fooled Smokey, this fraudster didn't appear to get any useful info."

"True," I agreed. "Of course, Smokey's embarrassed about it. He feels like he's less of a friend for not being able to tell the difference between me and the fake Jim."

"Tell him he shouldn't feel like that at all," Mouse assured me. "In fact, it was him being a good friend and knowing you that probably made your lookalike skedaddle."

I gave him a bewildered look. "I'm not sure what you mean."

"Think about it. Smokey had just asked him about the mission. Presumably, your double didn't know anything about it. He wouldn't be able to discuss it without blowing his cover."

"Or at the very least making Smokey suspicious," I added.

"Right," Mouse stated with a nod.

"It's too bad the League doesn't have cameras in the teen lounge," I lamented. "We might have been able to figure some more things out if we caught this guy on tape again."

"You super teens are under enough pressure," Mouse explained. "You need to have at least one place you can go and relax without feeling you're being scrutinized. So, no cameras in the lounge."

Unexpectedly, my cell phone vibrated, indicating a text message had been received. I pulled it out and glanced at it as Mouse continued talking.

"Anyway, your evil twin didn't learn anything," my mentor stated, "even though he got close to someone in your inner circle."

"Make that *two* people in my inner circle," I corrected, frowning.

I handed Mouse my phone, showing him the text that I'd just received, which had come from BT and confirmed my earlier suspicion about who the fake Jim had definitely made contact with. It stated:

Logs show you visiting Paramount twice this weekend.

265

Chapter 43

"You think you need to go talk to Paramount?" Mouse asked after viewing BT's text. "Maybe peek inside his head and see what happened?"

I shook my head. "Paramount's brain is still a block of Swiss cheese to a large extent. It's still regrowing, healing. Even if I did go and take a cursory glance at what's in his mind, between the seizures, the memory lapses, and everything else, I wouldn't know what was real and what wasn't. Moreover, if I go in quizzing him about this stuff, it may cause some type of setback — delay his recovery. It's part of the reason I didn't go into it when he said I'd already come by that morning. No…it's enough to know that my doppelganger visited him."

"That brings up another interesting question," Mouse stated. "Why visit Paramount? Given everything you said a minute ago, nothing your brother says is really reliable. He's not a trustworthy source. "

"It's more than that," I insisted. "Historically, Paramount and I weren't close at all — he didn't even know who I was. Even if he had known, he's not anyone I would have hung out with — especially after he put together that little cadre of teen supervillains, like Daemon, Goon, Incendia…"

I trailed off as I suddenly felt something tickling at the back of my brain. It was a stray thought, roaming around like an annoying fly that you can't quite lay eyes on but which keeps buzzing in your ear. After a few moments, however, it came into focus, making me recognize a connection where I hadn't seen one before.

Mouse, as expected, was ten steps ahead of me and was already on his cell phone, addressing the issue.

****

"Okay, it's confirmed," Mouse stated a few minutes later, hanging up his phone. "BT verified that, in addition to Incendia, several other members of Paramount's prior clique of sinister teens have been grievously injured."

"Was it the same guy?" I asked. "My evil twin?"

"Officially, no. There were three of them, and like Incendia, they were being held in nullifier cells. It appeared that there was some type of malfunction, and the equipment intended to subdue them in the event the nullifiers failed became active."

"Okay, that's the *official* story," I uttered. "And *unofficially*?"

"Unofficially," Mouse said, "with nothing showing up on any of the cameras that were in place, I think your double either became invisible or used telekinesis to do the same thing he did to Incendia. I assume he would have done something similar to Paramount but changed his mind for some reason."

"Or maybe he figured he's done enough damage," I tossed in. "After all, he's framed me pretty well now by going after people I arguably have a grudge against."

"Except he's only visible in the footage concerning Incendia," Mouse countered. "If everything he's done is some kind of set-up, why not appear as you every time he attacked someone instead of just that last assault?"

I considered his question for a moment. "You're thinking maybe this isn't simply a frame job."

"What I'm thinking is that his actions don't make sense if that's his goal."

"Hmmm," I muttered, pondering. "Maybe he wasn't ready."

"What do you mean?" Mouse asked, looking perplexed.

"I mean, what if he hadn't finished whatever process was necessary to make him look like me? If that were the case, he'd want to remain out of sight."

"Now I understand," Mouse said with a patronizing nod. "You're still thinking his resemblance to you is some type of surgery or something."

"Actually, it occurred to me this morning that maybe the guy has some kind of healing ability," I clarified. It was a thought that had come to mind when I was wishing my new talent for healing others could take away Sarah's heartache. "I know you said surgery usually leaves scars, but if he's able to heal himself like a lot of supers can, then scarring wouldn't be an issue."

"If he could heal himself, I would expect any kind of graft to be rejected."

Mouse's statement caught me by surprise, prompting me to ask, "Why is that?"

"If a super who gets hurt has a healing ability, his body usually goes back to its form and condition before any injury was sustained. If he gets a cut, it heals. If an organ is damaged, it mends. Lose a leg, it regrows."

I nodded in understanding. My own body had an exceptional ability to heal, so little of this was news to me (although thankfully, I hadn't been forced to try to regrow any limbs thus far).

"However," Mouse said, continuing, "if you try to transplant something — an organ, a limb, or even a face — to someone with that kind of healing talent, the body will reject it."

"Wait a minute," I interjected. "I thought there was always the risk of rejection with a transplant anyway."

"There is, because a person's immune system often recognizes transplanted material as being foreign — not an original part of the body — and attacks it. But in the situation we're talking about, it's less of a risk and more a certainty due to the fact that the body of our hypothetical super is already fixing whatever is wrong. If, say, his body is already regrowing a liver that got shot to pieces, it's going to identify a transplanted liver as being of unknown origin — because he shouldn't have two livers — and reject it."

"So with the fake Jim," I surmised, "a face transplant wouldn't work because his body would say, 'I'm already repairing this guy's face and it's going to be perfect when I'm done, so get your substandard transplant material out of here.' Assuming he has a healing ability, that is."

"In essence, yes," Mouse concurred. "But it's more than just that. Remember when we talked about molding the subcutaneous contours of his face to match yours? Those would start healing as well, going back to their previous shape."

"In other words," I concluded, "now that we've eliminated all other possible explanations for his appearance, I need to accept that this guy is most likely a shapeshifter and—"

I stopped as I abruptly sensed a wild flurry of panicked — almost crazed — emotions coming from nearby. I picked up feelings of dread and trepidation on a level that could almost be described as horror. And the source of it was heading in our direction like a jet.

Acting on instinct, I phased both myself and Mouse just as something seemed to strike the double doors that served as the main entrance to the lab with a sound like a mortar shell. The doors flew open, struck by a force that almost tore them from their hinges and which sent them swinging around so wildly that they embedded in the walls. And whatever had done it suddenly came streaking towards me, a blur moving at almost the speed of sound.

REPLICATION

Chapter 44

I shifted into super speed, ready to face whatever threat had just crashed into the lab. However, I was completely unprepared for what I saw coming at me: my father.

Something was obviously wrong. Alpha Prime was so keyed up that I hadn't even been able to recognize him, empathically, as the source of the feelings I'd picked up on. It was as though he was hardwired with a panic button that had somehow been pushed, setting off an endless string of emotional klaxons.

As he came towards me, I felt my father's panic subside slightly. At the same time, his speed began dropping precipitously, such that he was no longer flying at me like a rocket trying to break free of Earth's gravity. He was still far from his typical emotional state, but I didn't get the sense that he represented a danger. With that in mind, I matched him, switching back to normal speed while at the same time shifting Mouse and myself out of our phased state.

Sparing a glance at my mentor, I suddenly noticed that he had his right arm pointed at my father. More importantly, his right hand was curled into a fist and seemed to be encompassed by something akin to a metallic brace which extended just slightly past his wrist in the direction of his forearm. I had never seen it before, didn't know where Mouse had retrieved it from, and hadn't seen him put it on, but everything about the brace — which had a series of softly winking lights on it — seemed to scream "weapon." And from the intense look on his face, Mouse wasn't afraid to use it.

A moment later, however, I had no more time to dwell on the subject as my father stopped directly in front of me and began practically jabbering.

"Son! Son!" Alpha Prime essentially shouted as he gently but firmly gripped my head between his hands and looked me in the eye. "I'm sorry! I'm so sorry!"

"What…?" I muttered, perplexed, trying to take a step back. "I'm not…I'm—"

"Are you hurt?" my father asked, shifting a hand to my shoulder.

"No," I insisted, attempting to shake my head. "I'm alri—"

"I'm sorry," Alpha Prime cut in again, as if he hadn't heard me, and a moment later, we were completely talking over each other.

"I don't know what happened…" he said.

"What are you—" I began.

He placed both hands around my face again. "Are you okay, son?"

"Yes, I'm just—"

"Are you in pain?"

"Huh? No, I—"

"Do you need a doctor?" he asked, placing a hand to my abdomen and pressing like a paramedic trying to locate a contusion.

Suddenly frustrated at not being heard, I angrily slapped his hands away and belted out, "Dad, stop!"

Looking completely startled, Alpha Prime abruptly went quiet and just stood there, staring at me.

****

Later, Alpha Prime would say that it was my calling him "Dad" that had stunned him into silence. It was a term I had never used in addressing him before. (In truth, I couldn't say that I had ever actually planned on calling him that, so I was as shocked by it as anyone.) However, after getting over his surprise, he explained what led to him busting into Mouse's lab.

"I was here at HQ when I got a notice from the alarm system at the mansion indicating intruders," Alpha Prime explained to me and Mouse. "I pulled up the cameras on my cell phone and saw this."

He handed the phone to Mouse, who held it so that we could both see the screen. It showed an image that I immediately recognized as being one of the interior rooms of the mansion. Without warning, someone showed up in the middle of the frame, appearing out of nowhere.

"Hang on," Mouse said, tapping the "Pause" button.

He then pulled some cables from a nearby drawer and spent about thirty seconds using them to connect the phone to some of the equipment in his lab. When he was done, the video from the phone was showing on one of the larger monitors. As I could have guessed without being told, the person who had appeared looked exactly like me (although it was easier to note with the image enlarged on a bigger screen).

Mouse hit a button on the phone and the footage resumed playing.

"You are trespassing," said a robotic voice on the video. "You have ten seconds to vacate the premises or the use of force will be authorized to detain you. Ten…nine…"

273

The voice continued counting down, but my doppelganger didn't seem particularly disturbed. Instead, he seemed to be taking in the room, which housed some nice artwork on the walls. In fact, because his attitude was so nonchalant, it was almost comical when the countdown hit zero and a laser blast took him in the gut, passing through his body and searing a hole in the wall behind him. There was a look of complete and utter surprise on his face — like someone who had just discovered that fire was hot by touching the business end of a blowtorch.

"Whoa…" I muttered as my evil twin doubled over in pain. A moment later, he vanished — teleported somewhere.

"Uh, maybe you don't know this, AP," Mouse said as he stopped the video, "but it's illegal to use deadly force to protect property. To protect yourself, yes, but not things you own."

"I know that," my father said testily.

"So why are your automatic defenses trying to ventilate this guy?" my mentor asked.

"It was only supposed to give a light shock — like a stun gun," Alpha Prime explained. "The laser setting shouldn't have even been turned on. I'm guessing it was some kind of malfunction."

Mouse and I exchanged a glance, but didn't say anything.

"Anyway," my father continued, "once I viewed the footage I thought it was Jim and… Well, I guess I sort of panicked."

"No kidding," Mouse joked, nodding his head towards the double doors. After calming my father down, we had pulled them from the walls and put them back in place as best we could, but they no longer fit together quite perfectly. They'd need some work before they were fully functional again, but in the meantime the lab was made secure by a solid metal barrier wall that extended down from the ceiling behind the now-damaged doors.

"Anyway," Alpha Prime went on, ignoring Mouse's comment, "I made an emergency request for Jim's location to the League's computer system and was told that he was here. I came as fast as I could and the rest is history. Now, can someone tell me what's going on?"

Chapter 45

I let Mouse explain the current situation to my father in succinct fashion. When it was over, we had a quick Q&A with Alpha Prime to confirm that my double hadn't made contact with him. (From everything we could discern, he hadn't.) Then, after making us promise to keep him apprised, my father left.

Once he was gone, Mouse turned to me, asking, "Thoughts?"

"Yeah — lots of them," I said. "For starters, Alpha Prime mentioned making a request to track me down."

"That's through your cell phone," Mouse said. "However, it's only for emergencies. You're not supposed to use it to see if some super teen is out partying when he should be studying, or to see if a League member you're dating is two-timing you, or anything like that."

"Well, as luck would have it, I'm not asking about it for any of those reasons. I'm asking because I could still use an alibi, and if my phone were being tracked, maybe that opens the door."

Mouse shook his head. "That doesn't do anything for you. You could have left the phone at the party, teleported to put the kibosh on Incendia, then come back and retrieved your phone with no one the wiser."

"Okay, let's move on to Alpha Prime's mansion. Why go there?"

Mouse shrugged. "Don't know. But I have a theory about how your double got gutshot."

"Yeah — whatever 'malfunction' caused Paramount's old buddies to get injured in their cells happened at my father's place. But if my doppelganger's the cause, it doesn't make sense. I mean, why would he turn laser-fire on himself?"

"I'm not sure he did," Mouse said. "Or rather, I don't think that was his intent. You saw his face. Was that the look of a guy who expected to get shot?"

"No. He looked more like a guy who just got shoved into the water on an alligator farm."

"Right," Mouse said with a nod. "I think maybe he tried to disarm the system and somehow it backfired on him."

"So, you think he's in a hospital somewhere right now, getting treated?"

"Don't know," Mouse admitted, his brow wrinkled in thought. "But it's worth checking out. I'll ask BT to look into it."

"What should *I* do?" I asked.

"Go home. Get some rest. From what I've seen, you've been running around all morning. Have you even had breakfast yet?"

I had to admit that food had not been a high priority, but also stated that it wasn't an issue because I'd altered my systems so that I wouldn't get hungry. Mouse, of course, didn't care about any of that. He ordered me out of his lab, saying he didn't want to see or hear from me again until I'd had something to eat. Reluctantly, I teleported home.

REPLICATION

Chapter 46

I popped up in the kitchen. No one was there, but when I reached out telepathically, I could sense that everyone was awake. Mom was in her office typing, my grandparents were in the breakfast area, and Myshtal was in her room.

I switched my bodily systems back to normal and suddenly realized I was famished. I went to the refrigerator and rooted around for a moment before pulling out some cheese and cold cuts. A minute later, after getting my hands on a loaf of bread, I'd whipped together a sandwich, which I promptly began devouring while heading to the breakfast area.

My grandparents were seated at the table when I entered the room; Gramps was reading the paper while Indigo nestled next to him, her head resting on his shoulder. She sat up when I came in, and my grandfather folded the newspaper and set it aside.

"Anything good in there?" I asked, nodding towards the newspaper before finishing off my sandwich.

"A couple of articles about our party the other night," Indigo said, "which is great for your grandfather, since he likes seeing his name in the paper."

Gramps grunted in fake annoyance at her teasing, then turned to me and muttered, "Got your note."

For a moment, I didn't know what he was talking about, then I remembered the piece of paper I had hurriedly scribbled on when I'd left earlier.

"Good," I replied. "Hope you didn't worry."

"We always worry about you, *Sxibbo*," Indigo chimed in. "It's the privilege of being grandparents."

278

REPLICATION

"You can worry if you want," Gramps admonished. "I'm not going to fret over a kid who can outrun a bullet."

"Don't pay any attention to him," my grandmother said with a smile. "He worries about you more than anyone."

My grandfather merely grunted in response, causing us to laugh.

"So," Indigo continued, "how's your day been?"

She asked the question innocuously, but I could tell that she — along with my grandfather — were eager to hear my response. Unlike the day before, no one had bombarded me with questions upon my arrival. (Apparently a decision had been made to give me a little space in that regard.) Grateful for the short reprieve, I reached out telepathically to my grandparents and my mother and brought them up to speed. The only person I didn't mentally share with was Myshtal, whom I sensed was preoccupied.

When I finished, no one said anything — either verbally or telepathically. In terms of emotions, however, I could sense my family's concern and unease over the situation with my evil twin. I tried to reassure them, stressing that this thing would get sorted out soon, but they didn't appear convinced — especially Mom, who had left her office and joined us.

"Look," I finally said, "you guys are acting like I've been diagnosed with some deadly disease. This is serious, but it's not fatal."

"It doesn't have to be fatal," Gramps declared. "It just needs to be bad enough for them to justify kicking you off the planet."

"Then I'll travel the universe with you guys," I stated. "Although you're already dragging one bratty kid along."

As I uttered that last sentence, I cut my eyes at Mom, whose mouth dropped open in feigned shock as my grandparents started chuckling.

"Who are you calling a brat?" my mother almost shouted, smiling. Then she turned to Indigo. "You want to hear about bratty behavior, Mom? Let me tell you about the time your grandson…"

My mother then proceeded to tell the story of a temper tantrum I threw once while we were out shopping (and when I was much younger) that was so outrageous that it resulted in us being asked to leave the store. Although slightly embarrassing, it actually was kind of funny, and by the time she finished, we were all laughing. And just like that, the mood of the room lightened considerably, with the specter of my evil twin banished — at least temporarily.

REPLICATION

Chapter 47

I spent a little time hanging out with my family, just laughing and joking for the most part. Maybe it was the fact that we were all telepaths (and were therefore able to connect profoundly on several levels), but we really enjoyed being around one another and had an exceptionally strong bond. It would be weird for me once they left the planet — assuming I wasn't forced to go with them — and made it all the more important that I cherish the time we had together.

We had been sitting around the table in the breakfast area for maybe thirty minutes when Myshtal entered the room. She was looking lovely, as always, wearing a charcoal-gray bell sleeve top and faux leather pants. She stopped short as all of our heads swiveled in her direction.

"I'm sorry," she began sheepishly. "I didn't mean to intrude."

"Don't be silly," Indigo said. "Come sit down."

"Are you sure?" Myshtal asked as she tentatively stepped over and took a seat next to me. "It looked like you were having a family moment."

Mom pooh-poohed Myshtal's concerns with a wave of her hand. "Assuming that were true, you're part of this family now, so any family moments also include you."

"Thanks," Myshtal said in a sincere tone, at the same time blushing mildly.

Unexpectedly, I picked up on some quick telepathic chatter between my mother and grandparents. Not being part of the conversation, however, I didn't know exactly what had been discussed.

"Anyway," Mom said, interrupting my thoughts, "I should get back to writing."

"And we've got some errands to run," Gramps said, as he and Indigo rose to their feet almost simultaneously.

"Do you need any help?" Myshtal asked.

"No," my grandmother stated, and then began to give a quick overview of what she and Gramps had on their agenda. I took advantage of the opportunity to have a quick mental chat with my grandfather.

<What was all that?> I asked telepathically.

<All what?> Gramps responded almost automatically.

<That jibber-jabber between you guys and Mom. The three of you have a quick mental chat, and the next thing I know, you're all scrambling for the exits.>

Gramps let out a mental sigh. <Look, we like Myshtal and she likes us, but she doesn't want to be around us all the time. She wants to spend time around people in her own age group.>

<What are you talking about? She's like fifty! You guys *are* her age group.>

<You know what I mean. She's a teen by Caelesian standards — like you are by our norms.>

My eyes narrowed as I considered his statement. <What are you saying?>

<What I'm saying is that I know you have a lot going on, but I hope you'll remember that we have a guest, and that you'll treat her the way you'd want to be treated if your positions were reversed.>

REPLICATION

Chapter 48

With telepathy being a high-speed form of communication, my mental conversation with Gramps ended right around the time Indigo finished detailing for Myshtal the errands they had to run. Moments later, my mother and grandparents were gone, leaving me and Myshtal alone at the breakfast table.

Frankly speaking, my grandfather's words had embarrassed me. Having been the only Earthling on Caeles, I knew *exactly* how Myshtal probably felt as a Caelesian on Earth — and also how important it was to have friends in that situation. And while I had never been anything less than congenial towards her, I had been rather preoccupied of late, first with Electra and then because of the fake Jim. (The latter situation was obviously rather serious, but didn't give me carte blanche to ignore Myshtal entirely.)

"I hope this doesn't sound too vain," she abruptly said, interrupting my thoughts, "but how do I look?"

"Uh…you look, uh…you look good," I mumbled. "Most people would probably say beautiful."

I was a little surprised at the question. There was little doubt that Myshtal knew she was stunning, but she had never struck me as the type who solicited compliments on her appearance. In truth, I couldn't quite figure out why she would even ask.

Myshtal laughed. "No, not my looks. The clothes."

To emphasize her point, she stood up and spun in a circle, arms outstretched.

"Oh," I muttered, now understanding. "They're nice."

"Thanks. I made them myself."

I blinked in surprise. "You made this outfit?"

"Yes," she replied. "This morning."

"Is this what you were doing earlier?" I asked, suddenly recalling that I had sensed her being preoccupied when I had first teleported home.

She nodded. "I'm still trying to get a handle on Earth fashions."

"Yes, but to make an outfit in a single morning is pretty impressive."

"Less than you think," she stated, "in light of the fact that Caelesian clothing material is really more like malleable high-tech gear."

"Ahhh," I droned in an enlightened manner as I remembered the "mood clothing" she'd worn a few nights ago. "Regardless, you did a great job."

"Thanks," she said, beaming. "Well, now you know how *my* morning went. How was yours?"

"It had peaks and valleys," I remarked, and then went into detail about everything that had happened.

Myshtal listened attentively to what I said, seeming to absorb every word. When I was done bringing her up to speed, she looked at me with a worried expression.

"This double you have seems crafty," she said. "Do you think he'll try to fool *me*?"

I shook my head. "I don't think he'd risk it. You spend a lot of time around my family, and they can read minds. Approaching you probably brings him too close to their proximity. I don't think you're in any danger."

"I wasn't particularly troubled about being in harm's way," she said. "I was more worried that he might somehow get information from me that could be used against you."

"Oh," I muttered, a little surprised. "Well, thanks. I appreciate the concern."

"No problem," she assured me. "So what happens now?"

"I'm not sure," I admitted. "I'll probably go by League HQ to see if Mouse has come up with anything."

"League HQ?" she repeated, sounding excited. "Where I'll be staying?"

"Yeah, although you'll actually only be there part-time," I stated. And then I was hit with a sudden inspiration.

"How'd you like to see it?" I asked. "Your future room, that is."

"I'd love to," she declared with a grin.

****

As Myshtal was essentially ready to go, I teleported us within seconds of her expressing a desire to see her quarters. Once at HQ, I did a little running around (i.e., called Mouse) to find out exactly where she'd be staying. Once that info was in hand, we made our way to her new digs.

Upon reaching her door, I quickly realized I'd been neglectful in at least one area: we didn't have a key to get in. That, however, barely qualified as an impediment. I phased the door, and we walked inside.

Much to my surprise, Myshtal was incredibly excited about her quarters and eagerly went through the place, eyeballing everything like a kid in a candy store. Based on her enthusiasm, you would never have guessed that she had closets as big as a house back on Caeles. I suppose that it was a lot like someone going off to college:

their dorm room might be smaller than the room they had at home, but there's a certain thrill to being in a new place, being around different people, and adjusting to an unknown environment.

I, on the other hand, didn't get particularly excited initially. If my count was correct, this was the third teen suite that I'd visited in the past few hours. Even were that not the case, I was so thoroughly familiar with the teen quarters at this juncture that I could probably find my way through them blindfolded. I knew the layout, had a good idea of how they were furnished, and so on. In short, one would think that — with respect to me — any novelty associated with staying at Alpha League Headquarters had long since worn off.

That said, the opposite actually turned out to be true. Just looking at the room where she'd be staying made Myshtal wildly elated, and her mood was infectious. Before long, I was almost as enthused as she was about her taking up residence at HQ.

Her animated disposition continued after we finished looking over her new place, spilling over into a desire to see the rest of the facilities. With nothing else to do, I took her on a leisurely tour of Alpha League Headquarters.

Being a teleporter and a speedster, it normally doesn't take me very long to get where I'm going. However, one of the overlooked faults of having those talents is that you often lose awareness of things like space and distance. That had apparently happened to me, because as I began walking around with Myshtal, I garnered a newfound appreciation for just how sizeable HQ was. From the helipad on the roof to the training facilities to the rec area (which housed a pool and a weight room, among other things), the sheer number of amenities housed under one roof made it clear that the place was enormous — a fact that I should have remained cognizant of.

On her part, Myshtal seemed fascinated by every part of the tour. Naturally, there were some things that I didn't show her, like Command Central and Mouse's lab — the former because it was the room that basically controlled all of Headquarters, and the latter because Mouse was probably working (and I didn't want him distracted from the issue of my evil twin).

All in all, the tour took a couple of hours, with us finishing up in the teen lounge. At that point, some of my peers had started showing up, which meant that school was out. I waved to a couple of them as I guided Myshtal to a table, and then — remembering that we had pretty much skipped lunch — I ran to the kitchen area to see what kind of goodies were on hand. After a quick review of what was available, I settled for a couple of bottles of water, some bananas, and a few power bars. As I was heading back, I saw that Smokey had joined Myshtal at our table.

"Hey," I said to him as I reached the table and set down the food and water. "You want anything? I can just head back—"

"No, I'm good," he firmly stated. "But thanks for asking."

"I just took Myshtal on a tour of the place," I said as I sat back down.

Turning to her, Smokey asked, "So what did you think?"

Myshtal, who was just unwrapping a power bar, paused for a moment before responding. "I thought it was great! Everything just seemed wonderful. I really think I'm going to like it here."

"Well, it's not just the facilities that are great," Smokey noted. "The people here are generally nice, too."

"Oh, I know," Myshtal agreed. "Like at the party — you were all so congenial, and I appreciate how your friends made me feel included."

"No problem," Smokey said.

"Speaking of the party," I began, a little red-faced, "I don't think I apologized for the way Electra and I kind of ghosted on you guys."

"Don't worry about it," Smokey said. "Everyone understood and no one took offense. You did miss saying goodbye to Kane and Gossamer, though, since they went back home right after the party ended."

I nodded, but didn't say anything, as the swift departure of Kane and Gossamer was something I'd known of in advance and had expected. They had only come to show their support for me (although meeting Indigo had been a nice bonus).

"Vestibule also left," Myshtal added. "Shortly after you and Electra took off."

I winced. "Oh, man. I forgot all about Vestibule."

I excused myself and got up from the table, stepping away for privacy as I pulled my phone out. Aside from the text I'd sent, Vestibule hadn't even been a blip on my radar screen. With everything going on, I had essentially pushed her to the backburner. I did still owe her an outing, though, and — with a little time on my hands — felt the need to inform her that I intended to make good on it. However, it would probably have to wait until the situation with my evil twin was resolved, and as I dialed her number I was hoping she'd understand that.

She answered after the first ring. "*Bonjour, mon chéri.*" Even though she'd spoken in French, her voice had a suggestive edge to it that suddenly made me feel like the temperature had gone up a few degrees.

"Uh, hey," I said. "Look, I wanted to talk to you about our outing."

"Okay. Where are you?"

"I'm at League HQ — in the teen lounge."

"Alright, I'll be there in a sec."

A moment later, I heard a click that told me she'd hung up. A second after that, she popped up a few feet away from me.

She had her hair pulled back into a ponytail, and was dressed in a pair of dark, form-fitting leggings, and a red sports bra. The ensemble left her midriff bare, showing off a great set of abs and a well-toned figure in general. I hated myself for thinking it, but in all honesty, she looked hot. (And apparently others thought so as well, because quite a few eyes turned in her direction.)

Eyes twinkling, she almost ran towards me. Next, much to my surprise, she flung her arms around my neck and kissed me.

REPLICATION

Chapter 49

I was so stunned that I didn't do anything for a moment (although I'm pretty sure I didn't kiss her back). After realizing what was happening, I reached up and took her arms from around my neck and stepped back.

"What are you doing?" I whispered harshly, looking around to see who — if anyone — had seen what had just happened. (Judging from the emotional vibes I was picking up, almost everyone present had.)

"What — too soon?" Vestibule asked, seemingly not put off by my tone. "Come on," she said, reaching out and taking my hand. "Let's go."

"Go where?" I asked woodenly, still trying to make sense of what was happening.

"My place, of course," she replied.

"Your place?" I repeated, not sure what she was talking about.

"Not my *place*," she clarified, giggling. "My park — where I go to relax. Remember?"

"Huh?" I muttered, giving her a perplexed look.

"Come on," she said again. "Let me take you."

I felt something akin to a light tugging, like someone had pinched a bit of material from my shirt and was gently pulling on it, but on a metaphysical level. After a moment, I recognized what it was: Vestibule trying to teleport me.

One of the great things about being a teleporter is that you can go anywhere you want. However, a corollary of that rule is that you *don't* have to go any place where you *don't* want to be. For instance, if a teleporter is on a mountaintop and you manage to immediately transport him to a valley, his own power would take him right back to the mountain as if he never left. In short, no one — not even another person with the same power — can teleport a teleporter against their will.

At the moment, Vestibule was trying to take me some place, and I had to decide whether to allow it. Ordinarily, I wouldn't do it. Not that I had reason to suspect Vestibule of something nefarious, but I had once recklessly teleported myself into a trap. If I could do something like that to myself out of sheer carelessness (and I generally thought of myself as a cautious individual), then others could do it to me as well. It also didn't help that Vestibule was acting in a manner that could be described as overfamiliar, to say the least. It was if we had spent a bunch of time together and miraculously become best...

Oh, no, I thought as my mind abruptly latched onto a new idea, one that I prayed I was completely wrong about.

Suddenly eager to speak with Vestibule, I gave Smokey and Myshtal a telepathic heads-up that I had to leave for a minute. After getting their acknowledgment, I released the hold I usually kept on my teleportation ability and allowed Vestibule to spirit me away.

REPLICATION

Chapter 50

We popped up in a public park — a scenic venue with acres of lush green grass, majestic trees, and pathways lined with beautiful flowers that were just starting to bloom. There weren't many people around, but I noted that those present were mostly dressed in shorts and T-shirts. Given the fact that we were outdoors and seemingly in a temperate clime, I assumed that we were on the West Coast.

We had actually appeared near a lake, and I caught a picturesque view of a beautiful swan elegantly gliding across the surface of the water, followed by several of its young.

"They're called cygnets," Vestibule said.

I turned towards her to find that she had taken a seat on a nearby wooden bench.

"The baby swans," she explained. "They're called cygnets."

"Oh," I muttered. "That's interesting." Then I frowned. "So you read minds now?"

She let out a peal of laughter — a sound that was so pure in relaying her mirth and amusement that I was almost taken aback, as it bespoke of a depth of personality that I hadn't suspected.

"No," Vestibule said, still smiling as she shook her head, "but I saw you looking at the swans — everyone does — so it was a safe bet that 'swan babies' was running through your head at some point."

"I was actually thinking 'offspring,' if you want the truth."

She laughed again and then gently patted the space next to her on the bench. Taking the invitation, I walked towards her and sat down.

She didn't immediately say anything, merely spent a few seconds glancing around the park. As she did, I detected a surprising serenity in her, a calmness and tranquility that caught me somewhat by surprise. I had always considered Vestibule to be vapid and vain, but there was apparently more to her than met the eye. However, I didn't come here to ponder the depths of her soul. I was here for information, and was about to ask a question when Vestibule spoke.

"So," she said with a sly look, "couldn't wait for tonight?"

"Tonight?" I asked, eyebrows raised.

"Yeah — our date."

I blinked in surprise. "We don't have a date for tonight."

"Ha-ha," she quipped. "You're funny."

"I'm serious," I stated firmly. "We don't have plans for tonight."

"Sure we do," she insisted. "You asked me out again last night, right here in this park."

"*Again*?" I repeated in surprise.

"Yeah," she said with a nod. "Did you get hit on the head or something? After you wimped out on me yesterday, you actually showed up at my house later, saying that you wanted to keep your word."

I gave her a stern look. "Listen to me, Vestibule. We didn't go out yesterday. I didn't do anything last night except go home and go to bed."

She bit her lip nervously. "Okay, this isn't funny anymore."

"It's not supposed to be," I said. "There's a guy — presumably a shapeshifter — going around pretending to be me."

"What?!" she nearly screeched.

"You're not the only one he's fooled," I assured her. "He's been careful to avoid certain people who'd know he's a fake, like my girlfriend Electra, but—"

"Wait…no…" she muttered, shaking her head. "Your girlfriend? But…you broke up…you told me…"

"I'm sorry, but it wasn't me."

Now clearly on edge, Vestibule stood up, practically wringing her hands.

"But I…" she began. "We…I mean…the two of us…"

She continued mumbling, but wasn't particularly coherent. Hoping to make sense of what she was trying to convey, I took a telepathic peek inside her mind and saw much of what had happened: my evil twin taking her out, her showing him this park, him asking her on another date. I also noted several images that made it very clear why she had felt comfortable kissing me and holding my hand.

As I withdrew from her mind, she turned to me with a forlorn look and teary eyes. Emotionally, I sensed that she was coming undone to a certain extent and was on the verge of being completely distraught. The only thing she was holding onto at the moment was a slim hope that perhaps this was a cruel joke on my part.

I merely shook my head, not saying anything.

Vestibule's mouth opened, and she let out a piercing, undulating scream that carried across the lake like a train whistle, frightening the swans and making numerous people look in our direction. It was a sound of inconsolable distress and unsettling dismay, the resonant tone of a tortured soul wallowing in anguish.

And then she vanished.

REPLICATION

Chapter 51

I stayed on the park bench after Vestibule teleported, the sound of her scream still ringing in my ears.

My heart went out to her. Unlike Sarah and Smokey, my double hadn't just pulled the wool over her eyes — he had completely hoodwinked her.

Needless to say, I felt particularly bad because Vestibule hadn't been on my short list of people to talk to about my evil twin. Frankly speaking, she and I weren't close. Thus, I hadn't pegged her as someone the fake Jim would try to get close to because she really didn't have much info to impart (assuming, again, that my double was after details about me).

I frowned as my thoughts turned in general to my evil twin. It was one thing for him to home in on people in my inner circle — people who were expected to know me intimately. His actions with Vestibule, however, indicated a certain callousness and disregard for common decency. It wouldn't be a stretch to call what he'd done cruel.

Once again, I found myself pondering what my lookalike's endgame was. What was he after? Also, given what had just happened with Vestibule, were there other people I needed to add to my list and have a conversation with? Kane perhaps, or maybe Gossamer? My cousins? Other teens in the Alpha League?

I shook my head in frustration. I couldn't run down everyone with a tenuous connection to me. My gut told me that would probably be a waste of time. I needed to work smarter, not harder. I needed to—

"Penny for your thoughts," said a voice that was oddly familiar as someone seemingly appeared out of nowhere and took a seat next to me on the bench.

REPLICATION

I glanced at the speaker and then did a double-take.
It was my evil twin.

REPLICATION

Chapter 52

He looked like me, of course, except he looked *exactly* like me: same hair, same eyes, same face. More to the point, I could tell that this was *him*. And by that I mean that this was his normal, natural appearance — no augmentation, no shapeshifting, no nothing. I don't know *how* I knew that; I just *knew*. In essence, the guy really was my double.

I could also perceive other things about him. For instance, I would have known without being told that he was a super. In some way I can't explain, I could sense that — like me — he had a wide slate of powers, although I couldn't immediately tell what they all were. (I did note, however, that he wasn't a telepath.)

I spent a moment trying to figure out what to do. In a perfect world, I'd just teleport him — whisk him off to a nullifier or someplace that could neutralize his powers, or hand him over to the proper authorities. But he was a teleporter, so that wouldn't work. A world-class telepath could go inside someone's head and incapacitate them, but I had limitations in that regard. (Plus, despite his lack of telepathy, I could tell that this guy had first-rate mental shields — even a preeminent telepath would have trouble boring into his mind.)

Without many options, I decided to grab the low-hanging fruit and simply try to get as much info out of my doppelganger as possible. Shockingly, he actually offered to help in that arena.

"I suppose you have questions," he said unexpectedly, after sizing me up the same way I'd done him.

"That would be an understatement," I replied, although it felt bizarre to hear someone else speaking with *my* voice. "Who are you?"

"I would think that was obvious," he replied nonchalantly. "I'm *you*, of course."

"No, you're *not* me," I insisted. "But you've been doing a good job of convincing others that you are and framing me for things I didn't do."

"Is that what you think I've been doing?" he asked, eyebrows raised. Plainly amused, he let out a short bark of laughter that was cut off almost immediately as he winced and laid a hand gingerly on his midsection.

"Stomach issues?" I queried dryly, suddenly remembering that he had taken a laser shot to the gut earlier in the day.

He gave me a knowing look, one which telegraphed the fact that he knew that I knew the source of his discomfort.

"I'm on the mend," he declared. "Anyway, as to framing you — that's the last thing I had in mind."

I was incredulous. "Really? You run around with my face, doing everything from attacking people to dating, all while trying to convince them that you're me, and you don't think that's the same as setting me up?"

"First of all, it's not just *your* face," my double stressed. "And second, with respect to the dating thing, I thought I was doing you a favor. You've got your hands full these days in the romance department, so I was just trying to take some things off your plate."

"And help yourself to some off-menu items while you were at it," I added angrily. "Did you ever consider how Vestibule would feel after she discovered that it wasn't me who she went out with? That I wasn't the guy holding her hand or kissing her?"

"Will you relax?" the fake Jim said, brushing off my concerns with an indifferent wave of his hand. "She's a big girl, and can take care of herself. Besides, it's not like we did anything R-rated. It was PG-13, max."

"I know," I practically hissed. "I saw it in her head. But that still doesn't erase the fact that you humiliated her."

"Okay," my lookalike conceded, "you want to defend Vestibule's honor out of a sense of chivalry? I get that. But the same can't be said of the others."

"The others?" I repeated. "You mean the ones you attacked when they were helpless in their cells?"

"They needed to be punished," he responded.

"They *were* being punished," I said. "That was the whole point of them being locked away."

He shook his head, like a parent having a tough time explaining a simple concept to a child. "You don't understand."

"I understand that my brother Paramount was probably on your hit list," I retorted. "So what happened? You got there and found out that he wasn't in a nullifier — that with his power set it would be almost impossible to hurt him?"

"No," my evil twin stressed emphatically. "I got there and figured he wasn't worth the trouble."

I frowned. "What's that supposed to mean?"

"It means that someone else got there first. Whoever blasted away his brain saved me the trouble, because at his current mental stage, doing anything to him would have been like harming a child. I mean, he's just a hair above being the village idiot. What a re—"

My double's words were cut off as he suddenly found me standing over him, with one fist holding a handful of his shirt and the other cocked back, ready to punch him in the face.

"Say it," I hissed. "Say it. I dare you…"

His statements about Paramount had completely infuriated me. I was so enraged that I actually didn't recall exactly how I came to be looming over him. I didn't know if I had teleported, shifted into super speed, or just jumped up and grabbed him. I just knew that if he finished labeling my brother with the word he'd been about to say, I was going to beat the stuffing out of him.

My doppelganger smiled and held up his hands defensively. "Okay, okay. I was going to say what a re*covery* he's made, despite any current limitations. Nevertheless, I can see now that maybe I crossed a line, so I'm going to go while we're still friends."

A moment later, I was holding nothing but empty air in my fist. I lowered my arm, and began reflecting on the conversation I had just had. However, before I could figure out whether I had truly learned anything, my phone rang. I glanced at the caller ID and mentally groaned.

"Gray," I said as I answered. "This can't be a coincidence."

Gray laughed. "You're right about that, but you still don't know *Jack*. That said, how'd you like to learn?"

Chapter 53

"A clone???!!!" I roared. "Are you kidding me?"

"Unfortunately not," Gray replied. He was dressed, as usual, in a gray suit. I didn't know his actual age, but he had iron-gray hair that gave me the impression that he was in his sixties. However, despite his apparent age, he wasn't anyone that I would have considered feeble in any sense.

We were currently in the backseat of a chauffeured SUV, with a soundproof partition between us and the driver. After receiving Gray's call, I had teleported back home — to a downtown intersection Gray had identified. When I popped up, he was already there in the SUV, waiting, and I had climbed in. He had then proceeded to inform me of why the fake Jim was less of a fake than I'd assumed.

"What's wrong with you people?" I asked rhetorically. "Not only is it morally and ethically problematic, last time I checked, human cloning was illegal."

"Murder's illegal, too," Gray countered. "Unless the right people give you the green light — such as by, say, declaring war. Then you can blast the enemy to smithereens without anybody trying to slap cuffs on you. They might even give you a medal."

"That's different and you know it, but I concede your point. Some higher-up authorized this."

"That's usually how it happens."

I rubbed my temples. "This is all I need right now. I'm already dealing with things most sixteen-year-olds don't even think about."

"Oh, yes — you're engaged to a girl with money, beauty, personality, and powerful political connections. Must be torture…"

I gave him an evil look, but chose to stay on topic rather than respond to his barb.

"So why me?" I asked. "There are plenty of other supers out there who you could have cloned. Why single me out?"

Gray didn't immediately respond. Instead, he just stared at me with a blank expression, and a moment later the truth dawned on me.

I let out a depressed sigh. "I'm not the only one, am I?"

Gray made a vague gesture in response. "You have to understand the position of the decision-makers. There are a number of supers out there with the ability to destroy this entire planet — or maybe just conquer it, if that's what they decided to do. Something was needed to keep those individuals in check, should the occasion arise."

"I get it," I said with a nod. "Your enemy develops nuclear weapons, so you race to do the same thing."

"Pretty much."

"So what, you've got clones of every super growing in a lab somewhere?"

"Don't be absurd," Gray said, giving me a disparaging look. "Just those who might be considered a global threat."

"So what does that mean — every member of the Alpha League except maybe Mouse?"

Gray snorted in derision. "Ha! Your friend Mouse is the most dangerous one of all."

I had trouble hiding my surprise at this. He was absolutely brilliant, but as far as I could tell, Mouse didn't have any discernable super powers.

"However," Gray continued, "cloning your mentor hasn't been possible. There's some breakdown in his DNA that prevents the process."

I almost laughed. "So even without knowing what you were up to, Mouse has outsmarted you."

"*I* wasn't up to anything!" Gray forcefully insisted. "Had I known about any of this, I would have tried to stop it. As it was, this program was well under way before it came to my attention. At that point, all I could do was damage control."

"Yeah, right," I muttered sarcastically, "'cause you're a regular saint."

"You think you've got me pegged?" Gray shot back, instantly livid. "You don't know the first thing about me."

"I know you love your job and the power it gives you."

"Wrong," Gray shot back. "I hate this job. I would have retired twenty years ago if I could have."

"So walk away. No one's stopping you."

Gray let out a frustrated breath. "It's not that easy."

"Sure it is. People serve notice to their employers every day."

Gray rolled his eyes in agitation. "Okay, smart guy, let me paint the picture for you. Suppose that you suddenly get sick of being in the Alpha League — you just want to go out, have a normal life, and leave all this superhero business behind you. But the minute you leave, your powers go to someone else who's still on the roster, and not necessarily someone you'd personally choose. So maybe your abilities go to your best bud Smokey, or maybe your girlfriend Electra. Or maybe someone you've only waved to in passing. Or, if he was still in the League, imagine if they went to your brother Paramount. Not the Paramount you know today, but the guy he was a year ago — the arrogant jerk who went bananas and left a bunch of death and destruction his wake. Knowing all that was possible, do you just leave and don't worry about what's going to happen?"

"What are you trying to say, Gray?"

"I'm saying that I know you think I'm some kind of fiend, but some of the guys waiting in the wings are far worse. For instance, I've always tried to be respectful, such as giving individuals their privacy and so on. If I retire and certain people step into my role, you'll never have privacy again. Within twenty-four hours, your house will be bugged, and every conversation you have from that point forward will be recorded."

"Ha!" I scoffed. "Don't try to sell yourself as some great humanitarian or protector of the innocent. You've done horrid things, like kidnapping my friend Rudi."

"Your friend is one of the most powerful precognitives in the world," Gray said. "With her ability to see the future, she helped her parents turn a hundred dollars into sixty million in the stock market in less than three weeks. Impressive, but she was causing all kinds of issues in the world of high finance. Left unchecked, she would have wrecked the global market, so we took her into custody."

His explanation sounded plausible. Rudi was a young girl that my friends and I had rescued awhile back (along with her younger brother) from a secret government facility. As Gray had noted, she was indeed incredibly powerful. However, she was also a pre-teen, and may not have understood the consequences of her actions — assuming that Gray was telling the truth, and from what I could pick up empathically, he was being sincere.

"Okay, but what about Schaefer?" I asked. "You let that maniac release a virus that almost killed every super on the planet."

As I spoke, I reflected back on the incident in question. Schaefer had been one of Gray's agents whose hatred of supers had led him to release a virus that only attacked those with superpowers. He had ultimately been stopped, but his actions led to the destruction of the Academy, which had been a schoolhouse and training facility for teen supers.

Without missing a beat, Gray said, "Schaefer went off the rails. What he tried to do wasn't sanctioned."

"So you had no hand in that situation?"

"I know I seem all-powerful to you, but I'm in a very tenuous position, all the time. I can't be seen to be losing control of my organization, or let rumor spread that there are rogue elements in my establishment."

"So rather than disavow Schaefer, you retroactively approved what he did," I surmised.

"The damage was done," Gray protested. "Yes, I knew about the virus, but it was only devised to make sure we had a safety-valve in case supers went bonkers — something that would incapacitate those it infected. It was never supposed to be used to kill people, and I'm truly sorry for that."

Needless to say, his reply caught me off guard. From everything I could read of his emotional state, Gray was being truthful. But if that were the case, it would mean that I might have seriously misjudged the man. Was it possible that Gray was actually one of the good guys? I didn't even want to consider it…

"We've gone kind of far afield here," I said. "We were talking about this illegal clone of me that you had made."

"As I said, this program initially began without my approval," Gray corrected. "When I found out about it, it was too late to shut it down, so I inserted myself in the process just to ensure there was appropriate oversight."

"Well, your oversight leaves something to be desired, because your fake Jim is running all over the place, doing whatever he wants."

"He goes by 'Jack,'" Gray said.

I blinked. "What?"

"Your clone. His name's Jack."

I frowned. "Jack," of course, is a nickname for "John," which was my formal first name. They had really pulled out all the stops in making this clone seem connected to me. (Also, understanding now dawned on me with respect to Gray's *you-don't-know-Jack* punchlines.)

"With respect to him running all over the place," Gray continued, "that's because he's escaped."

Chapter 54

"Escaped?" I repeated with a frown. "Escaped from where? Was he on lockdown or something?"

"Not exactly," Gray replied. "Needless to say, you can't have a secret cloning program and then let said clones roam around like free-range chickens. Thus, for most of his life, Jack was housed in a specialized facility, with little access to the outside world."

"Housed," I echoed. "You make it sound like he was boxed up and stored in a warehouse."

"That's not far from the truth. Physically, he's your age, but chronologically he's much younger. We accelerated his growth and development using special hormones and unconventional biological techniques, among other things. That said, he spent a fair amount of time in stasis until recently."

"You said 'recently,'" I noted. "So what happened?"

"A couple of things, actually — first and foremost being that you left the planet."

"So what? I mean, it was a big deal for me, but I'm not sure what it means for a clone."

Gray's brow wrinkled for a moment, as if he were working out a thorny problem mentally.

"There's something in the cloning process that makes clones want to meet their originals," Gray began. "With his power set, it was tricky when you were here, but once you left…"

I picked up on his train of thought. "Once I left, you could let your pet out of his cage on a more regular basis because there was no chance we'd meet."

"Right. Letting him out, as you put it, was necessary to gauge his abilities, assess findings about the cloning methodology, and so on. But then you came back."

"Let me guess: at that point, you couldn't put the genie back in the bottle."

"Yes, but it was actually a little more complicated than that," Gray said. "Jack's stasis chamber was an upright, rectangular pod with lots of wires, tubes, etcetera — probably similar to things you've seen in the movies."

I nodded, understanding and able to visualize the type of device he was mentioning.

"Anyway, we discovered that Jack was leaving the pod at will."

"How?"

"Sometimes the equipment wouldn't complete the stasis process. It would just stop in the middle, like someone had hit an off button."

"He did it," I concluded. "Telekinesis."

Gray nodded. "That's what we assumed."

"Shouldn't someone have noticed that?"

Gray shrugged. "Like a lot of people, the scientists working with Jack fell into a routine. Once he was in the pod and they turned it on, they didn't stick around to make sure everything went off without a hitch. They left to do other things."

"I can follow that," I said. "It's kind of like people who let the garage door down when they get home from work. Once they see the garage door descending, they assume it's going to go all the way down without issue, so they simply go inside without making sure it actually happened."

"Exactly. Likewise, Jack just telekinetically shut things off — pulled a switch, pressed a button, whatever.

In addition, we think there were other times when he simply teleported out of the pod before stasis was complete."

"Okay, so he liked staying up past his bedtime," I said. "Big whoop."

"Except when he was supposed to be all snug in his bed, he was out there doing the types of things that you're now complaining about."

I spent a moment pondering his statement before responding. "Paramount's cohorts. Those times when Jack was slipping out of bed is when he attacked them."

"Yep. Guess he heard they were getting out and didn't like it."

"What?" I blurted out, unable to hide my befuddlement.

"Oh, you haven't heard," Gray said casually. "I'm not surprised, since it isn't common knowledge, but many from your brother's old crew are getting out of the orange jumpsuits."

"How's that possible? People died because of what they did."

"These folks were mostly minors when they got sucked into Paramount's orbit, plus some of them say they were terrorized into doing his bidding. In essence, they've done the equivalent of serving time in juvie, so…"

He trailed off, but I finished for him. "So their records will be expunged and they get to go back to life as normal." I shook my head in disgust.

"Well, there may be some community service requirements in one form or another — you know, using their powers for the greater good to make up for their misdeeds and all that."

"In other words, each of them was probably offered some kind of deal."

"I'm not at liberty to say, but that's a safe assumption."

"I have a better idea now of why Jack was saying they needed to be punished. He thinks they're getting off light."

"Probably, but he also feels an affinity and similitude with you, which may have also guided his actions."

"What are you implying? That he attacked Incendia and those others because he thought that's what *I'd* do?"

"More likely he attacked them because that's what he thought you'd *like* to do, without regard to whether it's something you would actually follow through on."

"That's crazy."

"I don't disagree. Anyway, when his actions were discovered, a decision was made to warehouse him — keep him in stasis — until we figured out a way to control him. Suffice it to say that it didn't go well."

"What happened?"

"I'll let his handlers tell you."

Gray reached into the inside pocket of his jacket — presumably for a phone, but instead pulled out what I initially took to be notecards. A moment later, I recognized them as photos. He began handing them to me one at a time.

"This guy, as you can see, got telekinetically staked through the heart with a chair leg... This other young man got flung through a plate-glass window — took a piece of glass through the neck that almost decapitated him... This fellow fell victim to Jack's teleportation power, and to be perfectly honest, we've never actually located the other half of him…"

I frowned in distaste as Gray handed me the photos, each more gruesome than the last. Looking at them gave little room for doubt that my clone was deeply disturbed.

"And finally there's this lady," Gray said, handing me a final pic. "She was having convulsions when we found her and it wasn't until we performed a CAT scan that we discovered the problem. Apparently Jack tossed a paper clip at her head and then phased it, but made it solid again as it passed through her brain. It was surgically removed, but there was some neurological damage, so she has a long road ahead of her in terms of recovery."

"And these were his handlers?" I asked, flipping swiftly through the photos once again. "He did this to the people he interacted with on a regular basis?"

"Apparently he felt strongly about being indefinitely put into stasis."

"What about you?"

Gray frowned. "I don't understand the question."

"Well, you say he killed or incapacitated all his handlers, but you mentioned that you became involved in the process as well. Why hasn't he come after you?"

"To begin with, I wasn't involved in the day-to-day operations, so he didn't necessarily associate me with those in the photos. In addition…"

Gray seemed to pause for a moment, then cleared his throat. "Ahem. In addition, there is a psychological barrier ingrained in him against harming me."

"Wait a minute," I said, focusing on what I'd just heard. "There's some kind of mental roadblock in place that keeps him from coming after you? How convenient."

"You assume he had a reason to come after me in the first place. The truth is that he doesn't. He's barely ever laid eyes on me."

"Still, no matter what else happened with this guy, no matter how many gaskets he blew or how many gears he had come loose, you were always safe. Unbelievable. I don't even know why I'm sitting here with you."

"You're here because I can help you deal with Jack."

"Help *me* deal with it?" I uttered, nonplussed. "This is *your* mess. You should be cleaning it up."

"Perhaps, but I'm not the one implicated by Jack's actions."

I just stared at him for a moment, and then, detesting almost everything I'd heard, I teleported.

Chapter 55

I popped up in Mouse's lab. My mentor, however, was nowhere around. Eager to speak with him and share what I'd learned, I called him on my cell phone. He answered on the first ring.

"Hey," I said. "Are you coming back to the lab soon?"

"Headed there now," Mouse replied. "We were at Alpha Prime's mansion, looking into what happened earlier."

"Who's 'we'?" I asked, curious.

"Me and BT."

"Okay, I've got an update."

"Great," Mouse said. "I'll be there shortly, but BT had something to do."

"Any interest in taking a shortcut?"

****

The proposed "shortcut" generally consisted of Mouse pulling over to the side of the road and informing me of his location. I then teleported there and brought him (along with his vehicle) back to HQ. A few minutes later, we were in his lab, at which point I relayed everything that had happened since I'd last seen him.

"A clone, huh?" Mouse muttered after I finished bringing him up to speed. "Fortunately, we have probably the world's foremost expert on the subject on speed-dial."

He was talking about BT, of course. Being part of a network of clones herself, she could probably expound on the topic ad nauseum. In fact, the same could be said of BT with respect to almost any topic. Information was her

314

stock in trade, and there was very little that she didn't know or couldn't find out.

"Unfortunately," Mouse went on, "she's out of pocket at the moment, but I'll get word to her that we need her expertise."

"Sounds good," I said. "So, were you able to find out anything at the mansion?"

Mouse nodded. "Looks like your clone Jack tried to manipulate the mansion's security system — presumably via telekinesis. However, instead of turning the laser off, he boosted it up a notch and ended up getting blasted in the stomach."

"Well, seeing as how his innards weren't falling out all over the place, I'm assuming he has an advanced healing ability."

"Maybe," Mouse intoned. "You said you sensed that he had other powers. Could you tell what they were?"

I shook my head. "Nothing that we don't already know about, like the telekinesis and teleportation. However, I did pick up on the fact that he's not a telepath."

"That's interesting," Mouse remarked, his brow wrinkling in thought. "And he's been attacking Paramount's former cronies because he thinks it's what *you* want?"

"That's the way Gray seemed to put it, but I don't think it's necessarily true. It's more like Jack self-identifies with me — if that makes any sense — and views an attack on me as an attack on him."

"And apparently he views injustice to you as injustice to him."

"Injustice?" I said, puzzled — and then I realized what he meant. "Oh, you're talking about Incendia and

315

some of the others getting an early release. Yeah, Jack didn't seem to care for that."

"What about you?"

"Me?" I muttered. "What do you mean?"

"Do you feel Paramount's little syndicate has paid their debt to society?"

"If they're getting out now, I'd say their punishment was like getting a hundred lashes with a wet noodle."

"So you're not wild about it either," Mouse noted, laughing.

I shrugged, then frowned as a new thought occurred to me. "Do you think we need to put out some kind of warning about Jack?"

Mouse seemed to consider the question for a second, then shook his head. "No, I think it's enough to just focus on your inner circle for now."

"Yeah, but I'm starting to feel like a newscaster out on assignment, having to constantly give updates."

Mouse chuckled. "So basically, you're tired of having to tell the same story over and over again — maybe to me, then your family, then your friends…"

"Something like that."

"So what do you want, a Jack-the-Clone hotline, where people can call in and get the latest?"

"It would be a start."

"Not gonna happen," Mouse said flatly, although I could sense that he was amused. "Look, I honestly don't know what you're complaining about. As a telepath, you can mentally convey almost any story you want in virtually any amount of detail — all in about two seconds. Is it really that tedious?"

I sighed. "It's not so much telling the same thing again and again. Given the current situation, it's necessary, and I admit that I can bring people up to speed a lot faster telepathically than I can verbally."

Mouse gave me a look of incomprehension. "So what's the problem?"

"In all honesty, I just don't like spending a lot of time running around inside my friends' heads," I confessed. "Things have a tendency to slip through."

"Huh?" Mouse muttered. "What kind of things?"

"Things a good friend probably wouldn't tell you, and that you most likely wouldn't want to hear," I explained. "I mean, do you really want to know that your friends think you're a terrible dancer, or that you look stupid in that hat, or they hate your chicken parmesan?"

"Hold on," Mouse said, looking gravely serious. "You don't like my chicken parmesan?"

I just stared at him for a moment, and then we both started laughing.

"Okay," he said a few seconds later, still grinning, "I understand your point. But right now, you're our fastest and most reliable form of communication regarding this Jack situation. More importantly, you're also the most secure method at the moment."

"What do you mean?" I asked, trying to make sense of his statement.

"Well, you said that Jack isn't telepathic, right? But you are. So, if you make everyone close to you aware of that fact, the next time you're looking to confirm your identity with them…"

"I just have to communicate with them telepathically," I blurted out, finishing my mentor's thought. "And that way everyone will know it's the real me and not Jack. It's genius!"

"Well, I wasn't going to toot my own horn," Mouse said, with a faux sheepish look on his face. "But if *you* say so, I'm fine with it."

We both laughed again, and for about the millionth time I marveled at how well Mouse and I got along, such as our ability to find humor even in serious situations. I wasn't sure that I'd ever said it out loud, but I counted myself lucky that he was my mentor, and I knew he felt the same with respect to me.

However, this particular meeting of our two-man, mutual admiration society was promptly dismissed when Mouse, after regaining his composure, abruptly stated that he had work to do.

"I've got some stuff I still need to look at," he said. "Why don't you take off, and I'll let you know when we can circle up again."

With no other real options, I agreed and took my leave.

REPLICATION

Chapter 56

After departing the lab, I went in search of Myshtal and Smokey. Despite everything that had happened since Vestibule teleported me to her park, I actually hadn't been gone particularly long — less than two hours. Thus, it wasn't that surprising that I found my friends exactly where I'd left them: in the teen lounge, presently engaged in a game of table tennis (which Myshtal showed surprising aptitude for).

Upon noting my presence, they cut their game short and — after confirming that he was in — we all went to Li's quarters. Once there, I gave everyone an update on recent events as we sat in the living room, although I didn't go into detail about Jack's interaction with Vestibule. (She was humiliated enough as it was; it would suffice for others to simply know that Jack had been in contact with her.)

"So your evil twin is actually a clone?" Smokey asked when I finished. "That's arguably worse than an evil twin."

"No kidding," I grumbled. "But at least you'll be able to figure out if it's me or not."

Smokey nodded. "If he doesn't give us the telepathic high sign, he's a phony."

"What about Li?" Myshtal interjected. "I don't think your telepathy works with him."

"I have my own means of discerning the true Jim," Li assured her.

Smokey's brow furrowed in thought for a moment. "So what do you think he wants? I mean, it's nice to know he wasn't trying to frame you — assuming that's true — but the way he's approached people has to mean something."

"I agree," chimed in Li. "His raining fire and brimstone down upon miscreants does not neatly dovetail into duping your confederates."

"Hold on," Smokey protested. "I'd argue that 'duping' is kind of strong. Rather than being duped, I think it's more appropriate to say I was—"

"Punked?" Myshtal suggested.

Caught completely flatfooted by her comment, Smokey just looked at her with an expression that seemed to combine amusement, shock, and bewilderment.

"Hoaxed," he finally declared after a few seconds. "I was going to say 'hoaxed.'" He then turned to me and, hooking a thumb towards Myshtal, said, "Your girl obviously ranks television as the leading authority on Earth culture."

A moment later — maybe tipped off by the look on my face — Smokey winced and added, "The princess, I mean. Myshtal. Not your girl. Not Electra." Then, clearly aware that he was rambling, Smokey muttered, "Whatever. My point is, you might want to have her crack open a book now and then."

Giggling, Myshtal stated. "I have read books extensively since I arrived. I have al—"

"Okay, okay," I interrupted. "That's enough of the sidebar conversation. Let's just assume that nobody got punked, nobody's a couch potato, and everybody loves a good book. Now, can we get back to the subject of Jack?"

"We were discussing what he might want," Li said. "What his goal might be in seeking out friends and close associates of Jim."

"You sound like you might have a theory," I reasoned.

"It is more conjecture than theory," Li admitted, "and stems from the fact that — aside from those he attacked — his demeanor when dealing with others has generally been reported as affable and congenial."

"So in terms of what he's after, what exactly does that mean?" Smokey asked.

"I believe it means that he wants friends," Li replied.

REPLICATION

Chapter 57

No one really bought into Li's hypothesis about Jack simply wanting some amigos to hang out with. Just the fact that he was out there pretending to be me gave the impression that a larger, more nefarious plot was at work. Thus, the rest of us spent a little time trying to blast holes in our friend's theory before Smokey announced that he had to get going. That was the impetus for me and Myshtal to leave as well. (I was also spurred by the sudden recollection of another situation that I had to deal with.) Thus, after saying our goodbyes, I teleported the two of us back to the embassy.

We popped up in the kitchen. Prior to my taking off with Vestibule, I had left Myshtal in the teen lounge with a power bar and some fruit, but I didn't know if she'd properly eaten. My teleporting us to the kitchen was a way to sort of make up for that, which I admitted.

"Thanks for thinking of me," Myshtal said of my gesture, "but I'm fine until dinner."

"Great," I said. "Also, while I hate to dash off, I've got something I need to attend to."

"No problem," she insisted. "Go, go."

"Thanks, but just so you know, you may be on your own for supper. No one's home at the moment."

I then explained that, telepathically, I wasn't sensing anyone else, which meant that my mother and grandparents were out.

"I'll be fine," Myshtal assured me. "Just go. I'll let everyone know what's been happening when they get back."

REPLICATION

As she spoke, she made a shooing motion with her hand, essentially telling me to leave. Chuckling, I did as instructed and teleported.

****

I didn't immediately leave the embassy; instead, I popped up in my room, then proceeded to pull out my phone and call Electra.

"Hello, my love," she said in a honeyed voice after the first ring.

"Uh, hi," I replied, a little surprised at both her tone and choice of words, as she usually avoided using the term "love" in reference to me. (Basically, it was a reminder that I — allegedly — didn't have her heart locked down yet.)

"As always, it's great to hear your voice, lambchop," she teasingly stated.

"Um, thanks. Listen, are you at home?"

"Of course. Where else would I be, sweetness?"

I frowned, thinking that the terminology she was using was distinctly out of character, but not sure what it meant.

"Well, I need to talk to you about something," I stressed. "Would it be okay if I came by?"

"Certainly, sugar lump. Whatever your heart desires."

Okay, something was definitely off. Electra would occasionally use terms of affection, but at the moment she was laying it on pretty thick. And then the truth hit me.

I let out a deep sigh and said, "You already know, don't you?"

"Know what, dear heart?" she asked, a hint of surprise in her voice.

323

"Vestibule," I said flatly.

"Oh. You mean that tongue-wrestling session the two of you had in the teen lounge? I may have heard a rumor."

There was a short silence (although it felt long and uncomfortable), that was finally broken by me saying, "Okay, that's what I wanted to talk to you about. If you give me a minute, I can explain everything."

"You've got thirty seconds," she replied, now sounding like her usual self. "And the clock's ticking."

Not wasting a moment, I teleported to my girlfriend's house.

REPLICATION

Chapter 58

As it turns out, I didn't need the full thirty seconds to convince Electra of my sincerity. As soon as I got to her house, I reached out telepathically and showed her everything I'd learned about my clone — including how he'd deceived Vestibule — in just a few moments.

"Oh my…" she began after I severed the mental link between us. "Jim…that's awful! I mean, Vestibule's not my favorite person, but what he did to her was horrible."

I nodded. "I know, but you can't tell anyone. Vestibule's embarrassed enough as it is."

"Of course," she uttered sympathetically. "I'd never say anything."

"Good," I stressed. "The only reason I showed you everything is so you'd understand what happened in the lounge."

"Honestly, I wasn't too concerned about that," she confessed.

I raised an eyebrow in surprise. "No?"

"Not really," she confirmed, shaking her head. "Unexpectedly kissing you is something Vestibule's done before, and from what I heard, that's essentially what happened."

"Then why act like you were upset?" I asked. "I brought along extra kneepads thinking I was going to have to do some epic groveling to get back in your good graces."

She laughed. "I *was* upset — but it was because you didn't tell me what happened. Instead, I had to hear about it through the grapevine."

"Well, in case you missed the other part," I said defensively, "I was busy focusing on locating my evil twin and finding out what his game plan is."

"Oh, quit pouting," she cooed as she stepped close, slipped her arms around me, and gave me a quick peck on the lips. "Better?"

"Not really," I replied, giving her a sly look. "Maybe you should give it another go, but act like you mean it this time."

She giggled. "I'm not falling for that one again." Playfully pushing me away, she added, "Besides, I have a project to finish for school."

"So, should I leave?"

"Not necessarily," Electra said. "You know where everything is here — the living room, the TV, the remote. Why don't you make yourself at home while I finish, and when I'm done, I'll order some pizza and we can watch a movie."

"Sounds great," I admitted.

A moment later I was heading towards the living room, hoping there was something good on television.

REPLICATION

Chapter 59

I spent the next few hours with my girlfriend, who had the ordering of pizza down to a science; it arrived at almost the exact moment she finished her school project.

"Esper and I order from this place all the time," she explained. "We pretty much know how long it's going to take them to deliver, give or take a minute."

Mention of Electra's guardian, Esper, brought to mind the fact that I hadn't sensed her when I'd arrived. Like my family, Esper was a telepath, so I usually had a pretty good idea when she was around. (Actually, I always got the impression that Esper *wanted* me to know when she was around, just in case I started getting any ideas.) It just so happened, however, that Esper was out on assignment, so Electra and I ended up without a chaperone on this particular occasion.

That said, we primarily used the opportunity to simply snuggle on the couch. Electra picked the movie, which turned out to be some schlock about space vampires, and we spent most of the film hilariously picking it apart in terms of the terrible plot, bad acting, and poor special effects.

However, as was typical when I was with Electra, the time just seemed to fly by. Before I knew it, the movie had finished and it was time for me to go. After getting a goodnight hug from my girlfriend (and stealing a kiss), I teleported home.

Popping up in my bedroom at the embassy, I gave a telepathic hello to my family (all of whom I could now sense were at home). I then stretched out on the bed for a moment, staring at the ceiling as I reflected on my day. It had been long and exhausting, to be honest, so saying I was tired was an understatement. I closed my eyes for a moment — just to think — and before I knew it, I was completely knocked out.

****

I woke up the next morning feeling refreshed; there's a lot to be said for a good night's sleep. I glanced at my cell phone and noted that it was still early — not catch-a-school-bus early (like the previous day), but early enough that no one could brand me as having slept in. I also saw that I had a text from Mouse asking me to meet him in his lab a little later.

With nothing pressing at the moment, I went through my morning routine at a normal pace for the first time in days, including taking a long, relaxing shower. Afterwards, I got dressed and went downstairs.

I found my grandparents in the breakfast area again, huddled up against each other as before while looking through the paper.

Indigo greeted me with a smile, saying, "Good morning, *Sxibbo*."

"Good morning," I said in response, then pointed towards the newspaper with my chin. "Wow, you guys are really getting into the periodicals lately."

"It's your grandfather," Indigo contended. "It's been awhile since he's seen his name in the paper, but after they ran that picture of us a few days ago, followed by articles about the party, he's become obsessed with seeing his name in print."

"Not true," Gramps protested. "First of all, I generally read articles online, but when they printed our picture, the newspaper also gave us a free, one-year subscription. So the paper in my hand every morning is a sign of free delivery, not egotistical obsession."

"Oh, just listen to him justify his actions," Indigo joked, giggling.

Ignoring her, my grandfather went on. "Second, if you must know, rather than scouring for something about myself, I'm actually reading an article about a congressman who voted to raise the minimum wage yesterday, even though he was opposed to the law up until a few days ago. Claims he must have been hypnotized or drugged, because he doesn't remember the vote at all."

My grandmother rolled her eyes. "Seems that politicians are the same everywhere — always trying to avoid taking responsibility for their actions."

Her comment was a subtle reminder that, back on Caeles, she was always neck-deep in political intrigue and hated every second of it. However, despite her disgust at the constant shifting of alliances, backroom deals, and so on, she was actually very good at it.

"Anyway," I said, "I've got some things to do, so I'm going to take off."

"Not without breakfast," Gramps admonished. "It's still the most important meal of the day."

"Yeah — right after breakfast," I concurred. "I was going to say that, but you didn't let me finish."

My grandparents snickered, then Indigo said, "That's your grandfather's ego again. He made pancakes this morning, so nobody's escaping today without trying them."

"What do you mean, 'escape'?" Gramps asked indignantly. "No one tries to get *away* from my pancakes. People run *to* my pancakes. Ex-cons break back into prison for my pancakes. Olympic athletes trade their gold medals for my pancakes. World-famous chefs call me, begging for the recipe so they…"

Chuckling, I left my grandparents and headed to the kitchen, with my grandfather's praise of his pancakes echoing in my ears.

REPLICATION

Chapter 60

After locating a stack of pancakes in the microwave, I wolfed down a couple of them in short order. Gramps may have exaggerated about their appeal, but not by much, in my opinion. He really did have notable culinary skills, and his pancakes (which were truly delicious) were just a small example.

Upon finishing, I noted that it was close to the time I was supposed to meet with Mouse. I told my grandparents that I would see them later and telepathically passed along the same message to Mom (who was once again in her office, working). Surprisingly, no one in my family seemed to express an interest in the situation with my evil twin. I took that to mean that Myshtal had done as promised and apprised them all of recent events. Then, after promising to be careful, I teleported.

****

I reappeared in Mouse's lab. My mentor was already there, along with BT.

"Right on time," Mouse announced, glancing at a clock on the wall.

"Please tell me you guys have something," I pleaded.

"We've got information," BT replied, "but there are a lot of moving parts. Where do you want to begin?"

"I don't care," I replied. "Start with anything that's going to distinguish this clone from me so I can clear my name."

"Well, for starters, he's not a clone," Mouse clarified.

REPLICATION

"What?!" I exclaimed, giving him a look of incomprehension.

"He said that Jack's not a clone," BT reported. "And he isn't. Not a true clone, anyway."

"You lost me," I admitted, shaking my head.

"Let's start with the basics," BT said. "Cloning generally refers to producing a genetic copy of some biological structure or organism, and there are actually several different types of cloning. Gene cloning, for example, involves making copies of a segment of DNA. Therapeutic cloning, on the other hand, relates to copying genetic material for the ultimate goal of providing stem cells for the treatment of injury or disease. Then there's reproductive cloning, which relates to creating an exact genetic replica of an organism."

I nodded in understanding. "I take it that last — reproductive cloning — is the one we're concerned with."

"Correct," Mouse agreed. "Without getting too far into the science, in reproductive cloning you take DNA from the original organism and use it to make a copy."

"And that's what they did to create Jack," I concluded.

Neither Mouse nor BT immediately responded. Instead, they exchanged a knowing glance and then BT spoke up.

"That's not exactly what occurred," she intoned.

"You know, that's the second time you guys have indicated that there's something other than cloning going on here," I remarked. "Can someone just give me the straight dope?"

BT sighed. "I've known you — your family — for a long time, Jim, and for most of your life I've probably been the closest thing you've had to a doctor. I've had numerous opportunities to examine you, check out your biological systems, analyze your blood and tissues. In the course of doing all that, one of the first things I realized is that your DNA doesn't lend itself to cloning."

"Hold on," I almost snapped, suddenly anxious. "Are you saying you tried to clone me?"

"Never," BT protested adamantly. "But based on my own experience, I could tell that traditional cloning methods aren't feasible with you. There's a portion of your DNA that, simply put, will not replicate the way typical genetic material will when cloning is attempted."

"So is that a good thing or a bad thing?" I asked. "Because it almost sounds like you're saying something's wrong with me."

BT laughed. "No, we're not saying it's bad. We're just saying it's different — your DNA simply doesn't conform to normal behavior."

"In other words," Mouse quipped, "even at the cellular level, you won't do what's expected of you."

"Funny," I said sarcastically, while trying (and failing) not to smile.

"We assume it has something to do with your singular genetic make-up," Mouse continued. "It's almost as if some part of your DNA recognizes that cloning is not a natural process and refuses to cooperate."

"So I've got good genes," I concluded. "But if my DNA isn't susceptible to cloning, how'd they create Jack?"

"We were able to retrieve some of his genetic material from the room in the mansion where he was shot," Mouse said. "From all appearances, they seemingly replaced the uncooperative portion of your DNA with some other genetic stock."

"Wait," I insisted, holding up a hand for emphasis. "How'd they even get my DNA in the first place?"

Mouse gave me a patronizing look. "So you've never had a haircut? Have you hung on to every toothbrush you've ever used? When you finish a bottle of juice or water, do you take it home with you and put it in a hope chest or something?"

"Okay, fine — there's a million ways to get my DNA," I conceded. "Apparently just from stuff that gets thrown out every day."

"Actually, Mouse may have slightly exaggerated," BT said. "When you get a haircut, the hair that's clipped is made up of dead cells that doesn't contain viable DNA — just like your outer skin."

"Huh?" I murmured, confused.

"She's talking about the stratum corneum — the outer layer of your epidermis," Mouse explained. "It's made up of dead cells and a ton of them slough off every day, but there's no useful DNA in them."

My brow crinkled as I considered this. "So you're saying that if you peel back the outermost layer of my skin, there's like a fresh new me underneath?"

"Sort of," Mouse said. "As I mentioned, there's a thin mantle of dead skin covering your whole body, but human beings don't discard it the way you're describing. There's not going to be some husk laying around like a snake that just shed its skin."

"Unless, I just teleport the portion of me that's beneath the dead skin," I suggested. "That would leave a husk."

Mouse just stared at me in disbelief for a moment, then muttered, "Why do I get the feeling that this conversation is foreshadowing some elaborate Halloween prank?"

I laughed. "What makes you think I'll wait until Halloween?"

We both chortled at that, causing BT to huff slightly in annoyance (while trying not to smile).

"If I can get you two juveniles back on point?" she chided.

"Okay, fine," I said. "We were talking about how Gray's minions might have gotten my DNA — basically from things I regularly toss out. I guess I just hadn't thought about the lengths someone might go to in order to get it, like digging through my trash."

"From what I've heard of Gray," Mouse said, "it wouldn't surprise me if he sent guys crawling up your sewer line, if it would get him what he wanted."

"Okay, that's mental imagery I didn't need," I muttered, causing BT to giggle this time. "Anyway, I think I understand now why you're saying Jack's not a true clone. Genetically, he's not a pure, one-hundred-percent replica of me because of the DNA substitution."

"Right," BT agreed with a nod. "He's maybe ninety percent you, max, with the remainder coming from some other genetic source."

I rubbed my chin in thought for a moment. "So, this replacement DNA — where'd they get it?"

BT shrugged. "Who knows? It could have come from anyone."

"Well, can't you guys look at the DNA string in question and figure all that out?" I asked.

"We appreciate the faith you have in our abilities," Mouse stated, "but it's not that simple. It's like finding fingerprints at a crime scene. Unless you can match them to a set on file somewhere, you can't say who they belong to without something more. So, unless you've got a genetic database for all the billions of people on this planet, we're a little stuck on that front."

"Not to mention the fact that the DNA segment in question might not have even come from a single source," BT added.

"You mean it might have come from more than one person?" I asked, a little stunned.

"It's unlikely they were successful in creating Jack with a single trial," BT said. "My guess is they tried various formulations — including hybridized DNA — until they hit upon one that worked."

I shook my head in dismay. "Okay, this is way more complex than I ever imagined."

"Don't get wrapped up in the minutiae," Mouse advised. "The exact composition of his DNA isn't pertinent. The main thing is that *having* his DNA gets us a lot closer to clearing your name."

"But like you said earlier, this is the equivalent of prints without a match," I argued. "We need Jack *in carne ed ossa*."

"'In the flesh,'" Mouse translated, impressed. "Kudos on the Latin."

I gave a brief nod to acknowledge his compliment, while BT stuck to the subject at hand.

"Holding Jack in place is easier said than done, given his power of teleportation," she noted. "That's one ability his handlers were effective in developing."

Her words striking me as odd, I gave BT a curious look. "What do you mean?"

BT appeared to reflect for a moment before answering. "Do you recall when your teleportation ability first manifested?"

"Yeah," I replied. "I was like five years old and getting whaled on by an older bully. I kept wishing he was somewhere else, and all of a sudden, he was."

"Using that as an example," BT said, "under the proper circumstances, your powers seem to develop when needed. It makes you possibly the most versatile super on the planet. Understanding this and knowing your power set, Jack's handlers were well aware of his potential."

"In essence," Mouse added, "they knew the types of abilities he was capable of developing. They simply had to coax them out of him."

"Coax in what way?" I asked.

Neither BT nor Mouse immediately answered. Instead, my mentor pointed to one of the large monitors positioned around the lab.

The screen suddenly showed an odd scene: several people in white lab coats standing around an odd glass cylinder that was about six feet tall and three feet in diameter. Inside the cylinder, wearing what appeared to be a pair of swimming trunks, was a young boy — maybe nine years old. At that moment, my mouth almost fell open when I realized something: the kid in the cylinder looked exactly like me when I was that age.

Jack, I thought.

He looked nervous, and apparently he had good reason to be, because a few seconds later, the cylinder started filling up with water — fast.

The folks in the lab coats — presumably scientists — watched in utter fascination as the water quickly rose. Jack's expression, on the other hand, had gone from nervous to anxious as the water climbed to his waist — and then to terrified as it reached his chest. By that time, he was beating on the interior of the cylinder (which I now recognized as a water tank), pleading with the scientists, beseeching them to let him out. There was no audio, but you didn't need it to see that Jack was begging for his life.

As the water continued going up, Jack rose with it, frantically moving his arms and legs and tilting his head back to keep his face in the small but shrinking pocket of air at the top of the tank. He also still appeared to be screaming for help.

"He's drowning," I said flatly.

"Technically, he's in aquatic distress," Mouse corrected.

"The main difference," BT chimed in before I could ask, "is that when you're in aquatic distress, you can still move your arms and legs voluntarily, as well as call out for help. When you're drowning, your body employs an automatic reaction known as the instinctive drowning response. When that happens, your arms move out laterally to the side and your head tilts back."

"And it's all involuntary," Mouse added. "You have no conscious control at that point. You can't even shout for help."

"That's not how they show it in the movies and on television," I protested.

"Then I just don't understand," Mouse uttered in mock confusion. "Because they *never* put anything inaccurate in movies or on TV — it would be like reading something on the internet that wasn't true."

I was immediately tempted to give a smart-aleck response, and was on the verge of doing so when BT cut in.

REPLICATION

"It's called 'dramatic license,'" she said. "Producers and directors portray certain things unrealistically to increase the drama or interest of the audience. But Mouse is right: actual drowning doesn't involve any flailing about or shouting. Thus, a person could be drowning ten feet from you, and you'd never know it."

As if giving credence to what I'd just heard, Jack no longer appeared to be calling for aid. His head was tilted back and his arms were out to the side, exactly as BT had explained.

"*Now* he's drowning," Mouse uttered dispassionately.

A few seconds later, there was no air left in the tank and Jack was completely submerged. He seemed to float for a few seconds and then slowly descend. As he did, his mouth opened, releasing a short stream of bubbles. A moment later, his chest expanded, and I cringed, realizing that he was breathing in water. His eyes, still open, began to take on a glassy look.

The attendant scientists abruptly began talking among themselves — hopefully discussing whether to get Jack out. However, the conversation was cut short as Jack, completely soaked, suddenly appeared on the floor in front of them, collapsing to all fours and spewing water from his mouth like a fire hydrant.

He had teleported.

An odd scene then ensued, with the scientists cheering, high-fiving, and otherwise enthusiastically congratulating each other, while Jack — still on his hands and knees — retched his guts out.

Chapter 61

"Okay," I muttered as Mouse turned the video off. "That was unexpected."

BT nodded. "As I stated, they had effective methods for developing Jack's abilities."

"You mentioned *coaxing* his powers out," I corrected. "You made it sound like they gave him a cookie if he did something right. I wasn't expecting this water torture cell."

"Their approach was unorthodox," BT admitted.

"Unorthodox?" I repeated. "Try *extreme*. What would they do if they wanted him to fly — toss him out of an airplane?"

Mouse and BT exchanged a glance, but neither spoke.

"You've got to be joking," I said. "They threw him out of a plane without a chute?"

"Let's just say we've confirmed that he can fly," Mouse responded.

Incredulous, I simply shook my head. I took a few moments to get my head back in the game and then said, "Alright, what else you got?"

****

We spent a little time watching more footage of Jack's powers (or the attempted development of them). The videos came courtesy of BT, who — as previously mentioned — took in information the way ordinary people breathe air. With clones presumably at the highest levels of government, industry, and academia, there was little she couldn't find out.

Of the other clips we viewed, the one that drew my attention the most involved an attempt to gauge Jack's telepathic abilities. This one actually had audio, and essentially involved a female scientist pulling what appeared to be playing cards from a nearby deck. (At a guess, I thought it was the woman Gray had showed me a photo of, but it was difficult to tell without her face being twisted by paroxysms.) Jack, sitting at a table across from her, would attempt to guess which card she held.

More often than not, he failed at the task. This would result in Jack getting angrily berated by the scientist, with each additional failure causing a notable increase in the verbal abuse. At one juncture, she grew so furious and frustrated that she actually leaned across the table and slapped him. The blow was so forceful that it snapped his head to the side, and the sound of it seemed to reverberate in the air long after he'd been struck.

"I'd say that supports the theory that he's not telepathic," Mouse commented after we were done viewing that particular video.

"Yeah, but we still don't know what he's up to," I said. "What's on the next page of his playbook."

"Maybe nothing," BT suggested. "Maybe he just blends into the background now. Disappears. If he's truly a shapeshifter, it should be easy enough."

"But if that's the plan, why reach out to Jim?" Mouse asked. "Why show up in Alpha Prime's mansion? Why go on a date with Vestibule?"

"Li's theory is that he wants friends," I offered.

Mouse seemed to consider this for a moment. "It's possible. I mean, it's not like his home life was warm and nurturing."

"And maybe it's easier for him to form relationships with people who already view him as a comrade," BT suggested. "Or rather, those who view Jim that way."

"Perhaps," Mouse droned, not sounding convinced. "Anyway, we've been going at this for a while now. I say we break for lunch and then maybe BT and I can tackle this situation from a fresh angle with food in our bellies."

"What about me?" I asked. "Aren't I included?"

"Well, you certainly aren't *ex*cluded," BT assured me. "I think Mouse was just making it clear that you aren't required to stay."

"At the moment, I've got nothing more pressing than this," I reminded them. "Plus, I'd probably be hanging out here anyway, even if we didn't have this issue with Jack."

Mouse glanced at BT. "He's probably right. He spends so much time here that it's practically his lab, too."

"How about this?" I interjected. "I'll run out and grab lunch — my treat — and we can figure out afterwards whether it's worthwhile for me to hang around."

"Far be it from me to turn down a free lunch," Mouse said. "Alright, make it happen."

REPLICATION

Chapter 62

For lunch, I teleported from Mouse's lab to Jackman's — a local grill owned by a couple of former superhero sidekicks. It was an eatery that was frequented by a fair number of supers, and not just in support of two of our own. They actually served great food. The place was also a favorite hangout for a lot of super teens, including me and my friends, and we usually came by at least once a week.

I popped up in the parking lot. Based on the number of cars present, there didn't seem to be a lot of patrons — a fact that was proved correct when I went inside the grill a moment later. (Of course, it was the middle of the school day, so the throngs of teens that I typically saw when I came here were all in class.)

I went straight to the takeout counter, intending to make a quick to-go order. When I got there, however, the waitress on the other side, a twenty-something brunette wearing a hairnet, placed a bag on the counter and pushed it towards me.

"Here's your order," she announced. "Right on time."

"Excuse me?" I muttered in confusion.

"Your order," she repeated. "I told you it would be ready in ten, and it was — almost on the dot."

"I'm sorry," I said, "but I think there's been some mistake. I haven't ordered yet."

She giggled. "Well, if it wasn't you, it must have been your twin brother."

"Except I don't have a…"

I stopped speaking, the words frozen in my throat as reality set in.

343

"Look," the waitress said, "it's already paid for, so you might as well take it."

She then walked away, headed back to the kitchen.

I stood there stunned for a moment. Jack had been here, not fifteen minutes earlier. Plus, bearing in mind that he'd ordered food, there was an expectation that he'd be back soon.

However, before I could make plans on how to best utilize that information, I heard a soft heads-up whistle that seemed to be directed at me. I turned in the direction of the sound and then stared.

There, sitting in a booth and waving me over, was Jack.

REPLICATION

Chapter 63

I frowned, suddenly ill at ease. By coming here, this faux clone was overtly invading another aspect of my life, and I didn't like it. However, understanding that there was an opportunity here, I decided to take him up on the invite to join him and began walking over. However, I hadn't taken three steps before he cleared his throat and then nodded towards the bag the waitress had placed on the counter. Rolling my eyes, I turned around and grabbed it, and then resumed my approach to his booth, with Jack smiling broadly the entire while.

When I reached him, I tossed his order onto the table and sat down across from him. Ignoring me for the moment, he opened up the bag and took out a burger and an order of fries.

"Oh, man," he practically gushed, "this looks great."

"What are you doing here, Jack?" I asked.

He gave me an appraising glance. "You know my name. Someone's done their homework."

I ignored his comment. "I'll ask again. What are you doing here?"

Having just taken a bite of his burger (which seemed to be loaded with lettuce, tomatoes, and everything else), he held up a forefinger to indicate I should give him a moment while he swallowed his food.

"I would have thought that was obvious," he replied. "Getting lunch."

"Yeah, but why *here*?"

"Why not? This is one of our favorite places."

"No, it's not one of *our* favorite places," I corrected. "It's one of *my* favorite places."

"Well, I'm you," he insisted.

"No, you're not. If you were me, you wouldn't have to avoid certain people because they can tell the difference between us. If you were me, you'd know I take my burgers with veggies on the side. If you were me, the security system in my father's mansion would have recognized your biometrics and gone passive instead of blasting a hole in your midsection."

"Well, I'm you to the extent it matters, such as for any major purposes."

"Major purposes?" I echoed. "What does that mean?"

Jack seemed to contemplate for a moment before answering. "You'd agree with me that there's currently conflict between countries all over the globe, right? Everything from border skirmishes to open warfare."

"Okay," I muttered, not sure where this was going.

"Now, just imagine for a second that the leaders of two warring nations suddenly sit down next week and sign a peace treaty. And then two more a few days later, and then two more shortly after that, and so on. We could be on the cusp of world peace within a month."

"It's a nice dream," I noted, "but good luck with making it reality. You're talking about armed conflict that, in some cases, has been going on for decades. Getting the appropriate politicians and heads of state to change their minds in a week — which is what you seem to be suggesting — simply isn't going to happen."

"I'm not talking about changing their minds. I'm talking about changing the person making the decision."

"What, replacing them? That involves new candidates for the requisite positions, them running for office, winning their respective elections, and so on. And all this assumes we're talking about countries with some kind of democratic political system as opposed to a dictatorship or a monarchy."

Jack laughed. "You're overthinking this. Isn't there a way we could replace them almost immediately?"

I frowned. "Not without somebody dying. And even if world leaders did start dropping like flies, there's always someone next in line, but you don't know if that person's going to care about things that are important to you. I mean, you don't know how they'll feel about global issues like world peace and nuclear proliferation, or even topics that hit close to home, like access to health care, education, minimum wage…"

I trailed off unexpectedly as my thoughts veered in a new direction, prompted by my brain suddenly connecting the dots between my current conversation and something I'd heard earlier.

"That congressman," I droned. "The one who voted differently than anticipated on the minimum wage law. It was you."

Jack gave me a sly smile. "You know, telekinesis makes it ever so easy to drug somebody." He nodded towards the end of our table, where a set of salt and pepper shakers were located. As I watched, the salt shaker rose up about an inch and then tilted slightly, spilling a bit of its contents upon the table before going back to its original position. However, the action was so subtle that, had Jack not called my attention to it, I might never have noticed it.

"So you inconspicuously slip him some knockout drops," I summed up. "Presumably something untraceable — maybe in his coffee, or juice, or the glass of wine he sips to relax after work — and then shapeshift into him and vote the way you want."

347

"Pretty much," Jack agreed.

"And now you want to step up your game — take it up a notch. Go from domestic affairs to global politics."

"It's the level where I think I can do the most good."

"Good?" I said incredulously. "You don't see anything wrong, morally, with what you've done or what you're proposing?"

He shrugged. "I guess I see it as the ends justifying the means. But in terms of the world peace I mentioned, I can't do it alone. I can shapeshift into one person, but not two — not at the same time, anyway."

There was no need for him to break it down any further. I clearly knew exactly what he was suggesting.

"You're crazy," I blurted out. "There's no way I'm helping you with this insane plan."

"That's hurtful, Jim," Jack said, but in a tone that didn't imply that he felt pained at all. "Especially coming from you, since we're the same person."

"We're not the same person!" I practically hissed, trying to keep from raising my voice.

"Well, we'll just have to agree to disagree on that point," he declared with a slight smile. Emotionally, I could sense that he found my position on the subject amusing.

"Regardless," he went on, "world peace is just the tip of the iceberg. There's so much more we can do, so much we can achieve, if we work together."

"There's no working together," I stressed. "Look, Jack, simply based on the things you've done, your moral compass is off. You don't seem to draw a strong distinction between right and wrong. That said, I don't blame you entirely for that. I know what they did to you — what they put you through to cause the development of your powers."

Without warning, I felt heated emotions — led by unbridled animus and fierce resentment — roiling in Jack like a tempest.

"You can't imagine all the things they did to me," he growled with balled fists. "The things they'd *still* be doing if I'd let them…"

There was a faraway look in his eyes, and from the emotional vibe I was picking up, I knew that he was remembering some deep-rooted trauma he had experienced. His pain seemed so palpable that even a person without empathic abilities would have picked up on it, and — despite the things he'd done — I couldn't help feeling sorry for him.

"But hey," he blurted, snapping out of his reverie, "that's all in the past. We've got other fish to fry. I'm taking off now, but just think about what I said. We can do great things together."

And then he was gone, along with his food.

Chapter 64

"I'm not seeing any lunch," Mouse noted critically when I teleported back to his lab.

"Change of plans," I said, then recounted my recent *tête-à-tête* with Jack.

"And this just happened?" BT asked when I finished.

"Yes," I confirmed. "A few minutes ago. I came straight here afterwards."

A solemn expression settled on BT's face. "Any idea where he went?"

"No," I answered, emphatically shaking my head. "But I think it's safe to assume at this juncture that he does not intend to go gently into that good night."

"No doubt," Mouse agreed, "but in speaking to you, he's given us info that we didn't have before."

"You mean his plans for world peace?" I inquired.

"More like world domination," BT asserted. "Because if you're talking about replacing world leaders — even temporarily — to significantly alter the course of global events, then there's no other term for it."

"Well, I'm not just focusing on that," Mouse said. "I'm also talking about Jack's power set. In pretending to be that congressman, he confirmed that he's a shapeshifter."

"Huh?" I muttered, puzzled. "I thought we already knew that."

"No," BT chimed in. "I think initially there was an *assumption* that he was a shapeshifter because he looked like you on tape. We've since learned that his natural features replicate your own. Thus, even when he was pretending to

350

be you, he never had to alter his appearance. This is the first indication that he can actually look like someone else."

"Hmmm," I droned, thinking. "So there's this broad overlap between his power set and mine."

"Yeah, but that's to be expected," BT contended. "Even though he's not a true clone, a good portion of his biology is sourced from you, so it makes sense that he has a lot of the same talents."

"But there are still some abilities I have that he doesn't," I noted. "Like telepathy."

"What's your point?" Mouse asked.

"It sort of begs the question," I said. "What powers does *he* possess that *I* don't have?"

Mouse and BT exchanged a glance, and I could tell from their expressions that my question wasn't one that they had previously considered. However, before either of them could comment, my phone rang.

I glanced at it, and then became immediately annoyed when I saw who was trying to reach me: an anonymous caller.

Gray.

Chapter 65

"First, let me say thanks for meeting with me," Gray began. "You took off yesterday before we actually had a chance to finish our conversation."

"No thanks necessary," I said. "Just get to the point, Gray."

We were in the back seat of the SUV again. After taking his call, we had agreed to meet up as we had last time, and I had immediately teleported from Mouse's lab to the appropriate street corner, where Gray's vehicle had been waiting for me.

"Well, I know that you've crossed paths with Jack a couple of times," Gray began. "I just wanted to tell you to be careful in dealing with him."

I didn't respond. Instead, I simply waited, sure that there was more to come, but after a few seconds it became clear that Gray had said his piece.

"Wait — that's it?" I asked in surprise. "You had me come all the way across town just to tell me *that*? As if I didn't know after the things he's done?"

"You act as though you had to take a taxi, the subway, and two metro buses to get here," Gray countered, chuckling. "And yes, I had you come so I could give you a warning, because I thought it was necessary."

"And why is that?"

"Because — even though you know what Jack's capable of — you're not likely to see that side of him. Generally, he's going to be on his best behavior around you."

"What's so special about me?"

"You mean other than the fact that he's basically a clone of you?" Gray asked sardonically. "In essence, he wants you to like him. It's important to him."

I frowned. Gray's words had a ring of truth to them, and Jack's demeanor did comport with what I was hearing.

"That's a tall order, considering the things he's done," I finally said.

"Paramount did things that were just as bad — maybe worse. You're best buds with him now."

"That's an entirely different situation, but I will say this: I don't blame Jack for being the way he is. I saw the things that he was put through. It was enough to unhinge anybody, let alone a kid."

Gray nodded. "I know what you're talking about, and yes — what happened to him was horrible. If I'd known about it, I would have stopped it. Putting a halt to those kinds of things is part of the reason why I got involved."

"Oh, come off it, Gray!" I snapped. "You don't get to say that you inserted yourself into the process as a way to keep bad things from happening, then turn your back and let them shoot this guy out of a cannon. Either you're a good guy or you're not. You can't have it both ways."

"It must be great to be young and idealistic," Gray shot back. "To see everything in simple black-and-white terms. Given everything you've experienced, I would think by now you'd realize that the world simply isn't that clear-cut. The lines between right and wrong get blurred a lot more often than you might think."

"Blurred lines?" I repeated, eyebrows raised. "You're the draftsman here. If there are any blurred lines, it's because you drew them that way. But you know what?

If it makes you sleep better at night to tell yourself a pack of lies, go right ahead."

"It's not lies," Gray said defensively. "And you can vilify me all you want, but as I stated before, none of this was my idea. That said, I can follow the logic of the people who authorized Jack's creation. They saw a potential threat and looked for a way to neutralize it, if that ever became necessary. From that standpoint, their actions are justifiable."

"And the end justifies the means, right?" I intoned mockingly. "You know, Jack said the exact same thing to me. It's starting to become clear to me where he gets his values."

Gray simply sat there silently, staring at me, but I could sense that my comment had irritated him.

"So today you justify cloning," I continued. "What's tomorrow — human-alien hybrids? Cyborgs?"

Gray unexpectedly gave me a look of surprise, but quickly recovered. However, his expression — despite being brief — indicated that my offhand comment had hit pretty close to home.

"Unbelievable," I muttered, shaking my head. "You people are just unbelievable."

"Maybe," Gray admitted, "but the job I've been tasked with is the most important work I'll ever do. Believe it or not, I've saved this planet a dozen times over, but no one will ever know. I'll never get any medals, my name won't appear in any history books, they won't be erecting any statues in my honor. And I'm fine with all that — I didn't sign up for any accolades. But at the end of the day, all this job will have left me with is three failed marriages, children who won't speak to me, and grandkids who don't know me."

His face took on a slightly pained expression as he spoke, and I sensed remorse and regret in him — emotions I would have doubted he had just moments earlier.

"You know," he went on, with a faraway look in his eyes, "I went to see my granddaughter play a talking tulip in a school play a few months back. She's just five, but she did a wonderful job. Afterwards, I went up to her to give her a hug, and she started screaming — like I was some stranger trying to kidnap her. She had no idea who I was."

Empathically, I picked up nothing but candor from him. Needless to say, his impromptu speech had been unexpected and revealed a side of Gray I didn't know about — would never have guessed existed. Caught flatfooted, I struggled for something to say. Thankfully, Gray saved me the trouble.

"Anyway, I think the focus here is supposed to be on Jack," he said, "so why don't we keep the spotlight on him?"

"That would be great," I proclaimed, "especially since *his* spotlight is squarely on me. I mean, he's infiltrating my inner circle, going to my father's house, popping up at my hangout spot…"

My voice slowly faded as something new suddenly dawned on me.

"What have you given him on me?" I asked pointedly.

"I'm not sure what you're asking," Gray replied.

"Well, Jack seems to know a lot about me. Who my friends are, the people I've had run-ins with, where I like to hang out. It strikes me that he's got far more info about me than he should, even given the fact that he's been able to hoodwink a few people into thinking he was me."

Gray sighed. "Remember, Jack was created to challenge you, if necessary. That being the case, he needed to know as much about you as possible."

"So what's he got?"

"Just a dossier. Mostly big-picture stuff — friends, family, favorite haunts. Light on minor details, like how you like your eggs, favorite video game, and so on."

I drummed my fingers on the seat for a moment, pondering. "How current is it?"

"It's pretty topical. Mentions your lovely new fiancée, that you lost your powers temporarily on Caeles, and — according to a time-traveling criminal — that you end up on the Caelesian throne at some point in the future."

I had to admit to being surprised. Gray had more or less cited the most notable highlights of my visit to Caeles, save perhaps one: the fact that I'd met a future version of myself, who had gone inside my head and manipulated some things. On the whole, however, Gray's info wasn't just up-to-date, but also incredibly accurate. I was aware of the fact that he had a wide array of resources, but I couldn't help but be impressed (although I wasn't going to let him know that).

After taking a moment to recover, I said, "Doesn't sound like it's error-free, but your profile on me is probably close enough to explain how Jack got the bulk of his info about yours truly."

"And he could talk to your friends to fill in the blanks on the negligible stuff."

"While pretending to be me," I added. "You know, it would have been nice if you guys had worked on instilling a nice set of scruples in Jack so he'd realize that kind of thing is wrong."

"You still don't understand," Gray stated in a patronizing tone. "He was created to be a weapon — no different than a gun or a grenade. When's the last time you heard of a pistol having principles or a code of conduct?"

"Okay," I snapped back, "forget a code of conduct. How about just a safety catch, or an 'off' button?"

A sudden gleam appeared in Gray's eyes, albeit only momentarily. However, it was enough to tip me off.

"Okay, what is it?" I asked.

"What's what?" Gray responded, feigning ignorance.

"You've got something else on Jack — something you haven't mentioned yet. What is it?"

"Very good," Gray said, nodding. "I do have other info, but unfortunately, it's highly classified. I can only share it with those having the proper clearance. That usually equates to members of my team — and those committed to joining us."

"So that's it," I continued. "That's the real reason you got me here. You've got something to sell me on Jack, and the price is me coming to work for you."

"No," he insisted. "That would be a nice outcome, but I'm not so foolish as to think we're there yet. So, my intention is merely to help you as much as I can within the bounds of my mandate."

"I think I've heard enough," I said flatly. "I'll be taking my leave now."

"Oh, so I get an alert before you depart this time," he muttered, chuckling. "I must be moving up in the world."

I rolled my eyes at his comment, but didn't say anything.

"Seriously though," he went on, sobering, "feel free to call me if you need me. In all honesty, Jim, I'm just trying to help."

"Your kind of help comes with too many strings," I declared, "so thanks for nothing, Gray."

He smiled. "You know, before all is said and done here, I'm going to have to think of a way to get you to call me *Mister* Gray."

"Keep dreaming," I almost growled. "A mouse has a better chance of marrying a cat and living happily ever after."

Then I teleported.

Chapter 66

I popped up in Mouse's lab. My mentor and BT were nowhere around, but I did see a note indicating that they had stepped out for a bite to eat, plainly intent on getting the lunch I had failed to bring back earlier. Not knowing when I'd be back, it was a fairly practical decision on their part, and I spent a moment debating on whether to try running them down. In truth, my discussion with Gray struck me now as a non-event for the most part, as he hadn't really imparted anything new. That being the case, I decided to follow their lead and get some sustenance myself. Thus, I spent a moment scrawling my own message at the bottom of the aforementioned note (stating that the meeting with Gray was anticlimactic), and then teleported home.

Appearing in the kitchen, I immediately sensed that no one was present but Myshtal. I telepathically reached out to let her know I was around — didn't want her to hear me making noise and think a prowler was on the premises. She mentally shot back that she was coming to join me, and a few moments later, she appeared.

"Hello," she said, smiling.

"Hey," I replied. "What are you up to?"

"Nothing — just reading a book." Then she added, "If you're looking for your mother and grandparents, they went out."

"No, I only popped in to get something to eat," I stated. Then I frowned. "Wait a minute. Have you been here by yourself all day?"

"Yes, but it's fine," she insisted. "Your family asked if I wanted to join them, but I decided to stay here."

"Oh?" I muttered, raising an eyebrow. It seemed to me that Myshtal spent more than enough time at the embassy. I would have assumed that she was dying to get out.

"They're getting ready to leave," she explained. "They're saying goodbye to old friends, favorite places, treasured memories... Everything that's familiar. Having gone through the same thing myself, I didn't want them to be burdened with having to babysit me while they severed ties with so much of the world around them."

"So they told you," I surmised. "You know they're leaving the planet."

"Yes," she answered, nodding. "But even if they hadn't mentioned it, it was going to become evident pretty soon that they went *somewhere* when they suddenly vanished without a trace."

"True," I admitted, chuckling. "But I don't think my family would leave without telling you goodbye. They would consider it impolite. Plus, they adore you."

"Really?" she asked. "So all the Carrows are fond of me?"

I blinked. Her query struck me as slightly odd — almost like she was posing two questions in one.

"Of course," I quickly uttered, hoping I hadn't paused too long before responding. "Everyone thinks you're wonderful."

"Great. I was worried that my being here was becoming a bit of a strain."

"What?" I blurted. "No...absolutely not. I know that we've been preoccupied lately — especially me — but all of us love having you here."

REPLICATION

"And on my part, I should make it clear that you've been wonderful hosts," she intoned. "Now, I believe you mentioned getting something to eat?"

****

It turned out that Myshtal hadn't had lunch either, so I ended up nuking a couple of cans of soup in the microwave for us. Afterwards, we sat in the breakfast area, discussing the book she'd been reading (one of Mom's romances) as we ate.

As always, Myshtal was bubbly and engaging, and it wasn't long before the conversation moved from books to a variety of other subjects. We found ourselves discussing everything from furniture to pets — mostly comparing Earth versions to their Caelesian counterparts — and I was so engrossed that I quickly lost track of time. It wasn't until my phone vibrated, indicating receipt of a text message, that I realized how long we'd been talking.

"It's Electra," I said aloud as I glanced at my phone. "She wants to meet in the teen lounge at HQ in about twenty minutes."

"Oh," Myshtal murmured. "I suppose you should go, then."

Empathically, I sensed that she was a little crestfallen. We'd been having a good time just chatting, and now I was about to run off again. Remembering my grandfather's earlier statements, I decided to be bold.

"You know what?" I began. "Why don't you come, too?"

Myshtal perked up immediately, but then seemed to become wary.

"Are you sure?" she asked. "I don't want to make waves."

"It'll be fine," I declared, with more confidence than I felt. Electra probably wouldn't be wild about the notion, but — with the rest of my family leaving soon — I needed to start acclimating her to the fact that Myshtal was going to be around more often than not.

With that in mind, I sent a text back to my girlfriend indicating that Myshtal would be joining us. Much to my surprise, she immediately responded, saying it wasn't a problem. (More specifically, she wrote, "The more, the merrier…")

With that, I asked Myshtal if she was ready and — upon receiving a reply in the affirmative — teleported us to HQ.

REPLICATION

Chapter 67

With some time to kill before meeting Electra, I actually took us to Mouse's lab. My mentor and BT were now back and greeted us cordially after noting our arrival.

"Got your note," Mouse said to me after the salutations were done. "Sounds like Gray didn't really have much to impart."

"Not really," I agreed. "I don't think he said anything worth noting."

"Hmmm," BT muttered. "With no new developments or information, we may be at an impasse at the moment."

"So what does that mean?" asked Myshtal.

"It means we wait until Jack does something else," Mouse replied. "Anyway, what are you two up to?"

"We're going to meet Electra in the teen lounge in a few minutes," I replied.

"Good," BT said, then turned to Myshtal. "I'm glad that Jim's current issues haven't kept him from showing you around."

"Oh no," Myshtal assured her. "He's been great. He even showed me the quarters that I'd be occupying here."

She then began to recount for BT our earlier visit to HQ, telling her what a wonderful tour guide I'd been. While she was talking, Mouse motioned me aside, indicating that he wanted to speak with me.

"What's up?" I asked after we had moved a few feet away from the others.

"The princess," he answered, inclining his head towards Myshtal. "Seeing her reminded me that if she's going to be joining us here, she'll probably need to be assigned a mentor."

"Makes sense," I noted with a nod. All of us who were part of the League's teen affiliate had mentors. Myshtal shouldn't be an exception.

"I've been considering the options," Mouse said, "but figured that it probably made sense to let you weigh in since you know the princess better than anyone else."

"Okay, who's at the top of your list?"

"Actually, I was thinking Vixen."

"No way," I declared, emphatically shaking my head.

"Why not?" Mouse inquired. "She's not mentoring anyone at the moment, and she's a solid member of Alpha League."

"Your girlfriend's also a Siren," I added, "able to manipulate the opposite sex. Do you really think it's a good idea to have her mentoring a girl I'm trying to break off an engagement with?"

"What, are you afraid she'll show the princess how to actually wrangle you into marrying her?"

I gave him an evil look then said, "Who else you got?"

"Luna," Mouse replied.

"Luna?" I repeated, frowning. Luna was a League member who derived her abilities from the moon. She was powerful, but drew her name from an ancient goddess who had inspired the word "lunatic." More to the point, Luna seemed to have a personality influenced by her namesake.

"I don't know," I finally admitted after a few moments. "Isn't she kind of — what's the word I'm looking for — crazy?"

Mouse chuckled. "She's not crazy. She's just extraordinarily passionate about everything she does."

"I suppose that's one way to put it," I muttered, reflecting on a recent incident where Luna literally washed a would-be mugger's mouth out with soap before turning him over to the authorities because he called her a name she didn't like. "Who else is on your short list?"

"Why don't we tackle this from a different angle?" Mouse queried in response. "Instead of me rattling off names that you might ultimately want to strike, let's talk about the things you're thinking the princess needs in a mentor."

"Fair enough," I said. "For starters, she needs someone who's going to be patient with her. Remember, despite her appearance, she's an alien. She's adjusted pretty well to Earth culture, but she's still going to have lots of questions and is bound to make missteps."

"That's reasonable," Mouse stated with a nod. "What else?"

"Someone mature. A person who's going to help her when she makes the occasional social blunder instead of making fun of her."

"Got it."

"She also needs a mentor who's accessible — someone she can reach out to at any time, day or night, if she's having issues."

"Hmmm," Mouse droned. "I'm starting to understand now why you never seem to respect *my* schedule."

I grinned, then went on listing the characteristics I thought would be important in any potential mentor for Myshtal. To be frank, I patterned my statements in large part on my relationship with Mouse. That fact wasn't lost on him; although Mouse didn't say anything about it, I felt a sense of satisfaction arise in him as he listened to my comments — gratification that he had been doing his job well. (I made a mental note to do something to let Mouse know that he'd been a great mentor — stellar, in fact.)

It took a few minutes, but by the time I was winding down, I felt that I'd provided a pretty good roadmap for fruitful mentor-mentee relations.

"Anything else?" Mouse asked as I seemed to come to the end of my index of qualifications.

"Yeah," I said. "A good sense of humor. You guys have a tendency to be way too stiff and form—"

I found myself cut off as lights began flashing throughout the lab and something like a mid-volume alarm clock began sounding.

"What's happening?!" I yelled at Mouse.

"It's Jack!" he shouted back. "He's here!"

I was about to ask where when I suddenly picked up a massive surge of emotions. The feelings I sensed ran the gamut, from fear to concern to anger, and I knew based on past experience that I was picking up on the collective emotional responses of a crowd of people simultaneously experiencing a specific event — like an earthquake or a fire. Moreover, the feelings all emanated from a central location: the teen lounge.

I teleported there without another word to Mouse — and almost immediately found myself under attack.

REPLICATION

Chapter 68

I popped up in the middle of the teen lounge. The first thing I noticed was that almost everyone in the room — about twenty people in total — was on their feet and facing the far wall, with their backs to me. I also realized that the place was a mess. There was at least one overturned table and another that looked like it had been smashed, along with all kinds of stuff on the floor: smashed glassware, spilled drinks, food and snacks… All in all, it looked like there had been some kind of stampede.

"There he is!" someone yelled. "Get him!"

Jack! I thought, as everyone turned in my direction. Suddenly sensing a bevy of antagonistic emotions coming from the other teens, I shifted into super speed and spun around.

There was no one there.

Confused, I turned back towards my fellows, only to realize that the entire room had seemingly launched a blitzkrieg against me.

The world around me had gone into slow motion for the most part, but from what I could see, there were at least three projectiles headed straight at me: a bolt of charcoal-gray energy that had seemingly come from a guy known as Nightshift, what appeared to be a wooden knife that had been flung by a fellow called Boomstick, and a bottle of water. I almost laughed at the last, until I realized it had been thrown by a teen named Actinic, who could change the chemical composition of materials. That meant that the liquid in the bottle was probably no longer water — a fact proven when I saw that whatever fluid it now contained was already eating through the bottle that held it.

REPLICATION

Moreover, although most of their fellows were moving in relative slow motion, I saw three of those present coming towards me at what seemed like a normal pace. That meant they were speedsters.

The first two I recognized as a brother-and-sister team of fraternal twins known as Haste and Hustle. I wasn't completely familiar with their power set, but apparently super speed was among their abilities. The other person coming at me was Dynamo — a guy who had generally been ranked second only to my brother Paramount when it came to powerful teens.

Trying to prioritize the potential threats in order of importance, it seemed prudent to deal with the people first and the projectiles afterwards. One of my patented methods for dealing with speedsters is to telekinetically trip them. People get shaken up from stumbling while walking at a normal pace; tumbling along the ground at Mach speed will really rattle you. However, these were my comrades-in-arms and I didn't want to hurt them. So, with that in mind, I teleported the twins to the middle of the swimming pool in the League's rec area.

I then turned to Dynamo, ready to send him on the same trip. However, as I was preparing to do so, I witnessed him getting tackled from the side by none other than Atalanta, who seemed to come out of nowhere. Her momentum sent the two of them smashing through (and obliterating) a shuffleboard table before breaking through a wall like it was made of paper-mâché.

Somewhat surprised but grateful for the Argonaut's interference, I turned my attention to the projectiles. With the speedsters out of the way, dealing with these were child's play, and I resorted to my usual method of avoiding harm: phasing. At the same time, I also stepped out of the path of the thrown items, became invisible, and then returned to normal speed.

The bottle thrown by Actinic seemed to have the lowest trajectory and hit first, striking the floor. The bottle was practically gone by that point, and the liquid it had contained splashed slightly as it struck. Almost immediately, noxious-looking fumes began to spew into the air from where the fluid had landed.

The wooden knife Boomstick had tossed struck the wall and exploded, blasting away plaster and exposing the interior wooden frame.

The third projectile — Nightshift's weird energy bolt — hit a dartboard hanging on the wall, which then swiftly became engulfed in some queer, viscous substance that looked like dark gray tar. It spread rapidly all over and was seemingly dense, as the nail the dartboard hung from began to bend with the weight.

I turned back towards my fellow teens, hoping now I could make my presence known without being attacked. However, they were still so keyed up emotionally that they were likely to shoot first, so to speak, and ask questions later. Fortunately, someone came to my rescue.

"Stand down!" said a booming, yet feminine voice. It was my girlfriend, Electra. I hadn't even noticed that she was in the room (as was Smokey).

"That was Jim," she went on. "The *real* Jim."

Sensing a loosening of the group's collective tension, I decided to take a chance. Making myself visible, I immediately dropped to my knees and placed my hands behind my head.

"I surrender," I announced to no one in particular.

REPLICATION

Chapter 69

"Well, the teen lounge is a war zone," Mouse said, "but the damage is pretty much cosmetic. We'll have it back to normal in a few days."

"Thanks," I murmured, as did Electra and Smokey.

"Now," my mentor went on, "does someone want to explain what happened?"

We were in one of the League conference rooms. In addition to myself, Mouse, Smokey, and Electra, others present included BT and Myshtal. We had congregated here after my "surrender" in the teen lounge in order to get debriefed.

"It's pretty straightforward," Smokey began. "I was in the teen lounge with Electra and Atalanta, waiting for Jim and Myshtal to join us. But instead of Jim, his evil twin showed."

"I knew it wasn't the real Jim the second he appeared," Electra said. "His bioelectric field was different. But I decided to play dumb to see if he'd say something we could use."

"Did he?" BT asked.

"Things never got that far," Electra said. "First thing he did was try to kiss me, and I kind of lost it."

"She blasted him," Smokey clarified. "And then, while he was a little stunned, Atalanta tagged in. She grabbed him and flung him across the room, where he smashed into a table."

"Nice of her to step in like that," Mouse noted, "sizing up the situation solely based on Electra's actions."

I didn't say anything, but it was a sure bet that Atalanta had known that Jack was a fake independent of anything Electra did. She would have seen his aura and

370

realized that it didn't match mine. However, I wasn't sure how much the rest of the League knew about her abilities, and it wasn't my place to out her like that.

"Anyway," Smokey chimed in, "Jack jumped up and started telekinetically flinging stuff around — chairs, tables, supers — and at that point, the fight was on."

"But it didn't last long," Electra interjected. "Next thing we knew, he was gone. And then Jim popped up, and the rest you know."

Mouse's brow creased as he seemed to consider something. "Was anyone hurt?"

Both Electra and Smokey shook their heads but it was the latter who answered, saying, "Just some bumps and bruises — nothing requiring more than a light bandage or an aspirin."

My mentor suddenly leaned forward, looking at each of us in turn.

"This has gotten far more serious," he said. "Before, he was incidentally causing people to think he was Jim because they look alike. Now he's actively trying to mislead others. It was bad enough when he was breaking into secure facilities to torture those he presumed were guilty. Now he's infiltrating our headquarters, fighting us in our own house."

"So what do we do to keep him out?" asked Electra. "Set up additional checkpoints? Establish passwords?"

BT shook her head. "No, that's not necessary. Jack's biometrics have been fed into the security parameters here. When he pops up, an alarm goes off — like it did today."

Curious, I asked, "How'd you get his biometrics?"

"The security system at AP's mansion," Mouse replied. "It recorded them when Jack showed up there — before he got drilled with a laser."

"Well, you might want to tweak whatever we're using to monitor his presence here," I advised. "The alarms went off in Mouse's lab when Jack showed up, but — now that I think about it — they weren't going off anywhere else."

"That was by design," BT stated.

My eyes went wide. "What?"

"Think of it as a silent alarm," Mouse explained. "If klaxons start going off all over the place when he shows up, Jack's going to know we're on to him. But if it only goes off in one place…"

"We can get the drop on him," Smokey said, finishing my mentor's thought.

"*Could* have gotten the drop on him," BT corrected. "Prior to today, he knew that technology could distinguish him from Jim. Now he knows that some of us can, too — assuming he didn't before. Regardless, he's not likely to try waltzing in here again."

REPLICATION

Chapter 70

With little more to be said at the moment, our discussion group disbanded, with Mouse and BT going back to the former's lab, while the rest of us retreated to Smokey's quarters. Atalanta was already inside waiting for us when we arrived, and I sent her a quick telepathic thanks for her help with Dynamo. (Knowing it was the real me, she had tackled him under the impression that I might have needed help with the situation.) She mentally replied that no thanks was necessary.

We congregated in the living room area, with Smokey and Atalanta sitting on a loveseat, while Myshtal, Electra and I sat on a couch (with Electra in the middle, of course).

Opening a telepathic link with Electra, I said, <Do me a favor — distract Atalanta.>

<Huh?> Electra replied.

<Distract her.>

<How?>

<I don't know — girl talk. Shoes. Purses. Shopping.>

Mentally, my girlfriend narrowed her eyes. <You know, because I realize you're under a lot of stress, I'm going to overlook how sexist and denigrating that comment is.>

Mentally, I groaned and was about to apologize, but Electra was already engaging Atalanta in a conversation, thanking her for jumping into the fray with Jack in the lounge. I took the opportunity to telepathically reach out to Smokey (which was the reason I wanted Atalanta distracted in the first place).

<Atalanta,> I said to him. <How much does she know?>

<You mean about Jack?>

<Yeah. How much have you told her?>

There was a slight hesitation on Smokey's part, and I sensed a mild degree of worry coming from him.

<Everything,> he said a moment later. <I told her everything.>

<Oh,> I murmured. <Okay.>

<Listen, man, I just felt like she needed to know. Jack had already gotten to Sarah, and pretty much had me fooled. Bearing in mind that he can't get over on Electra and Li, I was feeling like the weak link in the chain, and I kept thinking that Atalanta might be next on his list. Sorry if I made the wrong call.>

<It's fine,> I assured him. <I trust you and I trust your judgment. If you felt she needed to be told, then she probably did. I just wanted to know what she knew so I'd have an idea of how frankly we can speak in front of her. But you didn't do anything wrong.>

<Thanks, man.>

We then turned our attention back to the conversation between Electra and Atalanta, which was just winding down.

"Anyway, this wasn't how I anticipated the day going," Smokey said when the girls ended their chat. "So much for hanging out and having fun."

Electra sighed. "I don't know that having fun is going to be an option until we get this Jack situation resolved."

"She's right," I said. "His antics are hitting closer and closer to home. And now he's attacking people."

"I suppose there's an argument that we attacked first," Smokey noted.

"Oh, so I was just supposed to let him kiss me?" Electra said derisively.

Smokey shook his head. "No, I'm not saying that at all. My point is that — from Jack's perspective — we may have been the aggressor."

"In that case, he has a very twisted view of reality," Atalanta suggested.

"Exactly," Smokey said. "He went after Incendia and others who had never actually done anything to him. Today, he actually engaged in fisticuffs with people. What's he likely to do to them?"

Suddenly, the room was full of creased brows and frowns.

"Are we in danger?" Atalanta asked pointedly, looking at me.

Responding in kind, I said, "Frankly, I don't know."

Chapter 71

Unsurprisingly, my last comment put a damper on things, so we decided to call it a day shortly thereafter. Smokey and Atalanta indicated that they were going to stay in and watch a movie, while I offered to teleport Electra home. However, my girlfriend had driven her car to HQ and didn't want to leave it there.

"Just get Myshtal home," she said after we exited Smokey's quarters. "You can come by and see me later, if you have time."

I promised that I would, and then teleported myself and Myshtal to the embassy.

****

My family was still out when we popped up in the kitchen, and I relayed that fact to Myshtal.

"No problem," she insisted. "Thanks for taking me along with you today."

"My pleasure," I replied with a smile. "Sorry things ended on such a sour note."

"It's not your fault, and it's pretty clear that you're grappling with a lot of issues."

"Thanks for understanding," I said. "And I suppose I should have asked this earlier, but is everything okay with you?"

She raised her eyebrows in surprise. "Yes. I'm fine. Why do you ask?"

"Because you've pretty much gone mute since we were in Mouse's lab. You didn't say anything when we were in the conference room with Mouse and BT. I'm not sure

I heard you speak in Smokey's room, either. It just seems a little out of character for you."

She simply stared at me for a moment, and then sighed.

"My speaking around Electra always seems to create problems for you," she contended. "Regardless of the subject matter. I just decided to see if being silent would be beneficial."

"Well, that's kind of you," I noted, "but I don't think it's necessary for you to hold your tongue because of how speaking might affect me. Just say what you'd normally say, and whatever happens is what happens."

"Thanks," she said with a slight grin. "But you may end up regretting giving me free rein to say what I feel."

"I don't control what anyone else says. Why should it be any different with you?"

"Because I came back from Caeles with you and I'm staying with your family. To a certain extent, my actions are a reflection on you, and I realize that. Thus, I wouldn't want to say anything that embarrasses you or makes you feel awkward."

"Great, because I never did anything embarrassing or awkward on Caeles, right?" I droned sarcastically.

She laughed at that, obviously recalling the fact that I'd managed to make numerous missteps, in both word and deed, back on her homeworld.

"Fine," she said after regaining her composure. "I'll simply say what I feel, and you'll just have to deal with it."

"Sounds awesome," I replied.

"Famous last words…" she shot back, at which point we both started chuckling.

377

REPLICATION

Chapter 72

I hung out with Myshtal until my grandparents came home. She hadn't been present during the altercation with Jack in the teen lounge, but who knew what was going through my evil twin's head? There was no telling who he might decide to go after or why. That being the case, I was wary of leaving her alone at the moment. Thus, I made my grandparents aware of the day's events and that they should probably keep an eye out.

"We'll keep her safe," my grandfather assured me, after pulling me aside while Indigo and Myshtal chatted.

"Thanks," I said. "By the way, where's Mom? We need to let her know what's happened as well."

"She's still with the lawyers," Gramps replied.

I raised an eyebrow. "Lawyers?"

"Yes. All of your designated guardians are leaving the planet. There's a ton of legal stuff that has to be done so that you — a minor — won't have any issues when it comes to all the things you'll have responsibility for: money, property, living on your own, etc."

"Wow," I muttered. "I guess I never thought about all that stuff."

"So what do you think we've been doing when we're out all day?"

"I don't know," I admitted, shrugging. "Saying goodbye to people. Picking up some DVDs to watch on the trip. Stocking up on chocolate and other goodies you can't get outside the Milky Way."

Gramps laughed. "Yes, there has been some of that, but mostly we're making sure you're taken care of — and can take care of yourself — in our absence."

"Well, uh, thanks," I mumbled. "I honestly hadn't thought about all the ways your being gone will affect me."

It probably wasn't clear, but I wasn't just talking about the legalities Gramps had mentioned. He was the man who raised me, the only father figure I'd ever truly known. For most of my life, he'd also been my best friend. Last but not least, he'd always been my sounding board — someone I could always turn to for sage advice. I loved him, and I reached out telepathically to let him know that (and a million other things I'd probably have trouble voicing). Needless to say, the feeling was mutual.

"Anyway, it's not going to be forever," Gramps reminded me as he broke the telepathic connection. "We'll be back. But while we're gone, you're basically running the show."

"So wait — does that mean I'm being emancipated?"

"Hardly," my grandfather declared, chuckling. "Emancipation would mean that you would legally be considered an adult, despite not reaching the age of majority. However, there's a lot of gray area between that and still being a minor, and what we're setting up for you falls somewhere in that region."

"So semi-emancipated," I concluded. "I'm only shackled to my status as a minor by one ankle instead of both."

Gramps laughed again. "Something like that."

****

Shortly after my talk with my grandfather, I left, teleporting to Electra's house. I popped up outside her front door and rang the bell. About ten seconds later, Electra opened the door.

"Hey," she said, greeting me with a kiss as I stepped inside.

"I didn't call first," I remarked as she closed the door. "Is this a bad time?"

She shook her head. "No, it's fine. Plus, I did tell you to come over, so it's not like you were unexpected."

"So you just took it for granted that I'd show up," I remarked. "What if I'd had something else to do?"

She giggled. "Yeah, right. I can count on one hand the number of times you've turned down an invitation to come over."

She then stepped in close and slipped her arms around my waist. Giving me a flirtatious look, she said, "Of course, if you've got something more pressing, I totally understand."

"Uh, no," I responded, putting my arms around her. "I'm good."

Laughing, she stepped back, then took my hand, saying, "Come on," as she dragged me to the kitchen.

Once there, she guided me to a nearby breakfast table. On it was a half-full bowl of chips she'd presumably been eating when I showed up. Taking a seat, she popped a chip into her mouth as I sat down next to her. Delicately picking up another one, she then extended her hand towards my lips with the chip held between her thumb and forefinger. Taking the hint, I opened my mouth and took it.

"Mmmm," I mumbled as I chewed and then swallowed. "That's good."

"You think so?" she uttered with a hint of excitement. "They're homemade."

380

"Well, tell Esper she did a great job."

Laughing, she kicked me lightly under the table. "You jerk!"

I chuckled, enjoying the moment. I completely relished spending time with my girlfriend. Whether we were by ourselves or with friends, we always seemed to have fun. Seeing this side of her, it was almost hard to believe that just a few hours before she was trying to send a billion jigawatts of energy through somebody. And with that, my thoughts turned to Jack and I sobered immediately.

"Do you think we're taking this too lightly?" I asked.

She frowned. "What — the situation with your doppelganger?"

"Yeah," I answered. "It just seems like I should be out doing something instead of hanging out with you."

"Doing something like what?" she practically demanded. "You've still got to live. You've still got to eat, still got to sleep. No one's suggesting you stop doing those things just because a bad guy is out there. And there are always bad guys out there."

"I know, but…being here with you, like this… To someone on the outside looking in, it probably doesn't look like I'm taking it seriously."

She leaned over and took both of my hands in hers, then looked me in the eye. "Look, if all goes according to plan, you and I are going to have very dangerous jobs in a few years — as will a lot of our friends. That being the case, we're bound to lose people at some point. People close to us. People we care about. Knowing that, and having been around the League my entire life, I've learned that you have to take the little joys where and when you can."

"You really believe that?"

"Absolutely," she said with conviction, then kissed the back of my hand. "Remember our last little adventure, when we needed Vestibule's help to save the planet?"

"Yeah," I said with an uncertain nod, not sure where this was going.

"Just before she left for her part of the mission, she kissed you," Electra stated, now looking a bit stern. "I didn't like it, but she had the right idea. There was no guarantee that any of us were coming back or that the planet would survive, so — even though I wish she hadn't focused on my boyfriend — I don't fault her for trying to snatch what little joy the situation offered."

"Well, in that case, why didn't you kiss me then as well?" I asked.

"Ha!" she snorted derisively. "I'm supposed to kiss you after you've been swapping spit with Vestibule?"

"There was no spit," I countered fiercely. "Just a little tongue…"

"Shut up!" Electra screeched as she reached out with a grin and grabbed a handful of chips, then shoved them at my mouth. "Shut up! Shut up! Shut up!"

Chuckling heartily, I reached for her hand as she — laughing as well — pressed the chips around my mouth, grinding most of them into crumbs that went showering down onto the table and my lap.

"On second thought," I said, making an exaggerated chewing motion, "your chips are a little bland. They could use some salt."

There was a set of salt and pepper shakers on the table; I reached for the former — and then froze. Almost of its own volition, my head suddenly spun around — towards the kitchen's rear door, which led out to a patio.

REPLICATION

The door was mostly glass, covered with a set of blinds that were currently open. It was dark out, but after telescoping my vision (as well as cycling it through the light spectrum until I could see almost as well as in daytime), I caught sight of what I expected.

"What is it?" Electra asked anxiously, following my gaze to the door.

"Nothing," I said, trying to keep my voice emotionless. "But I have to go. I just remembered something I need to do."

"Huh?" she murmured incredulously. "You just got here."

"I know, and I apologize. I'll make it up to you."

"You'd better," she huffed.

"You have my word," I declared as I came to my feet. I then gave her a quick smooch and teleported.

I reappeared about a block away, with a clear line of sight to the back door of Electra's house.

Waiting there for me was Jack.

383

Chapter 73

Wearing a pair of khakis and a light jacket, Jack really wasn't dressed for the weather. However, if he could tweak his bodily systems like I could, he could make himself comfortable in any clime.

"I see you got my message," Jack said with a smile.

"Stop," I interjected heatedly. "We're not doing this here."

Jack suddenly looked confused. "Doing what?"

"Whatever you call this. Meeting, chatting, congregating... We're not doing it within shouting distance of my girlfriend's house."

"Okay," he said. "I'm fine with finding another spot to powwow. I can teleport us some place, but I don't think you'd let me. And needless to say, I'm not keen on *you* teleporting *me*."

"Maybe that's an indication that there's nothing for us to talk about."

"I'm not so sure about that," he countered. "Plus, I think I can find us an alternate venue. Follow me."

With that, he went floating straight up into the air. I was momentarily caught off guard — I'd forgotten he could purportedly fly — but then I quickly followed suit, rising up after him.

We moved up to a height of about fifty feet, and then Jack zipped away laterally. As before, I followed close on his heels, noting that he had impressive flight speed.

"This should be good," Jack declared after about half a mile. "High enough to avoid notice from anyone on the ground, but low enough that we don't have to worry about bumping our heads on any planes. And, of course, out of shouting distance of Electra's house. Any complaints?"

"It'll do," I grumbled.

"Now, I was asking if you got my message."

"If you mean the salt shaker, then yes, I got it. Would I be here otherwise?"

Jack smiled. "You have to admit it was pretty clever, though."

I grunted, but didn't immediately say anything. When I had reached for the salt shaker on Electra's table, I had seen it floating — just as I'd seen happen earlier in the day at the grill. I'd immediately known that it was Jack's doing — that he was around and probably had a direct line of sight to us. Once I looked out the glass door, it hadn't taken me long to peg him.

I gave him a frank stare. "Look, I'm going to make this perfectly clear: stay away from Electra. Stay away from my family. Stay away from my friends."

He smiled. "Why would I do that? They're my friends and family, too. So what's the issue — you're afraid they'll prefer the upgrade over the original?"

"The issue is that you're dangerous and unpredictable. I don't know what you're going to do, like what happened in the teen lounge today."

"Oh, that," he scoffed. "That was nothing — basically just horseplay."

"So you're not looking to get even with anybody about that little scuffle in the lounge?"

"No," he stated solemnly, shaking his head. "Electra's peers saw one of their own in distress and came to her aid. It's what I would expect, and I don't hold it against them. Plus, I'd never hurt anyone close to us. I mean, I tossed some people around telekinetically, but just to keep them off me, and I made sure nobody got more than a minor boo-boo."

"You shouldn't have been there in the first place," I noted. "I don't like having my friends in harm's way."

"Well, as I keep stressing, I'm not a danger to them. Even if I were, it's pretty evident that they can take care of themselves." He chuckled, apparently reminiscing, then added, "Our girl actually packs quite a wallop — that other one, too."

"She's not *our* girl!" I hissed. "And you're lucky Atalanta didn't tear your head off. Just stay away from us."

He didn't say anything for a moment, then cast his eyes down.

"Don't you think I would if I could?" he asked somberly, and I sensed an odd sadness and longing in him. "But being you is all I know. All I was ever taught. All that was ever drilled into me."

"But that's not your path anymore," I stressed. "The people who molded you for that purpose are gone now. You need to own up to the things you've done, but you're free to be your own person."

"Why would I want to be anyone else?" he demanded. "Why would I—"

Jack was cut off as a colony of bats abruptly swooped towards us, squeaking loudly. I instinctively phased, allowing them to pass harmlessly through me. I glanced at Jack, expecting him to do the same, and was caught completely by surprise by what I saw.

Rather than phase, my evil twin still appeared to be solid. Moreover, I saw a hazy blue glow forming around his eyes, and — knowing what was about to happen — I was immediately filled with dread.

"Jack!" I bellowed. "No!"

My shout came too late, however, as azure light shot out from Jack's eyes in several short bursts. Each beam hit one of the bats, which then seemed to simply vanish.

Inwardly, I cringed as the meaning of what I had witnessed became clear.

Jack had the Bolt Blast.

REPLICATION

Chapter 74

My father, Alpha Prime, was the most powerful superhero on the planet, and the deadliest weapon in his arsenal was his Bolt Blast — powerful beams of energy he could shoot from his eyes, and which would instantly vaporize, disintegrate, and obliterate anything they made contact with. My brother Paramount had inherited this incredible ability, and now Jack had somehow developed it as well.

Shock and fury welled up in me at what my doppelganger had just done. As the remaining bats scattered, chirping madly, I dashed towards him.

Gripping him by the collar of his jacket, I screamed, "What the hell is wrong with you?!"

"What's your problem?" he shot back, shoving me away. "They're just bats — flying rats, to be honest."

"And you just casually killed them, when all you had to do was phase or get out of the way!"

"Everybody wants me out of the way," he retorted. "My handlers. You. Bats… Well, maybe I'm tired of getting out of the way. Maybe it's time for the rest of the world to get out of *my* way."

"Or what?" I asked. "You'll blast them?"

"Maybe," he said hotly.

"And that's exactly what I meant earlier. You're dangerous, Jack. You'd rather kill an innocent creature than step two paces to the side. What does that say about you? About your character?"

"No," Jack contended, shaking his head. "You're wrong."

"On the contrary, I'm absolutely right — and you proved it by what you did to those bats," I insisted. "You're a menace. You need to step away — get help — before someone gets hurt."

"I disagree," Jack said. "You can't take what I did to some pests and say I'd do the same thing to people."

"Oh, I've seen what you do to people, and it's worse. At least the bats didn't suffer."

"Any people that I've harmed had it coming," he argued. "I'd never do that to anyone we cared about."

"You mean anyone *I* cared about," I corrected. "And there's no telling what you'll do, which is why I don't want you around my family and friends. And if you actually cared about them as much as you say, you'd keep your distance."

Suddenly his eyes narrowed, and empathically I felt ire and exasperation building in him.

"Why do you have to be so selfish?" he demanded. "It's always *your* family, *your* friends, *your* this, *your* that… Why does it all have to belong solely to you?"

I shook my head. "I never said that it did."

"That's precisely how you make it sound — like when you say they're your friends and not mine."

"Because you want connections and relationships with people that are usually built up over time. Friendship and trust are things that have to be earned."

"Earned?" he snapped. "What have you ever earned? Everything's just been handed to you on a silver platter, and it's still not enough."

"Huh?" I muttered. "What are you talking about?"

"Think about it," he said. "You've got enough powers for two supers, you're a prince in two different kingdoms, you've got a knockout girlfriend *and* a beautiful fiancée. Basically, your entire existence is a buy-one-get-one-free special."

"Most of that stuff — my powers, being royalty — is an accident of birth. It's not anything I had control over."

"And yet somehow you end up doubly-blessed in every way imaginable," he grumbled, "with enough for two people in almost every arena, and you still want it all for yourself. And to top it all off, you end up as king of an interstellar empire."

I was slightly stunned by his statement, and then I remembered: he'd had a dossier on me, including the fact that — in the future — I allegedly end up sitting on the Caelesian throne.

"I'm not trying to keep anything to myself," I professed. "The simple truth is that you're a walking hazard, Jack, and *that's* why I don't want you around the people I care about. Sooner or later, you're going to hurt somebody, just like you did those bats. As to me being king, the future isn't set. That story about me ruling Caeles could be entirely wrong."

As I finished speaking, an unexpected gleam appeared in Jack's eye and an impish look settled on his face.

"Maybe the part about you being king *is* wrong, but not in the way you imagine," he suggested. "Maybe it's not *you* sitting on that throne."

And then, looking crafty and exuding smug self-satisfaction, he vanished.

REPLICATION

Chapter 75

I teleported home in a somewhat disturbed state. It hadn't been direct or overt, but Jack had seemingly threatened me. (Or at least threatened to *replace* me, which didn't seem to bode well either.)

I popped up in my room, immediately collapsing onto the bed. Telepathically, I picked up on the fact that everyone was safe at home now (which gave me a sense of relief), and they — at least my family — sensed me as well.

I spent a moment rubbing my temples as I stared at the ceiling. Dealing with Jack was incredibly frustrating and left me mentally drained. It wasn't just that he was clearly a menace; it was also the fact that my options for dealing with him were absurdly limited.

As previously noted, I couldn't just teleport him, as I could with most bad guys. His own teleportation power prevented that, so there was no taking him into custody, popping him into a nullifier cell, or anything like that.

A true telepath — someone like Esper or my grandparents — could probably incapacitate him, assuming they could get into his head. Jack, however, had incredibly robust mental shields; if he was anything like me (and, as much as I hated to admit it, he *was*), getting into his mind was highly unlikely. Moreover, anyone making the effort was apt to give themselves away, and if Jack somehow managed to pin down their location (which wasn't entirely out of the question), all bets were off.

The option of taking him physically, in hand-to-hand combat, was also out of the question. Although I'd had years of martial arts training and didn't doubt my own skill in that arena, there's almost nothing you can do to a person who can phase.

At that moment, I suddenly grew pensive as an odd thought occurred to me. But before I could pursue it, I felt my grandfather reaching out mentally.

<You okay, boy?> he asked.

<Yes, sir,> I answered. <Just tired. It's been a long day.>

<Well, you should eat something.>

<I'm not hungry. I think I'll just turn in.>

<All right. Good night, then.>

<Good night, Gramps. See you in the morning.>

I broke the telepathic connection and closed my eyes, intending only to rest them for a moment. A few seconds later, I was fast asleep.

REPLICATION

Chapter 76

I slept fitfully that night, continually tossing and turning, as well as waking up with a start half a dozen times. When I finally woke up for good, I found myself plagued by vague but disquieting images from half-remembered dreams that left me with a sense of alarm and dread — and at the center of them all was my evil twin, Jack.

It was early and still dark out, but I decided to go ahead and get my day started. After a quick shower, I got dressed and then spent a moment contemplating what to have for breakfast. In all honesty, however — despite missing dinner the night before — I wasn't really hungry. It might have been the early morning hour, but I just didn't have much of an appetite.

With the decision to forego breakfast made, I sat down on the edge of the bed and turned my thoughts back to the problem at hand: how to handle Jack. Within minutes, however, I was right back where I'd left off the night before: other than talking to him (which hadn't paid any dividends that I could see), there didn't seem to be a reasonable way to deal with him.

I groaned in exasperation, increasingly vexed by my inability to come up with a solution. I was confident that there was an answer somewhere, but for some reason I just couldn't see it. I really needed to clear my head.

And with that thought, I decided to do the one thing that always seemed to relax me. I phased and then flew straight up, going vertically through the embassy until I found myself in open air. I continued on, flying high up into the sky.

I stopped when I was several hundred feet in the air. Taking a moment to glance down, I took note of how

393

far away everything seemed: buildings, houses, cars…all the signs of humanity's presence — and its problems. It all seemed so distant now.

I looked above me and saw the stars, twinkling merrily. As always, I found myself fascinated by them — how bright they were, how distant…how boundless and infinite the universe itself was. In the face of all that, it almost made my problems seem trivial.

Now feeling a bit more lighthearted, I zoomed away, smiling slightly as I zipped through the sky.

****

I spent about an hour soaring through the sky, simply reveling in the majesty of flight. As I had hoped, being aloft relaxed me by allowing me to leave my problems on the ground — at least for a little while. Soon enough, though, it was time to head back. Dawn had broken, and my family was probably awake and wondering where I was. Reluctantly, I decided to hurry back to the embassy before they started to worry. On the bright side, however, we'd all be able to have breakfast toge—

My thoughts were cut off by something akin to an explosion on the metaphysical plane. It was a psychogenic wailing of pain and anguish, but on a scale I'd never seen. On a supersensory level, it was the equivalent of a ten-point-oh-magnitude earthquake; mentally, it rattled everything in sight, and literally knocked the wind out of me.

Having experienced something similar in the past, I recognized the sensation and knew exactly what it was: the death throes of a powerful telepath — most likely as the result of some massive trauma. Psychic or not, almost everyone for miles around had surely felt the impact, and it continued to mentally reverberate.

As the telepathic keening lingered and echoed, I picked up the hint of something familiar about it — and then froze, reeling in horror.

Oh no…

REPLICATION

Chapter 77

I teleported back to the embassy, popping up in my room. Almost immediately, I picked up on extreme anxiety and duress, among other things, coming from several sources. At the same time, my mother and grandmother both began telepathically yelling at me — Mom almost hysterically. Although they were mentally talking over each other, I was able to make out where they were: the main living room. A moment later, I had teleported there and stood, dumbfounded, by the scene before me.

My grandfather was lying on the floor, with my grandmother cradling his head in her lap. Gramps seemed to be muttering something, but I couldn't make out what it was. My mother was on the floor as well — on my grandfather's right side, holding his hand, while Myshtal was on his left side doing the same. All three of them — my mother, grandmother, and Myshtal — were sobbing.

I dashed over at super speed, and then stared, completely aghast at what I saw.

The right side of my grandfather's head was caved in, liked someone had smashed him in the temple with a sledgehammer. However it had happened, the trauma had been so forceful that it had caused his right eye to pop out of its socket, and it lay dangling on his cheek. Beneath him was a widening pool of blood — my grandmother's clothes were soaked with it. And his brains. I could see his brains…

I dropped to my knees at my grandfather's feet, practically in shock. My vision got blurry as my eyes watered, and a second later, the tears started to flow, hot and heavy. I didn't try to stop them…didn't want to.

REPLICATION

"*Sxibbo*!!!" Indigo screamed, and I suddenly realized she had been calling out to me. "The Beobona!"

Of course! The Beobona! The ancient artifact had healed me on more than one occasion — saved my life, in fact. It could do the same for Gramps.

I nodded to my grandmother to indicate I understood, and then concentrated on where the Beobona was kept. A moment later, the armored, spider-like relic appeared near my grandfather's head as I teleported it.

Indigo looked up at the Beobona expectantly. I know what she was hoping, because I was wishing for the same thing: that the Beobona's chest cavity would open and it would shine its healing light on my grandfather. Unfortunately, the relic's torso stayed closed. Even worse, the Beobona turned and began striding from the room — presumably headed back to its normal spot.

I lowered my eyes. Pleading with the Beobona wouldn't do any good. The thing did as it pleased. My cheeks now soaked with tears, I reached out and laid a hand on my grandfather's leg.

Gramps was still muttering, and I could finally make out some of what he was saying.

"Birdsong?" my grandfather muttered. "That'll be bayside…the Prexin Twins…Indigo, don't want to…"

He continued rambling nonsensically, plainly the result of his head injury. However, as he spoke, his voice began to fade.

"John!" Indigo howled, obviously hoping her voice (and hearing his name) would be a source of strength. "John!"

At the same time, my mother fervently whispered, "Hang on, Dad. Hang on."

REPLICATION

On my part, I struggled to find words, but none would come. Instead, I simply closed my eyes and focused on Gramps — what he meant to me, all that he'd done for me, and how he'd always been there for me. I desperately wished we had more time together. More time to talk, more time to laugh, more time to build memories.

A harsh intake of breath interrupted my thoughts. I opened my eyes, and for a moment had trouble making sense of what I was seeing.

Gramps was encompassed by a soft blue glow that covered him from head to foot. Mom, Indigo, and Myshtal had all moved back, causing me to realize that the glow was actually coming from me — emanating from where my hand still touched my grandfather's leg.

I blinked in surprise, but managed to keep my composure as I realized what was happening. This was the power I had developed on Caeles, the ability that had saved Queen Dornoccia's life. And I knew without a doubt that it would save my grandfather, too.

REPLICATION

The blue glow faded after a few minutes. After it disappeared, my grandfather appeared to simply be asleep (albeit on the floor). Notably, the dent in his skull was gone, and his eye was back in place. Also, thankfully, I could no longer see any gray matter. (The blood was still on the floor, but there wasn't much to be done about that.)

"He'll be okay now," I said to no one in particular as I stood up. "Now, tell me what happened."

It didn't take long to get the story from the three women, and I could almost have guessed what had happened: my doppelganger, Jack, had shown up at the embassy.

He had seemingly gotten inside by using telekinesis to unlock the door. It wasn't clear what he'd wanted, but Gramps had told everyone else to stay back (presumably to keep them out of harm's way) and had then tried to subdue Jack telepathically. Jack had lashed out in retaliation, telekinetically whipsawing my grandfather around before finally smashing his head against a marble countertop. (Looking around as they told the tale, I could see that the living room was in disarray, with furniture thrown around helter-skelter, a bookshelf knocked over, and so on.) Shortly thereafter, I had shown up.

As I heard about what had happened, I had trouble controlling my temper. This was exactly the type of scenario I'd been worried about — the very thing I'd wanted to avoid — and Jack obviously hadn't taken what I said seriously. As a result, Gramps had almost died.

"I need to leave," I announced to everyone in general.

"Why?" my mother asked, voice full of concern. "Where are you going?"

"To find Jack," I declared bluntly. "I'm going to kill him."

REPLICATION

Chapter 79

After announcing my intentions with respect to my evil twin, I quickly teleported Gramps to my grandparents' bedroom at Indigo's request and then headed to my own room. Basically, I didn't want my mother trying to talk me out of what I now planned to do. It wasn't anything I had truly contemplated before, but in attacking Gramps, Jack had crossed a line.

Now that I was ready to go on the offensive, I found myself with a bit of a dilemma: I actually didn't know how to find my doppelganger. Upon reflection, Jack had always found me. I didn't have the slightest idea of where to even start looking for him — but I knew someone who probably did: Gray.

Unfortunately, I didn't have a number for him. Gray had given me a card with his contact info once a while back, but I had discarded it long ago. I had just never envisioned myself willingly reaching out to him, and it galled me to do so now. For a moment, I considered whether Myshtal could help, as she had a power that let her locate things, including people; however, it had to be something or someone she had a connection with, and Jack didn't count. Thus, it appeared that dealing with Gray was the only way to get what I needed.

That said, I couldn't contact him without the proper info, and I suddenly felt annoyed that I couldn't reach him as easily as he always seemed to reach me. And then the light bulb came on.

Why not? I thought. It was worth a try, and he'd specifically said to call him if I needed him.

I took out my cell phone and brought up the virtual assistant that was part of the phone's operating system. I

401

took a moment to get my thoughts together, feeling that the situation was completely surreal, and then found my resolve.

"Call Gray," I said.

Nothing happened.

Undaunted, I decided to try again. "Call Gray."

The virtual assistant still didn't respond.

I made a few more attempts, trying different types of inflection and tone, but nothing worked. I was about to throw in the towel when I realized there was one more thing I could try, but doing so rankled immensely. Still, I wasn't going to leave any stone unturned.

I wiped my face with my hand, completely irked by what I was about to do, wishing there was some other way.

Shaking my head in disgust at my own actions, I softly muttered, "Call *Mister* Gray."

The phone began dialing.

Chapter 80

"So, we have a deal?" Gray asked.

"Yes," I agreed without hesitation. "You give me what I need, and I come work for you."

"Excellent," Gray said with a smug grin.

We were once again in our usual meeting spot in the back of the SUV. My phone hadn't shown any digits, but it had definitely called Gray, who had seemingly been waiting for me to make contact. Two minutes later, I was in the back of the vehicle, making a deal with the devil.

"This is the dawn of a great new day," Gray continued.

"Well, the sun hasn't cleared the horizon yet," I countered. "You need to answer my questions — fully — or the deal's off."

"Of course," he responded. "And since you're officially joining the team, I can grant you temporary clearance so I can share information that was restricted before."

"Whatever," I said, rolling my eyes. "Mouse isn't going to believe this when I tell him."

"Hold on," Gray interjected. "You can't tell your mentor — or anyone else — that you're working with us."

"The hell I can't. I'm not keeping secrets from Mouse. *I* decide who to share pertinent information with, so either I tell him, or we can call this whole thing off before the ink's dry."

Gray appeared to contemplate for a moment, then shrugged. "Have it your way. Share whatever you want."

"Great," I muttered. "Now that that's out of the way, how do I find Jack?"

"With this," Gray said, handing me a metal device about the size of a cell phone, containing what appeared to be a radar screen. He had apparently anticipated the question, as he'd already had the device in hand.

"Unbeknownst to him, Jack has a small homing beacon implanted in his neck," Gray continued.

"A homing beacon?" I echoed, incredulously. "Really?"

"He was a high-value asset, and some folks at the upper echelons wanted their investment protected," Gray explained. "Anyway, that tracker will allow you to pinpoint his location."

"Hold on," I grumbled. "If you've been able to track him all this time, why haven't you tried to take him down?"

"Lack of resources," Gray admitted.

I grunted in disbelief. Gray had an army at his disposal, not to mention advanced weaponry and tech. It was hard to imagine him coming up short on anything he needed, but I decided not to delve into the subject.

"Next, what's the story on Jack's phasing ability?" I inquired.

"What do you mean?" Gray asked in response.

"Well, you told me that he used his phasing power when he attacked one of his handlers."

Gray nodded. "He did."

"Then why haven't I seen any evidence of phasing?" I demanded. "With most guys who can phase, you can't lay a finger on them in terms of physical harm. They just become insubstantial. But with Jack, he's taken a shot to the gut, gotten fried by my girlfriend, slung around by Atalanta, and I gripped him by the collar and shook him.

Maybe you get caught every now and then by one of those if you can phase, but not *that* often."

My narrative was the continuation of the notion that had occurred to me the night before — the train of thought I'd started developing just before my grandfather had telepathically contacted me.

"His phasing ability is limited," Gray replied. "Only small objects — pens, pencils, paper clips. Things along those lines in terms of size and density."

"And you couldn't tell me that before?" I huffed.

"Classified," Gray explained simply. It was an unsatisfying response, but I went on.

"So why is that?" I asked. "Why only little things? Is it the result of some kind of conditioning, like his inability to harm *you*?"

Gray shook his head. "It's not anything that was part of our program. It appears to be some kind of inherent psychological barrier."

"You're saying it's some sort of self-imposed limitation — some kind of unintentional roadblock he's constructed," I said. "Don't you think that's weird?"

Gray shrugged. "No more weird than a telepath who has trouble reading minds."

I ignored his subtle dig at me and moved on.

"How does he find me? Are you guys tracking me — maybe through my phone or something — and he somehow has access to that data?"

"No. Your friend Mouse has altered the telemetry and specs on all League communication devices. So, while we can call you on your phone, we can't track you using it."

"So how does he do it? How does Jack always seem to know exactly where I am?"

REPLICATION

For the first time, Gray looked truly uncomfortable, a sure indication that I wasn't going to like his answer.

"It's never been formally documented," he began, "but Jack appears to have a low-level precognitive ability."

"What?!" I screeched, eyes wide. "He can see the future?!"

"As I said, it's never been formally documented."

"Oh, you want to play word games?" I growled. "Fine. So how was it *informally* documented?"

Gray gave me a sideways look, then sighed. "When Jack's handlers were trying to gauge his telepathic abilities, they often did it using a card test."

"I know," I stated. "I've seen the tapes."

A look of surprise momentarily crossed Gray's face, then he went on. "From all appearances, Jack flunked the test soundly every time it was given. But upon review, it came to light that — while he generally wasn't able to peg the card that the tester was holding — he was actually identifying the *next* card in the deck. He would do that accurately eight or ten times in a row, which is far too great for it to be a coincidence."

"And nobody noticed that?"

"His handlers had tunnel vision on occasion. They knew his potential based on your power set, and they were so focused on those areas that they seemingly overlooked other talents he might have possessed. Thus, the person doing the card test just noted that Jack's answer to the pending question was wrong and failed to see the predictive pattern."

"Now I understand," I said, smoldering with anger. "This is why you've never gone after him yourself, and it's

406

got nothing to do with a lack of resources. It's because he'd see you coming."

"Resources doesn't just mean having a bunch of tools at your disposal," Gray countered. "It means having the right tool for the right job. If I've got the equivalent of a tactical nuke about to go off, it doesn't do me any good to send in an army of uneducated grunts. I need a bomb expert."

"And in this instance you found one — me."

"I don't deny that you're the right person for the task at hand, and sending anyone else would probably just get good people killed."

I let out a groan of frustration. "You know, you should teach a course on manipulation. This is your mess — you created it — and yet somehow, I'm tasked with cleaning it up. Moreover, at the end of the day, *I'm* indebted to *you*."

Gray chuckled. "Don't you get it? You're in the course right now."

I was about to give a wiseacre response when my phone rang. I glanced at the caller ID and noted who was ringing me: Mouse.

"You need to get that?" Gray asked.

"No," I replied, sending the call to voicemail and putting away the phone. "Now, we were talking about Jack's precognition. You called it 'low-level' before. What does that mean?"

"From what we can tell, he seems to only be able to see things in his personal future. That is, things he's personally involved in."

"So he wouldn't be able to see us if we were, say, colluding to plant a bomb in his car."

Gray nodded. "Correct. He might see the bomb going off in the future, but not the events leading up to it unless he was personally involved."

"So he can't see us right now," I concluded.

"No. Moreover, his precognition seems to be limited to a single, seminal event."

I shook my head in confusion. "You lost me."

"He only seems capable of seeing one crucial moment at a time. So if someone fires a rocket grenade at him in the future, he might be able to see that. But if someone launches a second grenade, it's not necessarily something he'd have gotten a vision of."

"In other words, he can see an initial threat that he might face in the future, but he doesn't get a hint of any hazards that may follow."

"Well, at some point the ability does reassert itself, but in terms of immediacy, you're correct. A second seminal event coming right on the heels of the first is not something he's likely to be aware of."

My brow crinkled in thought as I considered what I'd just learned. The fact that he was clairvoyant explained how Jack had accomplished a lot of the things on his résumé, such his getting inside maximum security stockades. He could waltz in, observe, take notes, whatever — all without being detected, thanks to his precognitive abilities.

"So I know now how Jack tracked me," I said after a few moments. "What about you? How'd *you* do it?"

Gray looked nonplussed. "I've already told you: we can't track you."

"And yet on multiple occasions you reached out to me right after I've had a chat with Jack. There's no way that's coincidence."

Gray laughed. "You're not putting two-and-two together here. We track *Jack*. It may take us a few minutes after he teleports, but we can usually get a bead on his location pretty quickly. Shortly afterwards, we're typically able to put eyes on him — sometimes by satellite if he's outside, or a building's security camera, or a direct line of sight by one of our agents, and so on."

"And naturally you can see if he's with someone," I added, catching on. "And in my case, once he left, you'd call me."

"Excellent deduction," Gray droned. "We're going to be lucky to have you on the team."

His statement brought up a question that I had never really gotten a straight answer to. I contemplated for a moment, and then decided to ask.

"So why me?" I asked. "What's the big deal about having *me* work for you?"

Gray gave me a frank look. "As I've said before, I hate this job. I'm ready to retire. But I can't just walk away — it would be irresponsible of me, especially considering who might be taking over when I leave. There's just too much power that goes with the position. And you know what they say about power."

"It corrupts," I quoted.

Gray nodded. "Right. So I need to bring in someone who won't be corrupted by what the job offers because they already have almost-limitless power."

"Hold up," I said. "Are you saying you want me to replace you?"

"It wouldn't be immediate," he countered. "I can't just hand over power and authority willy-nilly. There would be a transitional period."

"How long?"

REPLICATION

"A couple of years."

I frowned. "What's a 'couple'?"

"Five…maybe ten."

"Ten years!"

"Yeah, but it goes by fast," he said with a wink.

I shook my head in derision. "I can't even think that far down the road. But even if I could, what makes you think I won't get corrupted like others around you?"

"There's no guarantee you won't," he admitted, "but from what I've seen, I think it's less likely than most. I mean, you're incredibly powerful now, but you're not abusing your gifts the way others might. You're not sneaking into movies, stealing money out of locked vaults, teleporting people you don't like into City Hall naked, or turning invisible and slipping into the girls' locker room. You're using your abilities responsibly."

Empathically, it felt like he was being honest and forthright, with no hint of guile or deceit. Taken with the things he'd said, it almost felt like we could actually work together — something I couldn't have even fathomed a week ago. And then I remembered: this was a master manipulator I was dealing with, a guy who was using me as his stalking horse in the situation with Jack. I might be forced to work for him, but it would be a mistake to trust him or let my guard down around him.

"Why don't we cross that bridge when we come to it?" I suggested. "We need to deal with my evil twin first and then we can figure out the details of our future working relationship."

"Fine, fine," Gray intoned, nodding.

"So, is there anything else I need to know about Jack?"

"Actually," Gray muttered, his eyes narrowing, "there is one thing…"

REPLICATION

Chapter 81

I floated in the air outside a dilapidated, three-story building on the outskirts of the city. It was the former headquarters of a cement company that had shuttered ten years earlier during the last major downturn in the economy. Although the main entrance to the building had a sign posted that said "Keep Out," a busted lock and the way the door stood ajar signaled that the sign had failed to fulfill its duties. It was obvious that, over the years, various individuals entered and exited at their leisure. At the moment, however, I was only interested in one: Jack, whom the tracker indicated was inside.

Mentally, I went over my plan once again. It had pretty much been made on the fly following my meeting with Gray about an hour earlier. With little planning, it obviously wasn't perfect but was probably the best that could be achieved under the circumstances.

My thoughts were interrupted a moment later by my cell phone going off. It was on vibrate, but had been ringing almost constantly for the last sixty minutes. I knew without looking that it was Mouse.

I was tempted to simply let it go unanswered, as I had since my mentor had begun calling. However, bearing in mind what was next on my agenda, it was possible that I wouldn't get another opportunity to speak to him again. With that in mind, I hit the "Answer" button.

"Jim," Mouse said without preamble, "I know you're upset, but think about what you're doing."

"I already have, and I've decided."

"But you don't have to do this. Your grandfather's going to be fine, and he wouldn't want this."

"I know, but what if I hadn't been there? What if I'm not there *next* time? Do you know how I'll feel if somebody dies because of Jack — because I didn't stop him, or even try?"

"We'll find a way to stop him," Mouse argued. "I promise. But not like this."

"I'm sorry, Mouse," I said softly. "I have to go."

I hung up before he could say anything else and put my phone away. Then I phased and flew into the building.

****

I found my quarry on the second floor near the middle of the building, in what appeared to have been an office bullpen. The space was divvied up into cubicles, each of which had a desk and chair. A thick layer of dust covered almost every visible surface, indicating that it had been a long time since the space had been utilized for its intended purpose.

Jack stood in what appeared to be the main walkway between cubicles, dressed as he'd been the night before. He smiled as I flew towards him, then began to clap his hands in applause.

"It's about time," he said. "I was starting to think I'd have to do all the work in this relationship."

"You were expecting me," I noted as I stopped and hovered in the air a few feet away from him.

"Naturally. Nice to know you're willing to seek me out whenever we need to talk, instead of the ball always being in my court."

"You think I'm here to talk?" I growled angrily, letting my arms hang loosely at my side.

"Well, I was hoping you'd give me a chance to explain what happened this morning."

"Aren't you curious as to how I tracked you down?" I asked.

He shrugged. "I assume it was the homing beacon."

I raised an eyebrow in surprise. "You know about that?"

"Of course," he said, laughing, as he reached into a pocket. "Here it is."

He held his palm out towards me. On it was a small circular object about the size of a watch battery.

"I know that people are tracking me, so I usually have it on my person," he explained, "although occasionally I leave it somewhere random if I don't want my movements known."

Moving closer as I looked at the homing device, I asked, "Why's it in your hand?"

"Huh?" Jack murmured, frowning. "Oh! You thought it was…" He trailed off, pointing at his neck. "No, no, no. I took it out a while back. Teleported it out, actually."

"How'd you even know it was there?" I queried, sidling closer with my arms still dangling freely.

"Oh, this isn't the original," he explained. "The first one went on the fritz, so they replaced it. I woke up on the operating table during the middle of the procedure." He then whispered conspiratorially, "My handlers were bush league when it came to anesthetics."

Giving me a wink, he then went on, saying, "Anyhoo, I shut down my pain receptors and just listened for the rest of the operation and learned all kinds of interesting things. For the record, though, surgery without anesthesia? I wouldn't recommend — Ooof!"

Jack's words were cut off as he went sailing backwards through the air, bent over at the midsection, while I stood there watching, my hands gripping what most people would think was an imaginary bat.

The bat wasn't imaginary, however — just invisible, thanks to my power. I had worked hard to keep my arms positioned in what seemed a natural manner while gripping the unseen metal bat by the knob in one hand. Using the pretext of examining the homing beacon to get closer to Jack, I had then shifted into super speed, gotten a grip on the bat with both hands, and then swung at his torso for all I was worth.

The bat had struck around his stomach. Frankly speaking, given his precognitive abilities, I was actually surprised that the blow had connected, and the force of it sent Jack smashing through several cubicles before smacking soundly against the far wall and falling to the floor. However, he recovered quickly, and was already coming to his feet as I dashed towards him.

"Okay, that's your freebie," he announced.

"What?" I asked, stopping a few feet from him, still gripping the bat. (However, no longer having the element of surprise, I allowed the bat to become visible.)

"That's your free shot," he said. "I owed you that for what I did earlier."

Now I understood; my swing with the invisible bat hadn't caught Jack unaware. He'd let me hit him.

"For what it's worth, it was an accident," he insisted. "I'd never intentionally hurt Gramps."

"Don't call him that!" I hissed. "He's not *your* grandfather. You almost killed him."

415

REPLICATION

"Almost?" Jack repeated, sounding incredulous. "You mean he's alive?"

He seemed elated by the news, which was infuriating since he was the one who had caved my grandfather's head in. And then, rather than teleport Gramps to a hospital (which you'd expect had it actually been an accident), he had fled, leaving my grandfather to die. Just the thought of what he'd done set my teeth on edge. A moment later, boundless rage abruptly exploded in me, and I went on the attack.

Shifting into super speed, I charged, swinging wildly with the bat. On his part, Jack brought up his arms, obviously to protect his head, but it left a lot of target areas open: legs, sides, back, as well as the arms themselves.

I swung at him with abandon, with every blow connecting solidly as I dashed around him lightning-quick. Remarkably, he held his ground this time, absorbing the blows that rained down on him from all sides. As I continued pummeling him, I heard him muttering something.

"Enough," he uttered as the bat continued striking. "Enough. Enough! ENOUGH!!!"

His last utterance came out as a bellow, forceful and deafening in the office space. At the same time, he reached out amazingly fast and snatched the bat from my hands. Gripping it by the handle and the barrel, he then brought the bat down angrily as he jerked a knee into the air. The bat struck the raised knee and bent in half.

I stared in shock at what I was seeing. In addition to the Bolt Blast, Jack also had super strength.

"I said that's enough," he stated as he flung the bat away. (Oddly enough, bent as it was, it actually looked like a boomerang and I half-expected it to come back at him.)

Then, seemingly noticing something on the back of his hand, he wiped it against his pants leg.

"Now, I understand you're upset," Jack said, "and again, I apologize. But this continued assault on me isn't healthy for either of us. We need to find a way to move past it. With that in mind, I suggest…I suggest…I, uh…I…"

As he began stammering, Jack's eyes started to blink almost spasmodically and his skin took on an unhealthy pallor. He shuddered once, like he'd taken a sudden chill, and then a second time. Without warning, he turned to the side and, bending over, abruptly spat up what looked like black blood. (Except he didn't so much spit it up as send it spewing out, like projectile vomit, all over a nearby cubicle.) Eyes almost glowing with fury, he turned to me, scowling.

"What did you do?!" he screeched, his face contorting in pain.

I simply smiled, but didn't say anything. What was happening to him was the last thing Gray had told me about with respect to Jack — a final failsafe in case there was ever a need to shut him down permanently. Basically, Jack's creators had inserted an artificial organ in him. However, rather than serve a beneficial purpose, like one's heart or lungs, the purpose of this one was malignant. It was full of vile, venomous toxins.

"It won't kill him," Gray had said, "but when the toxins are released, it'll shut down his bodily systems and place him in a coma."

It didn't seem as good as having Jack dead, but it was a reasonable compromise, and so I had acquiesced. Getting the organ to release the toxins, however, required a specific catalyst — namely, a specially-developed bio-agent.

"The catalyst can be administered orally, intravenously, or directly on the skin," Gray had informed me.

"Well, if you guys have had this all the while, why haven't you taken him down?" I'd asked.

"Can you see Jack letting someone come up and inject him with a needle?" Gray had retorted. "Or pour some unknown liquid down his throat? Plus, the catalyst only remains viable for three seconds after exposure to air, so there's only a small window for getting the job done. All of that combined with the fact that he's clairvoyant just made it too risky for any of my people."

And so the job had fallen to me, and my personal window of opportunity had come while I was hitting Jack with the bat. At super speed, it had taken practically no time at all to pull out a little vial of liquid that Gray had provided — the catalyst — and squirt it on the back of his hand. The blows from the bat were coming at such a rapid pace at that juncture that Jack didn't even notice. (It wasn't until he flung the bat away that he seemed to realize that there was a foreign substance on him.) Moreover, the initial swing with the bat — the one he'd allowed to connect — had been the seminal event on this occasion, so the subsequent threat with the toxins was something he hadn't foreseen.

Watching Jack now, his face a grimace, I started to wonder if I had overreacted. Despite what he'd done to Gramps, did I have the right to play judge, jury, and executioner — essentially robbing him of any type of life going forward? I shook my head to clear my thoughts;

regardless of whether I'd had the right to do what I did, it was too late now. The damage was done. Or so I thought.

As I watched, Jack unexpectedly stood up straight. He had his right hand on his chest and was howling in pain. And then I did a double-take as I saw what was really happening. His right hand wasn't *on* his chest; it was *in* his chest. In an incredible display of iron will, he had dug his own hand into his body, through flesh and bone — and I had an inkling as to why. A moment later, I was proved right when he withdrew his hand, holding in his grip what look like a pulsing black heart. However, instead of blood, it oozed out a noxious green-black fluid.

Breathing heavily, Jack flung the item down, where it struck the floor and splattered the dark liquid in a wide arc.

"As…I…was saying…," Jack muttered, plainly winded by his ordeal, "you…gotta…get past…this."

"You're dangerous, Jack," I countered. "There's no getting past that."

He gulped, and I noticed that his color was coming back. "I'm still…gonna consider…all of this…part of…your free shot." He then gave me a stern look before continuing. "But if you come at me again…it's game on."

And then he teleported.

Chapter 82

"So you failed," Mouse said.

"That's subject to interpretation," I countered.

"What is there to interpret? You went after Jack, and you didn't get him. That's a fail."

I rolled my eyes, but didn't say anything. We were in Mouse's lab, where I had teleported immediately after my most recent interaction with Jack. I had just finished relaying everything to him, and was now getting the benefit of his frank criticism.

"Anyway," Mouse went on, "I can't say I'm sad about the outcome. I didn't like the idea of you killing anybody."

"For the last time," I uttered in exasperation, "the final version of the plan did not include Jack's death."

"Well, being forcefully put into a coma isn't considered one of life's great joys."

"He almost killed Gramps," I said somberly.

Mouse placed a sympathetic hand on my shoulder. "I know, and I agree that something has to be done about him, but I don't want you going off half-cocked or trying to carry out half-baked schemes."

"Well, we may not have time for full-baked ones," I countered. "The powers he has now, including the Bolt Blast and super strength, coupled with a callous disregard for life, make him infinitely more dangerous than we ever imagined."

"Then maybe the plan needs to be to take those powers from him."

"You mean like with a nullifier?" I asked.

"That's one way," Mouse replied.

I shook my head. "Forget it. He's clairvoyant, remember? You'll never get him within a mile of a nullifier."

"But you said he can only see the initial threat in any given situation."

I pondered on this for a second. "So what are you saying — attack him in some other way first and make the nullifier the secondary threat?"

"Exactly," Mouse said with a smile. "The only question is, what should the initial threat be?"

"From what I understand, it can be anything. A shotgun, a grenade, a rocket launcher…"

Mouse laughed. "How about we focus on something a little less likely to do damage to life or property?"

"Like what?"

Mouse shrugged. "I don't know. Jack's based on you. Aside from a nullifier, what would you consider a threat?"

"You mean other than death or being put into a permanent coma?" I asked sardonically. "Probably anything that would cause the permanent loss of my powers."

"Hmmm," Mouse mused. "I think we can work with that."

REPLICATION

Chapter 83

Typically, Mouse's plans are above reproach. His tactics are usually strokes of genius, his stratagems the best path to success. That said, I was not enamored with the plan he came up with pertaining to Jack. Frankly speaking, I hated it.

Not that the plan itself was bad. As with all of Mouse's ideas, it was actually pretty good. The problem was what it required me to do: Mouse's plan necessitated that I get the *crown*.

The crown was exactly what it sounded like: a bejeweled coronet that I had worn while on Caeles. Unlike its Terran equivalents, however, my Caelesian crown also had internal components that were designed to send minute electrical impulses into my brain in order to help me quickly learn the Caelesian language. However, the villainous Caelesian prince Vicra had rewired the crown to track the neural pathways used when I activated my powers, and then used the information to develop a neural blocker that stripped me of my abilities. Although I eventually regained my powers, I had treated the crown like a poisonous viper ever since, keeping it constantly under lock and key.

And now, despite my personal misgivings, I had retrieved my royal coronet and had it with me in Mouse's lab.

"Are you sure about this?" I asked for about the umpteenth time as Mouse took my crown.

"Yes," he answered, sounding exasperated. "But I'm happy to go over the plan again if it'll make you more comfortable."

"Sure," I replied.

REPLICATION

"Okay, once more," Mouse muttered. "I'll use the crown to develop a neural blocker. Since Jack is a replica of you to a large extent, the neural blocker should work on him, although I may tweak it to give it a broader range to account for any minor differences that might exist. We'll use the neural blocker as an initial threat, which Jack will see through precognition and avoid. We'll have a nullifier set up as a secondary threat, for lack of a better term, which he shouldn't be able to see in his future, and we'll use it to trap him. Got it?"

"Yeah," I said with a nod, "but why do we have to use an *actual* neural blocker? Can't we just use a placebo and pretend that's what it is?"

Mouse shook his head. "From the way it's been described, I think Jack's ability homes in on legitimate threats, and a placebo wouldn't fit into that category. So if we use a placebo…"

"It won't be viewed as a real danger," I concluded, finishing his thought as my mentor trailed off. "At that point, the only true threat will be the nullifier, and at that juncture it will represent a seminal event, which Jack would be able to see in his future."

"Now you got it," Mouse intoned. "And that's why the neural blocker has to be real."

"Well, why can't we use a gun or something? Wouldn't that work?"

"With his super strength, there's no guarantee that bullets will hurt him. And if he can't be hurt by it, his precognitive talents may not peg it as a threat."

"Which brings us back to using the neural blocker," I said in resignation. "Okay, so what can I do?"

"Nothing, in that regard," Mouse confided. "But I have another task for you."

423

"What?" I asked, eager to help.
"I need you to find your evil twin."

REPLICATION

Mouse was right. It wasn't going to do us any good to have a plan for stopping Jack if we didn't know where to find him. Moreover, for obvious reasons, Mouse thought I was the best person to figure out where he was holed up.

Personally, I thought it was a tall order. Being a teleporter, Jack could be anywhere, and he'd already shown he was crafty. On those forensic shows on television, they always use things like dirt on someone's shoes or fibers from their clothing to pinpoint an individual's location or movements, but we didn't have anything like that here. That being the case, I wasn't even sure where to start. Still, I teleported to my quarters at HQ to noodle on the problem, flopping down on the sofa as I considered everything I knew about Jack.

To be perfectly honest, I didn't know all that much. Our interactions had been limited, to say the least, and had grown worse in terms of temperament with each encounter.

Moving on from when Jack and I had crossed paths, I thought about what I knew of the other places he'd been in hopes that they might offer a clue as to his whereabouts. However, there wasn't much meat on the bone in that regard either. I could name a number of places he'd visited, but didn't think they offered much in the way of insight: Vestibule's park, my father's mansion, League HQ, my grandmother's embassy...

My thoughts suddenly shifted as I noticed a pattern in Jack's behavior. He had seemingly teleported into three of the venues I'd been thinking of — the park, the mansion, and HQ — but had picked the lock to gain entry

425

to the embassy. The reason for his different *modus operandi* at the embassy was obvious: he hadn't been there before. With the park, however, he'd previously visited it with Vestibule prior to chatting with me there. Likewise, as to HQ — specifically the teen lounge — he had spoken to Smokey there prior to his run-in with the teen supers the previous day. But my father's mansion…? When had he visited it prior to being gutshot?

The answer that immediately leaped out at me was my grandparents' party. That was the best opportunity for Jack to have gotten inside Alpha Prime's palatial home. Unfortunately, the security system was turned off that night (including the panic room monitors), so there was no video I could review for confirmation of his presence. However, there *had* been a photographer there — Matt Kroner.

Moreover, upon reflection, I recalled Kroner labeling me a "quick-change artist" when he took his picture of me and Electra. The comment hadn't made sense at the time, but now it did. Presumably, at some point prior to taking our photo, Kroner had seen Jack — most likely in a different ensemble than I'd been wearing at the time. Had they spoken? If so, had Jack perhaps said something that could be used to track him down?

Feeling that I was onto something (but unsure of what it was), I jumped up, intent on locating Matt Kroner. It was a long shot, no doubt, but I didn't have a lot of options or ideas (nor, at that juncture, a lot to lose).

Thankfully, running Kroner down wasn't particularly difficult; it just took me calling one of the newspapers where he freelanced and asking how to get in touch with him about his photos. Finding out where he actually was, on the other hand, came as a bit of a shock: according to the newspaper, Kroner was in the hospital.

REPLICATION

It wasn't visiting hours, so I turned invisible in order to slip past the nurse's station in the intensive care unit where Kroner was being treated. Upon reaching his door, I phased and went inside.

Kroner's hospital room wasn't completely full of cards and flowers, but had a healthy complement of them — enough to indicate that he was a nice guy and well-liked. Looking at him, it occurred to me that he needed all the well-wishes he could get. From all appearances, Kroner was practically in a body cast.

There was a space for his face, holes for his ears, and the top of his noggin was exposed, but otherwise his head seemed encased in plaster. Likewise for his neck and torso, as well as most of his limbs. About the only thing not currently wrapped and immobilized by casting material was his left arm and right thigh. He'd obviously had a serious accident recently.

He couldn't move his head, but he glanced in my direction as I made myself visible. His eyes went wide in fright, while panic and alarm surged in him with blazing speed.

"Easy, easy," I muttered, trying to keep him calm. "I didn't mean to startle you."

My words seemed to have something of the desired effect, as his trepidation began to subside and the fearful expression on his face was replaced by one of confusion.

"Jure nah him," he almost whispered between clenched teeth. It took me a second to translate his statement as "You're not him." At the same time, I realized why he seemed to be having trouble speaking: his jaw was wired shut.

428

REPLICATION

Before I could respond, I heard the doorknob being turned. I immediately went invisible and floated up into a corner of the room. A moment later, an attractive, middle-aged woman wearing a nurse's uniform stepped in.

"Are you okay, Mr. Kroner?" the nurse asked as she approached his bedside.

Kroner didn't respond. Instead, he simply looked at the spot where I'd been standing a few moments earlier, frowning in concentration.

"Mr. Kroner," the nurse repeated, "is everything okay?"

This time, the question seemed to snap Kroner back to the present.

"Yeth," he replied to the nurse. He then held up his left hand, revealing a nurse call button that I hadn't noticed before. "Thorry. Athident."

The nurse smiled. "No need to be sorry. The doctor said you might experience some muscle spasms, so if you accidentally hit the button a couple of times, it's okay. Let me know if you need anything."

She then turned and left. A moment later, I floated back down and became visible again.

Kroner gave me a bit of a smile. "Thorry. I—"

<Don't worry about trying to speak,> I said telepathically, cutting him off as I mentally reached out. <We can just communicate like this, mind-to-mind.>

<Works for me,> he replied.

<Again, I apologize if I startled you, appearing and disappearing like I just did. I'm sure you weren't expecting that.>

<Not *that*, specifically,> he corrected. <But if you're hanging out with the likes of Indigo and Electra, it

stands to reason that you have some level of super powers.>

    <It's a fair deduction,> I noted.

    <As I was saying, though, sorry about the nurse. I panicked and hit the call button — thought you were the other guy. I was afraid you — I mean, *he* — had come back to finish the job.>

    <Wait a minute!> I boomed, surprised. <My evil twin did this to you?>

    <Yeah, this is his handiwork,> Kroner confirmed, mentally nodding. <So he's your twin?>

    <Not exactly; I just call him that. How'd you know that I wasn't him?>

    <His demeanor was worlds apart from yours. Hard. Callous. Indifferent. Of course, my opinion stems from the fact that he beat me to a pulp, so I might be biased.>

    <But why would he do this to you?>

    <Because I didn't give him the photos from the party.>

    <You mean the party that was held for Indigo and Nightmare?> I asked, using my grandfather's superhero pseudonym.

    <Yeah, he showed up at my apartment a few days ago. I initially thought he was you and let him in.>

    <How'd he even know where to find you?> I asked.

    <I gave my card out like candy at the party,> Kroner replied. <I was hoping to drum up some more business, maybe develop a high-end client list.>

    I nodded but didn't say anything immediately, as it had occurred to me after I asked my question that Jack might also have used his clairvoyant abilities to figure out where to find Kroner.

<Anyway,> he continued, <your evil twin said he wanted the pictures from the party. I asked, 'What pictures?' — meaning which specific photos — but he apparently thought I was being a wise guy and insinuating that no such pictures existed. Next thing I knew, he punched me in the face. After that, he asked again, and when he didn't get the answer he wanted, he just went to town on me in the living room of my own apartment, slinging me around the place like I was a piñata he was trying to smash open. At some point I passed out, and when I came to, I was here.>

<I'm sorry,> I offered in sympathy. <Why didn't you just tell him what he wanted to know?>

Kroner scoffed. <Believe me, I would have told him that and anything else he asked about. Problem is, that first punch broke my jaw. It's wired shut now. Didn't you notice I could barely talk?>

<Yeah, but I thought maybe you were just hopped up on pain medicine or something.>

<Well, yeah, there's a little bit of that going on, too,> he admitted. <I could stand to have the dosage increased, but I'm not looking to get addicted to this stuff.>

<Guess you have a high pain tolerance, huh?>

<On the contrary, I'd argue it's pretty low. As I said, the only thing that kept me from spilling my guts was the fact that I couldn't talk, and I was passed out while he did the bulk of his damage — breaking my limbs, busting my ribs, cracking a couple of vertebrae in my neck and spine…>

<Geez, Matt,> I muttered, lowering my eyes. <Again, I'm sorry.>

<Hey, you didn't do anything wrong,> he acknowledged. <And I'm not trolling for sympathy. I'm just matter-of-fact about this stuff. But don't feel like you have to keep apologizing.>

<Thanks,> I said sincerely. <So, what happened to the pictures he wanted to so badly?>

<He may have gotten them,> Kroner admitted. <A friend went by to clean up my place the day after it happened. She found my camera flattened like a pancake.>

<So we can give up on pulling any images from the hard drive.>

<Or the chip,> he added. <From what my friend said, they're both lost causes.>

<That's too bad,> I said, trying not to sound disappointed.

<Yeah,> Kroner agreed. <Guess it's a good thing I made copies.>

REPLICATION

Chapter 86

It turned out that Kroner — having previously lost some photos due to technical issues — now made a habit of regularly copying photos from his camera to his laptop. Moreover, while his camera had been pulverized, said laptop (which was in his bedroom at the time of his encounter with Jack) had escaped the same fate. It was currently in the hands of the friend who had come by to clean up his place after the attack.

<Her name's Melanie,> Kroner said. <With people knowing what happened to me and that I'll be laid up here for a while, she took it for safekeeping — just in case an empty apartment proved too tempting to someone with criminal tendencies.>

After that, it was just a matter of getting Kroner to call his friend on my phone and convince her to give me his laptop. It was a little dicey with his jaw being wired, but in the end — with Kroner's blessing — she agreed to meet me in an hour and hand it over.

<Thanks, man,> I said as the call ended. <I wish there was something more I could do to show how much I appreciate your help.>

<Just get the guy that did this,> he replied.

<That's the plan,> I said. <In the meantime, maybe there's something else I can do.>

I then tried to use my healing power on him. After all, it had just saved Gramps when he was banging on death's door with a battering ram. Surely it could help Kroner, who wasn't anywhere near that condition. Much to my chagrin, however, it did not work.

Humbled by my failure, I thanked Kroner again for his help and then left.

REPLICATION

The meeting with Melanie went off without a hitch, and an hour after the call with her, I had the coveted laptop in hand. Still unsure of whether it held anything of value, I teleported to my quarters at HQ. Taking a seat on the couch in the living room, I opened up the laptop and pulled up the folder containing Kroner's pictures (which were, thankfully, grouped by date).

Turning to those from the party, I began quickly sifting through the photos, of which there were hundreds. Kroner had obviously worked hard to earn his pay, and he clearly had a good eye. Many of the pictures weren't just frame-worthy — they were good enough for commercial advertising.

For instance, one pic of a kid reading a book in my father's library could have been used in any effort to promote literacy. Another photo of a man and woman dancing while looking lovingly at each other could have graced the cover of any romance novel. An image of a group of friends having a toast at the bar seemed tailor-made for plugging a New Year's celebration (or something similar). In short, Kroner's talent was probably wasted doing freelance work.

Staying focused on the task at hand, I kept my eyes peeled for any photo containing my doppelganger. It took about ten minutes, but I finally located one. It was actually a picture of my grandparents, standing close with their arms around each other — with Jack basically performing a photobomb in the background, giving the two of them a fixated stare.

And just looking at it, I knew with almost certainty where to find him.

REPLICATION

Chapter 87

I immediately teleported to Mouse's lab (where my mentor and BT were still getting everything together) and reported the good news.

"That's great," BT said when I told them what I'd discovered. "We probably need about another hour before we're ready."

Neither she nor Mouse said anything else, but I got the hint: I was about to undertake a dangerous mission. If there were people I needed to spend some time with, there was a very small amount of time available to do so. With that in mind (and knowing that these kinds of opportunities didn't come along often), I told them I'd be back shortly and teleported home.

****

Once at the embassy, I gathered in the breakfast area with Mom, Indigo, and Myshtal. I gave them a brief overview of how the day had gone and let them know we had a plan for dealing with Jack (although I didn't give them the details). I then asked about Gramps.

"We had someone come by to check on him," my mother said. I nodded, understanding that she meant someone on a short list of physicians that we trusted. "The doctor said that Dad's fine as far as he can tell. He's just sleeping."

"But there's no telling when he'll wake up," my grandmother added.

"Can I see him?" I asked.

The three of them exchanged an odd look amongst themselves, and I sensed unusual emotions arising in each

436

of them. It wasn't anything that would make me think Gramps was in danger, such as anxiety or worry. It was more along the lines of bewilderment and stupefaction — as if they'd awakened and discovered a unicorn in the backyard. Before the silence got too awkward, however, Myshtal spoke up.

"Of course you can see him if you want," Myshtal said. "But even though the prognosis is that he's fine, he's obviously not at his best and probably wouldn't want you to see him this way — especially if there's a chance it will affect how you go about your mission today."

I frowned, contemplating. Seeing what Jack did to Gramps had certainly pushed me over the line earlier. (In fact, it wasn't too far from my mind right now.) Whether I saw him or not, there was every chance that what had happened to my grandfather would have an effect on the mission. That said, I didn't need to do anything that might put me more off-balance than I already was.

"Okay," I finally said. "I'll see him later."

****

I only spent a few more minutes with my family and Myshtal, then dashed to my room and called Electra. She answered after the first ring.

"Hello, sweet prince," she said.

"Hey," I said in response. "Listen, I don't have much time, but I was wondering if I could come by and snatch a little joy."

"Huh?" she murmured. "Oh! Oh, yes. Of course. I'm home now."

I hung up and teleported to her front door. Electra snatched it open before I even had a chance to ring the

437

bell. She closed the door and hugged me fiercely as I stepped inside — as if she never wanted to let me go. Eventually she did, however; stepping back and taking my hand, she guided me to a nearby loveseat and then pulled me down next to her. She then listened intently as I shared everything that had happened since I woke up. When I was done, she simply sat there quietly for a moment, plainly thinking about what she'd heard.

"You know," she finally said, "I don't often wish for the people I care about to fall flat on their face, but I'm glad you didn't succeed with Jack earlier."

I had trouble hiding my curiosity. "Why is that?"

"Because it was premeditated, Jim. It would have been murder. It's like a cop going out with the specific intent to shoot a suspect. It's one thing if it happens in the line of duty, but it's something else entirely if that was the objective."

"What everybody keeps forgetting is that I ultimately decided against putting him in the ground. I admit that if I'd seen him within five minutes of what he did to Gramps, I'd still be choking him. But again, the plan changed."

"So let me ask you something," she said. "Had everything gone as intended and Jack had slipped into a coma, what was supposed to happen then?"

"Huh?" I mumbled in confusion. "I'm not sure what you mean. The fight would have been over."

"But Jack would have been in a coma, right?" Electra queried. "What was the plan for getting him medical attention?"

"Wh-what?" I stammered.

"He would have been in a coma, with all his organs shut down. Surely you had a plan for getting him treatment? Perhaps a team of paramedics standing by? Or maybe you'd teleport him to a hospital?"

"Probably teleport him," I replied sheepishly. "To be honest, I didn't think much about what would happen after."

"But you knew your actions would have life-or-death consequences for him," she said. "And it would have been premeditated."

I frowned. As I'd told Electra, I really hadn't considered what would have happened had I been successful during my last encounter with Jack. Without psychoanalyzing myself, there was undeniably a part of me that wanted him dead. But did I subconsciously realize what would happen if he'd gone into a coma and just blocked it out?

"Anyway," Electra continued, "I'll repeat my earlier statement and say that I'm glad you failed. I don't need any more people that I care about locked up for no good reason."

I simply nodded, knowing without asking that she was talking about her father, Vir. It wasn't a subject that she generally talked about directly, so I showed my support by slipping my arm around her and giving her a heartfelt hug.

Chapter 88

The amount of time I had available to spend with Electra was short to begin with, and passed in the blink of an eye. We said our goodbyes (with me stealing one last kiss), and then I teleported to Mouse's lab. When I popped up, my mentor and BT were there waiting on me.

"All set?" I asked.

"Ready when you are," Mouse replied.

"My clones have everything in position," BT added, "so we're good on that front."

"So, that just leaves one final detail," Mouse noted. He then held out his hand to me, palm up. In it was a rectangular, wooden box. Mouse then opened the box to reveal a custom-fitted interior lining in which rested a narrow syringe with a barrel about six inches long and a protective cap over the needle. Inside the barrel, I noticed a peculiar, yellow-orange fluid.

"The neural blocker?" I asked as I reached out and gingerly took the box.

"Yeah," my mentor answered. "It's based on *your* synaptic patterns, as indicated by your crown, but — because Jack isn't an exact clone of you — we attempted to broaden the effective range. Also, it's geared to activate almost immediately once any form of contact is made."

"That includes the skin," BT tacked on, "so don't get any on you."

"Understood," I said.

"Also, bear in mind that there's no way to test this stuff," Mouse declared. "You and Jack are the only people it will work on because of your unique synaptic formation, so — short of you volunteering to be a guinea pig — there was no way to determine how effective it will be, such as how long it's likely to strip you of your powers."

"Great — just what I always wanted," I deadpanned as I closed the box. "So the takeaway is basically to be very, very careful with the syringe."

"That's the gist of it," Mouse agreed. "We ready now?"

"As ready as we'll ever be," I answered.

With that, I teleported myself and Mouse to the position he was going to hold while we sprang our trap on Jack. Next, I teleported home and grabbed a jacket from my closet. I didn't need it for the weather, but for subterfuge. The invisible-item-in-my-hand gag had worked once with the bat, but wasn't likely to be successful a second time. Keeping that in mind, I needed a place to keep the box holding the syringe until I needed it. The jacket I selected had a deep interior pocket, so I shoved the box in there and zipped the jacket up.

Now fully prepared, I took a moment to mentally prepare myself, and then teleported to the place where Jack had gone to ground.

Chapter 89

I popped up in the living room of my condo. It was a very nice three-bedroom, two-bath unit, but knowing someone had been killed there made it lose a lot of its appeal. Just thinking about it almost made be frown in distaste, but I managed to keep my game face on.

In confirmation of my suspicions, Jack was there, sitting on the sofa.

"We meet again," he said, giving me a short wave. "Nice detective work in locating me."

I shrugged. "Wasn't that hard. You wore a tux to my grandparents' party with a red bow tie. Gramps gave me that tie when I attended my first formal event a few years ago. He bought it for me, taught me how to tie it. I recognized it immediately. I also remembered that I kept it here."

Jack grinned. "Yeah, I got the feeling there was something sentimental about that tie as soon as I saw it. Guess I was right."

"Well, if you like it, keep it."

He gave me a look of surprise. "You're kidding, right? I mean, I know how possessive you are."

I shook my head. "No, I'm serious. Keep it."

"Thanks," he intoned softly, almost disbelievingly. "So, I take it you're here to pick up where we left off this morning."

"No," I stated, shaking my head.

"No?" he repeated. It obviously wasn't the answer he had expected. "Does that finally mean you're ready to join me?"

"I think I've made my position on your proposal very clear."

"But you don't even know what I'm offering," he pleaded. "I can show you the *secret*."

I frowned. "What secret?"

"How to get the Bolt Blast!" he exclaimed. "Super strength! It's an outgrowth of the things the scientists did when they were forcing me to develop powers like yours — something I learned to do. I can show you how to generate any power you want."

"Does that include telepathy?" I asked casually.

Jack looked taken aback for a moment, but then recovered. "Okay, that was a little below the belt, but I'll simply respond by modifying my original statement. I can show you how to generate *almost* any power you want."

"No thanks," I said, doing my best to appear to turn him down flat. (In truth, however, I had to admit to being intrigued.)

Jack's eyes narrowed. "So if you aren't here to join me or to fight me, why *are* you here?"

"Once I realized where you were, I remembered that I'd left something important here — something I wanted to keep."

"What?" Jack inquired. However, he'd barely started forming the word with his mouth when I switched to super speed, dashed into one of the guest bedrooms, then zipped back out again.

"Got it," I said, shoving my hand into my jacket pocket as Jack watched me, looking befuddled. "Alright, I'm good. You can have this place and everything in it. See you around."

"Wait!" Jack roared, coming to his feet. "What did you take?"

"Huh?" I asked, giving him a bewildered look.

"What did you take?!" he demanded, looking angry.

443

"Just something important to me," I insisted.

"Let me see," he ordered, holding out his hand.

I looked at his outstretched hand for a moment, then shook my head. "I don't think so."

"Give it to me!" he bellowed. "*Now!*"

"Make me," I said, then phased and went flying through an exterior wall to the outside.

A moment later, concrete, drywall, and various pieces of debris came erupting from the side of the building with a sound like a mortar being fired. It was Jack, of course, crashing through the wall at full speed and coming after me. Smiling to myself, I turned and took off, knowing he'd be right behind me.

****

My condo wasn't located too far from downtown, which was where I headed. I zigzagged between a couple of high-rises along the way — evasive maneuvers that Jack would probably expect, but nothing to throw him off my trail. In the meanwhile, as we drew close to the designated spot of our snare, I reached out telepathically to Mouse.

<We're almost there,> I said. <Are you ready?>

<Affirmative,> Mouse replied.

Inwardly, I sighed in relief. Bearing in mind that our plan required coordination, I kept the telepathic channel open between me and my mentor. Glancing back to make sure Jack was still in pursuit (he was), I headed towards my destination: four skyscrapers in close proximity which — when seen from above — could be viewed as forming the corners of a square, and a fifth high-rise that was centered between them.

REPLICATION

Mentally I crossed my fingers as I went through our strategy again in my head. In essence, BT's clones had placed specialized equipment near the roof of each skyscraper forming the corners of the aforementioned "square." When turned on, they would operate in conjunction to form a giant nullifier around the fifth building that was in the center. My job was to get Jack to the roof of that center building, and then attack him with the syringe containing the neural blocker. Assuming his precognition was effective, he'd see that threat and somehow avoid it. We'd then activate the nullifier equipment (which Jack presumably wouldn't have seen in his future), and at that point he'd be trapped on the roof without his powers and could be taken into custody at our leisure.

The real trick had been figuring out how to get Jack to the proper location. After tossing around numerous ideas, it had finally come to me that I could possibly use Jack's own nature against him. He was latching onto the things in my life that had meaning for me: friends, family, and so on. It had then occurred to me that if I took something of significance away from him (or pretended to), he'd be obsessed with getting it back. Surprisingly, it had worked, with me pretending to take something from the condo and Jack now manically pursuing me for it.

<Jim!!!> Mouse unexpectedly screamed, bringing me back to the present. <Veer off!!>

I acted instinctively, arcing away with Mouse's shout ringing in my head just before I reached the outer edge of the region that would be covered by our nullifier.

<What is it?!> I asked anxiously. <What happened?>

REPLICATION

<The nullifier accidentally activated!> Mouse replied.

<What?!> I screamed, as I suddenly had an awful vision of what would have happened had I flown into range of an active nullifier and then lost my powers.

<It's not on anymore,> Mouse assured me. <Now get Jack to the center building.>

Somewhat less confident now, I headed back to my original destination (and a quick look over my shoulder confirmed that Jack was still behind me). I felt relief a few moments later as I entered the square to be formed by the nullifier and managed to stay airborne instead of plunging to my death. However, as I angled towards the rooftop of the center high-rise, a shaft of blue light went hurtling by me.

Bolt Blast! I thought. Had Jack tried to hit me? Despite how potent it was, he had to know that the Bolt Blast was the one power he possessed that probably wouldn't harm me. In short, family members were immune to it — for instance, Paramount's Bolt Blast had no effect on me. Thus, since Jack was a near-clone of me, it seemed unlikely that he could injure me using that particular weapon.

I was tempted to track the Bolt Blast to see where it hit, but decided it was better to fully focus on the task at hand. (I did note, however, that it appeared to be headed in the direction of one of the buildings, although at this elevation — near the rooftops of skyscrapers — the odds were remote that it would put any lives in danger.) A few seconds later, I landed on the roof of the center building.

The roof of the building was incredibly expansive — tens of thousands of square feet in size, at the very least. It was generally flat, but across its surface was an extensive array of large AC units (each of which was perhaps four feet tall, four feet wide, and ten feet long), along with vents and a couple of satellite antennas. There was also an enclosed structure with a door and windows that I took to be some kind of electrical room. Finally, the south side of the roof was also home to a network of solar panels, which was housed on a metal racking system that rose approximately forty feet in the air. However, I barely had time to take everything in before Jack landed about a dozen yards away from me.

We stood there for a moment, silently facing each other. At this height, the wind was whipping strongly, but neither of us was bothered by the weather. We were like two gunslingers in the Old West, about to face off. (Truth be told, the only thing needed to complete the imagery was having a tumbleweed blow between us.)

"I want whatever it was you took," Jack said.

"People in the desert want rain," I responded. "You don't always get what you want."

I then reached out telepathically to my mentor, saying, <Mouse, what's going on? Are we ready?>

<We're having issues,> he stated. <Stall.>

"Why does it have to be like this?" Jack implored. "Why do you have to be against me? There's so much we can do together."

"Like denting the skulls of senior citizens?" I asked sardonically.

His face unexpectedly shifted into a mask of anger. Rising about twenty feet into the air, he said, "You want to be enemies? So be it. But I'll give you one chance to walk away from here today — just show me what you took."

447

REPLICATION

I didn't like having to look up at him. It's a psychological move, meant to imply superiority. Well, I wasn't going to play that game.

Rising up to about the same height as Jack, I said, "I'm not showing you anything. There are some things that are personal to me and me alone."

"Don't make me take it from you, Jim. It won't be a pleasant experience for you."

I was about to tell him that I'd love for him to try when Mouse's voice sounded in my head.

<Jim, inject him with the syringe!> my mentor ordered.

Here we go, I said to myself.

I gave Jack a solemn look. "Fine. If you're that interested, I'll show you."

I reached into my jacket's interior pocket and pulled out the wooden case. As expected, Jack began moving towards me, closing the distance between us as he stared at what I held. In my head, I began playing out the upcoming scene: *I'd pop open the case, grab the syringe and attempt to inject him. With his clairvoyance, Jack would see the threat coming and avoid it, after which Mouse would turn on the nulli —*

My thoughts were cut off as I abruptly dropped like a stone down to the roof of the building, as did Jack. I landed on my side and pain lanced throughout my entire body as the wind was knocked out of me. (Much to my chagrin, Jack seemed to land on his feet.)

<What the hell, Mouse?> I cried telepathically. <Did you turn on the nullifier?>

Then I realized I'd answered my own question: if the nullifier were on, I wouldn't have my telepathy. But in that case, why had I fallen? And why wasn't I able to turn off my pain receptors? (And believe me, I was trying.)

<Listen,> Mouse said. <You have to inject Jack with the neural blocker.>

<How's that?>

<When the nullifier came on before, *that* was the seminal event — the one Jack could see,> Mouse explained. <The neural blocker is now the second threat. It's the one he's unaware of.>

<So our whole plan's backwards now?> I asked.

<Basically.>

<Okay, but there's something weird going on with my powers. I can't seem to fly or manipulate my bodily systems.>

<It's the nullifier,> Mouse stated. <It's not fully functional. Something took out the equipment on one of the corner buildings.>

The Bolt Blast! I realized with a start. Jack hadn't been trying to hit me. He'd been taking aim at the nullifier equipment. For a moment I was worried, as Mouse was actually with the equipment on one of the other buildings. Thankfully, Jack had only fired the one blast (and from all indications, my mentor was okay).

<I'm working on a fix, but the end result seems to be that you won't have your full slate of powers,> Mouse continued, <but neither will Jack.>

Because of the speed involved in telepathy, the conversation with Mouse only took a few seconds. Needing him to concentrate on the nullifier, I broke the mental connection to my mentor. I then turned towards my doppelganger and saw him bending down to retrieve something. It was the wooden box holding the syringe; I had apparently dropped it when I fell to the roof.

REPLICATION

Somewhat panicked, I began trying to rise when I noticed two things. First, Jack turned the box upside down and shook it, but nothing came out. It was empty.

The other thing I noticed was the syringe. It was lying under an AC unit not far from my evil twin. It seemed that when I dropped the box containing it, the syringe had rolled free.

As I struggled to my feet, Jack apparently came to the same conclusion I did regarding the box's contents, because he bent down, gripped the underside of an AC unit next to him with one hand, and ripped it up from the roof almost effortlessly, bolts and all. My eyes widened as I realized he still had super strength. Fortunately, the syringe was not under the unit in question.

Rethinking his strategy, Jack unexpectedly got down on all fours, peering under the structures near him. Seeing that, I became decidedly more anxious. Assuming he retrieved it, Jack wouldn't know what the syringe contained, but it wouldn't take a genius to figure out that it wasn't anything beneficial. More to the point, if he got his hands on it, I had serious doubts about my ability to take it away from him as long as he had super strength.

Feeling somewhat desperate, I quickly did a sound check of my powers as Jack came back to his feet — specifically, those that might let me get the syringe before Jack.

Telekinesis? No.
Teleportation? No.
Super speed? No.

Nothing that might help seemed to be working, and I grew a little anxious as Jack began moving towards the AC unit that was over the syringe. As he bent down and gripped the underside of the structure, I made a last-ditch effort. All of my prior attempts to use my powers were focused on getting the syringe into my hands; this time, I attempted to use a power that would keep it away from Jack: invisibility. Much to my surprise, it worked.

The expression on his face was classic as, after lifting the AC unit and expecting to find the syringe, he saw nothing. He then glanced around, looking completely befuddled — until his eyes settled on me.

Up until that point, Jack had seemingly forgotten about me. Maybe he thought that I was unconscious. Or maybe he believed that the fall had killed me. Or maybe he was just hyper-focused on the contents of the wooden box. Regardless, he had suddenly become acutely aware of my presence, and that was a serious problem.

"What did you do with it?" he asked, stalking towards me.

"Do with what?" I asked, feigning ignorance.

Rather than respond verbally, Jack growled and leaped at me. Anticipating something along those lines, I turned invisible, at the same time ducking and diving to the side. Luck was with me because I managed to evade his grasp, but just barely. I then scrambled away madly as he turned around looking for me, his face contorted with rage.

"Where are you?!" he demanded.

Oh yeah — like I'm gonna answer that, I thought.

I quietly slipped around a couple of AC units, heading for the syringe. My vision had switched over to the infrared once I became invisible, so I didn't have any trouble spotting it. However, before I could get to it, I had my feet knocked from under me.

I landed on my backside, wondering what was happening since the entire building seemed to shake for a few seconds. An earthquake, maybe? Getting to my feet after the shuddering subsided, I looked around for Jack; he was standing in roughly the same area where he'd leaped at me, and as I watched, I saw him raise and then stomp his foot. In conjunction with his action, the roof shook again, and I struggled to stay on my feet.

So that was his plan. If he couldn't see me, then he'd simply try to prevent me from moving by keeping me off-balance. It wasn't a terrible idea, and with super strength, he could probably keep it up indefinitely. (Presumably, however, he'd only keep at it until he found some way to sweep the roof and locate me.) Not caring to wait until his plan unfolded, I came up with an idea. I employed my invisibility power once more, and then made myself visible.

Jack was in the process of raising his foot to stomp again when he saw me. Rather than say anything, he simply charged, growling menacingly. I stood my ground as he came barreling towards me — and then tried not to laugh as Jack seemed to run unexpectedly (and painfully) into an invisible wall of sorts. In truth, however, it wasn't a wall but rather one of the AC units that I'd turned invisible (and I had to hustle to get out of the way, as — with a screech of torn metal — the force of Jack's impact ripped it from its moorings and sent it skidding across the roof). It wasn't as satisfying as maybe punching him myself, but it was the next best thing.

The incident left Jack momentarily disoriented, and I used the opportunity to go after the syringe. Switching my vision to the infrared, I noticed that it had rolled away from its prior location — presumably because of Jack's earthquake mimicry — but didn't seem to be damaged. Gripping it in my hand but leaving it invisible, I looked back at Jack and saw that he appeared to have recovered.

REPLICATION

Jack rushed me again, with similar results as the first time, but he was obviously a quick study. It only took two more unexpected encounters with roofing structures to make him tire of this new game. A little banged up but none the worse for wear, he changed his tactics and gave up on charging at me like a shark that smelled blood in the water.

On my part, I was disappointed. I'd been hoping Jack would be so enraged by me evading him that he'd keep running into things until he knocked himself out. (Or, barring that, at least dazed himself sufficiently for me to inject him with the neural blocker.) Now, noticing the way he stared at me, I could tell that he was thinking of some new way to deal with the problem I represented.

There was about forty feet between us when Jack made his move. Unexpectedly, he reached for a satellite dish that was near him and, in one fluid motion, ripped off the reflector and flung it at me. Shaped like a dish, the reflector came in low and fast, and I instinctively jumped to avoid having it take me out at the knees. It was a critical error.

Once, years ago, I'd had a short stint playing basketball in an intramural league. We'd been fortunate to have as our coach a neighborhood mom who had played both in college and professionally. One of the things she'd taught us was that when you have the ball and someone's defending you, if you can get them to leave their feet you've got the advantage, because they're committed at that point.

That's exactly what Jack had gotten me to do. Jumping up had committed me to a course that I couldn't deviate from; once I was in the air, I couldn't do anything but go back down. And Jack, apparently guessing what my

453

reaction would be to the projectile he'd flung my way, had followed up on his throw by immediately leaping at me.

In the movies, it would have been one of those scenes where everything slows down: as Jack came at me, I would have brought up the syringe, popped the protective cap off, and put my thumb on the plunger. And then, as he reached me, we'd go down to the ground with him on top of me. A moment later, I roll him off me, with the syringe sticking out of his chest. Cue applause.

None of that happened.

Having left my feet, I saw him coming at me and realized there was nothing I could do. There certainly wasn't time to get the syringe in position to inject him. All I could really do was try to brace myself somewhat as he hit me like a missile.

I went down hard, banging my head soundly on the surface of the roof as once again I had the wind knocked out of me. At the same time, I lost my grip on the syringe, which went skittering off to the side. I was a little stunned and trying to get my bearings when I found myself hoisted off the ground by the neck. Jack, holding me aloft with one hand, smiled.

"I told you this wouldn't end pleasantly for you," he reminded me. "I'm sincerely sorry it has to be this way."

Slowly, he began to squeeze.

REPLICATION

Chapter 90

Feet dangling, I clawed and beat frantically at the hand gripping me, but to no avail. My efforts made no impression on Jack — I'm not even sure he felt them. As my body began to run out of air, I started to see spots before my eyes. In about a minute or less, I'd pass out and it would all be over.

Oddly enough, what flitted through my mind at that point wasn't nostalgic memories of my family, recollections of having fun with my friends, or reflections on time spent with my girlfriend. No, what popped up in my brain was what I considered the one silver lining that would come out of dying by Jack's hand: I wouldn't have to work for Gray now.

Gray! Just the name brought to mind a crucial fact I'd forgotten, and gave me a slim sliver of hope.

Almost in a panic, I began trying to alter my features. I didn't even know if I still had my shapeshifting ability, as I hadn't tried it since we'd been on the roof. A moment later, I felt a small sense of relief as I felt changes taking place with my countenance, but with Jack's iron grip around my throat, I was still deep in the danger zone.

Without warning, the vise around my neck loosened. It wasn't enough to let me drop to the ground, but I was able to draw in air again. After a few deep breaths, my vision cleared, and I saw Jack staring at me with a mix of bewilderment, anger, and determination. The hand that held me seemed to pulse, squeezing and loosening almost rhythmically. I understood what was happening: flexor and extensor muscles in Jack's hand were engaging in an epic battle, with the former trying to choke me out and the latter trying to let me go.

Jack's hand began to tremble with the conflicting effort, which was basically a reflection of the mental battle he must be going through. On the one hand was his desire to kill me; on the other was the fact that his conditioning wouldn't let him harm Gray, whose face I now wore.

"What is this?" Jack asked. "What have you done to me?"

Despite how dire my situation was, I laughed — right in his face. Jack obviously didn't know about the psychological barriers his handlers had placed in his head.

My amusement infuriated Jack, and he literally redoubled his efforts to strangle me by placing his other hand around my neck as well. Arms trembling and visibly straining with exertion, he continued trying to throttle me, grunting loudly. As much as he tried, however, his handhold never got any tighter. Finally, after about fifteen seconds of futile struggle, he released me, howling in exasperation.

I landed off-balance and flopped onto my rear. I put a hand up to my neck, gently massaging my throat while at the same time awkwardly scuttling backwards, trying to put some distance between myself and Jack. But it turned out that there was no need to rush, as my doppelganger was momentarily preoccupied.

Jack was staring at his hands in utter confusion, as if he didn't know what these weird appendages were that happened to be attached to the ends of his arms or where they'd come from. What had just occurred had to be unsettling for him; his body had essentially refused to obey him. It was akin to going to the fridge for a soda, but every time you try to reach for it, your hand grabs the milk instead.

REPLICATION

All of a sudden, Jack put his hands to his face, covering his eyes. It was an unexpected move on his part, and ostensibly, it gave the appearance that he was weeping. Somehow, though, I doubted that's what was happening; in my opinion, my evil twin wasn't the crying type, and in short order that was shown to be a correct assessment.

After a few moments, Jack removed his hands and I simply stared, not believing what I saw: his eyes were gone. The area where they had been was now featureless, unbroken skin.

At first I thought maybe he'd gouged his eyes out. (After all, he did reach into his own chest to pull out a toxic organ.) Then I realized that what he'd done was shapeshift in order to avoid seeing me since I was still sporting Gray's face. It gave him the appearance of something out of a horror movie, but would presumably be effective in regard to the conditioning that prevented him from harming Gray.

As if to test that theory, Jack all at once went down to one knee and smacked a fist almost exactly in the spot where he had dropped me, causing tremors to once again shake the building. Seeing what Jack had just done, I almost felt like *I* was precognitive to some extent, and I sent up a small prayer of thanks that I'd had the presence of mind to move after he let me go.

Once the shaking subsided, I noticed that Jack was still down on one knee. His face was close to the rooftop, and he seemed to be taking slow, deep breaths — as if he couldn't get enough air — although he only inhaled and exhaled through his nose. Without warning, he stood up and began to methodically turn his head from side to side while appearing to sniff the air at the same time, his actions putting me in mind of a human bloodhound.

457

REPLICATION

Jack looked in my direction and grinned. ("Looked," however, is probably a misnomer since he didn't have any eyes. It's more like he *faced* my direction and grinned.)

"You know, Jim, you really should have taken me up on that offer to help develop your powers," he said. He sniffed the air again and — waving an outstretched arm in the air in front of him — took a ponderous step towards me.

"My latest pet project has been enhancing the senses," Jack went on, sniffing the air as he spoke. "You know — sight, touch, taste, and all that."

He took another stride in my direction.

"Of course, I'm not using the eyesight right now," Jack admitted. "And the hearing's not where I'd like it to be yet. But smell?"

Without preamble, he tilted his head back and drew in a long, exaggerated breath through his nostrils. He embellished the act by simultaneously stretching his arms out to the side. The overall effect was one of a person inhaling a heady ambrosia.

"My sense of smell," he went on, "is beyond belief. For instance, I can smell your sweat…"

Hand out in front of him again, he put another foot forward. "The blood from the scrapes and bruises you've picked up on this rooftop…"

Jack took another step. "Your girlfriend's perfume from your being next to her…"

He shuffled another foot in a beeline towards me. "The soap you showered with this morning…"

By this time, I was already crabwalking backwards as Jack advanced on me, reciting the long list of things he could smell on me thanks to his super-sniffer. Sadly, I hadn't gone far before I found my retreat (which was what it was) blocked by the metal racking that held up the solar panels. Unable to go back any farther, I got to my feet as quietly as I could and then continued to fall back by moving parallel to the solar panels as quickly as humanly possible without making a sound.

Glancing back, I saw that Jack had reached the racking. He sniffed loudly, then turned his face in the direction I'd gone. (In the back of my mind, I realized that my comparison to a human bloodhound was a lot more accurate than I'd intended.)

Apparently not wanting to chase me across the roof indefinitely, Jack then did something completely unexpected. Reaching up, he grabbed the metal racking — and then pulled the whole thing down!

REPLICATION

Chapter 91

The network of solar panels didn't actually fall all at once. It was comprised of numerous interconnected sections, only one of which Jack had yanked down. However, that was enough to make the entire thing collapse. (It was easiest to imagine the solar sections like a line of trees in the forest that are tied together. Cut down the first tree, and as it falls it will pull down the next tree, which will pull down the next, and so on.)

As I watched the solar panels starting to topple, filling the air with metallic creaks and groans (as well as a shower of electrical sparks), my instinctive response had been to phase. Then, upon recalling that I no longer had that ability, I did the next best thing — I ran.

The goal, of course, was pretty simple: to get clear of the area likely to get smashed by the falling solar panels. I understood that, like a tree falling in the forest, the bottom part of the racking — the segment that was nearest the roof surface — would hit first; then, as it toppled over, the top portion would strike last. I had judged the height of the solar panel framework to be about forty feet. Thus, running from the side where the solar panels were located towards the center of the roof, I needed to clear a little less than fifteen yards in order to reach safety.

All of this flitted through my head in an instant as I ran. My footfalls were hard and loud in my opinion, but I doubted they could be heard over the metal framework that was collapsing all around me. (Assuming, of course, that Jack had told the truth about not having super-hearing, but I didn't waste time checking to see if I'd drawn his attention.)

Also, while forty feet wasn't particularly far to run, it felt like it was taking too long to cover that distance. Obviously, I had been spoiled to a certain extent by my particular power set, and perhaps didn't fully appreciate what "normal" people went through on a day-to-day basis. Nevertheless, despite moving at what felt like a snail's pace, there was no doubt that I was going to be okay. And then I skidded.

In essence, I was about two-thirds of the way to a point I had mentally marked as "safety" when my right foot came down on something loose — like gravel — and slid out from under me. I went down painfully, bruising my tailbone and cracking my elbow on the roof as well. That said, I didn't have time to nurse any injuries, as evidenced by the grating of metal-on-metal that seemed to be coming from all directions. Ignoring the pain, I scrambled to my feet and took off running again. Much to my surprise (and in spite of the tumble I'd just taken), it still looked like I was going to make it.

That's when someone bludgeoned me from behind and everything went black.

****

I came to lying on my back, surrounded by a fair amount of dark, broken glass. My head was throbbing violently, and there was a queer pressure bearing down on my waist. There was also dust in the air, and somewhere nearby I could hear an unusual metal banging — like a couple of guys facing off with iron quarterstaffs.

For a moment, I didn't know where I was. Reaching a hand behind me, I gingerly touched the back of my head. I flinched at the contact, noting that there was a

461

bump rising on my scalp. At the same time, I immediately remembered everything that had happened.

Apparently I had been premature in my assessment of how close I'd been to safety. From all indications, a piece of the solar panel rack had given me a love tap on the noggin as I ran. (Thankfully, it only appeared to have knocked me out for a few seconds.) Even worse, the odd pressure on my waist seemed to be coming from the fallen structure. In short, while it wasn't crushing me, I did seem to be effectively pinned.

The metallic banging noise sounded again, seemingly coming from the area where I'd last seen Jack. As I peered in that direction, the wind began to clear out the dust (which I assume had billowed up after the solar panels fell). A moment later, I saw him.

Jack still didn't have eyes, which wasn't surprising since he was obviously trying to avoid any conditioned response to my looking like Gray. As I watched, he gave his head a quick shake, causing a number of dark glass shards to fall out of his hair. Of course — when he had yanked the solar panels down, he had pulled them down on himself. Naturally, a falling wall of steel and glass is nothing when you have super strength, and he had apparently come through unscathed.

He was currently standing next to what had been the top of the solar panel array. In one hand, he held a length of metal piping that he'd presumably taken from the solar panel racking. Keeping the far end of it low to the ground, Jack swung the pipe side to side like a white cane for the blind as he slowly walked forward. As it oscillated back and forth, the pipe would regularly strike the top of the solar equipment, thereby making the metallic banging I'd heard.

"Hey, Jim," Jack called out without warning. "You okay, fella? You need some help?"

I ignored his taunting and instead focused on getting out from under the solar panels. With a little effort, I was confident that I could lift the racking enough to shimmy out, but it would take a little time, and certainly make noise. Needless to say, noise of any type was bound to bring Jack on the double, and I wasn't sure I could get away before he reached me. (And I had no illusions about what would happen if my evil twin got his hands on me again. Forget "game on." It would be "game over.")

"Come on, Jim," Jack went on as he continued to walk forward. "This is getting old. You can only evade me for so long."

I kept silent, but he was more right than he realized. He was walking a path that ran right next to what had been the top of the solar array, and I was pinned at the top of that same structure. In short, if he kept walking, he was going to run right into me.

"Say something, Jim," Jack said, continuing to step in my direction. "My nose tells me you were close by when I brought these solar panels down. If you're hurt, there's no need to suffer. I can put you out of your misery. Even if you're not, staying quiet isn't going to throw me off your trail — you're upwind of me."

I wanted to scream in frustration. The wind was blowing from me to him, taking my scent (for lack of a better term) to him, which meant he was probably locked in on me. Not for the first time, I wished I'd brought a weapon with me — a submachine gun or something along those lines, regardless of whether or not Jack could be hurt by it.

463

REPLICATION

Fighting a growing sense of desperation, I looked around but didn't see anything nearby except shards from broken solar panels. Casting my gaze farther, I didn't see anything in close proximity that could help — and then my eyes lit upon something potentially useful.

Not far from where I lay was one of the AC units Jack had knocked free earlier. It was leaking water that had pooled in a small recessed area near the top edge of the fallen solar panels. In addition, a shorn piece of electrical cable with exposed wiring extended from said panels to the water. If Jack kept walking along his current path, he'd step right into that electrified pool.

In short, Jack's own actions had created a potential weapon that could be used against him.

Once Jack stepped in the water, the ensuing electrical shock would hopefully — at the least — disorient him, as Electra had done in the teen lounge. At that point, I'd have to act fast. I needed to squirm free, locate the syringe, and then find a way to inject him without getting shocked myself (assuming he hadn't recovered by then). Taken altogether, it was a heady project to attempt without my powers.

With the thought of my abilities, my mind turned to Mouse. My mentor had said he'd try to fix the nullifier, and I was tempted to reach out to him telepathically, but decided against it. Communication with me would only distract him.

The sound of metal banging on metal — Jack's makeshift white cane striking the solar panel array — brought me out of my reverie. And then my eyes widened as a new thought occurred to me.

What if Jack banged the metal pipe against the solar panel just as he stepped in the water? What if, while still in the water, he collapsed against the solar panels? I was currently pinned down by that self-same structure, and not too far from where the electrified water had pooled. I suddenly realized that there was a very real possibility I could get electrocuted.

Now gravely concerned, I started to feel an overwhelming need to get out of my current predicament, but how? Jack was closer now than he'd been a few minutes earlier. If I didn't think I could wriggle free before he reached me then, the odds were much less favorable now.

With nothing to lose, I started cycling through my powers again, hoping something useful would work this time. For instance, if I could phase, any potential electric shock wouldn't harm me. Unfortunately, phasing didn't work. Neither did telekinesis. I then reached for teleportation again and — surprisingly — felt something there. However, it seemed a bit...off, in a way I didn't understand, but I was so overjoyed at having a life-saving power back that I just chalked up any odd sensations to the blow I'd taken to the head.

Feeling better than I had since starting this mission, I prepared to teleport out from under the solar panel, and then stopped.

Thanks to his super-sniffer, Jack was locked in on me. If I teleported, my scent would immediately go with me. More to the point, Jack probably wouldn't keep going — that is, step into the electrified water — if he didn't still think he was headed to me. On my part, I felt like I needed the advantage I'd gain by him getting shocked.

In short, I had a bit of a dilemma: I needed to stay in place in order for Jack to become vulnerable, but I needed to get away to avoid any risk of electrocution. It wasn't possible to do both, unless I found a way to lay down a false trail of blood, sweat, and tears (and whatever else he could smell on my skin) for Jack to follow. And with that, I got an idea, based on something Mouse had said.

According to my mentor, the outer layer of my skin — the stratum corneum — was comprised of dead cells. We had only mentioned it in passing, but it seemed possible to separate that portion of my epidermis from the rest of me. With that in mind, I closed my eyes and concentrated.

Typically when I teleported, I moved entire objects from one place to another, whether it be myself or something else. So if I teleported, say, a bottle of juice, I would do so with its contents inside; if it were a pencil, the lead inside would go with it. What I was attempting to do now was markedly different, like trying to teleport a car without the paint job.

If I'd had my powers — particularly, the ability to "see" and control my physiological systems — it might have been easier. In that scenario, I would have just looked internally and wrapped the part of me that was "living," so to speak, in my power and teleported it. (Even then, however, there would have been exceptions, such as hair, nails, and so on.) Without my full slate of powers, it was infinitely harder, but after a few moments, I felt I'd done my best. Taking a deep breath, I opened my eyes and teleported.

REPLICATION

Chapter 92

My first thought was that it worked. I was no longer pinned under the solar panels. I was, instead, near the center of the roof, close to where I'd lost the syringe.

No — wait, I thought. It appeared that I *was* still pinned down. I was still lying on my back in the same position I was before. But at the same time, I wasn't.

Something was very, very wrong. No, not *wrong*, I quickly decided. Just different. A moment later, I knew what it was: there were two of me!

One of me, as noted, was up and about (and dressed only in a pair of boxer briefs), while the other — wearing the rest of my clothes — was still under the collapsed solar panel equipment.

I had intended to teleport the "living" me under the stratum corneum to another part of the roof (along with my underwear so that I wouldn't be naked). That should have left something like a husk of me under the solar panels. Still draped in my clothes (and bearing my scent), it should have been enough to fool Jack. Rather than that, however, some new power had manifested, and it appeared that I had truly replicated myself.

I spent a moment looking around, marveling at what it was like to take in the world from two different vantage points. It should have felt bizarre, but it didn't. Instead, it felt…natural.

A metallic bang brought me — both iterations — back to myself. Wasting no more time, the second me (the one that was free) began looking for the syringe. Remembering the direction it had gone in, I headed there, scouring the area.

REPLICATION

Meanwhile, the first me (the one pinned on the rooftop) looked in the direction of the banging sound and saw that Jack had reached the pool of electrified water. At this point, however, he halted and sniffed the air. Frowning, he squatted down on his haunches and sniffed again. He then reached out a hand in front of him, where it hovered teasingly just above the surface of the water.

Come on, I said to myself. *Just another step…*

Unfortunately, Jack wasn't cooperating. Maybe there was the scent of ozone in the air, maybe he could detect an electric current in the water, or maybe some other ability was being employed. Regardless, he obviously could sense that something was wrong.

At that juncture, the Jim-2 version of me found the syringe lying near a vent and picked it up. It was visible now, and had probably been so since the brief moment when I'd gotten knocked out earlier. I then began hustling back towards the fallen solar panels.

As Jim-2, I apparently made some noise, because Jack suddenly jerked his head in my direction and stood up. As Jim-1, I saw his reaction, which prompted me to make a command decision.

"Hey, Jack," I shouted as Jim-1, drawing his attention to me. "Why do you think your handlers were so focused on getting you to develop the same powers I had? It's because a knockoff has to imitate the original if it's going to fool anybody, if it's ever going to be worth anything. But you know what? People in the know — people with refinement and discerning taste — will always be able to tell the difference. So if you take a designer bag and a knockoff, and then destroy the former, the bag you're left with is still a knockoff. That's you, Jack. A knockoff. And it's all you'll ever be."

468

REPLICATION

I had watched Jack's face as I spoke, and it had gone from surprise at hearing my voice to anger to unmitigated rage. After I finished my little speech, I expected him to suddenly charge through the water (and hopefully get shocked), but again he worked overtime to spoil my plans. Instead of rushing towards me, he jumped, clearing the electrified pool in a single bound and coming down almost on my head, making me grunt in surprise. That sound was apparently all he needed to pinpoint my position, as he reached down and — getting a grip on my shirt — yanked me free, heedless of the damage it inflicted on me. (For the record, it felt like my back got scraped with sandpaper, and my hip and a knee got hyperextended, among other things.)

Jack then proceeded to shake me wildly for a second, like a pair of maracas making the most beautiful sound he'd ever heard. He then flung me down with enough force that I cracked my head and saw stars. Lying on my back, I couldn't immediately tell if anything was broken, but — with almost everything aching from my head to my toes — it wouldn't have surprised me if something was.

"You should have worked with me, Jim," Jack said as he placed a foot firmly on my chest. "We could have made the world a better place. Now I'll have to do it alone. Funny thing, though: working solo is turning out not to be as hard as I thought."

I placed both hands on his foot and tried to shove it off. It didn't budge. With his strength, he probably didn't even notice that I was making an effort. Moreover, his foot had me pinned down as effectively as the solar panels had.

An odd noise off to the side drew his attention, causing Jack to jerk his head in that direction just as Jim-2 leaped at him, with the syringe poised to inject the neural blocker.

****

It wasn't the most original plan. While Jack was busy manhandling the Jim-1 version of me, as Jim-2 I had rushed forward with the intention of catching him unawares. It worked to some extent, as I was almost on him by the time he heard my approach, and had already sprang at him when his head snapped in my direction.

Unfortunately, that was about as much success as I could claim in this instance. With cat-like reflexes, Jack reached out while I was still in the air and caught me around the neck with one hand, while his other hand closed over the fist in which I held the syringe.

He sniffed the air and then muttered, "Well, I'll be damned! Two of you!" He shook his head in disbelief. "I mean, I saw it in my future, but it seemed improbable, and clairvoyance can be hard to rely on."

My eyes went wide. Jack had plainly foreseen my attempt to inject him as Jim-2. It explained a lot, including how — without eyes — he'd caught me in mid-air. But from what I understood of his powers, it shouldn't have been possible.

"How…multiple…threats…?" I croaked as Jim-2, barely able to get the words out with my throat in Jack's vise-like grip.

"Oh, so you know something about my precognition," Jack said with a laugh, clearly understanding my confusion. "Well, you'll be pleased to know that I still only see one threat at a time. However, I get images of the future more often now. This scene we're playing out now only came to me since we've been on the roof."

I felt despondent. We had severely underestimated Jack, and it looked like the price for doing so was going to be pretty steep (not to mention paid in blood).

"Anyway," Jack continued, "what's this you've been playing keep-away with?" He shook my fist — the one he held in his own grip — blatantly indicating the syringe.

"Vitamin…supplement," I managed to mutter.

"Really?" Jack chuckled. "In that case, let's make sure you get the recommended daily allowance."

With that, he began slowly moving the syringe towards my neck.

"NO!!!" I roared as both Jim-1 and Jim-2. Immediately thereafter, both versions of me began desperately trying to get away. As Jim-1, I squirmed violently under Jack's foot like a worm on a fishing hook, pounding fiercely on his leg at the same time. As Jim-2, I beat furiously on the arm that held me in the air with my free hand, while also bucking wildly in an effort to break his grip.

None of it worked. Jack was simply too strong, and he smiled with malignant glee as he continued guiding the syringe towards the Jim-2 version of me. Because of the angle at which he gripped my fist, it appeared that it was easiest for him to inject me behind the ear. Of course, he could have just taken the syringe from me (or broken my arm) in order to inject me in a preferred spot, but that obviously wouldn't be as much fun as making me do it myself.

My mind raced as I tried to think of what to do in the few seconds remaining before I was injected. Jack's grip around my fist made dropping the syringe impossible. There was a little wiggle room around the plunger which allowed me to take my thumb off it, but once the needle was inserted, Jack could press it himself. Still, wanting to delay the inevitable as long as possible, I moved my thumb off it anyway — just to make sure I didn't accidentally squirt any of the fluid out...

I blinked as understanding suddenly dawned on me. Throwing my thumb back on the plunger, I pressed down as hard as I could. The syringe's contents squirted out in a powerful jet, striking my ear and the side of my face, and then running down to my neck. And onto Jack's hand, which was still locked around my throat.

Without eyes, Jack couldn't see what I'd done, but he undoubtedly felt the neural blocker running over his hands. Plainly surprised, he stopped his efforts at trying to inject me with the syringe. Then he must have had some sort of revelation, because he simultaneously let go of my fist and throat like he'd just touched a red-hot poker.

The Jim-2 version of me dropped to the rooftop, but I managed to stay on my feet. As Jim-1, I put one hand on the heel of the foot Jack had on my chest and the other on its toe, and then I twisted. My action had the combined effect of getting his foot off me as well as throwing him off-balance, and he went sprawling.

As Jim-2, I let the syringe fall from my aching fingers before wiping its dripping contents from my face, then reached out my other hand to help my Jim-1 self to my feet. Nothing seemed to be permanently broken in either body, so I turned the attention of both Jims to my evil twin.

Jack had gone down on his stomach, and he lay there for a moment, making harsh breathing noises, as if he couldn't catch his breath. Slowly, he rolled over and sat up. As I suspected, his eyes were back. I interpreted that as meaning his powers were gone. It begged the question of why my own powers were still present (as evidenced by the fact that I was still two Jims), but I filed it away for later.

Jack looked at me with an odd expression that seemed to combine deep-rooted melancholy with profound loss and sadness. As both Jims, I took a step towards him and he recoiled slightly, at which point I realized that I was still sporting Gray's countenance — on both Jims, no less.

Switching both faces back to my own, I spoke as Jim-1, saying, "It's over, Jack. You're done."

"No," he insisted firmly as he got to his feet.

"Your powers are gone," I stressed. "It's time to face up to what you've done."

"You mean go back into stasis," he muttered, taking a step back. "Probably forever."

"You don't know that," I countered.

"It's you who doesn't know," he shot back. "They'll stick me back in a box, only this time it'll be for good. Powers or not, I can't go back to that. I won't. I'd rather die."

I should have seen it coming, should have known what he was about to do. Should have realized what he was capable of.

Without another word, Jack turned and raced towards the nearest edge of the roof. Being slow on the uptake, it was another second or two before I realized what he had in mind, and I took off after him.

I wasn't going to catch him; we were too evenly matched and he had a head start. Nevertheless, I shouted to him as we ran, begged him not to, yelled that he'd be treated fairly.

My words fell on deaf ears. Jack reach the edge of the roof and calmly stepped over the side without a word and without looking back.

REPLICATION

Chapter 93

Jack didn't hit the ground. The building we were on had a balcony that ran around the fiftieth floor, and that's where he landed. Fortunately, there had been no one around to see it. After the tremors Jack caused when we were on the roof, the entire place had been evacuated.

At present, I was actually on the fiftieth floor (known as the "Sky Lobby") of the building in question, sitting in a lounge chair. After Jack went over the side, I had reached out to Mouse telepathically, letting him know it was okay to stand down on repairing the nullifier. He had done so — turned it off, actually — and I'd immediately gotten my powers back. (I had been particularly grateful to have my healing ability back, as it quickly remedied the injuries I'd received at Jack's hands.)

I had then teleported to Mouse and given him a quick telepathic overview of everything that had happened, but not before bringing the two Jims together again. (Basically, all I'd had to do was want them unified again, and it happened.) Following that, we had coordinated with Gray, essentially telling him to come clean up his mess (although it was obviously a poor choice of words).

Gray had shown up with a small army, sealed off the building, and was now having a deep and intense discussion with Mouse in a far corner of the Sky Lobby while his people put things in order. Mouse had told me that I didn't have to be here, but — although others may have found it morbid — I had to see what had happened to Jack for myself. It wasn't pretty, and I'd been grateful when Gray's people, showing a decency I wouldn't have expected considering who they worked for, had covered the remains with a sheet before respectfully taking them away. Now I was primarily just hanging around to get debriefed by Mouse.

Eventually, the conversation between Gray and Mouse ended, punctuated — to my surprise — by a handshake. Then, while Gray stayed put, Mouse headed in my direction. I got up and met him halfway.

"Look," Mouse began, "you've had enough on your plate for one day. Let's just shoot for catching up in the morning."

"Does that include what you and Gray were talking about?" I asked.

Mouse glanced back at Gray before responding. "Yeah, we'll talk. For now, though, I think our mutual friend wants a word with you."

With that, Mouse gave me a time to meet at his lab the next day and then said goodbye. He turned to leave, but then expectedly spun back towards me.

"Also, I just wanted to add that it was a pretty gutsy move deciding to squirt the neural blocker on yourself as well as Jack," he said. "Most supers would have been too worried about losing their powers."

I shrugged. "My powers were going to be forfeited anyway if Jack injected me — or so I thought. That being the case, I didn't have anything to lose, and if nothing else, I figured it would stop him."

Mouse merely nodded in understanding before turning to leave, at which point I sauntered over to speak with my new boss.

"You rang?" I said when I got close.

Gray smiled. "I just wanted to say that I thought you did well — not just today, but during this entire episode with Jack. There aren't many people who could

476

have bested him on his worst day. Just proves I was right about having you on our team."

"And if Jack had killed me?"

Gray shrugged. "Then I guess I'd have been wrong." I gave him an incredulous stare, at which point he laughed and said, "I'm kidding; I'm kidding."

"Then why does it feel like all I've done today is literally survive some probationary period? And my reward is that I get to fix your screw-ups on a full-time basis now."

"Oh, come on — it won't be that bad," Gray insisted. "Especially after Mouse started haggling on your behalf. Your friend drives a pretty hard bargain."

I raised an eyebrow. "Bargain?"

"For having you on my team," Gray said. "Mouse negotiated some terms that I think we can all live with."

I frowned. "I don't think I understand."

"We had to figure out a way to coordinate things such that working for me doesn't interfere with your League duties."

"Wait a minute," I muttered. "I don't have to quit the League?"

Gray chuckled. "What gave you that idea? I've never intimated that you had to chuck your cape."

"Yeah, but that was back when you wanted me operating as a mole," I stated, remembering how Gray had first approached me. "I thought this would be more overt."

"You've got the wrong idea about us. We're very flexible."

My eyes narrowed in contemplation. "Mouse — he gave you something. What was it?"

Gray hesitated for a moment, giving me an appraising glance before responding. "Nothing really. We merely formalized some arrangements that had generally been casual in the past."

I shook my head in exasperation. "This is worse than I ever imagined. Not only have I gotten myself sucked into a decaying orbit around you, now I've done it to the people I care about."

"You're blowing things way out of proportion," Gray retorted. "I know you think you've sold your soul to the devil, but there are a lot of benefits to being in this organization."

"Like what?" I demanded.

"You tell me," Gray replied.

"Huh?" I muttered, not quite understanding.

Gray spread his arms in a magnanimous gesture. "Make a wish — anything you want. What's something you'd like to see happen?"

I just stared at him for a moment, thinking this had to be a joke. On an empathic level, however, I sensed nothing but truth. But Gray was wily; he didn't have to be lying for this to be a ploy of some sort.

"No thanks," I finally said. "I'm already in too deep. I don't want to be any more in your debt."

"This one's on the house," Gray stressed. "A goodwill gesture."

I spent a second deliberating before responding. "Alright, you can clear my name. Without Jack, it's going to be difficult to show I wasn't framed for some of the stuff he did, so feel free to take care of that."

Gray pooh-poohed my concerns. "That's done — took care of it days ago."

"What?" I practically growled.

"Well, I knew you were innocent," Gray declared, "so it was just a matter of informing the proper people that you weren't the guy." He then leaned in conspiratorially. "Now, come on. Give me a *real* challenge."

I pondered for a moment, then came up with something that I thought was sufficiently onerous.

"That's it?" Gray remarked, obviously unimpressed by what I'd asked for. "Consider it done."

"Just like that?" I asked, having trouble hiding my skepticism.

"Just like that," Gray confirmed. "Welcome to the big leagues. I'll call you when it's done."

I nodded and then teleported.

REPLICATION

Chapter 94

I didn't immediately teleport home after leaving Gray. Instead, I went to get something to eat.

One thing I hadn't shared with Mouse was that, after the two Jims became one again, I was famished. No, it was worse than being famished; it felt as though I hadn't eaten in years, and the hunger pangs were excruciating. I'd initially tweaked my systems so that I couldn't feel the pain, but now that we had seemingly wrapped up for the day, I knew I needed to get some food in me asap.

I addressed the issue by going to fast-food places, first walking into a burger joint and ordering everything they had under the heat lamp. (Or rather, as much as they'd let me order, since they said they had to keep something on hand for other customers.) I did the same thing at a second fast-food restaurant — this one specializing in chicken sandwiches — and then another burger place. (In retrospect, I probably should have just gone to a buffet, but they would have taken a severe loss that day.)

Eventually, I felt as though I'd gotten enough sustenance, and at that juncture I teleported home, popping up in my room. I immediately reached out on a telepathic level, letting my mom, Indigo, and Myshtal know I was fine. It just so happened, however, that they had already received the news. Mouse had told them.

Apparently my family had been eagerly waiting to hear about the outcome of the final encounter with Jack. (In fact, I learned that Electra — rather than wait alone at home — had joined them, only leaving after Mouse had confirmed that we'd been successful.) Although being told by my mentor that all was well put everyone's mind at ease, there was something about hearing it directly from me that seemed to give them an additional sense of comfort.

They were obviously relieved, but also buzzing with excitement on such an elevated level that I could have picked it up empathically from a mile away. Quite clearly, they had been extremely worried about me.

Mentally exhausted from the day's events, I asked quickly about Gramps and — after being informed that he was fine — told them I was turning in, and no one naysayed me. I stretched out on the bed and immediately fell asleep.

****

I slept soundly that night, and woke up the next day feeling completely invigorated. Performing a little psychological self-analysis, I chalked the good vibes up to no longer having an evil twin. I didn't like the way things had ended with Jack, but I was certainly glad not to be dealing with the problem anymore.

That settled, I hurried through my normal grooming and hygiene regimen before getting dressed and going downstairs.

I went into the kitchen and suddenly stopped short. There was a strange man standing at our refrigerator.

He was maybe an inch or so taller than me, with a solid muscular frame and a rich, chocolate complexion. He had a bright smile and a handsome face that made me peg his age as maybe mid- to late twenties.

He didn't immediately say anything — just stood there with a cocksure grin, but one which I somehow didn't find offensive. I couldn't put my finger on it, but there was something familiar about him. Hoping for a clue,

I reached out to scan the surface of his mind telepathically, and...

My eyes widened in surprise. "Gramps?"

He laughed. "In the flesh."

Before I knew what I was doing, I dashed over and gave him a fierce hug, which he returned. Then I stepped back, and looked him all over, still surprised by what I saw. Now I understood the odd response I'd received when I'd asked about seeing him, and perhaps what my family had been so excited about the night before.

"When did this happen?" I asked.

He winked. "You should know the answer to that. This is *your* handiwork."

Of course! I'd almost forgotten: when I had healed Queen Dornoccia back on Caeles, she had actually grown younger as a result. The same thing had apparently happened to Gramps.

"So what does this mean?" I asked. "Are you putting on a cape again?"

"Ha!" my grandfather barked sharply. "No, your grandmother and I lost a lot of good years. In a way, this gives us a chance to get those back, and I'm not going to squander it. Besides, I think the world's in good hands with this new generation of capes."

With that, he gave me another wink and clapped me on the shoulder.

****

I spent the next couple of hours at the embassy, first talking to Gramps, and then everyone else as they trickled down for breakfast. As I'd suspected, my grandfather's rejuvenation was why everyone had felt excited the night before, but they'd decided to let me be surprised. (Needless to say, they all laughed when Gramps told them my reaction upon seeing him.)

We were all having fun — it seemed like forever since we'd simply been able to enjoy one another's company without some issue hanging over our heads — but before long, it was time for me to meet Mouse. That being the case, I quickly said goodbye to everyone and teleported.

I popped up in the lab, where Mouse and BT were already waiting on me.

I thought we'd immediately launch into a discussion, but instead they had me put on an electrode cap (which, as the name implied, looked much like a swim cap with a bunch of electrodes attached to it).

"This has been slightly modified," BT said as I donned the cap as requested. "It's going to give us an idea of your synaptic patterns."

"I thought you guys already had that info," I stated. "Isn't that what you got from my Caelesian crown?"

"We're just trying to confirm," Mouse replied. "It'll take a few minutes to get any useful data."

"That's fine," I declared. "In the meantime, can we talk about yesterday?"

Mouse nodded. "That's the plan. Where would you like to start?"

"The neural blocker," I replied. "Jack lost his powers but I didn't. Why not?"

"Let's come back to that later," Mouse suggested.

"Fine," I acquiesced. "Let's move on to the nullifier. What happened to it?"

"You have to understand a little about the configuration first," BT began. "Each of the four corner skyscrapers housed part of the nullifier equipment. For power, we hooked them into the electrical systems of their respective buildings."

"Unfortunately, one of the buildings had an older power grid," Mouse said. "There was a short that caused a power surge, which in turn caused the nullifier equipment in that building to turn on. However, because all of the nullifier components were synced, the entire thing switched on."

"That's when you told me to veer off," I surmised.

"Right," Mouse acknowledged. "I figured you could do without the experience of zipping around skyscrapers and then losing the power of flight."

I merely nodded, as this was the same thought that had occurred to me when the event actually happened the day before. (Also left unsaid, but coming to mind unbidden, was how things had ended for Jack.)

"What followed next is pretty much elementary," BT declared.

"Yeah," I agreed. "Jack's precognition allowed him to see the nullifier threat, so he took out part of the equipment with his Bolt Blast."

"And with only three-fourths of the necessary equipment, I couldn't get a fully functional nullifier," Mouse admitted. "No matter how hard I tried."

"Well, it worked out for the best," I noted. "And I even developed a new power."

"So I heard," BT said. "How exactly did that come about?"

I launched into a quick overview of Jack's heightened sense of smell and how it played a role in the advent of two Jims.

REPLICATION

"Basically, I was trying to leave a portion of myself behind while at the same time go somewhere else," I explained. "The end result was that there ended up being two of me – one in each desired location."

"If you don't mind satisfying my personal curiosity," BT added, "was there any issue in controlling two bodies?"

I understood BT's interest in that aspect of my new power. As part of a hive mind, she was actually only one component in a network of clones, all being controlled by a single consciousness. It was only natural that she wonder how things worked for others in a similar situation.

"There was no issue whatsoever," I confirmed. "It took me a second to realize what had happened, but after that, everything felt completely natural. Controlling two bodies was substantially no different than being able to control your right and left hand."

Mouse shook his head in mock derision. "Man, with all these clones and copies running around, we're going to have to change your name to Kid *Replication*."

We both laughed at that — but only momentarily, as BT put us both back on point.

"Any side effects?" she asked.

"No," I initially reported, and was about to shake my head for emphasis when a crucial fact came back to me. "Uh, wait. There was something. When the two Jims came back together, I was completely ravenous — hungrier than I can ever recall."

"Hmmm," BT mused.

"What are you thinking?" Mouse asked her.

"The type of replication Jim manifested is incredibly rare," BT responded. "There are only one or two documented cases. But what Jim's describing in terms of

485

hunger is consistent with what's been reported before. In essence, the copies, if we can call them that, are all connected to a single core. For instance, they'll draw energy jointly from the same biological systems and processes."

"I'm not sure I follow," I said, admitting my confusion.

"Think of it this way," Mouse directed. "Imagine the human body — *your* body — is powered by an internal battery. When you do your dual-Jim thing, the two copies of you don't each have their own battery; there's now a single battery powering two of them. So, if that battery could power you alone for, let's say, an hour, it might only power two Jims for fifteen minutes."

I nodded. "I think I get it now. The multiple Jims all draw from the same internal resources, but use them up exponentially faster."

"Pretty much," Mouse stated. "Explains why you were starving after your copies became unified. Operating in dual-mode drained any energy you got from food in record time."

"Hmmm," I wondered aloud. "Not sure how wild I am about an ability that runs a chance of sucking me dry."

"Like a lot of other powers, practice makes perfect," BT reminded me.

"I'll take it under advisement," I promised. "Anyway, are we about ready to get this souped-up swim cap off me?"

"It's probably been long enough," Mouse announced.

Without another word, I pulled the cap off and handed it to BT while Mouse retrieved his laptop from a nearby table. With BT looking over his shoulder, my mentor tapped the screen several times and then appeared to study whatever data had been pulled up.

After a minute or so, he looked at me and said, "Alright, ask your initial question again."

"Why did Jack lose his powers but I didn't?" I asked. "I mean, the neural blocker got on both of us, and you said it was effective even upon contact with the skin."

"Okay, there's a couple of reasons why you may not have lost your powers," Mouse explained. "First and foremost, based on the info we just got from the electrode cap, it doesn't look like your neural pathways match those tracked by the crown."

I gave him a dumbfounded look. "What do you mean it doesn't match? It has to. I lost my powers on Caeles because of what that crown was able to do. Are you trying to say it was all in my head?"

"No one's saying that, Jim," BT affirmed. "We're just saying that the crown's map of your neural patterns doesn't sync with the way your brain's actually wired."

"And let's not forget that the neural blocker based on the crown's data actually worked," Mouse added. "Assuming Jack's synaptic patterns mimicked yours to some extent, it implies that the info from the crown was accurate."

"So it's not the crown that's the real mystery," I concluded. "It's me."

"Somewhat," BT agreed. "Some time between when the crown did its work and now, your neural pathways changed."

"But doesn't that happen naturally?" I asked.

Mouse shook his head. "Not to this degree. What we're talking about here is extensive."

"Wow," I muttered. "You make it sound like some interior decorators didn't like the feng shui of my brain, so they went in and started moving stuff around and..."

My voice practically died in my throat as I had a sudden recollection of an event from the recent past.

"What is it?" asked BT.

"Back on Caeles," I began, "I had a chance encounter with someone who seemed to be a future version of me. He went into my head and poked around some."

"I remember you mentioning it," Mouse said. "Do you think he could have reconfigured your neural pathways?"

I shrugged. "Not sure, but he was incredibly powerful. If pressed for an answer, I'd probably lean towards saying he could."

"Interesting..." Mouse noted, rubbing his chin.

"Moving on," I interjected, "you said there was another reason why the neural blocker may not have worked on me?"

"Yes," Mouse replied, coming back to himself. "There's a chance that you were inoculated against it."

"Inoculated?" I echoed. "You mean like a flu shot?"

"Exactly," BT agreed. "It's possible that when you were first dosed with a neural blocker on Caeles, it actually immunized you."

"Well, that's surprising," I admitted. "I didn't think there could be a silver lining regarding my previous experience with neural blockers. I guess you never know."

"Anyway," Mouse said, "we can't prove them one hundred percent, but those are our best guesses regarding why you still have your powers."

"Okay," I intoned, accepting their explanation on the neural blocker. "Any idea why my healing power works sporadically? For instance, I could heal Gramps, but not the photographer, Kroner."

Mouse was silent for a moment, then spoke up. "I have a theory, but it's pure conjecture."

"Please share," I implored. "I've got nothing else to go on at the moment."

"Based on when you've told us it manifested, I'd say it's an emotional response," Mouse conjectured. "When Queen Dornoccia was dying, when your grandfather was dying... They were both occasions that solicited powerful emotional reactions from you. I think that's what triggers your healing power."

"Well, I felt bad about what happened to Kroner," I countered. "Why couldn't I heal him?"

"Because I don't think it's a voluntary response," my mentor contended. "I think it's like tears. Some people can cry on demand, but others can't. For the latter, crying is strictly an involuntary reaction that they have no control over. I think your healing power is like that. It's involuntary and doesn't manifest unless there's something going on with people you care about."

My brow knitted in thought. "So you're saying that deep down inside I don't care about Kroner or what happened to him."

"No," Mouse insisted, shaking his head. "I'm saying you don't care *enough* about him. But that's not surprising seeing as how you basically just met him."

"I guess that also means I couldn't have saved Jack after he fell," I concluded. "Even if I'd tried."

"Excuse me?" Mouse uttered in disbelief.

"It's something that's flitted into my brain every now and then since yesterday," I said, which was true. It was more of a random thought than anything else, but I had wondered once or twice if I could have gotten to Jack in time to do something for him.

"Jim, don't torture yourself over this stuff," BT advised. "What happened to Jack wasn't your fault."

"Maybe," I droned noncommittally. "I just know we were lucky, considering the way Jack's powers were developing."

I then told them how Jack's precognitive ability had given him a second vision of the future while we were on the roof.

Mouse seemed to deliberate heavily on what that meant, saying, "I suppose that if Jack's visions of the future had ultimately started coming fast enough and often enough, eventually he would have seen all future threats and been able to avoid them."

"And that brings up my next question," I said. "Could he actually see the seminal events that we thought he could?"

BT looked nonplussed. "What do you mean?"

"Essentially, it seems like there were times when Jack should have been aware that there was a threat in his future, but he wasn't," I explained. "Like when he was shot at Alpha Prime's mansion, or when Electra shocked him."

"Well, with respect to the mansion, there were actually *two* lasers that had targeted Jack, and he shut the first one down," Mouse said. "As to Electra, in all honesty, we don't know what threats Jack may have encountered *before* she sent some volts through him. Maybe he almost got hit by a bus, someone tried to mug him, or something along those lines."

I didn't say anything, but what I was hearing made sense. (It certainly clarified why Jack was blissfully unaware of actual threats on various occasions.)

"All in all," Mouse said, "the plan didn't go as intended by a long shot, but we — especially you, Jim — managed to pull it off in the end. You should be proud."

"I guess," I replied, shrugging. "One last question, though: when I was fighting Jack on that rooftop, were you able to see us?"

My mentor nodded. "I had a pretty good line of sight. I occasionally glanced in your direction, but mostly focused on trying to repair the nullifier, as that would have brought things to an immediate halt."

"Well, when you did happen to catch a glimpse of what was happening, did you ever think that you needed to step in?"

"Not really," Mouse said. "I mean, it was touch-and-go a couple of times, but since you never reached out to me telepathically, I assumed you had it under control."

"I don't know about that," I admitted. "I just knew you were working on the nullifier and I didn't want to interfere with that because it was important."

"Then I'd say you made the right decision," Mouse noted. "In short, when we go on a mission, everyone has a job to do, and we need to trust the people around us to do what's expected of them. Think of the Dream Machine mission last week: we didn't race off to help the others with their tasks, and nobody came to help us. Everyone assumed that all of their colleagues were competent. If there's a risk that I'm going to leave something undone in order to make sure you're safe, or you're going to shirk your duties in order to help me, then one of us doesn't need to be on the mission."

REPLICATION

I nodded as Mouse finished speaking, as I was able to boil down what he was saying to its essence: he had confidence in me. It was a fact that made me proud.

REPLICATION

Chapter 95

I stayed in Mouse's lab just chatting generally with my mentor and BT until early afternoon. About the only other topic of note that we discussed was the "bargain" that Mouse had struck with Gray.

"We've agreed to something along the lines of a secondment," Mouse explained. "In practical terms, it means that you'll occasionally be on loan to Gray's organization."

In my opinion, there had to be more to it than that, but Mouse nimbly sidestepped all my questions on the subject. Ultimately, my tarriance in the lab (and my attempts to get more information about the deal with Gray) were cut short when my cell phone rang. It was Electra.

"Hey, you," I greeted her upon answering.

"Hey yourself," she replied. "So, were you planning to come see me, or do I have to beg?"

"Aren't you in school?" I asked.

"Today was a half-day; there's some kind of district teacher's meeting," she explained. "So, I've extended an invitation. What say ye?"

****

Five minutes after getting off the phone, I was sitting with Electra on the loveseat in her living room, after having quickly said goodbye to Mouse and BT. For the first time in days, however, we weren't alone in her house; Esper was there (although, according to my girlfriend, she was banging around in the attic looking for something).

From what I could sense, both Electra and her aunt seemed to be in an incredibly buoyant mood.

It hadn't taken me long to share what had happened with Electra (although I left out some of the more morbid details).

"At least it's over," she said when I was done, interlacing her fingers with mine.

"So, were you worried?" I asked.

She shrugged. "Not really. I usually just assume you can take care of yourself."

"Funny — everybody seems to think that about me. I wonder what the reaction will be if I actually get killed one day?" Changing my voice to a whiny version of my girlfriend's, I said, "'It was just a twelve-megaton nuke; I thought he could handle it...'"

Electra laughed. "Stop it! I do *not* sound like that."

"Agreed — your whining's a little more annoying."

For that one, she spent a few seconds tickling me as we both chuckled.

"Anyway," Electra said, "thank your family for letting me hang out with them yesterday."

"Will do," I promised. "And for the record, they enjoyed having you visit."

"Thanks, but it was a little calculating on my part. I figured they'd get word first once everything was over, so I just wanted to be there. Plus, it was better waiting with other people than by myself."

"Well, you've got an open invitation to come by any time," I assured her. "Apparently my family adores you."

My last statement was meant to be a compliment, but I felt a small spike of annoyance from Electra as I spoke. Familiar with this from past experience, I knew that my comment had somehow invoked the specter of Myshtal, and a moment later it was proven.

"I had a question about something," Electra began. "When I was there yesterday, I noticed that your grandmother called Myshtal by a different name — Isteria. I also remember her being introduced that way at the party."

"Yeah," I droned. "Isteria is her formal name."

"So is 'Myshtal' like a nickname, then?"

"Sort of," I admitted, suddenly not liking the direction of the conversation. "But it's also her name — one of her middle names, that is."

"So what does it mean?"

I cleared my throat before speaking. "Ahem. It's. uh, just a term of affection between women who are close relatives or good friends."

"And when a man uses it?" she asked.

"Excuse me?" I replied.

"You said it's a term of affection used between women," she explained, looking me in the eye. "You're not a woman. So what does it mean when a man uses it?"

I lowered my eyes. "For a man, it's, uh…it's uhm…it's usually an epithet for a woman he's involved with. Romantically."

Electra leaped to her feet, ire and irritation exploding within her.

"Are you kidding me?!" she screamed. "You've been calling her your girlfriend this entire time?!"

"No!" I insisted, rising as well. "It's how she was introduced to me, and by the time I learned her formal name, it was too late. Mentally, I couldn't think of her with another name."

Electra lifted her hands up as if trying to push away something invisible yet oppressive.

"I'm sorry, Jim," she finally said. "It's just...it's too much." She went silent for a few seconds, and then took a deep breath. "I think...I think maybe..."

No, I thought. *Don't say it. Please.*

Strengthening her resolve, she blurted out, "I think maybe we need to take a break."

And there it was. I lowered my head, trying to get a grip on what had just happened, but it was difficult. It felt like something deep inside me — something intricate and integral to my well-being — had just been removed. No, not removed: ripped out.

"Look, maybe it's the right time for this," she went on. "I just found out this morning that my father's getting out."

"Really?" I said, trying to sound happy for her but failing miserably.

She nodded. "Yeah, he's getting paroled and will be staying here with us."

"That's great," I mumbled.

She cast her eyes up to the ceiling for a second. "Esper's super excited. I think she's hunting around in the attic for some old memorabilia — pics of them together and stuff like that."

I muttered something, but had no idea what it was.

"Anyway," Electra said, "my point was that with my dad here, I'd want to spend some time with him, so maybe it's the right moment for us to take a step back."

"I disagree," I said solemnly. "I can make this right. I just need some time."

Electra shook her head, and I noticed for the first time that she was crying. "I'm sorry, but I just can't be like the mistress of a married man, waiting for him to leave his wife. That's what this feels like, Jim, with your continual promises but no results. I love you, I really do, but you need to fix this. Until that happens, we can't be together."

Chapter 96

I left Electra's house shortly after she broke up with me. For once, I didn't teleport — I couldn't think of where to go — so I just stepped out the front door and started walking.

I'd been wandering aimlessly for maybe thirty minutes, trying to pull myself together, when my phone rang. I looked at the caller ID and saw that the number was blocked.

Sighing, I answered the phone but didn't say anything.

"Carrow," Gray said. "My office."

And then he hung up, laughing.

****

A few minutes later, I was in the back of the SUV.

"Just wanted to let you know it's done," he said.

I nodded. "I heard. Thanks for keeping your word."

"No thanks necessary," Gray assured me. "On the other hand, I'm sure this won you major points with your girlfriend. You must really love her to use the freebie I offered to get her father out."

I merely shrugged, but didn't say anything. Obviously noting that I was out of sorts, Gray gave me a hard stare.

"Look," he said after a few seconds, "don't beat yourself up about what happened to Jack. It wasn't your fault."

I frowned for a moment, trying to figure out how we'd gotten on this subject, then understood. Gray had

498

realized I was despondent, but misidentified the cause. He seemingly thought I was upset about Jack.

"Moreover," Gray continued, "that was the only way it was going to end — with either him or you in the ground."

Wrinkling my brow in curiosity, I asked, "Why do you say that?"

Gray sighed. "Remember when I said that clones always want to meet their originals? It's actually more than that. The clones fixate on the originals, including every aspect of their lives. Eventually, they try to replace them."

There was a faraway look in his eyes as he spoke, and emotionally I felt not just truth from him, but a profound sense of understanding.

"This isn't just theoretical or abstract for you, is it?" I asked. "This is personal in some way."

Gray didn't immediately answer. Instead, he was silent for a few moments, as if wondering how much to share with me. Finally, he seemed to mentally flip a coin.

"I wasn't lying when I said I was ready to quit this job," he said. "I've wanted to retire for years. But as I explained, I couldn't just walk away. Considering who was slated to succeed me, it would have been chaos. An absolute disaster. So I tried to think of another solution."

"You had yourself cloned," I stated. It wasn't a question.

Gray didn't deny it. "He was supposed to take over the job for me, and on paper it sounded great. A version of me who knew all the ins and outs of the covert world I live in, but who also wasn't burned out and desperate to leave it all behind. He'd step in, and I'd slip away."

"So what happened?"

"Apparently what my position offered — power, authority, and so on — wasn't enough. My clone didn't just want my job. He wanted my *life*. My friendships, my relationships, everything. And towards the end, he was willing to do anything to get it, even if it meant putting me in the ground."

"I take it that didn't happen."

"Let's just say *some*body went in the ground," he stated, giving me a knowing look. "I've been against cloning ever since."

"Is it done, though?" I asked. "Is it over?"

Gray appeared perplexed. "With Jack gone, I would think so."

"No," I said, shaking my head. "The people who authorized Jack's creation — will they produce another one?"

"I doubt it," Gray replied. "Not when they learn what he was up to."

Now it was my turn to look bewildered. "What do you mean?"

"Jack wasn't just sitting on his laurels when he was out of your presence. He was out there doing stuff. We've got evidence that he impersonated a prince from an oil-rich kingdom in the Middle East, as well as a couple of third-world dictators."

Gray's words brought to mind Jack's rooftop statement about having to do things on his own. Obviously, it hadn't been idle talk.

"Believe it or not," Gray went on, "you can do a fair amount of damage on the world stage in some of those positions — even if the nation you represent is underdeveloped and non-industrialized, and your tenure's short-term. Thankfully, it's been contained, but it's pretty clear that he had much bigger plans."

I didn't comment. I was too busy thinking about the havoc Jack had wreaked on a local level to even contemplate what he'd done globally. There was a long line of people who'd been hurt by his machinations: Incendia, Gramps, Vestibule…

Oh, geez, I thought. *Vestibule…*

REPLICATION

Chapter 97

It took me about twenty minutes to track Vestibule down. After she came to mind, I had quickly brought my meeting with Gray to a close and then teleported to the West Coast.

I tried calling her first, but my call went straight to voicemail. Reaching out to my cousin Avis, I discovered that Vestibule had taken a few days of personal leave from the A-List Supers. Avis provided a couple of other contacts — Vestibule's friends and such — but no one seemed capable of pinpointing her location for me. (Not even her agent knew where she was at the moment.) Somewhat disheartened, I made a last roll of the dice and got lucky.

****

I found her in the park she'd taken me to a few days earlier, sitting on the same bench, looking out over the lake. Teleporting here had been a bit of a gamble, but I recalled that this locale seemed to provide her with a sense of serenity. Moreover, it struck me as a place she might retreat to if she were still troubled by what had happened with Jack, and it turned out I was right.

I walked deliberately towards the bench and took a seat next to her. She didn't say anything; the only acknowledgment of my presence had been a short glance in my direction as I'd approached.

The silence lasted a few minutes, although it didn't seem as awkward or uncomfortable as one might imagine.

Finally, Vestibule let out a sigh and asked, "What are you doing here, Jim?"

REPLICATION

"I just wanted to see how you were doing," I said, hoping she knew that I was being sincere.

With almost everyone else who had crossed paths with Jack, there was a support system in place — people they could talk to about what had happened. For instance (and taking myself out of the equation), Smokey could always reach out to Li or Electra. Gramps, as another example, had the rest of our family to turn to. I didn't know if Vestibule had anyone like that in her life. Even if she did, talking about what had happened with Jack would require that she reveal something painfully embarrassing (humiliating, in fact). Bearing all that in mind, I had felt the need to check up on her — to make sure she was okay.

"I'm fine," she insisted.

Rather than simply take her word for it, I reached out empathically, trying to get a sense of her feelings. I picked up on the fact that the experience had rattled her to some extent, but at the same time I detected a surprising strength in her — an inner resolve which indicated that she would not only get past this incident, but any other obstacle life threw in her path. Noting this part of her personality, I was suitably impressed.

"Besides," Vestibule went on, "what would your girlfriend think about you paying me a surprise visit?"

"I don't know," I answered. "If I had a girlfriend, I'd ask her."

"Oh," she muttered softly, looking chagrinned. "So you and Electra…"

I nodded, as she left the rest unsaid. "Yeah — we broke up."

"I hope not because of me."

I shrugged, not caring to verbalize a response.

REPLICATION

Unexpectedly, Vestibule leaned towards me, a somber expression on her face. "Look, I didn't really want to make trouble for you. I just find dating so hard. Most guys are intimidated by me — either my fame, or my wealth, or my powers. I'm a triple threat. And those who aren't intimidated are just jerks. They want me to do all the work in the relationship. 'Why do I have to drive when you can teleport?' Or they think that because I'm rich and like them that I should be their personal ATM. I just wanted to go out one time with a guy who would actually act like a guy and treat me special. And after I heard about you taking Electra to Paris…"

I sat there silently as she trailed off. I now understood Vestibule a lot better than I had just a few days ago, and realized to a large extent I had probably misjudged her. She didn't really want anything more out of life (and in particular, relationships) than anyone else, but — like my cousin Avis — her status made it more difficult.

"And I know what a lightning rod is," she announced abruptly, interrupting my thoughts.

"What?" I asked, a little befuddled.

"Back at the Alpha League last week," Vestibule said, "I referred to Electra as a lightning rod. Your friend started to correct me, trying to point out that a lightning rod doesn't actually create electricity. I just wanted to make it clear that I understand the distinction. I called her a lightning rod because it sounded good, but I know it's not an accurate comparison. I'm not stupid."

Caught by surprise by her narrative, I burst into laughter. There was clearly a lot more to Vestibule than I'd initially assumed. As if I needed more proof, she seemed to pick up on the fact that I wasn't really laughing *at* her and smiled.

504

Still smiling, I stood up.

"Come on," I said, holding out my hand to her. "I still owe you a date."

She gave me a sly grin as she reached out and took my hand. "Don't you mean an outing?"

We both laughed at that, and then I teleported us.

****

I had a fantastic time with Vestibule, and ended up hanging out with her far longer than I'd intended. Thus, it was close to midnight when I left her on her doorstep and — after receiving a platonic kiss on the cheek — teleported home.

I popped up in my bedroom, with the intention of going straight to bed. Those plans were immediately put on hold, however, by the presence of someone in my room standing near the window.

Rune.

"I know it's late," he said. "And I didn't want to disturb your family, so I've kept my presence hidden from them."

I had trouble keeping a straight face. With three powerful telepaths in the house (not to mention Gramps being back in his prime), it would be difficult for someone to enter the embassy and remain unknown. That said, I didn't doubt that it was within Rune's power.

"Don't worry about it," I replied. "However, I assume this isn't a social call."

"Unfortunately, no," Rune admitted. "Do you recall at the party that I said I might need your help?"

I nodded. "Of course."

"I'm afraid I'm going to have to take you up on that offer of assistance."

"Okay," I muttered, feeling unprepared but willing to do what I could. "Can you share any details?"

"It's probably best if I do so on the way," Rune noted. "And just to let you know, we might be gone a few days."

"That's fine," I said. "When do we leave?"

Rune didn't say anything, but the fact that he was in my home around midnight (as opposed to the next morning) spoke volumes.

"I see," I added softly. I spent a moment reaching out telepathically to my family and Myshtal to tell them that something had come up. I received a bit of pushback (namely because the situation with Jack had only just wrapped up), but in the end they understood and wished me well.

I turned to Rune and said, "Okay. Let's go."

He smiled at me, snapped his fingers, and we vanished.

THE END

Thank you for purchasing this book! If you enjoyed it, please feel free to leave a review on the site from which it was purchased.

Also, if you would like to be notified when I release new books, please subscribe to my mailing list via the following link: http://eepurl.com/C5a45

Finally, for those who may be interested, I have included my website, blog, Facebook, and Twitter info:

Website: http://www.kevinhardmanauthor.com/

Blog: http://kevinhardman.blogspot.com/

Facebook: www.facebook.com/kevin.hardman.967

Twitter: @kevindhardman